HE IS WATCHING YOU

An absolutely gripping crime thriller with a massive twist

CHARLIE GALLAGHER

JOFFE
BOOKS

Published 2018 by Joffe Books, London.

www.joffebooks.com

© Charlie Gallagher

ISBN-13: 978-1-78931-055-9

Author's Note

I am inspired by what I do and see in my day job as a front-line police detective, though my books are entirely fictional. I am aware that the police officers in my novels are not always shown positively. They are human and they make mistakes. This is sometimes the case in real life too, but the vast majority of officers are honest and do a good job in trying circumstances. From what I see on a daily basis, the men and women who wear the uniform are among the very finest, and I am proud to be part of one of the best police forces in the world.

Charlie Gallagher

Chapter 1

He turned off the hill with a sharp right. Dover's historic castle was now directly in front and in the distance. A low-lying mist concealed much of the green hill that it sat on, giving the impression that the ancient fort was floating, like something from a fairy tale.

The first hour of daylight was always his favourite. Even more so now that the United Kingdom was in the grip of an oppressive heat wave. He felt as if he could only truly *breathe* in these first hours. There was a freshness in the air that could almost be mistaken for a chill. The mist was holding back the power of the sun, but it wouldn't last for long.

The road twisted away and he accelerated. The short row of houses on the nearside of his pickup truck blurred into a grey line that ended suddenly and the surroundings changed to greenery where the trees closed in. The road narrowed. The scent through the open windows changed, too. It was delicious — dewy grass and cut wood. The nearside opened up into fields where sheep grazed with their heads bent. The far side had a metal fence marking the perimeter of the castle grounds. There was a row of thick trees, their ancient trunks scarred and gnarled as if they, too, had battled to keep back the invading hordes. Soon the castle was just a glimpse in the rear-view mirror. Then it was gone completely. The fence ran out, too.

He pushed further into the countryside. It was where he was least anxious. Fewer people was always a good thing, and even when the greenery disappeared momentarily as he crossed above a major road, there was nothing moving on the carriageway below.

The road became twistier. He needed to slow down. The greenery on the right was giving way to a distant view of the English Channel, laid out like a sheet of beaten steel that caught the morning light. The mist was already starting to burn away and he could make out strips of green and blue in the water. He needed to concentrate on the road — he braked for a tight bend. There were cliff-top parking points dotted along this road and he saw his first car of the morning, parked up and facing out over the views, its brake lights showing. He continued on. The road straightened out and the trees were soon gone completely, leaving just fields on either side. He had climbed as high as he could. The road was now flat and the sea constantly visible on his right, beyond the sloping fields and the coast guard building that looked from here as if it was hanging over the edge.

He slowed to turn off onto a farm track. The grass sprouting up from the middle was long enough to brush the underside of his truck. He followed the track for half a mile. An open-sided barn was the first building he came to. It was just as he remembered: the roof had fallen in on one side, and the wood frame and plastic sheets that had once been part of it were now draped over a solid, metal container. The container itself looked lopsided and clumsy now that two of the four paving slabs wedged under the corners looked to have collapsed under its weight. The container was rusty and the sides were slick with moss hanging down from the top. The doors were not visible from the track — they were on the other side, facing the wall of the barn. It was why he had chosen it.

He pulled up and the track's rain-starved surface threw up a plume of dust that he stepped into as he got out of the truck. He turned aside too late to protect his eyes from it. He stood still for a second, his eyes stinging and blinking while the dust settled, and then walked to the back of the pickup and opened the back door of the hard top. The hydraulics hissed as it lifted.

Her body was wrapped in a sheet of plastic, her feet just visible. He could see her blue trainers hanging motionless out of the bottom. They were stained a dark red, one somewhat more than the other. She was heavy. He had chosen a plastic sheet because it made it easier to move her. He still struggled to slide her towards him. When she was close enough, he was able to grasp her around the hips and heave her up onto his shoulder. He couldn't see her face — it was wrapped up tight along with the rest of her. He didn't want her leaking any fluids or shedding any hairs. She was wrapped so tightly that she didn't bend too well over his shoulder and he grunted as he backed away from the truck. The bundle caught on the top of the open boot. He managed to get around it but stumbled a little as he walked towards the container. He lowered her to the ground under the broken roof.

The padlock was stiff. He should have got a bigger one, the key was too small in his gloved hands and he cursed his lack of dexterity. He sucked in deep breaths of air to calm himself. He couldn't take the gloves off, so he just needed to focus. Finally, the key found its place and the lock clicked. He pulled the door to the container open. It was heavy. He hooked the padlock back in the door. The smell hit him all at once and a swarm of flies lifted up. They didn't make for the door though; instead, they just landed right back on the identical-looking roll of plastic that was already in there. The feet sticking out the bottom of this one were bare. He cursed. He remembered that he needed to turn her round. He grimaced at the smell as he leaned forward. He took hold of the plastic and spun the roll. As the head end came around, it shed a number of dark, bloated flies — maggots, too. Disturbed from feasting on the flesh, they writhed on the scuffed metal floor.

Satisfied, he walked back to the new addition. He lifted her so that her trainers pointed at the ground and heaved her back onto his shoulder. He walked her a few paces closer to the container's open door, rested her in a standing position then pushed her in. Her plastic covering slapped against the metal. She rolled so the fronts of her trainers pointed downwards. He spun her round too. It was awkward. The flies that had settled were once again disturbed. They rose as one like a black shadow. When the shadow fell back down it consumed both the women. The flies could sense death, they could sense when it was fresh. He held his breath to step in. He tugged off her trainers, one after the other, then he went back for the thin, outer plastic sheet — the only item that could have caught a fragment of his DNA. A solitary hair or a smear of sweat would be enough. There was thicker plastic underneath and she was wrapped tightly up to her shoulders.

The padlock snapped back shut. He could feel sweat running down his back and his forearms where it would pool into his gloves. Sweat was bad news but it could be managed. He walked back to his truck and sat on the metal boot-lip to catch his breath. After a few minutes he reached further into the truck and dragged out a bin-style incinerator, the sort you could buy in just about any garden centre or home improvement store. It hadn't been used before. The metal was still bright and reflected the low morning sun. He had bought it two months earlier, plenty of time for the shop's CCTV to have wiped itself. He walked it into the side of the barn where the roof was still in place. It looked fragile though: there was a clear dip in the middle and some of the panels looked as if they were only being held up by the spiders' webs that stretched between them. He put the bin down and turned his attention to his paper suit. It was brightest white; he had to squint to look at it as it caught the strengthening sun. He pulled the zipper down and peeled it off, careful to roll it away from his body. He pushed it into the bin, his shoes too. He took the gloves off last, he was careful to pull them off from the fingers not the cuffs. He dropped them into the bin. He had taped a paper sheet flat in the back of his truck that could catch anything that might have fallen from the plastic. He would need to go back for that. He rolled up her outer sheet and laid it in the bin.

He froze. The unmistakeable sound of an engine drifted into the barn and it was getting closer. The wonderful stillness of the morning was broken. He was no longer alone.

Chapter 2

Ron Beasle leaned forward to peer out over the top of the worn steering wheel. An air-freshener jerked and fidgeted in his peripheral vision. He could see a pickup truck pulled over near the barn. It was new looking, the sort with a hard cover over its flatbed on the rear. It was pointing right at him, the wheels turned at an angle and a man who Ron presumed to be the driver was bent forward, studying something on the bonnet.

'What have we got here then, Tucker?' Ron said. On the cracked leather seat next to him the sandy-coloured spaniel looked out eagerly, his tongue sucked in for just an instant at the sound of his name.

Ron stopped. He killed the engine and the driver's door squeaked as he clambered out, careful to keep Tucker inside. The dog jumped instantly over to the driver's seat, clutching a rubber ball in his mouth. The window steamed up where his nose pressed against it. Ron took a moment next to his bottle-green Land Rover. It was a Series 2 — a classic and Ron's pride and joy. His wife often commented that nobody else was even allowed in it, but the dog seemed to have the run of the thing. Ron couldn't argue.

That's what Land Rovers were for, though: muddy fields and muddy dogs.

The man was still bent over the bonnet. He half-turned and straightened up as Ron rolled the sleeves up over his scrawny arms. He checked his shirt was tucked firmly into his jeans.

'Hey!' Ron called out. He walked over to where the man was smiling back at him. 'What brings you up here? You know this is private property, son?'

The man held his smile. 'That's exactly what brings me up here! I work for a construction company. They're at the table looking to take this land on. There's been some discrepancies over the boundaries. I've been asked to come up here and square it up. I'll be honest though, I'm not surprised no one's sure. The boundary isn't clear.'

'It isn't, that's true. But you're well within it here. I've been told that nobody should be up here. I'm here to size the place up for gates. You're lucky we didn't fit them and lock them already or you wouldn't have been able to get out.' He chuckled nervously. It was a bluff. Gates were something they had talked about but there were no definite plans for them yet.

'I'm sure I would have found a way.' The man's smile dropped away a little.

'Not without causing some damage, you wouldn't. How about I take down your name and phone number? That way I can let you know when the gate is up and anybody who wants to get in touch can do so. Who was it you said you work for?'

'I'm not sure I did! But it's McCall's. From what I've been told they're the front-runner to take this place on.'

'And you work on the land acquisition side, do you?'

'I guess that's a pretty good description, yes.

'And your name?'

'Steve. If you need a number you can take McCall's general number. I don't take calls on their behalf.'

'Depends. Are you gonna be up here much longer?'

'I didn't get *your* name?' the man said.

'Ron.' Ron rubbed at his white beard, still trying to size the man up. There was something not quite right about him. Certainly he didn't seem comfortable with their conversation.

'Well, thanks, Ron. And, no, I don't reckon I will be up here much longer. I just stopped to have another look at the map here. The boundaries marked on here definitely aren't right. I think they've overestimated. I need to drive the boundary, best I can, and then I'll be out of your hair. I reckon thirty minutes. That's going to be okay, right?'

'Thirty minutes?'

'Thirty minutes. You'd have to be going some to get a gate measured up, delivered and stuck in the ground in that time right?' He smiled again, but it didn't seem natural to Ron.

'Well, okay. But it will be done by the end of the day. You should tell your people — McCall's — that they may be at the negotiating table but they aren't the only people there. This is still privately owned land. You can't just be coming on here.'

'I will pass that message back, Ron. But if I can just get my work done today I won't be needing to come back anyway. I guess they figure that they want to know exactly what they're bidding for. That makes sense, doesn't it?'

Ron shrugged. He turned and walked to the Land Rover. He still had a question though. 'What is it? Six in the morning? You made an early start, didn't you?'

'And it was just gone five when I left home. I've got two sites to do after this one. I'm self-employed technically, so I work job-and-knock. The earlier I start, the earlier I finish. I've never been one to lie in.'

Ron considered it. It made sense; he was an early riser himself and had once worked on the same principle. 'Well, you're lucky I didn't come up with the police. I thought I would come and speak to you first. The next time you're on here, I will have to get them involved.'

'Understood. Like I said, I won't need to be on here again. I'm just doing what I've been asked.'

'You and me both, Steve.'

'At least I know getting here early makes no difference. I didn't think I would be bothering anyone at this time of day.'

'Well, I'm not one for lying in bed either. I run a gun club — clay pigeon, just up the way. I have to set up this morning. The old man who owned this land was a good friend of mine, a fine shot too. He died real recent. I just want to be sure that the family he left behind don't have any problems. That means no travellers on the site, no rubbish to clear and no one sniffing around before they've done what they need to do to get the deeds.'

'Loud and clear, Ron. I don't get told the history of the land or any plans for it. I'm just the bloke reporting back.'

'Well, he was a good friend. A hard-working man all his life. All he wanted was for his estate to be passed on. That's all any man wants for his family. I said I would make sure it happened and that's what I'm going to do.'

'Understood. Obviously McCall's aren't aware you're keeping an eye on the place.'

'Oh, no one knows, son. It's just a promise me and the wife made to a man on his deathbed. I'd rather keep it that way.'

Steve held his hands up. 'Well that I can understand. Sounds like he was a lucky man to have a friend like you.' He started folding up the large piece of paper.

Ron had one foot on the Land Rover's step but let his eyes lift beyond the man's truck and into the barn. Something in there had been moved. Something was different. 'Have you been in the barn?' His foot thumped back onto the ground. Movement caught his eye; Tucker was back at the window. He ignored him and made for the barn.

'The what?' Steve pulled open the door on the passenger side of his truck and put the folded-up piece of paper on the seat. He sounded disinterested.

Ron persisted. 'The barn? There was a pallet tied up against the side. Someone tried to break into the container before. I don't know why — there's nothing in there — but it costs money if they damage it getting in.'

'The container? No. I have no business with the container. The cost of removing it maybe.'

Ron walked into the barn. 'What the hell? Where did this come from?' He could see a new-looking bin that had been pushed out of sight. There were drag marks in the dust on the floor. They looked fresh. He tugged off the lid and looked inside. There was a white all-in-one suit inside. He had used them plenty of times before when he was working with crop sprayers or when he was decorating. He lifted it out. It was a large size and it looked brand new. There was a plastic sheet and a black sack underneath it that had been tied shut.

'Has there been any work going on, on site? That looks like something a workman might wear?' Steve said. He had moved to the back of his truck. He was closer to Ron now. His casual demeanour had dropped away a little bit. He rested on the back of his truck, both his hands pushed behind his back. 'There'll be asbestos all round this place. Maybe somebody's been thinking about removing it already,' he lifted his eyes to the roof.

'Not that I know about,' Ron said. He moved towards the back of the container and paused at the door. He rattled a chunky padlock. He stepped back out so he could see Steve by his truck.

But Steve was closer still — in the barn, just a step away with his hands in his pockets now. 'What's the matter?' he said.

'You see this? This weren't here the last time.' Ron held the lock and bent to inspect it. 'I put my own on here. Have you messed with this? Did you put this on here?'

'Ron, please! I've told you my business up here. I have no interest in containers. Just land and existing buildings. I guess you need to get those gates in sooner rather than later!'

Whatever Steve said, there was definitely something not quite right about him. Ron couldn't put his finger on it. He had thought at first that the man was nervous but now he wasn't so sure. 'Right, well I've got some croppers in the car. This kind of thing has happened up here before. I thought it was gypsies. They go out on the rob and then they stash the goods on somebody else's land until the heat is off. There was a quad bike in here once that somebody had nicked.' Ron strode to the back doors of the Land Rover and pulled the rear doors open roughly. He told Tucker to stay where he was. Tucker jumped through onto the back seats, close enough to smell his freedom.

Ron picked out his bolt-croppers, big ones, designed for heavy-duty cutting. He struggled a little under their weight as he moved back past where the man was still leaning on his truck, casual with his hands in his pockets. A little way into the barn, Ron's front foot caught on a loose rock and he stumbled. He felt a drop of sweat on his brow as he lifted the croppers to the lock. He was breathing heavily. He had to step back. The handles were long and the cutting jaws were heavy and cumbersome. Too big — they couldn't fit within the metal arms of the lock. They weren't going to do it. 'Dammit! I haven't got anything smaller,' Ron said.

'You want me to have a look in my truck? I can see if I've got anything that might fit?'

Ron spun towards Steve's voice. He was almost leaning over him. Ron took a step away. He considered his options. He made a show of checking his watch and then he shook his head. 'I wouldn't worry too much. I'll be back this afternoon. I got a booked-out shoot to run all morning.' Steve was still close. He was staring at Ron, too, his eyes seemed to have gained intensity.

'Let me have a look. Just in case.' Steve lingered for just a second then walked back to his truck. Ron stayed put. Steve lifted the tailgate and the hydraulics hissed. He leaned in and there were scraping noises as he searched and then what sounded like a toolbox rattling. Ron took the opportunity to wipe his brow. Steve turned back towards him. 'I can't say I've snapped too many locks. I've got a toolbox full of gear — most of it I've never used. You can have a look . . .' He stepped away from the truck and gestured at the space within. 'See if anything in there'll do the job if you like.' Ron moved a little closer to see into the back of the truck. A metal toolbox had been dragged out onto the dropped-down tailgate. Beyond it, plastic sheeting covered most of what was inside.

Ron deliberately rubbed his chin as if weighing things up. 'You know what? It don't matter now. I'll be back in a few hours. I can have a look then.' He gave Steve a slightly wider berth as he walked back to the Land Rover. As he saw it, his options were to return later when he was on his own and he could cut the lock off and then call someone if he needed to. Or maybe this Steve had something to do with whatever stolen gear was in there and he would take the opportunity to get it out while Ron was gone. Either way, Ron didn't need to get himself involved with anything right now. The man's story was plausible. Now that he was closer and the paperwork had been removed he could even see that the man's truck had *McCALL'S* written across the front door. But there was still something about Steve that made Ron feel uncomfortable.

'I assume you'll be gone by the time I get back, son?'

'Don't you worry. I'll be long gone. I've got a meeting to get to myself today.'

'Well, okay. This is your last chance — don't forget. We should have those gates up soon. You make sure you do what you need to do.' Ron peered over at the container one last time.

'I'll make sure of it, Ron,' Steve said.

'I'll sort this out later.' Ron pulled the door shut and started the engine. He crunched a gear as he moved off. He looked in his rear-view mirror, watching the man called Steve getting smaller. He was still standing, leant back against his truck, his hands pushed firmly into his pockets. Ron's eyes snatched away from the mirror when Tucker pushed his wet nose under his hand. He patted his old companion.

'Well, Tucker. We didn't like him, did we?'

* * *

Ron exhaled as the last of the punters' cars accelerated away. As a final service to his clients, he had shown them back to the area of hard standing that served as their car park. Saturday mornings were hard work — amateur hour. But it was always a relaxing time when they were all gone, leaving him on his own to clear up a few bits and pieces and have a last cup of tea in the peace of the woodland setting. Ron and one other had taken a group each through the twenty stands where the punters each took their turn at hitting the spinning clays. They varied from first-timers to casual fanatics. Some were on a team-building exercise, some on stag weekends. All were a pain in his arse. He was getting too old to be babysitting. He much preferred the day-to-day running of the site that was his normal responsibility through the week.

He made it back to the club-hut. It was little more than a wooden shack really, but it did the job. From here he could cook the bacon rolls, fire up the urn for hot drinks and provide some covered seating out of the inevitable British rain. Not that there had been too much of that recently.

'Ah well, Tucker. Another shoot closer to retirement.' The only reply was the breeze through the leaves. 'Tucker?'

Tucker was never far from Ron's heels — apart from when the bangs started, then he would retreat and lie under a makeshift bed beneath the wooden table in the hut. Ron checked under the table. No Tucker — just a solid rubber ball with teeth marks and hair stuck to it. If Tucker wasn't with him then he would be with his ball. 'TUCKER!' Ron shouted and then froze, listening for the sound of paws running towards him. There was nothing. He peered out into the woods, spinning on the spot where he stood. He retraced his steps, back to where he had taken the group to their cars. The path was short with wild ferns and trees on either side. The sun was brighter where the trees thinned out for the car park. There was just his Land Rover left.

A bark!

He stopped still. He heard it again; it was Tucker's bark, over to Ron's left. He walked towards the sound, just a few steps. There it was again! He thought it was coming from the road. He walked to the entrance. The car park was solid mud and stones so the tarmac of the road was a relief underfoot. It was mud-stained and the sides crumbled into potholes left over from a harsh winter. He took a couple of steps out into the road. Tight country lanes led right and left. The turning for the gun club was on a bend and punters often overshot. A dusty mirror was fixed opposite to aid drivers pulling out. He stopped again. He could hear an engine, ticking over just around the bend. Maybe Tucker had been running out in the road and someone had stopped. It wasn't like him.

'Tucker!' He shouted. The responding bark was immediate and clearly coming from the other side of the road. There was a gap in the hedge opposite, part of a footpath with a stile. Ron moved towards it. Tucker came into sight in the field on the other side. He was straining against a rope tied off round his collar.

'What the hell?' Ron quickened his pace.

He was vaguely aware of the change in the engine tone and the sound moving towards him but his thoughts were fixed on his faithful spaniel and the mystery of why he was tied to a tree. As Ron moved across the sun-drenched country lane he didn't consider that the engine noise meant that the vehicle was coming for him — not until it was too late.

He turned to the sound. He barely had time to see movement. The sun was reflected so brightly in the vehicle's metal front that it was like being hit by a beam of light. Then he was aware of the engine sound moving over the top of him as it revved and surged. And then all was silent. The beam of light was gone and there was only darkness.

Chapter 3

She gasped for air. She didn't know where she was. She didn't remember falling asleep or how she got here. She tried to sit up. Her neck shot with pain as she tensed, her stomach too, and she cried out. She felt dizzy. She didn't know if it was pitch black because there was no light or because her eyes were shut. She tried to move her arms to feel her environment, to rub at her face. *Her arms were stuck!*

Other senses were coming back to her. She calmed her breathing enough to detect a rancid smell. It was thick in the air, palpable, like nothing she had smelled before. No, wait! She *had* smelled it before, but she couldn't think where. She couldn't think about much at all. Some of the fuzz was clearing from her mind. She couldn't move any part of her body and so she tried to focus on her breathing; she needed to stay calm, to work out where she was and why she couldn't move. There would be an explanation. There would be a way out.

Eventually, she was able to roll onto her back. The feeling of the cold metal against her cheek was gone but the chill and the pungent smell were evidence enough that she wasn't dreaming. She couldn't be; it was all so real. Her arms felt numb, her legs too. There were pins and needles in her hands and fingers now that she had moved. Little pinpricks of light came into focus above her. She centred on them, straining her eyes, trying in vain to make out what they were. She concentrated on listening instead. There was a buzzing sound, constant but changeable, like a tiny motorbike moving closer then further away. She had assumed it was part of the dizziness and her confusion. Now she considered that it might not be. It was suddenly loud in her ear — then it stopped. Something tickled her face. She tried to move her arms again. The sensation moved across her face, onto her lips. She slammed her mouth shut and shook her head and her neck flashed with a searing pain. She blew hard. The tickle was gone for just a few seconds before it was back somewhere different. Something walked over her eye. *Flies.*

She jerked, her neck shot with pain again. She tried to roll back onto her front, away from the buzzing. The movement made her feel nauseous and she retched. She tried to force her mouth shut but her lips opened in a spasm as she coughed out bile and froth. The pain in her stomach was sharp, almost unbearable.

She stayed as still as she could to try and recover. It took a while. Where her eyes had started to get used to the gloom, it now felt like the darkness was closing in around her. She couldn't move any part of her body. She stopped trying. She was overcome with exhaustion. Her face tickled again. She didn't even have the energy to react. The buzzing drifted away to silence.

Chapter 4

'Thanks, Dad!' Lisa Simpkiss forced a smile. Her stepfather's glance lingered on her. He was looking at her the way he always did when he dropped her at her meetings. He didn't need to drive her. She'd have been happy to walk, but her dad always said, 'I like to make sure you get there okay,' which actually meant *I like to make sure you go.*

Lisa stood up out of the car and pushed the door shut. She was conscious that he didn't pull away. When she made it to the door of the sometime Scout hut in the seaside town of Langthorne, the car was still ticking over behind her. She was thirty-three years old and her dad was actually watching her to the door of her Alcoholics Anonymous meeting. This was not the way she had envisaged her life panning out.

She made it through the door without looking back. An older lady with a smile so welcoming it verged on the patronising sat on a chair to the left. She looked expectant.

'Lisa,' said Lisa.

The woman held her smile. 'And are you here for the meeting?'

'Yes, please.'

'Okay, great. I'll just mark you in. There's tea and coffee in the main hall. It's on your left as you walk in.'

'Thanks.' Lisa knew the drill. She had been to enough of these now. She had argued the first time, though. She even made a bit of a scene when they asked her for a name. She just went off on one — not giving them time to explain. She remembered it like it was yesterday. It hadn't been a good time in her life and she'd been an angry ball of frustration, only there to please other people in her life. If she had taken the time to listen she would have known that you only had to give a first name — it didn't even have to be your own. It was about fire regs and noting how many people used the facilities, nothing more. It had been a perfectly reasonable request at a time when Lisa was anything but. Now she'd come to appreciate the pattern of her meetings and of her movements when she attended them. She had come to understand herself and grasp just how important a clear structure was in keeping her on track. If that structure slipped away she could never predict what direction her life might take.

She moved to the coffee laid out on a table and poured herself one from a flask. One sachet of sugar stirred with a plastic stirrer. She turned to the open room. The blinds were pulled across the windows. They looked like they were glowing, a hint at the strong sunshine outside. The light levels overall were low. *Perfect.* It smelled of dust and polish and the temperature was verging on too hot to be comfortable. The door to the kitchenette on the other side of the room was open and she could hear a bubbling urn. It wasn't loud, barely noticeable normally, but it was the only sound. Four people were in the room already and she recognised them all. The chairs were laid out in a sort of circle, the seated patrons spread out as much as possible. She didn't tend to talk to people at these things. Most didn't in her experience. Normally you got just one or two who would be desperate to tell the rest about how close they had come to not being there at all. Lisa didn't want to talk about her own experiences of it. But she did like to listen. She liked to hear the desperation, stories from around the room of people hiding from the world, ashamed at what they had become, and of how they were still lying to their friends and families — and to themselves. She didn't want to talk about it herself but she liked to hear it all. She took comfort from knowing that other people were doing it, too.

She moved to sit down. The seats were moulded plastic. Not comfortable. She tried the coffee. It was far too hot. She leaned down to put it on the floor and got her phone out. It told the time as 12:53. The meeting would start in seven minutes. More people came in and they all made for the flasks. There was some hushed conversation and Lisa looked over. Two of the regulars were sharing a joke. One laughed a lot harder than the other. He sat down first. The quieter guy sat a few chairs away. The first man looked as if he had expected the other to sit closer and to continue the conversation. He looked put out. She liked to watch people, to see how they interacted with the world. She was still watching when a chair scraped to her right.

'Shit!' It was a man's voice. Her leg suddenly felt warmer. She looked down. He'd knocked her coffee over. The liquid ran against her trainers, the steam rose up against her bare leg.

'I'm so sorry!' She looked up. A man was standing over her with his palms out towards her. 'I didn't see it on the floor there. Hang on!' He jogged to the kitchenette and came back with a roll of tissue. He tore off several sheets and laid them out on the floor. Immediately they stained brown. He dabbed at her trainers.

'Don't worry,' she said, hurriedly.

'I don't think I got any on there. It's just round the bottom—'

'Don't worry! It's fine!' she snapped. She turned away, back towards the coffee. She considered getting another. Maybe he read her thoughts.

'Let me get you another one.' He was still stood over her. She had kept her eyes down but looked up at him now.

'Honestly, I'll go get my own. It happens.'

'Least I can do!' He smiled. He was about her age and had dark features and nice eyes. His head was shaven close to his scalp and he had two-day-old stubble. He wore a designer polo shirt buttoned all the way up so it gripped tight around his neck. He was good-looking in an effortless kind of a way. 'How do you take it?'

She shrugged. 'One sugar.'

He stepped away immediately and she followed him over to the table with her eyes. He wore tight-fitting jeans over white trainers. His back looked strong and broad, his white t-shirt strained over it as he bent forward to sugar her drink. He came back to where she was sitting, two cups in hand.

'I figured I would get one for myself while I was over there.' He smiled again.

'Thanks.'

'Sorry,' he said.

'Don't worry about it.' She fell silent. She moved her attention back to her phone, scrolling idly through it. She didn't care for phones. She barely used hers aside from as a prop to repel conversation.

'Is this your first?' He persisted. Her prop had failed.

'No.'

'Oh. Mine neither. I haven't been to one here before, though. Any good?'

Lisa looked up from her phone. 'I don't know if they're supposed to be *good* are they?'

'I suppose not.'

A man walked in carrying his own chair. Lisa recognised him as the regular host of the meeting. He called himself Ian and told the same story every week. Sure enough he ran through it again. It was a standard tale of woe, of how he had once had a wife, a nice house and a future but alcohol had taken it all away from him and now he was doing what he could to get it back. Weren't they all? His story was for the benefit of any new people. It was also to break the ice, to get people talking about their own experiences. There didn't seem to be a shortage of people wanting to do that. Some meetings were like that. Lisa sat quiet the whole time. The man with the nice eyes was quiet until the very end, when the host solicited him to speak. It took a couple of prompts but he relented.

'Yeah, okay. I've been to a few of these. Not here though. I have a . . . an addiction. A problem. I take my hat off to the people around the room that have spoken so far and are able to say exactly what they are. I'm not there yet. But I know I have an addiction. And I slipped up really recently. I didn't want to but I didn't feel like I had a choice. I had been a few weeks clean, I was planning on getting to a month but then I slipped the once and one thing led to another . . .' He paused. Lisa dared a look over to see if he was getting emotional. He was shaking his head and his eyes were down. She couldn't tell.

Ian took advantage of the pause to get his own voice heard. 'So today is day one. And it's okay to have a few of those. As many day ones as it takes. You made it here, though. You should be positive about that. You know your problem and you want to change. I don't know your story but I bet you're a lot further along than you were. We've all been there. Don't beat yourself up too much for taking fourteen steps forward in those two weeks and then slipping one step back. You're still closer to where you want to be.'

'I guess that's true.'

'No doubt about it.' Ian was beaming. Lisa always thought he was a little too delighted with his own advice. Like he saw himself as more than just the bloke who sent out the time for the meeting. He was still an addict who needed these meetings. Just like everyone else.

There were some murmured voices of support around the room. The man flicked those handsome eyes left to meet with Lisa's and offered her a smile. She returned it awkwardly.

The meeting came to an end and she stood up. She refilled her coffee cup from the flask. It was part of her routine. She would walk it to the bench over the road, the one that overlooked the park. She would sit there and finish her drink and then walk back home. She liked to walk home. Her route took her past two off-licences and a pub called The Mariner. Sometimes she would even drop into the pub and buy a coke. She would sit at the bar on her own and drink it while she watched the regulars with their beers and wines. It was the only time she ever wanted to go there. Saturdays were her day to show the world that she was winning. It was a symbolic day for her. The weekends used to be when she was at her worst. It was how all this had started. You could always justify a drink at the weekend.

Today, she fancied just the bench. The road outside was busy. She had to jog across while balancing her cup. She made it to the other side and sat down.

'Mind if I join you?' The man with the nice eyes stood over her.

'No,' Lisa lied. Straight away she was thinking of how long she would have to stay before she could get up and leave without offending him. She even considered getting up straight away. Saturdays weren't about making friends. They were about hiding from her former self. He sat down. She kept her gaze forward and shuffled a little to increase the gap between them on the bench.

'Do they help?' he said.

'Sorry, what?'

'The meetings . . . do they help?'

'Depends what you want help with.'

'I just want to stop. I notice you didn't talk in there. I wondered if maybe you thought they were a waste of time?'

'It's not really why I go — to talk about it, I mean. Everyone's different. But, yeah, they help me.'

'Sorry, I didn't mean to bother you. I guess I'm just looking for someone to tell me how I do this. I've had enough of people telling me that it's something you have to do on your own.'

Lisa looked over at him. He was gazing straight out into the distance. His tone was tinged with melancholy and desperation. She remembered being there. 'You have to want to do it. No one can do *that* bit for you. But once you do it, other people can help, sure they can. It's a big thing to go to one of these meetings. You're trying to make it better at least. That's the best I can offer you.'

'Thanks.' He sounded genuine.

'No problem.' She stood up quickly; it was like a reaction. She even surprised herself. Her coffee slopped over the sides of the cup and onto her hands. She sucked the liquid off her fingers. 'See you next week?' She didn't know why she had said that. It was like a panicked reaction. She didn't want to see him next week or any week. That wasn't what Saturdays were for.

He looked up at her. 'Maybe!' he said. His grin seemed tinged with mischief.

Lisa walked hurriedly away.

Chapter 5

'Harry Blaker! I heard there was a Major Crime Senior Officer on the way but I didn't realise they were going to have to dig one up!'

'I'm not dead yet, Vince. How are you? Still ugly as hell I see.'

'I seem to remember your wife disagreeing.'

'You've moved on from the mum jokes at least.'

Inspector Harry Blaker took up Vince's hearty handshake. The grip was crushing as always. With men like Vince Arnold, handshakes were more of a competition than a welcome. Harry had worked with Vince a number of times. Vince was generally his go-to man if he wanted someone bringing in — the more dangerous the better. He was a man who loved to nick a murderer. A dying breed.

'I'm sure I've got a mum reference somewhere,' Vince said. He was short and squat, almost as wide as he was tall. His hair still looked like it was shaped by the army, his freshly shaven face likewise.

Harry, in comparison, was well aware that he was perhaps the *anti*-Vince. He'd been two days without a shave, he had lost the ability to shape his hair into anything a long time ago, and age and a lack of desire to stay in shape had seen his strong frame become somewhat smudged around the edges. 'I don't doubt it. So what have we got that you can't handle? And it had better be good.' Vince and Harry were standing in a clearing in the thick woodland that doubled as a car park. There were already a number of police vehicles on the scene but they were all silent and vacant, a CSI van among them. The side door was popped and he had seen a blur of white suit walk in and out of it already. The closest vehicle to him looked a lot more suited to their rural surroundings: an old style, bottle-green Land Rover. It looked clean and well cared for.

'Hit and run, I hear,' Vince said. 'I'm sure they've saved a special briefing for you though, *sir*.'

'I'm sure they have. I assume you had the one where you can just sit and colour-in if you want to?'

Vince roared and slapped Harry on the shoulder hard enough for it to sting. 'The dead fella is out on the road. There's a club house just through the woods there. Have you been here before?'

'Been here? No — should I have?'

'I'm a regular. It's a clay pigeon place. I've got my own shotgun now. It's a lovely way to spend a morning up here. Twenty stands, pretending each spinning clay is your wife's face.' Vince lifted his arms like he was holding a weapon and closed one eye to squint down its imaginary barrel.

'Is this *your* wife now, Vince, or still mine?'

'Listen, I've got a very specific set of skills — you know me! If you need something sorted, I can do a little something. Mate's rates!' That roar of laughter was back again. A uniform sergeant appeared at the entrance to the woodland. He was clearly awaiting his time to interrupt. Harry got the hint and made his way over.

'I'll sign you in. I appreciate you're too important to write your name out these days!' Vince called out after him as he followed the uniform sergeant into the woodland.

'We're down this way, sir,' the sergeant said. Harry was a few paces behind. The path was well worn, lined with ferns and bushes on either side as well as mature trees. The path led to another clearing. This one had a wooden hut in it. The side facing them was open and the roof had an overhang. A Portakabin lay just beyond it and was signposted as a toilet. From here a number of other paths spread off. Some of them had labels high up in the trees. *STAND ONE* was the most prominent and a thick black arrow that had run some of its colour pointed the way there.

Under the wooden overhang was a picnic bench that was being used to hold police paperwork and kit. There was a sort of counter over to the left-hand side. A few kitchen facilities punctured the surfaces behind. An older man in khaki trousers and a short-sleeved t-shirt stood behind it. He was still and quiet, as if he was taking in all of the activity. He also wore a quilted vest with deep pockets in its sides. He had his hands thrust into them. He looked every bit the shooting enthusiast.

'We're using this as a bit of a point for kit. I'm Sergeant McCallister — well, Paul. So what do you know, sir?'

'Dead guy. Came in as an RTC, right? That's about it.'

'Not much then. Well, it doesn't look like your standard RTC to me. The poor fella damned near had his head taken off. The traffic boys don't reckon the driver even slowed up. That *Town-and-Country*-looking gent back over by the kettle is John. He was working with our victim this morning. He was gone before anything happened but he came back when he heard the commotion. He lives local and knows the victim well.'

'Has anyone spoken to him?'

'We've got his details. That's about it.'

'Okay. I'll have a chat with him.'

'Did you want to do that first? He seems very keen to be making everyone tea. I think he needs to be busy. Or did you want to go and see our victim? He's still in situ.'

'He won't be going anywhere any time soon.' Harry looked over towards John. His expression hadn't changed. His eyes seemed to have lost their focus, his lips were pulled back in a sort of permanent grimace. Sure signs of shock. 'I'll speak to John. Then he can go home.'

John was quick to offer tea. The sergeant was right. Tea making had become his purpose and he was clinging on to it.

'Not for me, thanks. Are you okay, John?'

'Not really, you know. I don't know what to make of it all, really. I've done this a thousand times. I come here most days. Ron does too. He runs the site. Not always at the weekend but he was covering today. We got let down.'

'What do you do, John?'

'On Saturdays I run the groups. We get parties down here . . . stag parties, office outings or a just a few mates getting together. It's pocket money, really, but I get to shoot for free when I want to. And it gets me out the house. I walk them round the stands, give them a bit of coaching where I need to. Nothing too stressful.'

'The skipper over there, he said you had gone already when the accident happened?'

'Accident? Is that what you're saying now? When I got here I was asked to stay because you lot thought it was suspicious.'

'And what do you think?'

'It doesn't seem right to me. They say he got run down out front. I can't think of any reason why he would even have needed to go that way. Not out of his Landy.'

'Landy?'

'His Land Rover. The Series 2.'

'Ah, so that's his in the car park. I did see it. The site doesn't go over the other side then?'

'No, not at all. It's a public right-of-way on the other side. We don't have any stands pointing that way for obvious reasons.'

'And do you keep records of who's been here?'

'Yes, of course. We have to for safety reasons.'

'Have you handed those details over to anyone yet?'

'No. I'll look them out.'

'Did anyone stand out? Did Ron get into any disagreements, anyone complain or make a scene?'

'No. We don't get complaints. I can't remember any at least. Not ever. And Ron's such a good guy . . . or at least he was.'

'Okay, John. My colleague has your details. You don't need to stick around if you want to get home.'

'I don't really know what to do. I think I might stay and lock up. I might be able to help. I said I would take Tucker back to John's wife, too. I'm kind of putting that off, you know?'

'Tucker?' Harry repeated. John looked to the ground behind where Harry stood. Harry turned and stooped to see what he was looking at. He could just see a furry nose at first. He squatted down until he could see the full face of a handsome spaniel peering out through sad eyes. 'Hey, Tucker!' he said. 'Will you come say hello?' Harry had much more time for dogs than people.

'Only if you've got a biscuit for that one. He doesn't come out for anyone but Ron. Never left his side.'

'Like all good dogs.' Harry moved a little closer. Gently, he lifted his hand. Tucker strained towards it, his nose twitching. When he realised Harry had nothing for him he moved back to resting his chin on his paw. He was sandy coloured and his collar displayed his name in big letters. A piece of frayed rope stuck out from under it.

'Where is he normally tied up, John?'

'I've never seen him tied. Where he is now, that's where he takes himself when the shooting starts.

Otherwise he's on Ron's heel. He never bothers anyone. He's a good dog.'

Harry reached in to pat Tucker on his soft head. He stood back up. He thanked John and moved back to where Sergeant Paul McCallister was talking into his phone. He finished his call as Harry approached.

'He okay?' he said, gesturing towards John.

Harry looked back over. John still looked in shock. Harry shrugged. 'He will be.'

'Did you want to go and see him then?'

'Yes.'

They walked to the scene. He noted that the sergeant's demeanour changed a little as they approached and when they reached the roadside he pointed the way and excused himself. Harry had never been one to worry about gruesome scenes. Death was inevitable. It was coming for us all and the best you could hope for was to go out with your trousers still pulled up. This was not something Ron had managed. Ron's body was laid out at the side of the road. Harry guessed it was as he had been found. He was a bit of a mess. Harry would often find bodies laid out straight, their heads tilted back, their clothes cut open where those first on scene or ambulance crews had tried to breathe life back into them. It wasn't his preference; it hindered an investigation. It wasn't the case with Ron. Anyone would have seen that he was beyond saving. His body was bent in half. And not the way it might naturally bend. He was facing down into the ground, too, and his head was flatter than it should have been. His body was filthy overall, his trousers had been dragged down to his ankles by the forces in play and he was mixed up with bits of the hedgerow. The bank itself was scarred; a chunk was missing from it and strewn all over the road. The CSI stood up when she became aware of Harry's approach. She stepped away from Ron and pulled her mask down.

Harry spoke first. 'Looks like he was dragged a fair way.'

'And how are you, Harry? Still skipping the niceties, I see. We talked about this didn't we?'

'We did. I think I told you then about teaching an old dog new tricks.'

'I can't imagine a time when Harry Blaker was anything but an old dog.' Harry couldn't help but smile. Charlotte 'Charley' Mace pulled the hood down that was fitted to her paper suit and ran her fingers through her short hair. Harry had worked with her any number of times on everything from minor burglaries when he was in CID all the way up to the more serious end of the scale. Harry liked her. She was very competent, she knew her job and she had the edge about her that you needed to manage a crime scene effectively.

'So, *how are you?* Is that what you were after?'

'Well, it's a start. I've been better, Harry.'

'There you are, that's the problem with small talk. Now I've opened up to hear your woes.'

'I wouldn't waste my breath on anything personal — don't worry about that. I take it you've come from the hut up the path? I told that sergeant that it all needs cordoning off. If we think this man's been done in and the suspect was up there this morning, why are we not treating it like any other scene?'

Harry scowled back towards the way he had come. 'I get the impression everyone seems to be happy this is a hit and run rather than a murder. We're missing any sign of a motive, right? The only answers are going to be on Ron here. Any early thoughts?'

'That's a big call this early.'

'It would be. We're not making any calls. First impressions?'

'Well, the Serious Crash Team have already been out and done their bit. They took photos of the scene, measurements and all that. They can't find any evidence of a car skidding, braking or even swerving before our friend was hit. Either he jumped out and surprised them or this was done on purpose. I think they're the reason you got a call.'

'Cars would shift along here. There's no limit is there?'

'No, but the traffic lot . . . they reckon he was hit at a lower speed. Too fast and you're thrown straight up apparently. You have to be going slower to drag someone under the wheels. That's another reason why they called it as suspicious. To hit someone at a lower speed you have to mean it. You would be able to stop, rather than dragging him twenty metres.'

'So the driver meant to hurt him.'

'Or kill him.'

'It would have been useful if Crash had stuck around to talk to me about their theories.'

'It would. They had some good ones, too. If you look further up there you can see some skid marks. One theory is that they're linked to this scene. They're certainly fresh. They reckon he might have kept the momentum up until the body came free from the underside, *then* slammed on the brakes.'

'To make sure he was dead?' Harry was still scowling.

'That's one theory. No one could think of another reason. Shock maybe? I'm sure it will all be in their report. But I reckon that's why they don't stick around, that way you can't question them before it's done.'

'We'll see about that,' Harry growled.

'I'm sure you will!' Charley broke into a smile. Her hands moved to her hips and she looked down at her subject. 'I'll do a body map. That will give you a full forensic lift. With the slower impacts we can struggle to get anything, though. When you get someone thrown up and over they can pick up paint flecks, bits of headlight or windscreen glass or dirt from somewhere else — stuff that can help. In this case he might not have come into much contact with the body of the vehicle at all. He's been battered by the road and crushed by the wheels. I'm not sure what answers you're going to get.'

'Okay. I'll get some doors knocked. See if we can find a witness.' Harry stepped out into the road. He could see small yellow markers. They looked like tiny sandwich boards with numbers written on their faces. Every one marked something that might be significant. He counted six along a fifty-metre line that had been drawn in chalk. He guessed that to be the trajectory Ron had taken after being hit by the car. It still astounded Harry what the Serious Crash Team were capable of determining. Charley was right, though: he would have to wait for the full report. And they wouldn't do him any favours getting that done quickly. He had a little history with that team.

He pulled his phone from his pocket. He pressed to dial Chief Inspector Julian Lowe, the man who had sent him in the first place.

'What you got down there, Harry?'

'As you said, really. A dead body and probably dead after he was hit by a car.'

'Any idea why?'

'Not much. The traffic boys said something about it being a low speed collision. I think that makes intent more likely but they've not stuck around to explain that any further. I'll have to get back onto them.'

'Yes, they can be a bit funny those traffic boys.'

'They can. Charley Mace is here too. She's doing what she can with what is left of our victim. I don't think she's hopeful of getting much from him.'

'Okay, no problem. Thanks for turning out. I'll see you when you get back in?'

Harry was walking as he talked. He'd gone beyond where the Serious Crash Team had apparently marked as the point of impact. There was a stile on the left side of the road. It was coated in dried mud and the path leading away from it was well worn. He peered out into the field beyond and then was suddenly aware that the boss was still talking.

'Harry? Are you still there?'

'Yeah, sorry. Yeah, I'll come and see you when I get in. I've got to go.' He hung up the phone and pushed it back into his pocket. He stepped over the stile and dropped into a sparse-looking field. The closest feature was straight ahead in the form of a solid-looking tree. A tattered old rope was tied off loosely around the bottom. He squatted over it. Then he paced back to the stile.

'Charley!' He had to shout to make himself heard. She was kneeling over Ron Beasle's body. Harry could see that she had started layering him with stickers. She would cover his whole body with small, square stickers around the size of post-it notes. They would be labelled and photographed, then peeled off one by one, and bagged and tagged. It was painstaking and, in this case, quite probably pointless. It was designed to capture any fibres, paint flecks, alien DNA or anything that might have transferred during the incident. It could take hours — much longer with interruptions. She stood bolt upright. She made up the ground quickly.

'This had better be good,' she said.

'There's a tether round the tree in here. Can you get a picture in situ and then seize it?'

'I can do. I assume you have another end for comparison?'

'I might have. Around Tucker's neck.'

'Who's Tucker?'

'Ron's cocker spaniel. He's looking rather sorry for himself under the table back at the hut.'

Charley was rubbing her chin. 'I assume he's something worth crossing the road for?'

'I would, wouldn't you?'

'Yeah, I would. I'll need to do the same with the other end. Don't you touch the dog. And you need to tell that sergeant to cordon off this whole site like he should have done from the start.'

Harry didn't disagree. He made his way back towards the hut in the woods to break the news.

Chapter 6

Maddie Ives swept through the foyer of a luxury Manchester hotel with the stride and the air of someone who knows that she is turning heads. Attracting attention. She had chosen her outfit for that very purpose. The dress was a tight-fitting black number with the side cut into a violent slit almost to the hip that flashed a whole leg with every stride and another section carefully shaped to reveal her lower back, finishing just above her bottom. The shoes were jet black with thin straps and killer heels. She needed to be seen, but by one man in particular.

Eddie Flint was always easy to spot. He sat on one of the high stools at the bar. A drink was placed in front of him as she entered. It was a short glass on a cotton coaster. The ice still swirled in the glass as she pressed up against the bar beside him. He was dressed down today. The day before he'd been wearing an expensive Italian suit and two-tone designer shoes; today he'd opted for a brown jacket and jeans. He looked like he was trying to blend in as best as anyone could in the bar of one of the more exclusive five-star hotels on the bank of the Manchester Ship Canal. Even if Maddie hadn't known him from his reputation, his watch would have given him away. She knew her watches. She found them to be the most reliable method of spotting wealth — in men at least. Sometimes the well-heeled millionaires of the world wanted to just blend in, to not draw attention to themselves. His clothing smacked of that but his twenty-thousand-pound vintage Rolex watch? That told a different story.

He didn't look over. He reached out for his drink and pulled it in front of him. He was leaning forward, both his hands resting on the bar. It wasn't just his clothing that was a marked change from twenty-four hours earlier; his whole demeanour was different. Yesterday he'd been the centre of attention, buying drinks for anything in a skirt and even some in a shirt — looking every bit a man on the hunt. Maybe that was when she should have made her move, but he had been surrounded by women, all looking for the same thing. There'd been no way for her to stand out; she would have had to chase *him* and that simply wasn't her style. It was for different reasons that this evening didn't feel right, but at least she could get access to him easily enough. And she hadn't put this dress on for nothing.

Maddie placed her clutch bag on the bar. She made sure the metal clasp clanged off the surface. He didn't look up, let alone look over. The barman moved towards her and looked expectant. 'Madam?'

'I'm not quite sure what I fancy this evening,' she said. She flicked a glance back over. Eddie Flint was still staring into his drink.

'What's that you're drinking?' she called out towards him.

Eddie didn't react. He didn't even look up.

'It's a Cuban. Would you care for one?' The barman answered for him. But the barman was no damned good to her.

'A fine choice,' she said, loud enough to be overheard. 'Thank you.' The barman turned away to prepare her drink. She leaned over to speak to the man who still had his head bent. 'I haven't had a Cuban in a while. Thanks for the inspiration.'

Eddie did now turn his head. His eyes were wide, his lips were pulled back over his teeth. Maddie wasn't sure if he was tense or on something. 'What?' he snapped.

'Cuban, right?' She gestured at his drink.

'Yeah.'

'I was looking for inspiration. Thank you for providing it.' She swept her long, brown hair out of her eyes and over her shoulder.

'Oh, yeah, you're welcome.' He moved back to staring into his drink. The barman pushed a cotton coaster in front of her. The drink quickly followed.

'I wonder if I might have made a mistake?' she said.

The man bit down, his cheek creased and he turned back to face her. 'What?' he said again.

'I said, I wonder if I might have made a mistake. It's just you don't seem to be enjoying it too much. I can be a good listener, you know.'

He turned back to his glass. He picked it up and lifted it to eye level. He swirled it, staring intently at the movement of the liquid. 'I should be enjoying it. I should be savouring every last drop of it. This is my last drink.' He dropped it clumsily back onto the bar. The liquid fidgeted and brushed against the top.

She smiled at him — not that he would notice — he was back to looking down at the bar. 'I've said that a few times in my life! I gave it up once for real. Lasted a few months. I figured I could do without it. You know what I realised?'

He spun to face her. The intensity had grown in his expression. 'They're going to fucking *kill* me!' He snatched his eyes left, just for a millisecond then he was back hovering over his drink. He scooped it up and downed it in one. He tapped the bar. The barman immediately started making another.

Maddie picked up her own drink. She used the glass to hide her reaction. She hadn't been expecting that. She took a mouthful. She let her eyes scan lazily around the room. The stool had a top that spun and she used it to twist her body. It was just after 6 p.m. — still early. There were a few men and women in business suits. Some on their own and a couple of groups. She guessed they were having a drink straight from work. It was a large area, a modern space with subtle white backlighting. The seating was mainly green leather with thick studs down the sides and tables with clean edges. At the far end against a wooden mesh, a table stood out — or at least its occupants did. They stared over at her. Two men together, both solidly built, their necks pushing against their shirt collars. They were both sat facing her, with jackets done up despite the heat. Nothing about them was natural. Casually she turned back towards the bar, inwardly chastising herself for not noticing them on the way in. She took another mouthful of her drink. It wasn't her tipple, far too sweet. She fought back a grimace. She heard a sound, it sounded like a sniff at first. Another followed quickly. Eddie Flint was *crying*.

'Are you okay?' she said. She tried to hide her surprise. Everything she knew about this man screamed at her that he was not alright. He was not the sort of man to shed tears.

'How did it get to this point?' He was still facing down his drink. A drop of water balanced on the end of this nose. He sniffed again.

'Do you want me to call somebody?' she said.

'A fucking bodyguard — scrap that — a whole fucking squadron of them might help me get out of here. Who knows after that?'

'Are you in some sort of trouble?' She was now facing forward herself, certain that they were being watched closely.

'Big trouble, love. Big fucking trouble!' His voice was strained. Again, all the confidence that she had seen him exert in the past, albeit from a distance, was gone. It was as if she were drinking with a different man, one whose life was falling down around his ears. He was terrified. 'This is it for me,' he said. He was shaking his head. 'They told me to drink up. Then I've got to go for a walk. Down by the canal.'

'Just don't go,' she hissed. 'Why would you?'

'If it's not me today, it's my family tomorrow. I need to keep these people away from my family. This is the only way.' He threw his head back and necked the rest of his second glass. He slammed it back down on the bar. The ice rattled.

The barman walked back over. 'Another?' he said.

'No. That's my last.' Eddie Flint pulled out his wallet and dripped some notes on the bar. It looked like far too much. 'Have one on me, yeah? When your shift is done.' He turned towards the door.

'Thank you, sir!' the barman called after him.

Eddie Flint walked behind where she sat; she felt him brush against her. She turned to watch him leave through the side door. He stopped just outside. The door was floor-to-ceiling glass, through which he was clearly visible. He lifted his hands to his head then they fell back to his side. He checked behind him just as the two men who had been sat at the table appeared in her periphery. They walked past her and towards the same door. He must have seen them. He slipped his jacket off and threw it over his shoulder. It was hooked over his finger as he sauntered away to the left, in the general direction of the canal. He was in no rush. The two men stepped through the door. They stopped too. They both faced the direction he had walked in. One of them produced cigarettes from an inside pocket. They lit one each. One of them glanced back over at her. It was too late to turn away; she met his glance and held it. Thirty seconds later they both moved to the left and out of sight.

'Shit!' Once they were clear she moved quickly. She strode across the floor to the ladies, pushed through the door and stepped in. As far as she could see, she was alone. She pushed each of the cubicle doors as she walked through. They were all empty. Resting on the side, she stared at her reflection in the mirror.

'Alpha, alpha,' she said out loud. The concealed earpiece in her right ear emitted a double-beep, confirmation that she had been heard. 'Subject is out, *out* of the side entrance. He went left — *left*. States he is walking to the canal. Two white males followed him out, both large build, black suits, short hair. Both lit cigarettes on exit. They pose a serious threat to the subject. They will require interception. Two beeps for message received.' She paused and held her breath. She heard one long beep, followed quickly by another. 'Two beeps to confirm intercept,' she said, and waited again. The two beeps came quickly — then a third. That was a negative. They were *not* going to intercept. 'Shit!'

Her heels clacked as she moved back out of the toilets and across the polished floor. A man in a formal suit and white gloves pulled the exit door open as she approached. She stopped immediately and looked left.

'Does madam require a taxi?' the man asked.

'No, thank you.'

She looked to the left. She could see the canal from here. There was an obvious path that led directly towards it. She had walked it before. It split when it got to the canal bank: the right path continued as a stone walkway towards a shopping centre; the left quickly became a ribbon of grit over worn grass and mud. She set off. Within thirty seconds she could see the back of the two men from the bar. They had taken the left fork. Just ahead of them she could see Eddie Flint. He was still at strolling pace, as if he didn't have a care in the world. She knew different. The two men following were very aware. They both saw her almost immediately. She could make out a rushed conversation and one of the men turned around. She was now at the fork; she could still veer right towards the shopping centre and away from the canal — away from trouble. She took the left; she was committed. The man was now walking directly towards her and he filled the path. She felt her shoes crunch stones and gravel. She cast a quick look at the canal that was just a few metres to her right. It was slower moving here and was an opaque green. It looked deep. To her left was an area of wasteland that was part rubble, part wild grass. A bridge rose up from out of it, its side coated in colourful graffiti.

'Sorry, love. This bit's closed for now.' The man had a noticeable lisp.

'My friend . . . he forgot his wallet. Can I just give it to him?'

'His wallet? Ah, I'll make sure he gets it.'

'I'm not giving it to you! I'll just call him back.' She strained to see beyond the man as he loomed closer.

'You can't, love, okay? So fuck off.'

She looked at his expression. He didn't look like he was about to let her past any time soon. She pushed her luck.

'Who do you think you're talking to?' she started to ask. The blow to her face was as instant as it was stinging. She never saw it coming. Her head was turned with the force, her hair thrown across her face. The sting seemed to emanate mostly from her lip. She raised her finger to it and it came back dripping with blood.

She shook her head. 'That's my f-favourite sh-shade of crimson,' she stammered. *Crimson*. It was the agreed safe-word. Uttered in any context it would call in her backup. And they were not far away.

If the man looked bemused for a second, he was shocked rigid when the shouting began, shouts that seemed to come from every angle and signs of movement from every side. Then everything happened at once. Two men emerged from the wasteland to the left and were on her attacker before he even had time to turn to face them. He was bundled to the ground, the barrel of a sidearm pushed into his face. 'ARMED POLICE! STAY WHERE YOU ARE! HANDS WHERE I CAN SEE THEM!'

The big man lifted his hands over his head. His eyes were wide as they flicked from the two armed men to Maddie. His wrists were snapped into cuffs and he was rolled onto his back for a hurried search. Maddie squatted down beside him, still dabbing at her lip.

'You know, I never saw the point of stilettos. They're uncomfortable, you can't move quickly in them and your calves ache for hours after. It's a whole load of discomfort just because of some notion that you men might like them. At least that was what I thought. But, y'know, there is a point to them. Something guys shouldn't forget about.' She stood back up to her full height and swung her right foot over the man's crotch. She shifted her weight to step onto him. She could feel that she had at least part of his appendage trapped beneath her heel as she shifted her weight to her front foot and pushed off to walk away. The man screamed in agony.

Maddie moved towards where the other would-be attacker had his hands in the air further up the path. He was being restrained by two men wearing black baseball caps with *POLICE* emblazoned on their fronts. A little further still up the path, Eddie Flint was an untidy mess laid out on the ground in handcuffs.

'Ah, thank God!' he exclaimed. 'Thank God!'

She sighed — part relief, part regret. This was not the outcome she had envisaged and it certainly wasn't the one anyone wanted. But her three-year operation was over.

Chapter 7

The buzzing sound was the first thing she was aware of this time. She was still wrapped tightly and could barely move any part of her body. She could wiggle her fingers and toes, blink her eyes and open and close her mouth — that was all. She was on her side and her head was hanging a little so her forehead rested on the metal floor. The flies seemed to have increased in number and felt massive as they crawled on her face and neck. She thought there was something wriggling on her belly but she couldn't be sure. Otherwise, she felt nothing anywhere else. Whatever it was that was wrapped so tightly around her covered everything except her face.

The smell was still strong and it was getting worse. It mixed with the stale, unmoving heat making her feel dizzy and she could feel the throbbing pulse in her temple. She kept waking then dozing off again soon after. She seemed totally bereft of energy; just trying to move any part of her body or to roll onto her side brought on complete exhaustion. She couldn't give up though; she had to keep trying. She knew she was in a lot of trouble. She couldn't recall how she had ended up in this place and that added to her distress. She tried calling out for help but her throat was so sore she couldn't manage the faintest sound.

She had been focussing on the tiny spots of light above her. She was pretty certain it was daylight shining through. At times they were so bright it was as if the slenderest of lasers were shining down. At other times they were far dimmer or couldn't be seen at all.

Another sensation was new to her: dampness. She could feel it around the tops of her thighs. Her legs seemed to be slightly freer too. She didn't think she had soiled herself but she couldn't be sure; her normal bodily functions seemed to have shut down — or at least she was unaware of them.

She smacked her lips together. They were so dry that they were sore as she parted them again. She longed for some water. Her thirst was driving her to fidget more, to push harder to try and free herself. She had worked out that her hands weren't tied together as she had originally thought; they were moving independently of each other though held tight against her body. She was trying to focus on her hands. If she could just work them free. She could pull them up a centimetre or two and then they would fall back, but when she'd first started trying there had been no movement at all. It was slow, painful progress but she used it as something to focus on. She kept on pulling her hands up and letting them fall until exhaustion took hold again. Her last thought was of the wriggling sensation in her abdomen. But the darkness reclaimed her.

Chapter 8

'What the hell was that, Maddie?' Superintendent Alan Jackson bawled the moment DS Maddie Ives crossed the threshold of his office. He was seated at the desk directly in front of her and there was a meeting table to her left with chairs tucked in under it. She didn't attempt to sit. She got the impression this wasn't that type of meeting.

'Can you be more specific, sir?'

'Don't be smart, Maddie. Yesterday, on the canal bank. You blew an operation that was years in the making. We were nearly there. You just needed to keep your nerve for a few more days — a week tops.'

'Keep my *nerve*?' Alan Jackson was not a man who was used to being interrupted. She stopped herself making it instantly worse. His expression was stoical. She got the impression he was trying to make her squirm. She was too angry to squirm — too stupid maybe. Jackson had never worked a covert job in his life, not as a player, not as a detective receiving information from a live subject that blew a job right open. He'd overseen them, sat on the other side of a radio — maybe worked a fixed observation point at best, but anyone could sit in a house overlooking a front door and call up when a subject left. Maddie's speciality was getting right in among them, right in harm's way. She'd never been compromised in over a decade and even this time it had been for all the right reasons.

'Yes. Your nerve, Maddie. You were given a very specific task and at no point did your instructions include chasing down a canal path after our main subject and putting the lives of every one of your support team in danger.'

'And what about Eddie Flint's life? They were going to kill him. He was a dead man walking. They were waiting until he got to the best place for them to dispose of his body. He knew it. Somehow the bastards had made sure he was aware of their plans. He told me in the bar he was having his last drink. The search teams found weights for his feet on the can—'

'I know what we found! I know what he told you! I was back here listening to every word. I was making decisions based on every word, as is *my* job. *Your* job was to get information off his phone. A quick data transfer, pure and simple. I'm the man tasked with keeping him alive. But you decided that getting his phone wasn't enough for you — you wanted to be fucking Wonder Woman or something, so you went stomping after him. There were contingencies in place. We were going to intercept, but in a way that didn't blow us all out. That didn't ruin three years of covert work. That didn't put all of our undercover assets at increased risk of coming to serious harm.'

Maddie took a step back. His words hit her like the slap in the face had. *Pure and simple* struck her the hardest. Like getting hold of the phone of one of the most dangerous men in the North West was either *pure* or *simple*. It could easily have gotten her killed. She swallowed hard. The events were still a turmoil in her mind. Maybe she had been too quick to react? Maybe this was her mess?

'So what now? There are other subjects working with him that I can get to. They will still have incriminating—'

'Maddie, stop! You've fucked up. The operation is one thing — I'll need to pick up the pieces around that. But now I have to consider *you*. Your personal safety. You're at risk. A target. I need to make sure the risk to you is nullified.'

Maddie had a bad feeling. It had started when she'd first gotten the phone call instructing her to come into a central Manchester police station for a meeting and it had been intensifying ever since. In the previous ten years, she had been in a police station only a handful of times and all of those were when she'd been arrested to keep her cover. Covert assets didn't report to police stations, and they certainly weren't summoned there by senior officers who knew this rule better than anyone.

'Okay. So, again, what now?'

'I need to move you. Away from here. A long way from here.'

'What do you mean, away from here?' Maddie was tired. She had been filling out paperwork pretty much since the incident the day before. Her long day was taking its toll.

'I've put out a few feelers. I've managed to come up with something. I want you to consider it, but I think it's the best option for you.'

'Come up with what?'

'There's a force down south. They have some posts for sergeants going begging. They can provide one that suits you. I'm not entirely sure of the details yet.'

'It'll be whatever shit no one else wants, I assume?' Maddie snapped. She wished she hadn't the second it dropped out of her mouth.

'You're probably right. But what else would you have me do? Your covert career is over, Maddie. You must recognise that. You've been gathering evidence against high-level OCGs. You always knew that being burnt would mean you were out of the arena. Instantly.'

'Who says I'm burnt? I used the safety word. There's nothing to say it was me that called that strike. It's not a big leap to assume that Flint was under surveil—'

'Maddie, please!' The superintendent was shaking his head. He held a sneer. 'These people are not stupid and we should not assume that they are. This is your life we are talking about and I cannot be putting it at risk. And, trust me, Maddie, you were burnt.' He rifled through some papers that were laid out on his desk. He pulled one specific piece and read from it. *The male was detained on the floor. I could see DS Ives had a visible injury. She was bleeding from her bottom lip and it was also swelling. She addressed the male, telling him what her heels were for. She then stepped onto his crotch area.'* He looked up. Maddie could hardly argue with the account. 'The same officer does go on to write an assurance in his statement that the placement of your foot was purely accidental, of course — you were merely trying to step over him so you could go and check on the other male and the welfare of Eddie Flint. But let's be honest, if you wanted to make sure you stuck in someone's mind, Maddie, stepping on their testicles might be in the top three ways of accomplishing that, don't you think?'

'Why name me? And as a DS? I'm never normally named in police statements? That's a basic, surel—'

'MADDIE!' His raised voice caught her out. 'You're not a covert officer anymore. It's that simple. I told them to include your name because he's complaining about the nature of his arrest and making an assault allegation. Specifically, this is against — and I can quote him here — *the slutty whore who stepped on my bollocks.* That allegation I should be able to make go away but his memory is another thing altogether. We will redact your name and your role. We're already feeding our sources that you were a female escort caught up in the incident. That might limit the effort they put into finding you. But it's a fair bet that they'll still try. Certainly you cannot pop back up with the same legend. You are finished as an undercover asset. Is that now clear enough?'

'So I just go down to the Met and take up a post doing whatever keeps me quiet. Which probably means going out and about introducing myself as a copper. And that makes me safer down there does it?'

'No. You go further south than that. Lennockshire have a role. Your old force, I believe. The Met won't have you — seems they also see you as a massive risk to yourself. Lennockshire have just the job. They mentioned something about missing persons, a sort of single point for the force. It sounds interesting and you shouldn't have any concerns about meeting any members of organised crime groups down there.'

'Lennockshire! The force I left just as soon as I could to go and get some action!'

'Yes. And the last thing you need right now is any sort of action. You need to get your head down and disappear for a while. If that's true of Lennockshire then it sounds like the perfect place for you. Look, I know this is a bit of a change but you have to understand the situation you have put yourself in. I've struck a deal. You will still be a Greater Manchester Police officer. You will go down to Lennockshire and take on this job as a secondment, not a permanent transfer. While you are down there, Lennockshire will support you in getting through your Inspector's board. You just need to make sure you pass your exams and then you'll be back up here with some cushy, non-customer facing, inspector role. I know a lot of people who would love this opportunity, Maddie. Covert policing takes a toll on your life. I know you have had to make a lot of sacrifices. You haven't really had much of a life at all these past three years. This is your payoff. I see this as a good thing for you. How old are you now?'

'What the hell has that got to do with anything?'

'Nearly forty, right? You don't see many UC officers at forty years old, not doing the sort of work you were doing. And an inspector by forty is not to be sniffed at. With your experience, your CV, you won't need to stop at inspector.'

'I'm thirty-five. Proper washed up, aren't I, *sir*? With respect—'

'LET me stop you there, DS Ives! All of the most disrespectful things I have ever heard from subordinates have started with that phrase. Consider what you say while this offer remains on the table. The alternative is a suspension while the assault allegation is dealt with and then being grounded to a rural outpost in the arse end of the Pennines. Think hard.'

Maddie gave herself a second. She flopped in one of the chairs, no longer caring about formal etiquette. 'But I like customer facing.'

'You'll still have that. Just a different sort of customer. The sort that aren't going to get you killed.'

Maddie sighed again. This was happening. He was still trying to push the positives but she couldn't see past leaving a job that she loved in a town she adored.

'When you said there was an option you wanted me to consider, you didn't really mean there was a choice, did you?'

Jackson huffed. Some of his earlier anger had dissipated but there were signs it was coming back. 'This hasn't been easy, Maddie. The options up here were to get you wiping the arses of the new recruits in a training environment or out counting sheep on a night shift. I still can't guarantee your safety in either of those roles. You know these people, Maddie — you better than anyone. What do you think they would do if they realised who you were and what you had been doing? I want you out of the North of England. Simple as that. You can refuse. In which case I will look to have you removed from the force in some other way so that when you turn up dead or dying

I can at least tell myself that I did what I could to prevent it. So, no, this is not a choice.'

Maddie got to her feet. 'Then, *with respect,* sir. I need to get going. I've got a lot to do.'

Chapter 9

The next morning, Maddie Ives stopped to take in the frontage of the police station in the city of Canterbury, despite the steady rainfall. It was still very warm, like a storm was brewing. It felt ominous in more ways than one. The station stood next to a far larger, more modern building that announced itself as *South East College* in huge letters. There was a compound on the left side where cars were parked, some marked *Police*, some not. Most looked like civilian cars — the officers' own. It was a far cry from her Manchester experience, where huge, block-shaped stations were stuck up in out-of-town industrial estates with grilles over the windows and vicious, impregnable fencing.

She had travelled down the previous day, the same day as the conversation with her superintendent. It was perhaps a sad reflection on her life that she could just pick it up and move it to the other end of the country without a second thought. She had learned to live lightly. Her work had demanded ultimate flexibility and she had never complained because the work was always good; she was making a difference. But this was not the same. Her hotel was booked out for a month by Greater Manchester Police. They reckoned a month would give her enough time to find somewhere more permanent to live. She was pretty certain they had plucked that figure out of the air. She certainly didn't foresee spending four weeks in a hotel. She couldn't stand such places.

The city centre was a stone's throw from where she stood. She was from this county originally, but not this area. She had been to Canterbury when she was much younger: a school trip to the impressive cathedral that had dominated the skyline for the best part of a thousand years. The previous night, Maddie had made a brief exploration. There was a subway entrance just a short walk away that ran under busy roads and a roundabout she could see to her right and came up pretty much where the High Street began. Canterbury was a pretty city: the streets were cobbled and tight and its medieval origins were clear. It still managed to maintain the look of a place that had been built around the horse and cart.

The reception area of the police building was empty. Maddie dropped the hood on her jacket and ran her fingers through her hair. Her shoulders were dusted with spots of rain. A woman walked from a back room to greet her and looked blank when she explained who she was and what she was supposed to be doing here. She had a name to quote — Detective Chief Inspector Julian Lowe. That seemed to get a spark of recognition at least, but nothing more. Maddie sat down. The woman made some phone calls but none of them were hurried. At one point she got into a conversation about her recent four-day stay at a holiday camp. Maddie had to stop herself getting up to remonstrate.

Eventually she was walked through the station by a PCSO who didn't seem to be any better informed.

'I've just got instructions to take you to the range, I'm afraid,' she said.

'The range?'

'Yeah. It used to be the firing range, see. Where firearms trained before it all moved to headquarters. Now it's offices.'

'I see. I was wondering if you just put all of us from other forces up against a wall and shot us,' she quipped. She got no reaction.

They walked up a steep, windowless staircase, the only light coming from a weak, circular ceiling light at the top. She turned left and was led through a door where space opened up in front of her. Its origins had been rather crudely papered over; it was still a long, thin, open floor. She could see right to the other end. Desks were scattered in between. Photocopiers and shelving had been stuffed in wherever there was a gap and even where there wasn't. She was led the full length of the room, and people stopped to look up and over as she passed. Some offered awkward smiles, most faces showed no expression at all. They were all dressed in smart, plain clothes. Their desks were covered in white files. Some of the dual screens played CCTV footage or showed legislation websites. The whole place stank of detection, something Maddie had never wanted to go back to in her own career. As she was led through a door at the end and into a small office, her feelings were a blend of foreboding and the anxiety of being the new officer — despite a decade of dealing with some of the worst criminals the country had to offer. The PCSO announced DCI Julian Lowe as if he was some sort of lord and then scuttled away.

'DS Ives?' the DCI said. He stood behind his desk and chair, pushing books around on a shelf. His office was small and windowless — at the opposite end to the stairs but with the same atmosphere.

'I suppose so, yes.'

'You *suppose* so?'

'Sorry, sir. The DS bit. I've never gotten used to it.'

'You are a detective sergeant, though, DS Ives?'

'I am. The detective part is from a long time ago it seems.'

'As I understand. I suppose you've not been doing any real police work for some time. I am told that you've been deployed largely as a covert asset. Is that correct?'

'I've been undercover for most of my career, sir. It's some of the most effective *police work* you can ever do in my humble opinion. We've had some big hits against some of the most dangerous organised criminal groups in the—'

'Yes, yes. All very impressive.' His lips curled into an almost sneer, though he tried to conceal it. But one thing Maddie was good at was reading what people were trying to hide. She was used to a negative reaction to undercover policing. Much of what was involved was neither measurable nor known.

'And I was not expecting you until the middle of the week. I understand you were being given some time to organise your affairs?'

'Call it enthusiasm!' She grinned. 'And I had nothing better to do. I figured the earlier I got started, the earlier I could work out what I'm doing down here.'

'Yes, quite. Well, we have been able to find you a vocation here in Canterbury. It may not compete with running round with OCGs but it's good work. Essential work. Have you any experience in missing persons?'

'Missing like abducted?'

The DCI snorted. 'Well, I mean it is a possibility, but you may have to adjust your expectations a little. I think it's fair to say that the majority of our missing people have an altogether different explanation for their disappearance.'

'Okay. Well no, then. I don't have masses of experience around missing persons but I'm sure I can learn.'

'I'm sure you can. We need a missing persons coordinator. It requires someone of a sergeant rank. You will hold missing persons for the area overall as part of your portfolio. The actual tasks around *searching* for these individuals will fall to uniform patrols in most instances. You will have more involvement from a risk assessment point of view. Have you completed a risk assessment before?'

'I've written covert operations orders. More than I can remember. Most of that is risk assessments and—'

'I think you might find these a little different!' Lowe snorted again. 'Once again, DS Ives, I feel I need to advise you to adjust your expectations a little bit. I understand you are to work your way towards completing your inspector's exam. You will also need to build a portfolio around that. Risk assessments, identifying vulnerable persons and pro-actively identifying measures to reduce the frequency of our regular missing persons will provide all you need in your journey to the next rank. I will need to endorse it, of course. I can assure you I'm not a difficult man to impress. Toe the line and work hard and you'll see that for yourself. And we will have a wonderful working relationship. I will arrange for you to be shown the ropes, as it were. I'm sure that someone with your background and ability will be able to pick up something like this very quickly indeed.'

Maddie bit down on her tongue long enough to stop the first thing that flashed through her mind from coming out of her mouth. 'I'm sure I will, sir.' She managed eventually.

'Your desk is the first one you come to on your right. There's a tea fund. Marilyn runs it. I have no doubt she will make herself known to you. Now, I do have a phone conference. I will be sure to check in with you later today to see how you are getting on. Could I ask that you push the door shut for me?'

Maddie stepped out. Back into the low level din of clacking keys and clicking mouse buttons. Every occupant seemed hunched over their keyboard and now nobody was looking up. Her desk stood out as the only one with no clutter. She had a dusty keyboard that looked to be from the previous decade and a monitor to match. Castoffs, equipment no one else wanted. Maddie was beginning to think that it was rather appropriate.

* * *

The woman woke suddenly. The pain in her stomach was so bad she felt like something was moving around inside of it. She was on her side — she didn't know how; perhaps she had moved in her sleep and that was what had woken her up. She tried to roll back and had to tense her stomach to do it. The pain spread instantly until it felt like it was consuming her whole body. The nausea came again and she froze where she lay. She couldn't be sick again — the retching was agony.

She tried to focus on her breathing. She needed to stay still and calm and maybe she could start to think of a way of getting out of this. She closed her eyes and thought about home, about how she had once had a life with so many plans. She knew if she got out of this she could get that life back. She just knew it.

She managed to calm down and her breathing reverted to normal. She could still hear the buzzing but there was *something different*. She had shifted enough for the sharp pain in her stomach to ease to a dull ache. And she was able to concentrate again — on listening. There was a tapping sound as if somebody was drumming their fingers on metal in a steady rhythm. Her hands were a little looser, especially her right. She had been working on freeing them every time she was awake. She tried to lift them again. Her stomach flinched, but it was bearable. She tried to focus on her right arm and it gave another few millimetres. She moved it again. There was nothing else to do. It was exhausting. Every attempt sapped more and more of her energy. She was aware of the buzzing still. The flies seemed worse. She could feel them almost everywhere now. They tickled her neck and she shook her head. Her neck shot with pain but no longer enough to stop her. The flies lifted only to land right back on her skin. She flinched again. Her breathing quickened. She could now feel flies on her legs, too. Sometimes she could feel them on her feet through the numbness. *What if they were eating her alive?* Did flies eat people? Perhaps they could lay eggs under her skin? Her mind ran with horrific possibilities. She wasn't even sure if the tapping sound was real or if it was just in her mind.

She flinched again, this time with her whole body. The pain was bad. She tried to shout but nothing came out and it made her neck throb. Her whole body stiffened as she tried to push against whatever it was that was holding her so tightly. It didn't budge. She flushed with adrenalin and could feel herself starting to panic. She wriggled a little more and it felt like her stomach was tearing as she did. She didn't feel the pain through the adrenalin but her energy was draining away. She had one last push in her. She tried to scream. Her throat stung, her stomach flashed with pain, she wrenched her arm hard as she rolled onto her back. Her arm was still stuck; it could be looser but she didn't have the energy to move it again. She concentrated on her breathing. She thought again about her family. The panic was ebbing, to be was replaced by exhaustion. Her mouth lolled open. She felt a drip on her mouth. She smacked her lips.

Water!

Another drip followed quickly after. Water was dripping through from somewhere. She waited for the next and adjusted her position just a couple of centimetres. The drops were falling right into her mouth. Suddenly she didn't care about the flies or the pain. The drips were coming fast and they were constant. She was getting a drink.

* * *

Maddie's computer was finally working after a twenty-minute conversation with an ironically named 'help desk.'

She needed a break. She scanned the room. No one stood out as somebody she could ask where the coffee machine was. She was aware of movement to her left. A man stepped out of the inspector's office. It wasn't the inspector. It was a taller man, older too — in his fifties, she reckoned, maybe half way to sixty. He had a crooked smile and his shaved head reflected the light. He had a look about him that was not unlike a few of the career thugs she had met. He made a beeline for her.

'Maddie Ives?' His voice was a low rumble. His face gave nothing away and she wondered if she might have done something wrong.

'That's me.'

'You're the misper coordinator, right?'

'So I've been told. If you need something, you might have to bear with me.'

'I don't. I did it for a bit. The boss asked me to talk to you.' The man didn't seem impressed by this. Not at all.

'Okay. And you are . . .?'

'Busy,' he replied.

'I see. Well, thanks but I'm sure I can pick it up.' She turned away, feeling her face flush as she fought to keep her anger under the surface.

'Inspector Harry Blaker. I'm not good at jokes. That was a joke.'

Maddie wasn't convinced. She turned back to him. 'No, you're not. So you did it for *a bit*. Not for long then?'

'No. I was somewhere else and I upset somebody. They suggested I take a break. This was my break.' His eyes roved her sorry-looking desk.

'I see. So it's a punishment posting.'

'It was for me.'

'Brilliant. I get the impression it is for me too.'

'You upset someone too?' His tone hadn't changed; it stayed low and flat. She couldn't read him.

'Yeah. I saved somebody's life.'

Finally his face flickered a reaction but she couldn't tell what it was. 'I can see how that could cause some inconvenience.' He moved to perch on the empty desk next to her, looking a little more relaxed — or just less pissed off.

'You don't want to be having this conversation, do you?' she said.

Harry's attention had drifted to a passing noise, then snapped back to her. 'Sounds like neither of us do, really.'

Maddie chewed on her lip. 'Alright. You have to speak to me. I have to listen. How about we at least go somewhere that does a decent coffee? I'm desperate to get out of here, just for a little while, and I get the impression you might know somewhere.'

'What good cop doesn't? But I've got a lot on. I came to introduce myself, then put you off.'

'You have a certain honesty about you, Inspector Harry Blaker. But I'm not easily put off.'

'Sounds like you might need that attitude, kid. Especially if you're gonna keep saving lives.'

'I just need half an hour. I'm done with sitting here clicking "refresh" on the BBC news site. At least give me a clue what the hell I should be doing and I promise I'll leave you alone. If you put me off now I could be a real pain in your arse.'

He hesitated. His resting expression seemed to be one of general disdain, but he looked even less happy at this moment.

'I may have to make a few calls. You can leave your phone in your pocket or take it out of that case. And you're buying.'

Maddie looked down at her mobile phone on the desk. The case was bright pink with faux diamonds. It had been a gift. She hated it but used it out of politeness. She considered ditching it now — one upside of her move. She snatched it up, along with her newly issued passes and

almost jumped to her feet. She had to get out of here.
Even with this misery of a man. She needed the air.

Chapter 10

He reacted to the vibration of his watch as if it were a sharp pain in his arm. *Proximity*, the notification read. He knew exactly what it meant. He was in his kitchen, having just got home with an uncut loaf and some cheese and chutney. He'd had a nice lunch planned.

Now he was pulling his phone out of his pocket and hurriedly opening the security camera app. It was a relatively new tech — for the domestic market at least. You could link CCTV to your phone and smartwatch from just about anywhere in the world. 'Smart cameras,' they were called. Everything was smart these days. They could be set to lie dormant, only activating when they detected movement. *Proximity* meant there was movement on one of his.

He moved through the menus. The screen showed that he had movement on camera four. *Camera four!* That was the one on Leonard's Farm. That land was a long way off being sold — nobody should be anywhere near it. Somebody must have opened the container door. They would have discovered the bodies. It was a shame but it didn't matter, he told himself, he had been careful.

He pressed to *view*. His screen turned pitch black. Only the camera label in the top right told him that his phone was still switched on at all. He hadn't expected darkness. Not if the door was open. He had fitted a *smart* light, too; it used the same Wi-Fi source. They were designed for your home so you could switch on your lights without the irritation of having to use a switch or to scare off would-be burglars from a distance. But they also worked on desolate farmland if you wanted to admire your own work, to watch it *change*. He pressed to activate the light. There was a few seconds' delay. Then the light came on strong and the screen suddenly flared a bright white before settling into focus. He could see the two rolls of dark-coloured plastic. The camera was pointing down at the end by the door. It still looked firmly shut. He had made sure their heads were in the shot so he could see their faces. It was the faces that changed the most. On one of the girls the flies had been busy. Much of her face was slipping and her eyes were gone already. He could see a layer of shuffling black where they still worked. The lighter coloured maggots were in contrast. They wriggled and flexed in the sudden light.

The other girl was holding up better. It had only been a few days for her. She was on her side, facing the camera. Her eyes were shut. Her mouth hung open. A fly moved out of it. The lips flinched. The mouth shut then opened again.

She was moving!

It couldn't be! He moved the screen closer and held his breath. Maybe he had imagined it? He could still remember her face when he had pushed the eight-inch blade into her gut. It had been like a beautiful embrace. She hadn't seen it coming — how could she have? He had savoured that wonderful sound when the breath left her body in a sort of coarse whisper. He had lingered for just a moment. Then he helped her to the ground. Down to the plastic sheet laid out behind. He was gentle, like lying down with a lover. Then in two flashes of violence he wrenched out the knife and slashed across her throat. He had wrapped the plastic around her immediately. As tight as he could to catch all the mess. He knew he had done enough. He had felt the life leave her body; he had *watched* it!

He stood in his kitchen, still staring at the phone. There was no more movement. He was less sure that she had moved. Less convinced. There could be no way. But was her face at a slightly different angle?

And then he considered it. He considered that she was still alive, that he might get to watch her die all over again. His face contorted into a grin. He practically clapped his hands — oh, how he hoped she was still alive!

He checked his watch. He was pressed for time. He would have lunch and then he had another job for the day. This evening he would connect his phone up to his television screen. He would get some nice food, a bottle of wine maybe. His entertainment was set. He just needed to get his work done. He would have more time this evening, he could be sure of that. And if he detected any signs of life he could watch her for a while. But in the morning he would need to go and finish what he had started. It was a nuisance; it brought its problems, but he couldn't help but hope she was alive, that she would last the night, so he would get to do it all over again.

He pressed the screen of his phone to turn off the light. There was work to do now. But later he would be able to savour it. It took a few seconds to take effect but then his screen turned back to black.

Chapter 11

'It doesn't matter where you are in the world, it seems like these places are all the same.' Maddie made a second attempt at small talk. She toyed with her drink. They were sat at the back of a popular chain of coffee shops. Lunchtime was fast approaching and it was busy. Harry was stirring his own drink. He didn't look up.

'I suppose so.'

'You don't talk much, do you, sir?'

'Talking gets you in trouble. And call me Harry when we're out of that place.'

'So I call you Harry and you call me *kid*, is that how it works?'

'Did I? Force of habit.'

'One could almost think you sounded bitter, *Harry*.'

'You do this job long enough and it can happen.' His tone had changed enough for Maddie to detect some sarcasm.

Silence fell back over them. 'Well, at least there's a bit of life in here,' she offered.

'You mean compared to CID?'

She looked at him closely. Was that humour she detected in his eyes, or was he just testing her? 'What is that about? It's like someone has vacuum packed the place and sucked out all the joy. Right bunch of miserable shits.'

'No bad language, not around me. I don't stand for it.' He seemed dead serious. Maddie was a little taken aback. The most foul-mouthed people she knew were all coppers; it was almost a prerequisite.

'You don't swear?'

'I need to be very angry.' His growl was back. She lifted her palms and he continued. 'And it's a difficult job for detectives at the moment. You think the cuts on the street are bad? The detective roles have taken an even bigger hit. They're all massively overworked. No one seems to want to be in there anymore. That used to be where you aspired to be.'

'It'll go full circle. These things tend to, right?'

Harry lifted his eyes. She got the impression that every time he looked at her he was inspecting her, sizing her up. He was a big guy himself. She reckoned she knew exactly how the criminals felt. Eventually he spoke. 'I've seen it a few times. Reinventing the wheel. It's the rank and file that take the hit for someone getting promoted on an idea. What's your story anyway?'

'My story?'

'You don't want to be here either. So how did that happen?'

Maddie toyed with her drink. 'I didn't want to leave. I loved my job and I loved where I did it. Maybe it was the right decision. I've had a few days to reflect.'

'Yours?'

'No.'

'I didn't think so.'

'What makes you say that?'

'Because you don't really believe that. I assume you weren't a misper coordinator up north?'

Maddie resisted the instinct to bite back. He had a nonchalance about him, as if he knew everything about her already. He definitely didn't.

'No. I've spent the last ten years working as a UC asset in the North West. Manchester mainly. Infiltrating organised crime groups. Just a few days ago I was on the ground and I made a decision in the heat of the moment that I believe saved a man's life. I knew it could have ramifications for me . . . I guess I just thought my team might have backed me a bit more.'

'And instead they moved you to the other side of the country?'

'Exactly.'

'To go to meetings with school head teachers and social workers, to work out how you stop kids from going missing when you know the only answer is to give them a bit of a slap.'

'Oh, God. Is that what the job is?'

'A big part of it.' He actually chuckled. Sure, it was at her expense but she joined in. She was a little surprised that he could actually laugh but when he did it was quite catching.

'I didn't realise you ever laughed,' she said.

'I try not to. I have a reputation for being miserable to uphold.'

'Really?' Maddie did nothing to hide her own sarcasm.

'Hard to believe, right?'

'Nope.'

A smile flickered across his face again. It was gone just as quickly.

'So what about you? I assume you're not in CID anymore?'

'No. I've been in Major Crime for most of my time. I got moved out for a few months. They soon realised that they couldn't live without me.'

'I'm sure. Major Crime, eh? I take it the atmosphere is better there, is it?'

'Yeah, generally. It's a bit strange at the moment. A lot of new people. Major Crime used to be run out of Langthorne, but they had some high-profile incidents that were picked up by the media and it didn't reflect well on them. They had some changes in personnel — the supervisors mainly. I was brought down from Major Crime in the West. The DCI was brought in from where he was working Counter Terrorism. But, yeah, it's a good atmosphere. You get a room full of people who want to be doing the job, it's going to be better. We're strapped for resources, just like the rest of 'em. But you put in the extra effort because of what you're chasing . . . murderers, rapists, kidnappers. The people who do that don't give a damn that we're tired or overworked.'

'That's the most passionate I've seen you.'

'It gets tested.'

'Do you get many murders in Lennockshire? I have a bit of an impression of the place. I lived in the Medway towns once. This county's called The Garden of England, right? Hardly a murder hotspot?'

'Every garden has its compost heap.'

'I suppose so.'

'You get murders everywhere.' Harry suddenly sat up straighter. Maddie could hear the vibrating noise in his pocket. He stood up and stepped away. No apology, no explanation. Maddie watched him go. She supped at her coffee. She could only concur with his reputation: he was a miserable bastard. But she could see the passion in him too. She found him interesting if nothing else.

His call was brief. When he came back over he pushed a lid onto his coffee and made no attempt to sit down.

'I assume you're needed?' she said.

'Yeah. There was a hit and run over the weekend and we've got a burnt-out vehicle that might be linked.'

'Hit and run? I thought Major Crime investigated murder? That's a traffic offence, isn't it?'

'Depends on why they hit him.'

'You think it was on purpose?'

'My gut does. And now I might have a burnt-out murder weapon.'

'Hit and runs, murder weapons . . . sounds so much more interesting than what I'm going to be dealing with.'

'Investigating murder is never as exciting as it sounds.'

'I remember.'

Harry had been gathering up his bag before he stopped and turned. 'You've worked Major Crime?'

'The fringes. I started out as a detective. A few years on the street, a few years as a detective. A long time ago, before I was headhunted for UC work. I was a good detective too. Or at least I had the potential to be. That's half the reason why they asked me to switch. The best UC assets have an investigator's mind set.'

'I'm sure they do.'

'So you can bear that in mind. That lack of resources you're talking about. Don't forget they've got me down here doing some made-up job at a desk down in CID.'

'I'm sure it's a very essential job.'

'You obviously didn't think so.'

'True.'

'So keep me in mind.'

Maddie stayed while Harry made his exit. He didn't reply. She watched him leave. He was already on his phone by the time he walked through the door. He turned left and out of sight. She knew she ought to go back, too — not that she thought anyone might be missing her. She let her eyes wander round the busy coffee shop. Most of the tables were occupied now, filled with people talking to one another. Maddie imagined they had interesting things to say and places to go afterwards. She was considering another coffee. Fifteen years into a career she adored and that had consumed her life, she had never felt so lost.

Chapter 12

The bingo hall bustled with people and activity. The speaker system was loud and the calls were quick. It was hot, too. Lisa Simpkiss knew that her mum was not going to last long but she had been insistent. Lisa knew better than to argue with her when she was in that sort of mood.

'This okay, Mum?' She put her bag down on a free table towards the back. Her friend Naomi Wood looked over at her, her smile was reassuring. Naomi sat down.

'This looks okay to me, love. I don't mind where we sit.' She took the chair her daughter was holding out for her.

'I'll get your stuff sorted, okay? What are you drinking?'

'Just a soda water for me, please, love.'

'One soda water.' Lisa knew her mother wouldn't drink it. She lingered on her as she sat with a straightened back and placed her hands out in front of her. Her fingers fidgeted and drummed on the table. Her eyes fidgeted too. They moved from one noise to another. She looked nervous, fearful almost.

'Are you getting that coke or not, Cathy?'

'I'm Lisa, Mum. Cathy's not here.'

'I know who you are.'

'I'll be right back.'

Lisa swept her bag back off the table. She walked to the bar and picked out some pens and game boards. Naomi appeared next to her. She leant against the bar, still looking over towards their table.

'She gonna be okay?' Naomi said.

'No,' Lisa replied curtly. Her mother hadn't been okay for the last five years at least. And it was getting worse. She was forgetful, confused, anxious — and so spiteful at times. She fiercely resisted going back to the doctor. Lisa knew why: she didn't want to be told she was getting worse or that she needed to be taking her medication every day — not by someone she might have to listen to. Lisa couldn't get across the argument that she might be able to delay or even stop whatever it was if she would just do as she was told. And it *was* an argument. Every time. They couldn't just talk about it; her mum was too terrified.

'How long do you think she'll last?'

'Don't get comfortable.' Lisa said.

She ordered the drinks. She stuck with the soda water for her mother. She was expecting a complaint.

'I wanted a coke.'

'Ah, yes. Sorry, Mum. I'll take it back.' Lisa had put the drink down and her mother reached out to stop her taking it away again.

'Don't worry about it now, Cathy, I'll drink it.'

'I'm not Cathy, Mum. She's your other daughter.'

Her mother looked at her closely. 'I know who you are. You're the drunk!' Her last words were said with such venom that Lisa had to bite her tongue. She took a second.

'Not anymore, Mum. I'm done with all that.'

'Oh, you've given me nothing but trouble, young lady! Your father . . . he would be turning in his grave if he knew what you were doing to yourself.'

'So you keep telling me, Mum. I don't do that anymore.'

'Well, good. I always said you should stop, didn't I?'

'You did, Mum. Oh, this is our game!' The PA system gave a sixty-second warning. Lisa handed out the game cards, one to her mum and one to Naomi. The pens followed. The sixty seconds were up.

'And here we go! Eyes down for the next game, ladies and gentlemen. We have a big game with a thousand pounds up for grabs! So listen in.'

There were whoops and cheers. The noise subsided quickly and the hall fell silent. The caller pulled his first number.

'Here we go . . . first ball. Two little ducks to start us off! Two and two, twenty-two.'

Lisa scanned her card. Then she scanned her mother's. She could see twenty-two on there. Her mother's pen hovered; there was a tremor to her hand.

'On its own, number three!'

Lisa checked her own for number three. Her mother's pen still hovered.

'Four and one, forty-one!' Lisa could see forty-one on her mother's card. Still it was unmarked. She leant over.

'You've got that one, Mum.'

'I know what I've got!' Her mother lashed out with the back of her right hand and caught Lisa lightly in the face.

'Okay, Mum.'

'One dozen! Number twelve.'

Her mother's eyes lifted towards the caller. There was clear desperation in them. 'He's going too fast! I can't . . . Can you tell him? He's going too fast!'

'I can't, Mum. There are other people here. I can just help—'

'I DON'T WANT . . .' she stopped herself. Her voice was raised enough that the caller stopped. Lisa looked up as her mother struggled to her feet then walked to the door through which they had entered just a few minutes earlier. Lisa watched her step through. She expelled her breath. She fought back the tears and dipped her head. The caller started up again. The world around her returned to normal.

'Do you want me to . . .?' Naomi whispered.

'I'll go,' Lisa said. She stood up and straightened her vest top. She took another deep breath and then she made for the door.

The sunlight was bright, the air warm and unmoving. The bingo hall faced out onto a busy road. The traffic was barely edging past in front of her. Her mother was over to the left, sitting awkwardly on a low wall and looking out over the traffic — beyond it, perhaps, to where Canterbury's cathedral filled the skyline over the row of houses on the other side of the road. Lisa sat next to her. She didn't speak. Her mother spoke first.

'I know I'm difficult. I know I am. I don't mean to be. I don't want to be.'

'Payback, I guess, Mum. It's not like I've been easy to bring up, right?' She chuckled.

Her mother relented enough to flicker a smile. 'The numbers. I can't get the numbers anymore, that's all.'

Lisa took hold of her mother's hand and rubbed the back of it gently.

'It wasn't so long ago that I had a big birthday and I was panicking that I was letting it all slip by — life, I mean. You said to me that the numbers . . . they don't matter. That's what you said. You said, "Life isn't about numbers, it's about moments." Do you remember that?'

Her mother's smile was more than a flicker now. 'I do. I was right, too.'

'You were. So those numbers in there. They don't matter.'

'They don't, love.' She lifted watery eyes to meet with her daughter's. 'But these moments . . . they really do!' A tear leapt from her eye. Lisa reached up to wipe her tear away then she grabbed her mum and pulled her in for a hug tight enough to hide her own.

Chapter 13

The heat rolled over Harry with an almost tangible weight as he stepped out of a car that had been loud with the sound of air-conditioning. He hadn't realised just how loud it had been until it was silenced and he had pushed the door open to the gentle sound of birdsong. He was back out in the woods. He had taken a farmer's track leading off a country lane and down to a ploughed field. The field was actually an expanse of scorched mud ruts, like a rough sea frozen in time.

He was in the corner of the field. On his left stood a police officer, his head bent over his notepad, his pen scribbling notes furiously. The air was tinged with the smell of burning and chemicals. The source of the smell was just beyond his colleague — a blackened husk still making metallic *pinging* sounds as it cooled — Harry's burnt-out murder weapon.

'DI Blaker, right?' Harry turned towards the voice. A middle-aged man in black cargo trousers and a blue polo shirt emblazoned with the force crest. As he spoke, he peeled a pair of gloves from his hands.

'Yeah.'

'I would shake your hand there, sir, but I don't think you would appreciate it. It's warm work out here today.' He flicked droplets of moisture from his hand.

'Don't worry about it. You're the vehicle forensics guy?'

'Yeah, for my sins. The name's Tom.' He pulled a tissue from his pocket and ran it over his hands. He used a second one for his glasses. 'I have to say though, sir, I'm not sure I can be of much assistance today. I got a chassis number but that's just about the only useable thing.'

'Well, it's a start. Have you fed that up the line?'

'I've added it to the running log. I don't usually run the checks myself. I figure that's something the investigators usually like to do.'

'No problem. I'll get my team looking at that. So there's nothing else you can tell me?'

Tom turned back to take in the husk. Harry did too.

'Not really. The ground's so solid at the moment I can't even say for certain which way it came in, although you could take a good guess. I'm not going to get any tyre lifts for comparison with your scene. Anything left on the front when it hit is going to be long gone. It would have gone up quick and hot. We're lucky it didn't set the whole place alight.'

Harry noted the ring of ash neatly framing the collapsed chassis. He paced around it. The plastics of the interior had largely melted away; there was some of the dash left, but it had twisted and warped in the heat to the point where it was barely recognisable. The position of the two front seats had been marked by their springs and metal frames. The gear lever was a scorched metal pole and the steering wheel was gone completely. The back seat was easy to pick out, too; the square frame of the bench seat met with the flat, metal panels that once formed the truck bed. The four corners of the vehicle were supported on blackened steel wheels, their tyres burned off completely. The whole thing was in the shade of a huge tree whose lower branches were all scorched. Higher up the green was tainted with grey ash. Harry could see what Tom meant. There had been some rain recently, but not enough. Everywhere was still so dry and the heat would have been incredible.

'Do we know anything else about it at this stage?'

'Well, I can tell you it was a truck. It has a flatbed at the rear that would have had a lid on it. The lids are mainly plastic, so it's pretty much gone. It was white too — I'm pretty certain of that. I've got some paint scrapings for analysis. Sometimes I can find a paint match, which can help if it's a rare type, but a white truck? It's gonna be a flat, common shade. I've found a few Volkswagen references on some of the internal components that would suggest to me that this was a VW Amarok. I'll be able to confirm that, but I'm pretty happy to stake my reputation on it. Your chassis number should confirm that, too.'

'But we're not getting anything here that will link this car to any crime scenes, right?'

'Forensically? No. But if you have a witness who says he saw a white VW Amarok making off from your scene then I could be useful yet. No matter what they tell you is registered against that chassis number, you'll still need to be able to say for certain that it was right. The number's etched into the engine mount so it's pretty fire-resistant. I can show you if you like?'

Harry held up his hand. 'No need, thanks.'

'No problem. I've taken photos. I'll submit them as part of my report.'

'Thanks, Tom. I'll let you finish up. I'll be getting a couple of search officers out to do the surrounding area here. I'll make sure they don't get in your way.'

'Don't worry about me. I'm almost done.'

Harry moved away. He walked along the edge of the field, staying in the shade of the tree line. He called the Major Crime hunt number and the call was picked up by Mitch Evans, the team's civilian investigator who majored in putting intelligence together. Just the guy Harry needed to talk to.

'Mitch, I'm out at the burnt-out car linked to the hit and run. The link is tenuous. Good enough for me but it won't be good enough for court.'

'What is the link, sir?'

'It's in the right area. Right now, that's about it. There's a chassis number that has been added to the log. I need some work done on that, please.'

'I did see it actually. I ran it through and put the results on there. It matches with a VW truck registered to a local construction company.'

'What company?'

Mitch hesitated. Harry could hear the scuffle of paperwork. 'McCall's. I don't know much about them yet but I'll put something together for you.'

'McCall's? Yes, please. I assume it didn't bring up any person's name specifically?'

'It didn't. It might be someone's allocated work truck, though, which would be a place to start. I'll make an approach to McCall's and see what we can find out.'

'Yeah . . . we need to do that. But Mitch . . . be subtle about it, okay? Let's try and find out who was supposed to be driving it without sending out too many alarm bells. I'll want to speak to this person without them expecting it.'

'No problem. How are you looking to talk to this person? Do I need to be getting together home addresses and a risk assessment?'

'I'm going to arrest him if that's what you mean.'

'Of course you are, and that's exactly what I meant. So much for a tenuous link!'

'Well, I said it was tenuous for a court. It's more than enough for me.'

'Understood. I'll have a look at the call log, too — see if anyone's reported a stolen truck. Would that change things?'

'It might. If it's been reported, I'll need to know the circumstances. We have a list of people who were at the shoot that morning, too. Make sure we check them all for any links to this construction company.'

'Understood. Leave it with me, sir. I'll try and have something for when you get back in.'

'Thanks. One last thing . . . the team were out doing house to house in the area. Can you have them revisit anyone they got details for? We'll need to ask them specifically if they saw a white truck in the area.'

'Got it. Leave it with me.'

Chapter 14

'Goddammit!' Maddie's frustration boiled over. Unfamiliar computer systems, any number of new passwords and not knowing where the hell she should go to for help were conspiring to ruin her day. For maybe the first time in her career, she couldn't wait for her shift to be over.

'Sorry . . . Sergeant Ives?'

Maddie looked up. A young-looking, slim girl in a police officer's uniform hovered at the end of the row of desks. Her black t-shirt was sucked in around a non-existent waist and tucked firmly into black, baggy trousers. Her dark hair was tied back and she had pretty, dark eyes that managed to stand out on a pretty face.

'Yes! Damned passwords! They're the bane of my life.'

The girl offered a tentative smile. 'I . . . er . . . I wanted to ask you about something. You're the misper expert — is that right?'

'Expert! Goodness, no. Right now I am a fraud and an imposter, I'm afraid.' Maddie sensed that her sarcasm was lost on her young visitor. 'Sorry, I think I am *supposed* to be the misper expert, yes. I'm a little way from that, but maybe I can help. Wassup?'

The girl looked down at the post-it note she had been clutching tightly. She seemed to be hesitating.

'You know what, it doesn't matter. I think I might have answered my own question,' she said.

'Oh, come on! I've achieved the square root of bugger-all so far today and I go home in one hour. This might be my big chance! At least run it past me.'

'Really, it's okay. I was told not to bother you with this. My sergeant . . . he doesn't even know I'm here. He told me just to drop it. He was right. I'm just out of my probation — I know I can get ahead of myself sometimes.'

Maddie sat back from her desk, turned her chair to face the girl and folded her arms. 'What's your name?'

'PC Davies.'

'That's not your name, is it? What's your *name*?'

'Rhiannon. Some people here seem to call me *Rhi*. I don't think I like it.'

'So Rhiannon then. I'm Maddie. I don't have a clue what I'm doing here to be honest. This is my second day in Lennockshire. But I'll level with you, Rhiannon . . . none of us do, really. You've got thirty-year coppers out there and I promise you they're stumped at least once a day, probably more. Don't listen to what people say about your length of service. For example, I bet you can work this computer system, right? And I sure as hell don't know who your sergeant is. I couldn't squeal on you even if I wanted to!'

The girl seemed to relax and stepped closer. She pointed at the keyboard. 'Do you mind? It might be easier if I show you what I wanted to talk to you about.'

'Oh, please do.'

Maddie watched as Rhiannon moved confidently through menus and typed quickly so that the changing formats on screen were just a blur. For the younger generation, it seemed to be second nature.

'I don't know what you know about our body-worn camera system . . . Basically we all have one and we upload the footage to here at the end of every shift.'

'Okay, makes sense.' Maddie was aware that body-worn was pretty commonplace in modern day policing. She had seen it introduced in Greater Manchester. The cameras had been issued to firearms officers first but rolled out to all uniform roles soon after. She had never operated one herself. Covert cameras were more her thing. All uniform officers now had bulky cameras jutting out from their chests. In her previous job it would have been rather counterproductive.

'I went to a call, Friday last week. It was a report from a neighbour of screaming from the flat below. When I got there the door was answered by a Lorraine Humphries. She's reasonably well known around here. The flat's her home address. She said that nothing had been going on and the screams must have come from somewhere else.'

'And you didn't believe her?'

'I didn't. She looked pretty scared to me. I know I'm new, but you get a feeling, don't you?'

'You do. The good cops do at least.'

'I talked her into letting me in. I had a look around as much as I could. My being there seemed to make her even more nervous, even more insistent that there was no one else there. I got the feeling that she was trying to tell me something — I just couldn't work out what. It got to the point where I couldn't stay there any longer.'

'Okay.'

Rhiannon checked her post-it note and typed in a counter time. A woman appeared on the screen, frozen mid-movement. The image had a *play* symbol across it. The woman on the screen had long brown hair that she wore down. It looked like it needed a brush dragging through it. Her eyes were red, as if perhaps she had been crying. Her cheeks and nose had a red hue to them too.

'So this is her? This is Lorraine? Well, I agree she doesn't look happy.'

'This is my body-worn. I was leaving at this point. I just wasn't sure about the whole thing. I couldn't stop thinking about it so I watched it back.' Rhiannon leaned over to click again and then straightened back up. The video started playing. Lorraine Humphries was animated, her movements jerky and rigid, consistent with someone feeling tension. She thanked Rhiannon over and over for coming, though she seemed desperate for the officer to leave. Over-politeness was another sign of tension.

'Well, she's not telling you everything. And she's definitely scared of something.'

'She is, but it's not her. Watch again, but look behind her.' Rhiannon started the footage again. Maddie leant in and concentrated. The shadow moving across the hall behind her was now easy to spot. It was quick. Blink and you'd miss it. Maddie didn't miss it. She moved away from the screen. Rhiannon paused the recording.

'So there *was* someone else there?'

'Yes. And Lorraine's now missing.'

Maddie felt a spark of excitement flash through her. The sort she'd feared she might never feel again.

'And you think something's wrong?'

'I don't know. She was terrified. You can see that, right? And there was a back door to that place. I had a look at it. It's the ground-floor flat. It took me a while to talk my way in to have a look around. I was on my own at the front door. Someone in the house could have gone out the back in that time no problem at all. I wouldn't have known and I wouldn't have found them.'

'So they hung around and came back in.'

'They did. And maybe they were angry. I just had a bad feeling when I came away. It was like there was bad feeling in that house and I kinda brought it out with me. Am I making any sense?'

'It's your gut again. Not everyone is blessed with that instinct. You're right to listen to it. Hang on, though . . . your sergeant said not to worry about it?'

'Yeah. He knows Lorraine Humphries only too well. They all do. She's a bit of a drinker. She's known to us for night-time economy offences, but also for anti-social stuff during daylight hours. She's been missing before, too, quite a few times, I think. You know what it's like when you get your regulars. My sergeant said that she'll probably be in a gutter somewhere covered in her own sick and sleeping off a binge. He's probably right.'

'But he could be wrong.'

'I've met her a couple of times and she's always hammered. She wasn't that night — not from what I could tell.'

Maddie was trying to click back through the computer systems. Missing persons were handled on a totally separate system from everything else. Her password was rejected for the umpteenth time.

'It's case sensitive. Your caps lock is on. Knock that off and give it a go,' Rhiannon said.

Maddie did as she was told. She took her time and the system let her in.

'Ah! See? Teamwork!' A menu loaded. She had no idea what she should do next. 'Can you bring her up? Lorraine Humphries, I mean. I assume she has her own screen?'

'Yeah, they all do.' Rhiannon's hands were a blur again. The screen changed. The new one had *Lorraine HUMPHRIES* at the top then underneath was her home address, date of birth and **Sixteenth report** in bold letters.

'Sixteen reports? I assume that means sixteen times missing?'

'Yes. And that's just the times we have on record. I had a look into her background. When she lived with her husband, he used to report her missing a lot. Since they split it's hardly happened. I guess she lives alone and no one knows if she's missing or not. He reported her this time too, but by then she had been missing a few days.'

'What made him report it?'

'He called in when she missed an appointment to see their child. The daughter lives with him. He said it was *out of character*. We're duty bound to take it as a missing person report because he said that bit. Otherwise there is no way we would be looking for her. As it was, my sergeant was going to write it off, but then we had a second call, an anonymous one, saying something similar. That she was missing and it was out of character. He had to allocate it out then.'

'Anonymous. That is a shame. We could do with knowing who that was.'

'Well, actually, in this instance we kinda do.'

'Oh?'

'Yeah. It was me.' Rhiannon immediately brought her hand up to her mouth like she had said something horribly wrong. 'God! I don't know why I'm telling you this! You're not going to get me in trouble, are you?'

Maddie felt herself smile for the first time that day. 'I'd give you a medal first. That's good thinking. You weren't being taken seriously so you thought outside of the box. I reckon you're going to be alright, you know — at this policing lark, I mean.'

Rhiannon blushed. Then she smiled broadly.

'So how can we tell what's been done?'

Rhiannon moved back to the computer. The screen changed again so it looked like a spreadsheet. This one had a more obvious layout. Maddie could see a chronological list of actions that had been completed with notes next to them. It was all stuff that smacked of standard procedure. The home address had been attended. They couldn't gain entry and they had knocked at a few neighbours' doors with no real results.

'Is this it? This is all that's been done?'

'So far. I only made my call yesterday. Before that, nothing had happened at all. I called after my shift. I was passing, see, and I went to check if she was in. The mail was stacking up and there were no signs of life that I could see. It's been a week. In his call, her husband said he knew she attended a meeting on Fridays. My call out was the day before that so she must have been okay that night. I was just going to finish up here and try again today, but . . .'

'That feeling.'

'I can't shake it.'

'Not much has been done. Do you fancy going back?'

'Now?'

'Why not?'

'Because you said you were off in an hour?'

'Less than that now. But I'm used to a finish time being more of a guide. I was kinda hoping it would be like that down here too. Let's go and make sure your girl is okay. I assume you have a police car, right? And I haven't been in one of those for a long, long time.'

Both girls grinned as they swept out of the office.

* * *

He closed the door to his flat gently. He felt instant relief at shutting out the weak daylight — along with everything else. All his blinds were tightly shut, just how he liked them. He could almost convince himself that the rest of the world didn't exist. His afternoon's job had taken much longer than he had anticipated; the traffic had been congested on the motorway, closed for a time in both directions. He had been forced to sit and wait. He wasn't good at waiting. It was worse today.

But he was home now. He leant on the back of the door, lingering on the sensation of the wood against his hands. He could smell the paint and polish. His whole body shivered with excitement. He wanted desperately to fire up his phone immediately and sit there in the dark, streaming the images from the remote camera to his television. But he was making it last. He was fooling himself that he might not even watch it all, that it was wrong to do so. But he knew what he was. He was an addict and he needed his fix.

He took off his shoes and socks. His hands trembled and he struggled over the laces. He sunk his bare feet into the thick carpet, relishing the feel of being so grounded. He moved through to the bathroom, finally turning on a light, and leant on the sink. He took a moment to take in his face in the mirror. His eyes were backlit with excitement, his lips slightly parted and his breathing quick and shallow. He shook his head briefly. He knew the real turmoil would come later, after he had got his fix, when his release came. He would hate himself. Maybe even punish himself, too. His right hand ran over his left forearm. He turned it over so he could see where the scar tissue stood out from his skin. Years of self-chastisement, years of trying to inflict pain on himself — recompense for the pain of others. He wanted to stop. He had tried. He used to cling onto that. He wasn't so hard on himself any more, though, despite knowing that it was escalating. You were what you were.

He could wait no longer. He turned away from the mirror and tugged the light switch. The blackout blinds did their job effectively; there was just enough light to navigate his way to the kitchen. He took out a glass. He had left a bottle of red wine on the side. He walked it back through to the living room and sat down. He poured a large measure and placed it carefully on a low table. The technology to project his phone onto the television screen was fired up with one button. The screen fell black with only a digital time showing in the top right-hand corner. The camera was active. He had to control the shake in his hand so that he could work his phone to turn on the light. He bit down on his lip. His heart raced as he moved to the edge of the seat. His whole body was tensed with excitement. He pressed the screen and lifted his head. There followed a few seconds' delay . . .

Chapter 15

She was pretty sure she was dreaming. It was a comfortable dream. She was wrapped up tight in a soft blanket. It had a strong smell that she couldn't place. Her mother was holding her and she was looking down and smiling. She was tickling her belly and telling her everything was going to be okay. It was dark and she could only just make out her face. Her frizzy hair, her soft skin, her dark eyes.

Then she was gone. Replaced by a bright light that was all-consuming — it was as if she was inside it. She slammed her eyes shut and turned her head towards the floor. Her neck shot with pain. Her eyelids still glowed white where the light was forcing its way through. She twitched involuntarily as something landed on her mouth. She didn't think she was dreaming anymore. With her head turned away from the light, she opened her eyes a little. She could see a ridged, green floor. It was blurry, something was moving — it was small, white and moving from side to side. It reminded her of old computer games, the sort she used to love as a child, where the aliens moved in predictable patterns so you could avoid them if you timed it right. She tried to move her hands to swipe it away. They were still secured, wrapped against her body. She could feel the effort of trying to move them through her stomach.

Her eyes adjusted a little more. She could see the moving pattern in more detail.

A maggot!

She sucked in a mouthful of air in a panic. A lump came with it. She spat it out instinctively. A thick, black fly fell onto the floor. It landed on its back. It bucked and fidgeted to right itself. It had a green, shiny back. She fought back the urge to vomit. She knew how much that would hurt. She shut her eyes for just a few seconds so she could focus on her breathing. She needed to stay calm.

She lifted her head. She was in some sort of metal container. The walls were filthy, running with slick, brown mould that was shiny with moisture against the matt-green paint. Maybe that was the source of the smell? She tried to turn over. The source of the light seemed to be right in front of her, bright in her eyes. Her stomach hurt, her neck, too. One of her shoulders was exposed; she could feel bare skin against the metal floor. She channelled all her energy and started to rock. It took a few goes to build up enough momentum and her head rolled close to the floor as she did so. She could see a lot more maggots; they fell around her from somewhere. She tried to shut her mind to that. All her focus was on her movement.

Finally she rolled. Now she could see across to the other side of the container. It was bigger than she had imagined. There was a roll of what looked like a light-coloured, patchy carpet next to her. Its surface looked fuzzy, like it was moving. She shook her head to try and clear her eyes, doing her best to ignore the pain in her neck. Black bits were lifting off and falling back onto it. It wasn't fuzzy. The surface was a mass of flies! The buzzing was suddenly prominent. She had been used to it, but now seeing the source seemed to make it louder.

She took in more air. This time she sucked in through her nose, her lips tightly pursed. She could feel the panic rising up through her but she fought it with all she had. She slammed her eyes shut again and tried to focus on something else — *anything* else. She twitched her hands. Her right one had some give at least. She pulled it upwards and it moved a couple of inches. She ignored the pain and used her growing panic as a source of strength to push it back down and pull it up again, trying to work it loose. It was working. It was still painful, but it was working. If she strained her eyes she could see down her own body. She could see the flies bustling and jostling for position, but she could also see the plastic sheeting that was wrapped so tightly around her. Her panic subsided enough for her to feel tired. The exhaustion started to consume her; it came over her like a cloak. She opened her eyes to fight it. She tried to study her surroundings, to pick out details. Something to focus on.

The wall on the other side was cleaner.. It looked dry and there was no mould. There was a sticker in the top right corner with letters and numbers that didn't mean anything to her. She looked further down, back at the roll of plastic lying next to her. It was a dark grey and spotted with darker stains — mainly in shades of rusty brown. Her eyes moved up to where the plastic ended. At the top was a clump of black wire, maybe, or fluff. It was curled up and stained red in places. She looked closer. The wire was moving. It was alive with maggots! They writhed and fell, spilling out of what seemed to be the source of them all. She felt the panic rising up again. Her exhausted and confused mind was catching up. The smell suddenly seemed stronger. It clung to her like an extra layer. That wasn't wire or fluff, it was something else — *it was someone!*

She rolled away a lot quicker as panic surged through her, adrenalin with it. She bucked and twisted in the wrap. Her right arm suddenly worked free. She was able to push it down into the floor and push herself up. The tight plastic still restricted her movement but she could work on that now. She could unravel it maybe. She concentrated on finding the end. She had to block everything else from her mind. She found it under her hips. She dared a glance to her right. Now she was sitting up she could see the side of a woman's face. It looked red raw. What was left of her skin was a washed-out white. The eye sockets wriggled with the white bodies of maggots. Flies fidgeted across it. She tried to tell herself it wasn't real — just a horror movie prop put in here to scare her. But she had to stop what she was doing. She had hold of the end of the plastic but she leant away to heave. Only bile came up. The pain in her stomach returned at once and it forced her back down on the floor. All the strength in the arm holding her up was gone. She could feel the coldness of the metal again against her cheek. She wanted to close her eyes to the horror all around her.

Her exhaustion was back with a vengeance. She looked at her hand; how pale her skin was! She knew she was in a lot of trouble. She must have lost a lot of blood. She felt so weak. She knew she was meant to die here. Just like that other girl. She felt a sudden determination for that not to happen. If she could just stay calm . . .

She planted her hand back on the floor. It took every ounce of strength left in her but she twisted back to a sitting position. She found the start of the plastic again, the point where she could start freeing herself from its grip. She bit down hard, using her pain to fire her determination rather than let it cripple her. The outer layer of the plastic unravelled by an inch, maybe two.

Then the light was gone. The darkness was thicker than ever, the flies louder. She sucked in air again. She tried to speak, to shout out for help, but her throat wouldn't open. She managed a sob. It was excruciating but she could do nothing about it. More followed and the pain brought her back down to the floor.

* * *

He leaned right forward, almost out of his seat. He was barely breathing.

She was alive!

She was moving and she was fighting. He had actually seen the moment when she realised what was lying next to her. He could see the fear on her face! He nearly dropped his phone in his haste to activate the *record* function. He could save five-minute chunks at a time. That should be enough for what he had just seen. Already he wanted to review it. That would be when he would have his release. But he had to focus now. She was moving a lot more than he'd have thought possible. Now he realised he had a job that needed finishing. He was certain there would be no way out of that container, even for someone who was fit and well. But he wouldn't leave that to chance. He didn't want to. His excitement started to peak again. He walked back to the bathroom. It was a ritual of his . . .

He ran his hand over his sleek head. There was no need to shave it again. It was already close enough to his scalp that he could be sure he wouldn't shed any hairs. He lifted the blind that was covering the bathroom window. The daylight was diminishing. It would be dark soon. He considered that he didn't like to work at night. It gave an element of cover from prying eyes but also tended to hide the approach of other people — potential witnesses. Dawn was just a few hours away. He already had an early start planned for a job. It wasn't so far from the farm. He could be there by mid-morning. That way, he would blend in with the traffic. He knew a place he could park and wait so that no one would see him access the land. But even if they did, he had his reasons for being there. It would all check out. He just needed a few minutes on that land — to open that container door, to finish what he'd started. And to savour every second of it.

He walked back into the living room. He dropped to his knees and bent in front of his sofa. He reached under. His fingers bumped against something solid. He pulled out the long, vicious, jagged knife he had taken out of the truck. Tonight he would scrub it, then wrap the handle tightly in fresh sterile bandages, as tightly as he could manage. The next day, those bandages would burn in a metal incinerator.

This time he would make sure.

Chapter 16

Even on approaching the house Maddie was pretty certain there wasn't going to be anyone inside. It sat in complete darkness. She hung back and let Rhiannon ring the bell, then tap on the front window. The house was one of a number of newish builds that still managed to look rundown overall, flat-fronted and featureless. Some white weatherboarding clung to the top half of the front. Up close, she could see it was coated in a layer of grime. The place looked tired and unloved in the unforgiving white glare of the LED streetlights.

This was the home address for Lorraine Humphries - — occasional home address at least. From the tale of woe Rhiannon had told on the way over, Maddie got the impression that she tended to spend the night anywhere there was alcohol. And with anyone supplying it. She had explained how Lorraine had been married once with a young child. The marriage split up when Social Services had found her lying face down in the street while her nine-month-old daughter crawled around her, dragging her own dirty nappy. Her husband came home from work, picked up the child and left. Lorraine had barely seen him since, save for supervised child access.

'What's round the back?' Maddie said. The house was at the end of a row of three. The middle one incorporated a sort of arch over a slip of tarmac that went through to an open space. She could see waist-high lights on poles, through the gap.

'Car parking. It's like a courtyard.'

'And she's the ground floor, right?'

'Yeah. It's a bit misleading. They look like houses but they're split up into flats. The top flat runs over the arch.'

Maddie walked through the arch. On the other side was the rear of the ground-floor flat. A double door led out from it onto a small, enclosed garden. A light clung to the wall and it came on with her movement. The grass was overgrown and scorched to the point that it had a straw-like appearance. There was a low gate. She stepped over it to get to a back door that had frosted glass panels. There was also a window to the left. She pushed up against it. She could see into a kitchen that looked untidy rather than dirty. She knocked on the back door and immediately moved back to the window, watching for any signs of movement. There were none.

'Patrols that came here before . . . they spoke to the neighbours, right?'

Rhiannon shrugged. 'They spoke to a bloke who lives opposite and doesn't have much to do with her. He just said she was a drinker and a pain.'

Maddie lifted the lid on a wheelie bin that had been pushed to the far side of the window. The lid was sticky. Maddie suspected it hadn't been opened for a while. She leaned over it. It was two-thirds full: wine bottles and cider cans. Nothing that could be of help.

'I reckon we should try a bit harder,' Maddie said.

The front door to the flat that ran above Lorraine's address was back under the arch, next to Lorraine's. Again it had a frosted glass panel and Maddie could make out a flight of stairs on the other side. The doorbell was loud. It still took more than a minute for any response. Maddie was pressed up against the glass waiting for movement. The voice shouting down from above made her jump.

'Yeah?'

Maddie backed away. A woman looked down on her from an upstairs window pushed wide open. She was black with a round face. One of her arms was visible where she held onto the window.

'Hey, sorry to bother you. Do you have a minute?'

'Not really. I got the telly on. What yous want?'

Even though Maddie was doing the talking, the woman in the window kept her eyes fixed on Rhiannon who was standing a few paces behind her. Maddie guessed it was the uniform.

'We're worried is all — about your neighbour. We just want to ask a few questions. Have you seen her?'

'Who? Larry?'

'Larry? No. Lorraine, she lives in—'

'Larry, yeah. That's what she gets called. I ain't never heard no one call her Lorraine.'

'I see. Well, Larry, then. Have you seen her recently?'

'Nah, not for a while, actually.'

'Are you friends? You and Larry?'

'Friends? I wouldn't say friends, you know? Sometimes I go round for a can of cider or what not. She don't come round here though. My man, he don't like her. He thinks she's trouble. She can get a bit rowdy, you know what I mean?'

'I think I do, yeah. When was the last time you saw her?'

'I dunno. A week. Two weeks maybe. I got a busy life. I don't go round checking on no people to see what they got going on.'

'I'm sure you don't. Tell me about her though, Larry I mean. She's been reported missing. Are you surprised by that? Does she often go off for a few days?'

'She can do. I mean I don't really know the girl, yeah? I just live above, like. But I'm not surprised. She'll be somewhere having a right good drink. She likes a few beers. Probably somewhere being rowdy right now!'

'Let's hope so. Have you got a number for her?'

'A number? Like a phone number? Nah, we don't call. I got her on Facebook, see.'

'Facebook. Does she put stuff on there often?'

'She does yeah, quite a bit, stuff about her ex and her little girl an' that. Some people put too much of that shit on there, you know? I dunno why they do that.'

'Can you have a look? See when she last posted anything.'

The woman made a sound like she was sucking on her own teeth. Then she was gone. Maddie looked to Rhiannon and made a face. She had no idea if the round-faced woman was coming back. They both stayed in the garden, their necks craned upwards. The woman did come back. Her face was lit from the chin upwards by the phone in her hand.

'There's been nothing new on there for a while. Late last week she put something up about wanting to have her life over again or something. The usual sort of stuff. It's a bit of an attention thing, I think, but she's got her issues. Ain't we all?'

'That's true. Look, can I leave you my number in case she comes home. If you could just let me know if she does so I can stop worrying about her that would be great.'

The woman sucked her teeth again. She leaned out to look down at her own front door. 'I ain't coming all the way down there for that. Just stick it through the letterbox, yeah? I know where it is then, if I need it. She's out on some bender. She'll be having a beer and she'll come home when the party's over, you see if I'm right.'

'I'm sure that's all it is. We just want to be sure.'

'I get that. She's got some ex-husband. She talks about him a lot. I think they still talk. She might be with him, whatever. He's the man to talk to. I don't know who he is or where he lives but I think he's somewhere round here. Talk to him. I ain't no babysitter. If she comes home, she comes home. She's an adult, ain't she?'

'She is. Thanks for your help.'

The window was closed without another word. Maddie and Rhiannon carried on knocking doors. They did all the houses that were in view of Lorraine's front door. The story seemed to be the same: no one knew her well but they all knew she liked a drink.

They were soon back in the car.

'There's not much else we can do tonight, is there?'

'Do we know where the ex-husband lives?'

'We do. Someone's already been round there.'

'I'd go back. He seems like the best person to me to give us a bit of insight into her life. That's got to be how you find people, don't you think?'

Rhiannon chuckled. 'I don't know. That's why I came to you, remember? You're the expert!'

'Ah yes, I keep forgetting that. Well, then, that's what we should do next.'

'You want to do it now? You were supposed to finish hours ago.'

'I was. I'm living in a Premier Inn, Rhiannon. I am in no rush to go back to an oversized bed in a fog of purple. And this feels like police work. I get the feeling I should cling onto that.'

'I'll call up FCR for an address then.'

Maddie watched in mild awe as Rhiannon changed the channel on her radio and then used all the right talk to get her enquiry across. The last radio handset Maddie could remember using was very different. The address came back as a ten-minute drive. Rhiannon started for it.

Benjamin Humphries looked every bit the hassled dad as he answered the door on the third knock. Maddie could hear the baby before the door was opened.

'What?' he said. He was in cotton trousers and a vest top with a brown-stained muslin thrown over his shoulder.

'Sorry to bother you, Mr Humphries. I know you reported Lorraine missing and we were just following up. Can we talk to you for just a second?'

'Again?' he snapped. 'You'd better come in.' Benjamin turned away and made straight for the source of the noise. The crying was much louder and more cutting when Maddie stepped into the house. Benjamin picked up a baby that was wearing just a nappy and commenced with swaying from side-to-side while jigging at the same time. The TV played cartoons in the background. Some screwed up pieces of toast littered the floor around his feet. Maddie guessed they had come from a Peppa Pig themed plate that was on the low table. This was her idea of hell.

The baby settled down enough for Rhiannon to ask a question. 'You reported Lorraine missing, is that right? Or should I call her Larry?'

'What? Larry? No, that's what her piss-head mates call her, I think. No, it's Lorraine and, yes, I reported her. She was supposed to come round and see our daughter. She gets supervised access. She missed the first visit, which wasn't a massive surprise — I mean, even though she's been better recently. Then she missed the second one and I knew something was wrong. My first thought was that she had probably drunk herself to death in some gutter somewhere.'

'But you don't believe that anymore?'

'If it was eight weeks ago I probably wouldn't have even called. I might have tried to find her myself for a bit, or just waited for her to turn up with her latest excuse. These last eight weeks, though, she's been sober. And I mean sober. Something clicked with her. She's told me before that she's been off the drink but you can always tell. You don't have to live with an alcoholic long to know when they've been drinking. She was clean. I thought . . .

well, I dunno what I thought. That she might be getting somewhere maybe.'

'So this is out of character?'

'Going missing? Well, no. You lot should already know she goes missing a lot. I've reported her before, when we used to live together. She would go missing for a few days at a time fairly regular. But I think this is out of character now. For the first time in a long time I don't think she's somewhere drunk.'

'Does she have friends who she spends time with?' Maddie said. 'Is there a man on the scene?'

'Not that I know of. Her life has been chaos for a long time. She would spend time with anybody who could get her a drink — she wouldn't care who. I got the impression these last eight weeks that she's been a lot more insular. When she beat it before she locked herself in. She had to. She only goes out for her meetings.'

'Meetings?' Maddie said.

'AA meetings. Alcoholics Anonymous.'

'How often are they?'

'Weekly, up the top end of Canterbury. Sturry area. They're in a church hall on the main drag. I can't remember the name of the church it's attached to but you'll probably pass it on the way back out. It's every Friday. They help her, to be honest.'

'Sounds like it. Alcohol dependency can lead to money troubles. Do you know if Lorraine was in any financial trouble?'

'I know she doesn't have any money if that's what you mean. She's always been hand to mouth, that woman. When she got her benefits, she always tended to hand them straight to the nearest off-licence. She might have saved something up over these last eight weeks or so but I doubt it. Something else usually takes over. The last time she quit the drink she started chain smoking. That's not a cheap pastime these days, is it?' The baby offered another whimper. Her eyes had closed, but Maddie could see that they were now rolling open. Sure enough, she started to mewl again. Maddie thought she was building up to another full-blown wail.

'It certainly isn't. Would she borrow money if she needed it? From people she knew, or maybe people she didn't?'

'No. I've never known her to. And I can't see anyone lending her money. You wouldn't need to spend long with her to realise you weren't getting it back, no matter what you did.'

Maddie nodded. 'Well, I can see you have your hands full. I'll leave you my number if you don't mind. Please let me know if you hear anything, or if she turns up.'

'I will do. Let me know if you hear anything too.' He lingered on Maddie.

'You okay? Was there something else?' she asked.

'I do still love her, you know. It's ridiculous when I think about what she's put me through, but the sober version of Lorraine is all I ever wanted.'

Maddie was a little taken aback. 'We'll keep you informed.'

They said their farewells. Maddie sat back in the passenger seat. She peered back at the house. Rhiannon started the engine.

'He's really worried about her,' Maddie said.

'He seemed it.'

'And being married to an alcoholic for a few years . . . it must take a lot to worry him.'

'You think he knows a bit more than he's telling us?'

Maddie turned to look at Rhiannon. 'No, that's not what I mean. Just that this is more out of character than it might look. I know how missing persons used to be treated. An alcoholic who has been missing a million times before and always turns up? We would barely have taken details.'

'But you have a bad feeling, right?' Rhiannon said.

'Like you do.'

'Like her husband does.'

Maddie's gaze drifted away and she began staring out of the window again. 'Well, we've done all we can today, I think. But we do need to find her. All this bad feeling can't be good for any of us, can it?'

'I agree, but my skipper . . . I think he'll be taking me off it tomorrow. He said as much. He's passing the enquiries over to community officers. I'm not sure they'll be too bothered.'

'I'll keep on it. I probably can't get you out of your other work but I'll keep looking.'

'Thanks,' Rhiannon said.

'Don't thank me. I'm glad of it. It's either a day out looking for our Lorraine or in the office trying to work out my passwords!'

The two girls shared a brief chuckle as they set off back towards the station.

Chapter 17

Harry paced along the path. He was keeping close to the frontage of the block of flats. His target lived in a ground-floor flat: number 4. Mitch had been able to find out some information that he could use. The keys to the burnt-out vehicle were signed out to Jonathan Lee. A thirty-year-old with previous for domestic violence and minor theft offences. Nothing that had stuck — not yet at least.

He got to the communal entrance and stopped to peer through. He was at an angle so he wouldn't be seen by anyone looking out. He could see a bright strip light on the ceiling. It made the entrance glow a vibrant orange against the darkness of the night. He was here much later than he wanted to be, already a good few hours after his shift ended, but this was a lead that he didn't want to put off until morning.

He signalled to the uniform officers behind him to move up. There were two of them — and two more around the back. He would have liked more, but two would be just enough to get his man under arrest and back to the station — leaving two to carry out an evidential search at the scene. That was the plan at least. There was a panel on the wall that had a grid of numbered buttons. He pressed numbers 3 and 5 at the same time. Someone answered. The speaker crackled in response. The voice was muffled and low, and Harry couldn't make out what was being said. He spoke anyway.

'It's the police. We need access to your building.' He paused. The speaker fell silent. A few seconds passed. He was about to select another button when the door buzzed. He pulled it open and moved into the light. He held the door open and the two officers moved quickly in behind him. Harry stepped back to let his colleagues knock on the door. The taller of the two officers hit the door with his fist. It was a hammer blow. The sound echoed and bounced round the sparse hallway. It would have travelled up the concrete steps that were central to the building. Sure enough, he heard a door open on the floor above. It closed almost straight away. They all fell silent for a few seconds then the officer hammered the door again. There was still no response. The officer dropped to his knees, pulled the letter box open and flattened the bristles to see in.

'Lights are off, boss,' he said.

'Any signs of life at all?' Harry said. This wasn't ideal. He would rather they got him in now, rather than having to come back out in the morning. It would only take a nosey neighbour to let the occupant know that the Old Bill had been knocking at his door and before they were able to come back they could stand to lose key evidence.

'Someone's in!' the officer said. He stood up and took a step back. There was a noise from behind the door and then it was pulled open. A man stood in just a pair of shorts. His eyes were half-closed; he looked like he had been woken up.

'What the hell is this about?' he demanded.

'Jonathan Lee?' the officer with the heavy hand replied.

'Yeah. What do you want?'

'Can we speak to you inside, mate? I'd rather not do this out here.'

'No, you can't. Do what?'

'Okay then. Jonathan Lee, you are under arrest for murder. You do not have to say anything but it may harm your defence if you do not mention something which you later rely on in court. Anything you do say may be used in evidence—'

'What the fuck? Did you say *murder*?' He expelled air through his nose in a sort of laugh.

'You'll need to get some clothes.'

'Well, yeah. I mean, I reckon I will, won't I? What the hell is this all about?'

Harry stepped forward. 'Jonathan, I'm Inspector Harry Blaker. I work in Major Crime and we are investigating an incident where we believe a man was unlawfully killed. I need to talk to you about it. I won't do it here.'

'What? You need to talk to me about what? Murder? I just got back, like, this morning. I don't know what this is all about?'

'And why would you? I'll explain all in interview. Back at the police station.'

'Jesus . . .' The man shook his head. He seemed to be coming to terms with his predicament. 'You better come in, I need to get something on at least.'

Jonathan backed into the flat. Harry thought his shock seemed genuine. He just couldn't tell for certain what had caused it — being arrested for something he knew nothing about or just being caught. The uniform officers bundled in after him. They followed their suspect through to where he could get some clothes on. Harry stepped into the lounge. His first impression of the place was that it was sparse: a few chairs faced a large flat-screen television and very little else. The kitchen was just off the lounge and there it was a similar story. The work surfaces were clear except for a toaster and a kettle. It looked more like a base than a home. Certainly it smacked of a man living alone: all functionality and nothing more. It was just a few minutes before Jonathan reappeared. He still looked shell-shocked. He ran his hands through hair that was cropped close to his scalp. It was a similar length to the stubble on his chin.

'Can I have a glass of water?' he said.

'Sure. Which cupboard are your glasses in?'

'I'm not allowed to help myself?'

Harry fixed him a look, that he hoped was stern enough to give him his answer. 'I get nervous in kitchens,' he added.

'This is ridiculous . . . the cupboard there, over the toaster.'

Harry filled the glass with water. The man took a couple of swigs. He was wearing a jumper now and jeans that fell over new-looking trainers. He put the glass back down.

'You ready?' Harry said.

'I suppose so, yeah. I mean, this is all shit. Let's just get it over and done with. I've gotta go to work in the morning.'

'Bring your boss's number,' Harry said.

'I don't have a boss. I have a meeting.'

'Bring whatever number you need to explain you ain't gonna make it.'

'You're joking! This is a joke! I've done nothing wrong!'

'I've never met anyone who has,' Harry said. Then he spoke to the officers stood either side of him. 'Let's get our friend back to the station, shall we?'

'Can I lock up at least?' Jonathan said.

'No need. I'm staying. We'll be searching your place.'

'This place?' Jonathan snorted a laugh. It was incredulous rather than amused.

'This very place.'

'Mate, you can tear this place apart. There's nothing here, I'll tell you that now. Nothing here that makes me a murderer. This is ridiculous.' Harry sensed that he was starting to wind himself up. He also noted the phrase *nothing here that makes me a murderer*. He would bank that one for later.

'I'll try not to tear anything apart.'

Jonathan Lee was led out, still protesting his innocence. Harry heard him on the way out. His protestations increased in volume when the uniforms stopped at the door for handcuffs to be applied. He heard one of the officers explain.

'It's standard, mate. I do it with everyone. Do you want me to get you a jacket? We can lay it over the top so no one sees you in the cuffs.'

'Let's just get this over and done with, can we? You're really starting to piss me off. This is a joke! Don't push me!' Jonathan's voice was moving away. Two different officers stepped into the kitchen.

'He didn't seem too happy, sir!' A young girl with a sweet smile. She was pulling search gloves onto her hands.

'They rarely are.'

'Anything you want us looking for in particular?' she said.

'He didn't have a phone on him. That'll be here somewhere. Apart from that, you have the victim's details and the car's details. Anything that links him to either or both — or anything that makes him look more like a murderer.'

* * *

She had drifted off again. She must have. She could remember the light and the panic. It had taken her over. It was still dark. She felt for the end of the plastic sheeting again, ignoring the buzzing as best she could. Her body hurt so much. The pain in her stomach was enough on its own, but her movement was causing her neck to hurt too. It felt like it was burning hot. The numbness in her lower legs and feet was wearing off, but as the feeling returned it brought painful pins and needles with it. She could move her toes now, but she could feel the movement of the insects more too, all the way down her legs and on her feet. She knew they must have been there all the time but that did nothing to ease her discomfort. She needed to stay calm. She tried to block out the horrors that had been revealed by the light. She thought about the light itself. She considered there was a switch somewhere and she had knocked it; she couldn't think of another explanation. It would have to be on the floor for her to have done that. She plunged her free hand to the floor and scrabbled around. It seemed like everything was damp and moving. She pulled it back in disgust.

She concentrated on her breathing. She realised for the first time that she was hungry. She focussed on that as a way of distracting herself. It was a new feeling, distinct from the other pains in her abdomen. She was thirsty too. She didn't know how long ago she had taken the water that had dripped from above. Time meant nothing. She didn't know how long she had been lying there. She considered that it could only have been a few days. She was still alive. Had she been trapped here much longer, she didn't think she that would be the case.

She moved to sit up. It was easier now that she could plant her right hand. She reached again for the start of the plastic sheet that she knew was somewhere under her hip. If she could unravel it just a little bit, the wrapping around her would surely loosen enough for her to crawl out.

She felt for the end. She pulled on it, lifting her hips at the same time. Her abdomen tensed and the pain took her breath away. She tried to moan but her neck was too swollen to let any sound out. Her mind flashed with doubt. This was not going to be possible.

She took a moment. She got her breathing back under control. There was no rush. This was all she had to do, but she *did* have to do it. She had to get out of here. She had to get her life sorted out. She had made mistakes and hurt the only people in her life that she cared about. When she got out, she was going to tell her husband that it had all been a mistake, that she could be somebody different — or even somebody the same . . . the same person that he had married — and they could be a family again.

She took a firmer hold of the plastic and tugged harder. Her abdomen reacted instantly but she was able to keep tugging long enough to drag the sheet under her hip. It came free. She fell back to the floor. Her head ran with cold sweat. The flies that had been disturbed landed on it. She closed her eyes and concentrated on her breathing. She would recover — she knew she would. She needed to wait out the pain and then she could go again. She was inching closer to getting free.

* * *

Harry Blaker moved through the custody area to commence his interview with Jonathan Lee. He had waited until the search was complete in case anything came up that he could use in interview. It had been a waste of time: they had found nothing, not even his phone.

Jonathan had a solicitor: Karen Wilson. Harry had clashed with her a few times before. There were very few solicitors that he hadn't clashed with at some point in the past. He understood the purpose of a state-funded solicitor scheme — that they should never return to the bad old days of oppressive interviews and false confessions from prisoners who couldn't afford counsel. But Harry wasn't interested in false confessions; he was only after the truth. It seemed to him that things had gone too far the other way; solicitors now seemed to see it as their job to block the truth or to make getting at it as difficult as possible. Karen Wilson had a large build and cheeks that always seemed to flush red — as if just sitting there was an exertion. She pushed her glasses up her nose as Harry entered. He was accompanied by the night turn DC who would act as scribe, a guy called Tony Seddon. He was a good detective from what Harry knew; he worked CID and had done for some time. He was a little like all the rest — worn out. Harry didn't need him to be sharp; he just needed him to be able to write and to stay quiet.

Harry had already spoken to Karen before she had met with her client, the part of the process that was called *disclosure*. This was where he told her what he thought he knew. He'd then given her as long as she needed to spend with her client in private while they discussed the best strategy for blocking his way to the truth. Karen had a reputation for encouraging her clients to give *no comment* interviews. Harry was prepared for that.

He skipped any pleasantries and started the tapes before launching into the formal bits. It was nearly 10 p.m. and he was starting to feel tired himself. Eventually he was able to ask a relevant question.

'So, Jonathan . . . You understand that you have been arrested on suspicion of driving at someone and causing their death. What can you tell me about that?'

'What do you mean, what can I tell you? I can't tell you anything, man, I—'

'Can I remind you, Jonathan, that we discussed this matter and I have given you clear advice,' Karen Wilson interrupted. She put her hand on his arm.

Jonathan sat back in his chair. He had been leaning forward with anger written clear across his face. Harry had been hopeful. Angry people were often loose lipped. They talked fast and often without thinking and made mistakes. Instantly Jonathan became more measured.

'I got no comment,' he said.

Karen took up the talking. 'My client would like to provide a prepared statement that I will read on his behalf . . . *My client Jonathan Lee was out of the area on the date on which this incident is said to have taken place. He was staying with family in Suffolk and can provide any number of people who will confirm this. He also has a travel railcard and other receipts from shopping outlets used while he was away. He visited several town centres and he is confident that they will have some sort of CCTV coverage. The locations with possible CCTV are listed below — I see no point in reading these out. Further, my client wishes to make clear that he travelled by train and has not driven a vehicle for a period of more than seven days. He has certainly not driven any vehicle in any incident that could even be considered similar to the one he has been arrested for. The only vehicle he has had access to in the last month is a work vehicle, which was returned to his place of work before he went away. Any number of people have access to that vehicle. He wishes to make no further comment.'*

Jonathan Lee was sitting back in his chair. He had his arms crossed now and his face was the very picture of smug. Harry's first instinct was to grind it into the table. Instead, he fixed Lee with a glare.

'I still get to ask my questions,' he said.

'Go right ahead. That's all you need to know, though. Get it over with so I can make my complaint, yeah? You lot drag me down here in cuffs, you take my DNA, my fingerprints and treat me like a criminal — and for what? Just because you can't do your job!'

Harry sucked in a deep breath. His eyes never left the man sat opposite. 'I'm a police officer, Jonathan. It's my job to treat people like criminals.'

'No, it ain't! What happened to innocent until proven guilty?'

'I'm all about the proving guilty part. Don't forget that. Which brings me on to the fact that a truck signed out for your use ran down and killed a man on Saturday 18th August. How can you explain that?'

Jonathan leant forward, the emotion was returning to his face. Karen Wilson's arm moved across him. Her hand now rested on top of his. 'Remember what we discussed, Jonathan. I believe we've told Inspector Blaker all that he needs to know.'

'No comment.' Jonathan broke out in a grin. Once again Harry flushed with the urge to slam him face first into the solid table. He gave himself a moment, and he reminded himself that interviews were rarely the part of an investigation where convictions were won. Patience was the name of the game. Anyone sitting in an interview room accused of something that fell under the *Major Crime* remit was not of a mind to start making admissions. Murderers rarely liked to make things easy.

Chapter 18

Maddie was in early — 7:30 a.m. — and she was shown to the Major Crime floor by a cheerful cleaner who didn't appear to speak a word of English. Maddie was concerned that she was being led somewhere completely wrong when they crossed a yard to a separate building entirely, but then the woman gave a beaming smile as she pointed at the words *Major Crime* above a set of double doors. Maddie thanked her and pushed through.

It was open plan. Rows of desks were laid out in threes in a similar fashion to the CID floor over in the range. A little more spacious perhaps. There were rooms coming off it that looked as if they'd been set up as meeting rooms. In one, the glass panels in the door were covered crudely by yellowing sheets of A4 paper stuck down with clear tape. She could see Harry Blaker sat at a desk down the far end of the room. He was facing her but he was looking down and hunched over an open book, a silver ballpoint shuffling furiously. A cup steamed next to him. She was aware that Major Crime detectives generally started at 8 a.m. but somehow she had known that Harry would be in already. She scuffed her shoes on purpose as she approached. He didn't look up. She moved closer. Still he remained bent over his book. His pen stopped.

'Hey, Harry.' He took his time. He looked up but didn't change his position.

'How you doin', kid?'

'The kid thing . . . Any chance we could move on from that?'

'Maybe it's a term of endearment.'

'Or maybe it's a term for a junior.'

'You're in the Major Crime office. This is for experienced detectives. Maybe you *are* a junior?'

'I'm no one's junior,' Maddie bit. She immediately wished she hadn't. She got the impression he had been trying for one.

'Noted. I'll try and remember that.'

'How's your luck? Did the burnt-out vehicle give you a result?' She moved the subject away.

'We got someone in the bin.'

'Oh really! They in now?'

'No. Last night.'

'And?'

'And now they're back out again.'

Maddie smiled. Day two of Harry Blaker and she reckoned she was already starting to work him out. She reckoned he was short with everyone so they didn't come back and bother him. He certainly wasn't much of a people person and persisting with him was probably the best way to piss him off. And she was nothing if not persistent.

'You bailed him?'

'Early hours.'

'It's like pulling teeth with you, Harry. But I like a challenge.'

Harry adjusted his position so he was sitting back a little. 'And what makes you choose me as your challenge?'

'Maybe you want to be chosen.' She chanced a smile. He immediately bent back into his notes. His pen started moving again.

'If you bailed him in the early hours . . . have you been home yet?'

'Briefly.'

'Quick change of pants?'

Harry stopped again. 'Did you have something you needed from me, kid? It *was* a long night. I *am* tired. If you think I was a challenge yesterday, try me today.'

'I didn't come to try you. I just wanted to run something past you is all. I can come back?'

'Later? I'll be worse. What do you need?'

Maddie moved to lean on the desk. 'At what point does a missing person become someone Major Crime might be interested in?'

Harry let his pen fall onto his pad. 'When we suspect foul play.'

'How much cause for suspicion do you need?'

'What have you got?'

'On the surface, not much. I've got an alcoholic who has been missing umpteen times in the recent past who hasn't come home. Reported by her ex-husband because she missed two appointments with their daughter. A uniform cop responded to a concern for welfare call that was put in by a neighbour who claims to have heard shouting at her address. Our missing person told her there was nothing doing and that she was home alone. The officer's camera shows that someone was moving around in the background. The ex-husband has a bad feeling about it all. He says she's been clean for eight weeks and has turned a corner. I don't know . . . I just don't like it either.'

'You want us to take it on? Based on that?'

'No. I want to keep it. I just wanted some direction and I didn't want to be stepping on anyone's toes. If this is the point where you would normally look at it, then I don't want to be the *junior* messing up on her first day.'

Harry picked his pen back up. 'It's all yours.'

'Understood. I know she could just turn up with the mother of all hangovers but this is the longest she's ever been missing. I guess I'm more interested in looking for this one woman than reading through the twelve other cases. I've had a brief glance. They're all crap.'

'There's a lot of that. You do realise that *looking* for missing people isn't actually your job?'

'I do. But no one's told me that yet.'

'I just did.'

'And I didn't hear you.' Maddie was walking away.

'How long has she been missing?' he called out after her.

'She was reported on Monday but she was last seen on the Friday before that. At an AA meeting.' She called back over her shoulder.

'An alcoholics' meeting?' The interest in Harry's tone was sudden and clear.

'No. It was a get together of roadside mechanics.'

'Don't dick about, kid.'

'Well, I thought you weren't interested! Yes, then, Harry. Alcoholics Anonymous. A meeting in Canterbury. Why's that important?'

Harry had stood up. He chewed on his bottom lip. 'It probably isn't.' He sat back down to his notebook. 'Send me her name — now you've made me aware.'

'Will do.' Maddie continued out of the office.

Chapter 19

He had to press firmly on the brakes and pull the steering down hard left to make the turn into the track that led through Leonard's Farm. He nearly overshot it. He had planned to park up in the lay-by that was just twenty metres further back. He was going to wait until he was sure there was no traffic, until he was sure no one could see him pulling onto the property. But he was angry. He knew he was and that it was putting everything at risk. His eyes flicked to the rear-view mirror. He was kicking up a big trail of dust behind him that would be visible for miles. He eased off the throttle and took a deep breath. He was going too fast. He wasn't thinking straight. He wasn't being careful.

He pulled up next to the derelict barn and glanced over at the container. It looked identical to when he had left it a few days earlier. He didn't know what he'd been expecting. The door to the truck was heavy as he pushed it open as far as it would go. The dust cloud was still moving; it caught him out again and quickly filled the cabin. He turned his face away and held his breath. He chastised himself mentally: he was still being hasty, still making mistakes. It was the anger, the fury that had been building up inside him. He needed to unleash it. He needed to get this finished. He stepped out and moved to the back of the truck. The hydraulics hissed. He reached in for a fishing box. It had tackle in it: weights, lines, lures and even a spare reel. It was all ancient, none of it functioning, but it gave him a plausible excuse for the other thing that he was carrying in that box. He lifted out the vicious-looking knife, its handle wrapped tightly in a sterile bandage.

He stepped away from the truck and took a moment to take in the scenery. He tried to hold his breath, to calm his racing heart so that he'd be able to hear any other vehicle — or person — approaching. There were some bird calls, the sound of the plastic roofing clacking together in the breeze, a rodent moving at the back of the barn. Nothing was out of place. He was alone. He reached back into his vehicle for a paper suit and slipped it on over his clothes. He closed the truck back up.

He gripped the knife tightly in his right hand. He could feel the weighted handle through two pairs of gloves and the layers of bandage. He could feel his heart racing, too, as he moved towards the container. He passed the bin, the recent scorch marks tainting its metal, and he stopped at the container doors. He listened again . . . still nothing. The doors were still shut and the padlock secured. This close he could smell the odour of death — just a whiff of it in the air. Inside, it would be overpowering. Only the door was holding it all back.

He pushed the key into the lock and twisted it. The lock snapped open and he pulled it clear. It banged against the metal, loud enough to make it audible from the inside. He put his left hand on the door and stopped still, listening for movement but, more than that, he wanted to savour this moment. It had almost been ruined but he was here now.

There *was* a sound! It was so slight he almost dismissed it, but it came again, a scraping noise, louder and stronger. Definite movement from inside. His pulse increased with his excitement. He tensed his arms and chest. He clamped his fist tighter round the handle of the knife.

He pulled the door open.

Chapter 20

Canterbury had more church halls than Maddie had envisaged and it hadn't been easy finding the right one. This was it, though. The doors were open. She could hear beating music and loud instructions being called out by a breathless-sounding woman. She walked along a corridor lined with faded blue boards with notices and charity appeals that had slipped to hang at an angle. There was another door at the end. She pushed it open to reveal the main hall. It was hot and musty. Double doors on both sides hung open. She could see around fifteen women in Lycra outfits stretching in unison. Each stood in front of a mat and they were all heavily out of breath and flushed with exertion. It looked to Maddie like a warm-down, the end of the class. There were wooden benches running along one of the walls. She moved over to take a seat. She would wait.

Only one of the women was facing her. She seemed to be in charge. She led the stretches and she had a microphone taped off around her ear.

'If it hurts now, it just means you've worked hard!' she hollered. 'No pain, no gain!'

Maddie thought she could see a lot of pain around the floor. She wasn't sure about the gain. A few more stretches, a lot more looks of anguish and the class finished.

Maddie stayed seated. She was certain the woman leading the class had seen her. The participants all moved away through the same door she had come in. The woman wiped herself down with a towel. She stacked up a few of the mats that were closest to her, then walked over.

'Thinking of giving it a go?' She held out a card and Maddie took it. It read: *Kelly Dower, Throw some shapes to change your shape.*

'Nice slogan,' Maddie said.

'It works too. You get a room full of people dancing and they don't even know they're working out. It's a great way to get what you want while having fun.'

Maddie grinned through the sales spiel. Her mind flicked back to the exhausted faces that had just filed out. She was pretty certain those women had known they were in a workout. 'I'll bear it in mind. I am new to the area. This is the sort of thing I might be interested in.'

Kelly Dower stopped dabbing her brow. 'That's not why you're here then?'

'No, actually. Sorry . . . Kelly. I was actually after speaking to whoever arranges the bookings for the room. Would you mind helping me out?'

Kelly's eyes shifted to look her over. 'You after running a fitness class as well?'

'No! I'm not the competition, Kelly, don't you worry about that. I'm just looking for someone who comes to one of the other groups in this hall. I was hoping someone here might have her details. They may be able to help me find her.'

The woman was still eyeing her suspiciously. 'I'm not really into helping people find people. Some of the groups here . . . you get participants who'd rather not be known.'

Maddie had a realisation. Her hand snatched to her rear pocket. She pulled out her police badge and opened it up for Kelly's benefit. 'I really should have said this bit from the start!' she chuckled. 'I'm a police officer. I specialise in looking for missing persons. One of the women we're seeking, the last confirmed sighting of her was in this building. There are a lot of people concerned for her safety. I'm one of them.'

Kelly relaxed visibly. 'A police officer! Yes, you really should have said that. Sorry, I thought you were just some random trying to find someone. I don't like getting into other people's business. Did this girl come to mine?'

'No. There's an AA meeting run from here, I understand?'

'There is, yeah. It runs on a Friday morning. I had a dance class that used to start straight after it before I changed the time. I assume it's still going.'

'Do you know who set it up?'

'I've got the number I use. I guess it's the same person. Just let me get hold of my phone and you can have it.'

'That would be great, thanks.'

She watched the woman walk to the back of the room. She dug around in a bag and walked back over with a pen. 'Do you still have that card I just gave you?' Maddie handed it back. She watched Kelly scrawl a number out on it. She also wrote a name: *Jeremy*.

'Do you know anything else about him?'

'I don't. I don't really have much to do with him. I set the class time up as a regular thing and I drop money in a lock box in one of the rooms here. I run my own list of attendees, mostly over Facebook.'

'Understood. Thanks very much.'

'No problem. And bear me in mind, yeah, if you fancy a bit of a workout. We're a good bunch and you certainly look like you can keep up!'

'I will do, thanks.'

Maddie waited until she was back in her car before she dialled the number. She was just about to give up when it was answered.

'Yeah?'

'Oh, hey, is this Jeremy?'

'Yeah.'

'Jeremy, my name is Maddie Ives, I'm a . . . I'm a detective sergeant from just down the road at Canterbury police station. I was hoping to talk to you regarding an investigation I'm running at the moment.'

'You don't sound too sure about it. About being a detective or whatever.'

'It's a bit of a new thing for me. I've been a cop a long time but the detective thing is new. So I need your help.'

'With what?'

'A missing person actually. It's nothing to do with you as such and certainly nothing to worry about, but—'

'I don't know anything about no missing person.'

Maddie took a second before answering. 'No, of course not. And how could you? I haven't even told you who she is yet!'

'I don't get involved with people like that. I don't get involved with the police either to be honest. You could be anyone.'

'You're right. I tell you what . . . how about I come meet you. I can show you my ID and we can talk about what you might know. Does that sound okay?'

'Not really. I get busy, you know?'

'I'm very busy, too, Jeremy. I'm not calling you up to waste your time, or mine. You might be one of the last people to have seen a vulnerable young lady before she went missing. That makes you important. I suggest you make time.' Maddie was aware of a very obvious huff from the other end of the phone. She didn't bite. She let him consider his options for a few seconds. He spoke again.

'What do you need me for?'

'You arrange the use of the church hall, right?'

'Some.'

'Fine. The AA meetings, do you arrange those?'

'I run those. So what?'

'Great. So there you are. You are more important than we realised. One of the members of that group hasn't been seen since she attended your meeting. I need to talk to you to see if you remember her, to see if she said anything that might help and to talk about who else was there.'

'It's *anonymous.*'

'I get that, Jeremy. Thank you.' Maddie took a second to quell her anger.

'I don't know who they are, they don't know who I am. It's a safe environment.'

'It got a lot less safe for one of the members when she left. I'm very concerned about her. If I could just come and talk to you—'

'No, I don't think so. I don't talk about those meetings. That's what the whole thing is built on.'

'I appreciate . . . hello?' the line was dead. Maddie swore loudly. She wiped her mouth and peered out of the car. She pressed the redial button. It rang out. She pressed it again — same result. She waited. She would sit there for thirty seconds and try again. She would keep doing it until he picked up. She was stubborn when she was pissed off.

The phone rang in her hand. It was a concealed number. She considered that it might be Jeremy calling her back.

'Hello?'

'Maddie Ives?' The voice was gruff with a flat tone — instantly recognisable.

'Harry Blaker, if I'm not mistaken.'

'Very good. Where are you?'

'I have no real idea. I'm just off a major road leading out of the city. Sturry Road, I think?'

'Okay. You need to head back in. We have a meeting in ten minutes.'

'We do? Did I miss something? I wasn't aware—'

'No, you didn't miss anything. Ten minutes.'

For the second time in quick succession someone hung the phone up on her.

* * *

Maddie was a little longer than ten minutes. She headed for the Major Crime office. She could see Harry standing in one of the meeting rooms off to the right. When she walked into the room she could see a big flat-screen television projecting a video conference. DCI Julian Lowe's image filled half of the screen. He was sitting at a desk. The upper right quarter of the screen showed five people in smart clothing, all seated at a round table and looking attentive. The final quarter, at the bottom right showed Harry Blaker but, much to her embarrassment, became filled with her face as she stood too close to a wall-mounted camera. Harry spoke.

'This is Maddie Ives, who brought it to my attention. Maddie hasn't been party to any conversations prior to today. She doesn't know about the Hastings case. Dee, could I ask you to give her a brief summary?'

'Yes, of course.'

Maddie backed away from the camera but remained standing. On the screen, one of the women among the five seated people shuffled in her seat. She sat a little straighter and began.

'Sorry, Maddie, I don't know what you've been told already so I'll cover the basics and you can ask any questions. Five weeks ago we found a body. A young woman we now know to be Priscilla Earnest. She was found in a locked store room that was part of a derelict factory. It looked as if she'd been there around three weeks. Forensics are certain she wasn't killed there. We don't have a kill site. She had a stab wound to her abdomen and her throat was cut. Either wound could have been fatal and they were sustained at the same time. There is another job, too. Ellie Perkins was found in scrublands at an industrial estate on the other side of the county. She was out in the open and there are a few months between the two jobs but we are linking them for now because the murder method looks to have been the same. There are other similarities too — smaller details that you probably don't need. Any questions at this point?'

Maddie had loads, the most pertinent being why the hell was this woman telling her this? She shook her head, though; she was aware that Harry was looking over at her. He would be the best person to answer those questions.

'No questions. That all seems to make sense.'

'Indeed. Another link we have, which up to this point seemed rather tenuous, is around their lifestyle. Both were addicts of a sort. One alcohol, one painkillers — well, drugs, but painkillers largely. They both attended AA meetings, albeit in different locations. We appreciated that their addictions made them vulnerable, but what we didn't consider — until DS Blaker called us this morning with a hypothesis — is that these women could have been selected as potential victims *at* their support group meetings. The killer may even have befriended them there. DS Blaker has made us aware of a missing person in your county who was last seen at an AA meeting. Firstly, is that correct?'

Maddie's throat was suddenly dry. 'Well . . . yes . . . as far as I can tell, but there's still work going on to confirm her last known movements. We are all waiting for her to turn up somewhere after an extended drinking session.'

'I'm sure you are, and that may still be the case.'

DCI Lowe interrupted. 'Where are you with that investigation, Maddie? Have there been any advances?'

Maddie took a moment to get her thoughts in order. 'Sir, I revisited the neighbours last night and also the ex-husband. They didn't really tell me much else. I've just come back from the church hall where her AA meetings are held. I have contact details for the man who organises them. I was hoping he might be able to talk to me about her and about anyone else who was there, but he doesn't seem to want to play ball.'

The woman on the screen interjected. 'We've had the same issues. The AA community take their anonymity very seriously. As they should, of course, but it does cause problems.'

The DCI spoke again. 'Harry, can you take that up alongside Maddie, please? Let's find this man and find out what he knows. Now that Maddie has a little more of the picture I'm sure you understand that we may need to be a little more persuasive.'

'Sir,' Harry said in confirmation.

Maddie continued, 'I haven't exactly taken no for an answer, sir. I was far from giving up.'

'That's what I like to hear. This will now be a Major Crime investigation until we have bottomed out the cause of her disappearance. Harry has asked for you to be assigned to the case with him. I will try and oblige as best I can, alongside your own role of course.'

'Understood.' Maddie looked at Harry. He was sitting on the edge of the table. He was looking away.

'Major Crime will be treating this as a priority case. We do not have any definite links, but I think we should work as if we believe there to be foul play behind her disappearance. I'm at headquarters for today, but I'll be looking to catch up tomorrow. I'll leave you to compare notes with our Sussex colleagues.' The DCI disappeared from the screen.

One of the men from the Sussex team spoke next. 'I've spoken to the team and we are going to send copies of everything we have. We've no active leads as we speak. We're almost waiting for another victim and hoping he slips up. It's not a great place to be, as you can imagine. Not that I'm saying that we hope your girl is it. Hopefully she turns up with a sizeable hangover.'

Harry rubbed at his face. Maddie thought he was wearing even more of a scowl than usual. 'Yeah, send down what you have.'

'Some of it may need to be hand-delivered. My job for today is to review it all. You should expect it all in the next forty-eight hours.'

With that, the meeting was over and Maddie was still reeling. Harry Blaker was still sat on the table. He fixed her with a stare.

'You okay, kid?'

'I'm not sure what just happened. This morning I was doing a made-up job no one cared about, looking for a hopeless drunk. Now what? We're hunting for a serial killer and she's his latest victim?'

'I don't know. But I figured you might want to be involved at least, rather than us just taking it out of your hands. Or you can go back to your made-up job if you like?'

'And you want me to work it? With you?'

'*For* me.'

'Oh I see. Because I'm the *kid*.'

'Because I'm the inspector. You'd want this on your own, would you? I saw your face when you were listening to what Sussex had to say. You wouldn't know where to start.'

'I was on the spot. You made sure of that. You could have warned me, given me a little bit of a heads-up on the phone before I came in.'

'I'm not a big fan of saying things twice. You got what you needed.'

'I got some.'

'You need more? Sussex have two dead girls. Both were murdered with a big knife. Stabbed and their throats slit. They were both found naked, wrapped in thick plastic sheets and then dumped. They weren't too well hidden. The killer would have known that we would find them eventually and he didn't care. He's forensically aware.

We've got nothing from CSI. And do you want the kicker?'

'The kicker?'

'The bit that kicks you in the face. He was watching them rot.'

Maddie tried to form a facial expression. She took a step to her left, she found the table with her left hand and it steadied her.

'He was what?'

'The girls were both lying under a camera. One of these internet things — I'm not up on the modern technology. He'd set up a hotspot using an untraceable SIM card. He could stream live pictures anywhere. They reckon he could watch it on a computer, a tablet or even his phone.'

'He wanted to watch them decompose?'

'Well, Sussex have a theory that he was watching for when the bodies were found and maybe that's what the camera was for. The one on the industrial estate was pointed at the door, but it covered the victim too. But I reckon I know different. That's how I know the killer is a *he*. It was so *he* could tune in whenever he wanted. He gets off on it, he must do. The murders were sexually motivated. He's probably sat at home with his trousers down and his—'

'I get it, Harry. Christ! I get it.'

His face lit up for a brief second. 'Welcome to Major Crime.'

'The girls. They were raped too then? You said sexually motivated.'

'No. That's a bit of a fallacy. Sexually motivated killers get their rocks off somehow, but most just like to toss off over what they've done. Hence they take their little trophies or they set up cameras so they can have another bash.'

'He took trophies?'

131

'Well, the women are whole. Nothing's been cut off, but . . . are you okay, kid?'

'I just need some air.' Maddie moved to the door and out across the floor. Her stomach had suddenly twisted tightly, she felt like she might be sick. It had gone by the time she bundled into the loo. She splashed her face with water. She stared at herself. Wide eyes stared back. She cursed herself for leaving like that, for looking weak in front of Harry Blaker. She'd seen far worse than what he was describing. Maybe it was the nervous tension of being thrust into a meeting with people she didn't know, discussing something she knew nothing about. Harry was probably testing her. She cursed again.

When she got back to him his fixed expression had dropped away a little. 'You okay?' There was maybe even a flash of concern.

'Yeah. Been a long few days.'

'It's gonna get longer.'

'I can handle it.'

'I know you can.'

She fought to restrain the smile that wanted to form on her lips. 'So, what now?'

'Your mate who sets up the AA meetings . . . you said you spoke to him on the phone already?'

'I did, yeah. He won't pick up to me now. He said that the members respect their anonymity and he won't do anything against that.'

'That's next then. We need to go back to him.'

'I agree. I was going to try and look him up on your local systems. A lot of addicts come to the attention of the police. He said he runs the meeting, which means he'll have been an addict himself at some point. I figured if I could find a home address for him he might find it a little more difficult to ignore me.'

'Okay, that makes sense.'

'But he won't be happy,' Maddie said.

'If he gives us the same answer again, he definitely won't be.'

Chapter 21

It didn't take long to find *Jeremy* on the local police system.
It was amazing what could be achieved when you had
someone who knew what they were doing. Harry brought
up the address from where the AA meetings were run.
There were a number of people linked to it on the
intelligence system — mostly because they had been
sighted by local patrols going to or coming from it — but
a male with the full name *Jeremy Lennox* appeared for two
reasons. One report linked the location to drug dealing
while it was noted that Jeremy was running a session at the
time. The second link was stronger: Jeremy had offered it
as a bail address following his arrest for drunk driving. All
in, it didn't paint a very favourable picture of him and
maybe offered a reason as to why he hadn't been keen to
help the police.

Jeremy Lennox had been refused the church hall as a
bail address. He had been forced to provide a domestic
address, which appeared to be his mother's. That was
where they were heading to now.

'How far away is this place?' Maddie asked from the
passenger seat.

'Twenty minutes in this traffic,' Harry grunted. They were still waiting to enter the flow of cars passing the police station. Someone flashed them out. Harry edged forward a few feet.

'Twenty minutes, eh?' Maddie didn't relish the thought of twenty silent minutes. Harry's car was unusual. It was a new-looking Land Rover Discovery but it looked like it had been jacked up on the suspension to make the seating position even higher and there were little modifications dotted over the bodywork. Her view was obstructed by a thick plastic tube that trailed up the windscreen on her side. All the crime cars she had seen in the last ten years had been well used, small and unloved. This one certainly stuck out.

'What's the deal with the car?' she said.

'What do you mean?'

'It's not really a detective's car, is it? I mean, where are your crime scenes generally? Up a mountain!'

'It belongs to the Marine Unit.'

'I've never sat so high. And what's with the drainpipe?'

'It's a snorkel. Something about wading into seas and rivers. The guy who handed it over will happily bore you all day with the details.' Harry fell silent again. Like that had offered her any explanation at all.

'Major Crime get cars with snorkels then, do they?'

'No. I injured my arm. I needed an automatic and this was the only one that was available. It's a short-term thing. Couple of weeks.'

Maddie tried to be subtle as she looked down at his arm. It was resting on the gear-shifter, like a man who was using to driving a manual. He had the sleeves of his shirt rolled up. Among the body hair she could see a small, white track running up the centre. There were three white dots either side of it too. He must have seen her looking. He flipped his arm over.

135

'The scarring is mostly on the other side. They put in some metal and bolted it down. It just aches now. I told them not to worry, but the boss sorted me this.'

The scarring was indeed more obvious. The line that ran up the underside started as a jagged line butted up against his hand. It ran half the length of his forearm. The six white dots were more prominent; she guessed they were the points where the pins had been put in.

'You must be fun at airports.'

'I'm fun everywhere, Maddie,' he said. The silence returned and they were still in sight of the nick.

'You married then, Harry?' Maddie tried again.

He momentarily flicked his eyes to meet hers. They edged forward to the approach of a roundabout. His fingers drummed on the top of the steering wheel.

'Yes.'

'Kids?'

'Grown up.'

'Well. I feel like I know you better already.' She didn't care if her frustration was obvious.

'I need to go and speak with someone about the hit and run job straight after. Do you want me to drop you back?' Harry said.

'Do *you* want to drop me back?'

'I'd need to come back through this traffic to drop you. So, no.'

'I'll come with you then, sure. What's it about?'

'You don't need to get involved.'

'Okay, but what's it about. Maybe you could trust me enough to share something with me every now and then.'

He broke from staring at the traffic to face her. 'It's not a trust thing. I need to find out a few simple things today. It should be a simple job. The more people you talk to about it, the more opinions you get in the pot and the more these sorts of jobs can get complicated. No offence intended — this is not a respect or a trust thing. I just know what I need to do.'

The traffic shifted. They moved round to the left and picked up speed. She could see signposts for a university campus. They passed a train station on her side. The rest of the journey was silent but Maddie didn't feel awkward about it anymore. She had tried at least. It was twenty minutes, almost to the second, when they stopped outside of a row of terraced houses jutting off another road jammed with traffic. They got lucky with a parking space. Harry pushed the gate that was almost directly next to her car door. She followed him up the path. An elderly-looking female answered.

'Yes?'

Harry had his badge out. Maddie dug around in her bag for her own. She needn't have bothered; the woman had already invited them in. She confirmed that Jeremy was at home and immediately bawled up the stairs to let him know he had visitors.

Who is it?' The voice that came back down the stairs sounded agitated.

'It's the police, Jeremy. They say they need to speak to you.'

'Fuck's sake, Mum! What did you let them in for?'

'Sorry, Jeremy . . . I . . .' She flustered. The strength and volume in her voice dropped away. She turned to the detectives. 'I'm really sorry, he's a good boy, but he is prone to bad language on occasion.'

Maddie's eyes lifted to a sound on the landing. A head appeared over the top. The police system had him at forty-four years old. He looked older. His long, greying hair dripped down his face as he leaned forward. From what she could see, Maddie reckoned he was topless.

'What do you want?' he said.

'The same thing I wanted on the phone, Jeremy. I just need to talk to you.'

'You're the one I talked to on the phone? I told you all I'm going to tell you. You're wasting your time, love.' The head was gone. Harry was looking over at her. His jaw was tensed, revealing dimples in his cheeks. Jeremy's mother spoke again.

'I'll go up and see him. He shouldn't be so rude.'

Harry raised his hand to stop her. 'Don't worry, madam. Would you mind if I popped up to speak to him?' He smiled. The smile carried a warmth that Maddie had not yet seen or thought possible from him.

'Well, no, officer. If you want to. But he can be a bit cranky. You might need to be patient with him.'

'Oh, don't worry, madam. I'm blessed with a lot of patience for people like your son.'

Harry moved up the steps. Maddie gave the woman a reassuring grin of her own and followed him up. They turned back on themselves on the landing. The door at the top of the stairs was open. A toilet hissed as the cistern filled. The next door was also pushed open. It was a big room and light bundled in through the window, shining on an immaculately made bed with floral bedding on the duvet and pillows. The next door was firmly shut. It had a cracked indent around halfway up, as if someone had hit it with something solid. Maddie guessed that the "something" had been a fist. She stopped, expecting Harry to do the same and knock. He didn't. He twisted the handle and pushed it in forcefully.

The curtains were drawn. The room was small and very cluttered. The door only half opened, bouncing back off something.

'What the FUCK?' Jeremy was laid out on the bed with a computer games controller in his hand. A large flat screen was fixed to the wall and it played a shoot 'em up game of some sort. Harry was close enough to reach out and snatch the controller from him. He threw it immediately and it clattered into the wall under the window.

'WHAT THE HELL ARE YOU DOING? YOU CAN'T DO THAT!'

'Sit *down!*' Harry's last word was delivered with such venom its impact was as if he had physically pushed Jeremy and he slumped backwards. He was indeed bare-chested. He had jeans on his lower half and no socks.

'You can't just burst in here like that — not without a warrant.'

Harry stood silent at the foot of Jeremy's bed — he was good at silence — and glared down at Jeremy. Jeremy's eyes flicked from Harry to Maddie. She could tell he was uncertain, scared almost.

'What the hell? Is anyone going to speak to me? Are you retarded or something?'

'A woman is missing,' Harry said. 'A *young* woman. She was last seen at an Alcoholics Anonymous meeting that we believe you organised. Were you there?'

'Am I under arrest?'

'No.'

'Then I don't have to tell you anything.'

'Why would you not help us?' Maddie said. 'What does it matter to you? You know we're just trying to find someone we're worried about.'

'I told you. We're all about *anonymous*, that's the idea. The clue's in the name, yeah? I can't help you — even if I did know the girl's name and I don't.'

Harry spoke again, his voice even more gravelly. 'So you don't have the names of people that attend your meetings?'

'No. Sometimes people send me emails with questions or call me up. They might sign off with a first name or tell me it — sometimes their full name. But I don't care, that's the thing. I'm not doing this for them. I don't care who turns up, just that a few people do. I need them. The people that go, they need them too. What they don't need is some copper turning up and asking about a really private part of their lives. Now, I've got nothing more to say, and if you've damaged that controller then you will need to pay for it, yeah? Criminal damage. Am I right?'

'If I've damaged your controller consider that it might be the best thing that has happened to you.'

'How the hell do you work that out?'

'It might give you a rocket up your arse. You might get out there and do something worthwhile with your life, maybe even move out of your mother's house.'

'You're a big man to come up in here and judge me. You don't know anything about me.'

'I know you're forty-four years old and living with your mother. You're unemployed and you're playing war games with a bunch of teenagers at best. You're a drinker, probably because you're a loser with no prospects. It's far easier to get drunk than to face up to this, isn't it?' Harry gestured at the room. 'And open a window. It stinks in here.'

'You can't just come up here, throw my stuff around and call me a loser!'

'I figure somebody should.' Harry pulled a piece of paper from his pocket. He unfolded it to show the image of a young woman: Lorraine Humphries. It had been taken in happier times, her expression was warm.

'Do you know her?'

'I told you, I'm not speaking to you. You couldn't even ask nice.'

Harry used silence again. He took the time to look around the room and to inhale deeply. 'No, I couldn't. I was going to try, but I couldn't. What I *could* do, however, is search this room. Pull it apart, top to bottom. I'll get a whole team in here. Until I find your cannabis and probably something else. What are you into? A bit of amphet maybe?'

'I don't touch the stuff. I'm an addict, yeah. Recovering. I have an addictive personality, one bag of that shit and I would end up dead. Guaranteed. And you can't search this place. You definitely need a warrant for that. I know my rights.'

'I'm lawfully on the premises. Your mum invited me in. Now I'm here, I can smell the cannabis. It lingers for ages that stuff. Especially if you don't open a window. So that's reasonable suspicion of an offence. I can search where I want, how I want. Or you can answer a few questions and I might forget to look into it any further.'

'You can just come in here and search, can you?'

'If I'm invited in by the homeowner and then I discover offences. Like I said, Jeremy, you need to move out of your mother's place.'

'There's no weed in here. I don't touch it no more.'

'You sure?'

Jeremy stared right back at him. But he broke first. It was inevitable.

'Jesus! I can't be sure about nothing! I was in a real bad place, yeah? Fine, what's the picture?'

Harry held it out.

'Yeah, she's familiar. She's been to a few.'

'Recent?'

'I think she was at the one last Friday. She's been regular recently.'

'Does she go with someone? When she turns up?'

'I don't know if she goes with him. I think they met there, maybe.'

'Him? Who's him?' Harry said.

'I don't know, I told you that.'

'Tell me about him.'

'I don't know anything about him. It's not really a social thing.'

'Is he white, black or . . .?'

'White. Younger — like, thirty, maybe thirty-five, I dunno. Short hair — really short and stubble. Looks like he works out — bit of a gym body. He doesn't look like the normal sort we get through the door, I remember thinking that.'

'And they were together?'

'They sat together most weeks — always recently. They were talking before it started and I think after.'

'Is there any CCTV at this place?'

'No! Definitely not. It's a big reason why places like church halls are used. It's a private place. It's a private thing. It's a group of strangers in a room who feel comfortable enough to talk about their deepest secrets to people who won't judge. But they want to stay strangers at the end of it all.'

'And are they always together?'

'I don't know! I don't really take much notice. This ain't fair, all this. He's not been coming long. Not as long as her. Maybe a couple of months — twelve weeks at the most.'

'You said people email or call. How did he get in touch?'

'I said that some do, yeah, but most don't. He didn't. I stick out a time and a place and people turn up. Some people like to find out a bit before they do. It can be a bit intimidating, I suppose. These people are vulnerable. Most addicts have some sort of mental health problem at the core of it all, you know that right?'

Maddie stepped forward. She made sure her tone was soft. 'You're being a great help, Jeremy. If that girl is in trouble and she knew we were here, she would want you to help. I've been to similar meetings, further up the country. People speak, right? They talk about themselves, about their lives?'

'Some do, yeah, of course. Some just sit and listen.'

'This girl and the man she was with, did they speak?'

'She's a regular. She'll talk most weeks. The usual stuff . . . how hard it is . . . how the world wants her to drink . . . how she still craves the escape. I think she was doing better but I don't know nothing that will help you I don't think.'

'And the fella. Did he talk?'

'He talked about being an addict, about struggling with it like we all do, I guess. Nothing stands out, though. I remember he got really emotional one week, but that's what it's for. We all have.'

'About what?'

'I dunno. About being an addict, about having no control over your own life. It's hard, you know. None of us choose it. He didn't . . . I didn't — no matter how much of a loser your man here thinks I am.'

'Sometimes the members have sponsors, right? Other members of the group that can be on the end of the phone for support. Do you know if either of them had a sponsor?'

He seemed to look at her more closely. 'Were you an addict, then? You said you've been to a meet?'

'No such thing as *was*, right?'

'Fair point. I don't know about sponsors. Sometimes you do get to know who's helping who. I'm supposed to have an idea but I don't run it like that. I didn't get that from them two anyway. It's possible, I reckon, that they talked outside of the group.'

'Did you notice them talking to anyone else?'

'Not specifically, no. She was quite friendly. She would talk to people but it was general small-talk type stuff, I think. The usual stuff you get when you get a room full of nervous people.'

Harry took back the questioning. 'Was there anything that stood out about them? Anything about them we haven't asked that you think might be relevant?'

'I dunno, really. I dunno what you want me to say. The fella, he didn't speak much, he was the quiet type. The week he did speak he seemed different. That was when he got emotional.'

'Different?'

'Yeah. I think he'd had a slip. He didn't say it outright. He just talked like he might have. A lot of people, when they have a drink, they can't bring themselves to say it. He was talking about how hard it is an' that but it was all about how much he was hurting other people. I guessed he has a wife, a girlfriend at least. But I think he's a long way from winning. Doing this as long as I have, seeing the people you see every week, I could see it in him. He still gets that big thrill from it. He still yearns for that. He isn't ready to stop.'

'So you think he'll relapse?'

'If he hasn't already.'

* * *

They walked back to the car. Jeremy Lennox only just stopped short of apologising to Maddie and her gruff colleague on the way out. She had not seen that coming.

'What did you make of him?' It was the first thing Harry said when the doors were pulled shut on the Discovery. Maddie looked over, happy that he was asking her opinion like it mattered.

'If you're asking me if I think he was telling us all he knows, then, yes, I would say he is.'

'I agree. You seemed to know a little bit about those meetings. You said you've been to one.'

'A lot more than one.'

The car was ticking over but Harry didn't drive away. He looked over at Maddie like he was waiting for her to continue. She recognised that he was using his silences on her now and as difficult as he was to read, he might have looked concerned.

'*God grant me the serenity to accept the things I cannot change. The courage to change the things I can. And the wisdom to know the difference,*' Maddie said.

'What the hell is that?'

'The prayer. The meetings I went to . . . you said it at the start. Every time. It's not a bad mantra as they go. Certainly it gives the addicts something to cling on to.'

'And you still remember it?'

'You say something enough times . . .'

144

'I didn't have you as the type.'

Maddie laughed. 'You wouldn't believe what I've done, who I've had to be.'

'It was a UC thing then? Playing a role? Makes more sense.'

'It was. But that doesn't mean that I didn't need it.'

'That might explain your choice of phone case at least.' Harry's face flickered a smile before he selected *Drive* on the gearbox. He seemed to stumble over it a little. The car fell back into silence. Maddie broke it.

'We've got your enquiry to do now, then. Do you want me to sit in the car while the adults talk?' She chuckled, but she was testing him.

'No. You should come in. I don't want to leave you in here. Just in case you press something you shouldn't.'

Maddie was pretty sure that Harry Blaker had just made a joke.

Chapter 22

Maddie knew nothing about McCall's Construction but the impression the reception area gave was that of a reasonably large outfit. A middle-aged woman in a McCall's branded shirt sat behind a desk. The walls were plain white, broken up by pictures of men and women in high visibility clothing and hard hats shaking hands with people in suits with what Maddie assumed were examples of their finished work in the background. There were a couple of awards up on shelves, too, and rows of recent health and safety certificates. The woman picked up a ringing phone. She held out a finger towards Harry as he approached. Maddie could sense his frustration. The call was short.

'Can I help you?' the woman said. She stood up to speak. The desk was high and she needed to stand to be seen properly.

'I hope so. I'm Detective Inspector Blaker and this is Detective Sergeant Ives. We're here about the truck.'

'Ah yes, of course! We were expecting a visit. I've got a number to call from our fleet manager for when you did. Would you like to take a seat and I'll check if he's on site.'

She gestured at a row of benches softened by a long cushion. Maddie moved to sit. Harry walked over but stayed standing, facing out of the large window. Maddie's eyes were drawn to it too. It overlooked a busy-looking yard. There was a lot of movement from heavy goods vehicles, diggers and trucks. Raw materials were laid out like they were there to be picked up and taken away. A big warehouse was visible over the other side of the concrete yard. Everyone wore something blue with the McCall's branding on it.

'Good morning.' Maddie turned to see a man walk out into the reception area. His choice of McCall's branded clothing was a blue polo shirt. The buttons were done right up so the collar gripped tight around his neck. He had a warm smile. In his right hand he carried a clipboard. He pulled a pen from one of the side pockets in his black workwear trousers. Harry moved towards him and took his offered hand. Maddie did the same. 'I'm Ryan Clarke, the fleet manager here. I'll just sign you in,' he said, 'then you can come through and I'll put the kettle on.' He scribbled on the clipboard and left it on the desk. He made for a door that was off to the right.

As soon as they moved away from the customer facing part of the company, it was obvious that the attention to detail and clean lines of the décor was lost. They moved down a corridor. It was still white, but the plasterboard was chipped and scuffed, even coming away in places. Where the ceiling met the wall what looked like a water stain could be seen and the plush carpet of the entrance gave way to bare, pock-marked concrete flooring. There was a door halfway along. As soon as Clarke pulled it open the din of a roaring diesel engine was all-consuming.

They crossed the yard when it was safe and were led to a large Portakabin with steps up to the door. The quiet returned as Maddie pulled the door shut behind them.

'Sorry I couldn't take you to one of the nice meeting rooms in there. Those are for senior management. They get the hump if people like me go trampling in there in my big safety boots!'

'It doesn't matter where we speak,' Harry said. The gruffness was well and truly back in his voice.

'This is about the stolen truck, I assume?'

'It's about the truck, yes. I don't believe it was reported stolen.'

'Well, nobody here realised it had been. I got told it was stolen and burnt out. Did you want to take a seat? Two teas?'

'Sure,' Harry answered. Clarke walked to an area clearly assigned as the kitchen. It consisted of some work surface and a sink. The kettle was next to a row of upturned mugs. A small fridge sat underneath. He spun three mugs round. Each of them was branded with *McCall's*.

'You people really like everyone to be sure where they are!' Maddie said.

'Sorry?' Clarke stopped what he was doing.

'I haven't seen much that doesn't have *McCall's* stamped on it yet!'

'Ah! Yes, I know. An accountant explained it to me once. Companies get to a certain size and they need to lose some of their extra cash. Branding seems to be a popular way.'

'Couldn't they just spend it on your salaries?' Maddie said.

'Well, that was my suggestion, but they went for mugs. I mean, I could complain, but they're nice mugs.' He finished the tea and put one down in front of her. He lingered for a second.

She smiled. 'So it would seem.'

He gave the other mug to Harry then pulled two black plastic chairs out from under a desk on the far side of the cabin and moved them over. He pulled off some kitchen roll and dabbed at the seat meant for Maddie.

'Everything gets so dusty here. Not much we can do about it, I'm afraid.'

'It's fine,' Maddie said, sitting down. Harry sat next to her. Ryan Clarke moved to sit round the other side of the desk. The desktop itself seemed to be very orderly. He had two stacks of trays at either end. The keyboard and mouse were lined up just so and he had a coaster for his mug. It was one of two desks in the cabin. The other was more like Maddie might have expected: a mess of paperwork, clutter and teacup rings.

Harry took out a notebook. 'So, you're Ryan Clarke, the fleet manager here?'

'I am. I do a bit of surveying, too, but the fleet is more my thing these days.'

'Fleet manager — is that what it says on your contract?'

'It does.'

'What does that mean? What are your daily responsibilities?'

'Well, I look after the vehicles. We have a number of company cars for senior and middle management, pool cars for the likes of us down the bottom of the chain and also plant vehicles. The vast majority are leased. My job is the day-to-day running of those leases but also making sure that we have the right sort of plant on the books when we need it and that we're not paying out for it when we don't.'

'You say you "look after" the vehicles, but you didn't know this one had been stolen. Is that right?' Harry's pen hovered.

Clarke's gaze flicked from Harry to Maddie before he answered. 'No. That's right. I guess saying that I look after them isn't quite right. I'm responsible for making sure we have enough of the right types and the admin. The truck was signed out to someone and so it wasn't being kept here. There was no way I could have known it was stolen.'

'Assuming it was?'

'I can't help you with that bit.'

'So, tell me about this truck.'

'Not much to tell you, really. We have four trucks on the books that are for the use of the surveyors. We have six surveyors — some of them use the trucks, some of them don't.'

'Volkswagens?'

'Yeah, VW Amaroks.'

'And where are the surveyors based? Are they here, too?'

'No, they work from home — or remotely at least. There's not the need for them to come here, unless they're picking up one of the trucks or some gear.'

'So they will take the trucks home and have them for a period of time?'

'They can do, yeah. Like I said . . . some do and some don't. Their jobs have changed recently . . . they've all become self-employed, but they have contracts with McCall's.'

'So what does a surveyor do, exactly?'

'That's a fair question. It does seem to be a changeable role. I started here as a surveyor. At that time the firm would buy a piece of land then send me to view it and I would work out what could go on there and give a good idea of the value once it was built. There's more to it now. Surveyors need to do the leg work themselves. They will go to the auction houses, the farmers or factory owners to try and drum up a sale. Then they come back to McCall's with a proposal, if that makes sense?'

'Not really,' Harry said. 'Try again.'

'Right . . . the paper mill down in Dover, for example . . . One of our guys gets wind that the company running it is having financial problems and is looking for a buyer. He makes an approach to see if they'd consider selling it for development and a proposal is put together. That surveyor is given access to the site by the proprietor and is able to work out exactly what could go on there . . . How many flats, the construction costs, what they could sell for, etc. The surveyor then comes back to McCall's and tells them that Dover Mill is available for X amount and provides a detailed proposal. If McCall's take the project up, the surveyor gets a commission.'

'And what sort of money would we be talking about?'

'Every project is different. It's a percentage of the overall profit.'

'It's worth their while though?'

'Well, yeah. These blokes don't work for free.'

'And you do that, too?'

'Not so much now. I've been here a while so I'm a direct McCall's employee with a salary and a pension. The fleet keeps me busy. The logistics of the plant take up most of my time. I still have a few contacts at the auction houses and a few of the commercial estate agents. I can secure a project every now and then. I don't need the hassle so much. You have to invest a lot of work and a lot of time to see it through to your commission. I had a result with a country pub recently via an old contact. That wasn't too bad.'

'So you have six surveyors and they all share the trucks?'

'Exactly.'

'There must be a system, though — so you know who's got what and they can book them out?'

'There is, though it's not fool-proof by any means. They self-manage. There's a board with the keys. They sign them out when they need a vehicle and then back in again when they bring it back. I think somebody from your lot came and did some poking around to find out who had the truck. I wish you'd come to me straight away. I could have explained the system and shown you how it's not exactly perfect.'

'We didn't want to make too much noise. I'm sure you can understand why.'

'I suppose. But then you arrested someone. I could have explained it from the off.'

'Where are the keys?' Harry's tone changed. Maddie recognised that Harry wasn't looking to be questioned. She reckoned she already knew the answer to Harry's question; she could see a whiteboard with a number of different car registrations on it. Handwritten notes identified who was driving what. There was a metal hook next to each one. Only one of the hooks had keys hanging from it. They all started *GN66* and only the last three letters were different. The top four had *(TR)* after them, which Maddie guessed were the trucks. Ryan was pointing at the same board.

'Over there. You can see it's not a fool-proof system but it works well enough. We don't need nothing complicated.'

'So you knew that Jonathan Lee was last to have possession of the truck.'

'This is what I would have explained. It was signed out to him but the system's flawed.'

'But he would have had the key at some point.'

'He might have had one of the keys. We've got spares for all of the truck keys. That's what's happened with this one, I reckon. The spare key's not here. They're all kept in the drawer below. These blokes are out on busy sites. They're getting in and out all day, we get keys going missing or locked in the trucks so we have to make the spares available. A lot of the blokes will drop the trucks back and then clear off with the key still in their pocket, too.'

'So you keep spares in the drawer.'

'That's right.'

Maddie could see that Harry was looking round the interior of the cabin. He looked over to the door. 'How many people work here?'

'Two of us is the maximum number in here. Sometimes this place is used as an overflow if—'

'I meant at this site — for McCall's.'

'Oh, shit, I don't know. You get forty people here most days if you include the office staff. This is the head office. We've got a few satellite offices elsewhere and a few cabins that are set up on the big sites. Then you got all the agency staff. We use a lot of them — it's that sort of business. One day you're building seven houses at the same time on a good sized site and the next you're renovating a few outbuildings and redecorating a farm house. A lot of the building trade use agency or trade staff. You can just bring in the blokes you need. No point paying men to sit around on their arses.'

'So access to this place — access to those keys . . . do you lock this place up when you're not here?'

'No. Just when I go home at the end of the day or if I'm going out and I know I'm not coming back. But even then there's a key at reception in case anyone needs it. And the surveyors all have one, too, in case they need what's in here or the keys to a particular truck. They work some funny hours. They can be here at all times of the day.'

Harry rubbed at his face. Maddie could sense his frustration. She knew that he wasn't getting anywhere with this line of questioning.

'So the forty people that work here and the untold agency staff . . . in theory, they all had access to the spare keys of the truck Jonathan had?'

'I guess so, yeah.'

'And is there CCTV that covers where they're parked?'

'I don't think so, no. CCTV covers the yard out there and the warehouse. The trucks are in the side car park. There's no cameras there.'

'The yard CCTV would cover people coming and going from here? If they were after the keys, I mean.'

'Yeah, I guess it would. The CCTV would cover anybody coming in and out, but I don't see how we would know if they left with a key in their pocket.'

Harry sighed. He sat back and took his time sipping at his tea.

'So you can't say for certain if the truck was brought back here, you couldn't say who by and there's no way of knowing who took the spare key and drove it away again if it was?'

'That's it. In a nutshell.'

'Brilliant,' Harry growled. 'I'll need the names and addresses of the six surveyors. Well, five. I've got Jonathan's.'

'No problem. What's the deal with Jon anyway? Can we have him back here?'

'That's your decision, or a decision for someone here at least.'

'Is he still under investigation? I heard a bit. I heard someone got hit by that truck and died. You have to know that weren't Jon — he's not that sort of lad at all.'

'I don't know anything right now. Your processes here aren't helping me either. Or him for that matter.'

'I guess not.'

'What about mileage?' Maddie chipped in. 'Surely they have to record the mileage they do and justify what they've done? Otherwise they could all use your trucks for their weekly shop.'

'They write the mileage on the board when they take one out and they put the new mileage up when they get back. They pay for their own fuel as part of being self-employed. The company takes the wear and tear on the chin. It's a perk. I don't know how long they'll continue the lease on them cars, I think it's another tax relief to even have them on the books.'

'So you don't record what mileage has been done by whom?'

'Not like in a historical record, if that's what you mean? Was it not melted? The clocks an' that?'

'We can sometimes retrieve some information,' Harry said. 'I'm thinking about the other trucks . . . if we knew who was definitely in the others it would be a start. Do they have black boxes?'

'Black boxes? You mean like trackers?'

'Well a tracker would be wonderful, but a black box that records when the vehicle is in motion — the speeds, braking, that sort of thing?'

'No. Nothing like that. I'll be honest, no one really cares. They are there for the use of the surveyors. The company sort of runs on the back of their work, you know? They're important. If those six blokes don't find us the next project, everything comes to a grinding halt.'

Harry sat back. His body seemed to sag. This was a lost cause. Maddie knew it and it was obvious her colleague did too. He turned back to face the board with the keys hanging from it.

'You've got one of the trucks here?'

Ryan peered over to the board, too. 'That's mine at the moment. My car's out for a new tyre today. They didn't have one on the mobile van. I'm hoping to get it back later.'

'Can I have a look at it?'

Ryan scowled like he was confused. 'If you want to. It should be just out the front.'

Ryan picked the keys off the board and they stepped back out into the din. They moved back to the hallway that ran along the back of the building. Then, rather than heading right towards the reception, they took a left out through a fire exit. Immediately Maddie could see two identical-looking trucks, parked nose-in. They were in a separate car park that was fenced off as its own compound. It would be visible from the front. There were other vehicles, too, including a couple of small vans emblazoned with the McCall's brand.

'Ah, see?' Ryan said. 'There's actually two back. One of the blokes must have kept the keys for one. He'll probably come back for it.'

Harry shook his head. Ryan pointed the key at the truck and its lights flashed.

'Did you want to look inside it, or . . .?'

Harry didn't answer. He pulled the door open on the passenger side and peered in. Maddie stood behind him. The car looked tidy, much tidier than the builder's vehicles she had come across in the past. Harry moved to the front and ran his hand along the top of the bonnet. Maddie moved to the back. She pulled idly at the boot catch. The back lifted under its own steam. The hydraulics hissed. Ryan was standing a few steps away from the truck. He was watching Harry but he looked disinterested overall. He looked over at Maddie and smiled. She smiled back. She looked into the long boot. It had a metal floor. The back was orderly enough, too. It had a new-looking hi-vis jacket and a safety helmet still sealed in a clear bag. There was also a battered-looking metal box. It looked out of place. It reminded her of something her granddad had used a lot when she was a girl. He'd been a keen fishermen. She pushed it open.

'Fishing tackle!' she announced, surprised at her own recollection. She looked over at Ryan, who seemed a little confused.

He shrugged. 'Like I said, they pay for their fuel. They can take them fishing if they want.'

'You're not the fisherman then?'

'Me? I don't have the time for fishing. Could be anyone's.'

Maddie looked over at the truck next to it. It was identical except that it was noticeably dirtier. She flicked back to the truck Ryan was using. Water still dripped from the underside and there were damp patches on the floor close to the wheels. The one next to it had the standard layer of dust that seemed to have affected everything else.

'Someone cleaned this one,' Maddie said.

Ryan nodded. 'I did, yeah. They're supposed to keep them clean. There's a jet wash round the back they can all use. They do get filthy. You can imagine the muddy places they go.'

'Not recently, though,' Maddie said. She lifted her head to the blazing sun.

'Nah, she was just a bit dusty. Quick blast with the hose. I get told to make sure they're clean by the bosses, so I do it. I guess it's a first-impressions kind of a thing.'

Maddie pushed the boot shut. Harry was finished too. It was written all over his face.

'Shall we?' he said.

'Sure, if you're done.'

Harry turned back to Ryan. 'Like I said . . . the names of the surveyors, their dates of birth and their home addresses. You can put them in an email for me.'

'Okay, I should be able to do that straight away.'

They shook hands again. Ryan took Harry's card and showed them back to their car.

Once inside, Maddie chanced a conversation. Harry's mood was clear.

'What was the thinking? With looking round the car, I mean. I'm interested.'

'I wanted to see it for myself. The height and shape of the front. The victim was pushed downwards and dragged. Now I've seen the truck it makes sense.'

'There isn't a doubt what was used though, is there?'

'I like to see things for myself. I've had somebody out to take pictures of the truck already. I had an idea of what it would look like, but sometimes you don't know a thing until you've run your hands over it.'

'The child in me is desperate to make a joke right now.' Her smile disappeared immediately when she saw his reaction. She went back to looking out of the window. She waited for Harry to speak next. It took him almost fifteen minutes.

'I need to go to Aylesham. They have some property there.'

Maddie was looking for the question in there — or the option. There was none. 'Okay. And I assume I'm coming with you?'

'It's a just-job. I need to pick up some bits that were found in my victim's car. I said I would run it back to his wife.'

'No problem.'

Another minute or two of silence passed. 'And then we can go back to looking for your girl,' he said.

Maddie didn't reply. She felt like she knew better.

Chapter 23

The recovery yard was on the outskirts of a village called Aylesham. Maddie had never been there before but it still looked instantly familiar. Up north she was aware of a few ex-mining villages — whole communities built round the pits and collieries — and this had that same feeling about it. Sure enough, they soon drifted past a huge site that had all the hallmarks of a disused mine. Some of the buildings still remained but they were just blackened shells. The housing stock as they moved through the village became more modern, tighter packed and less interesting, but the atmosphere of a mining community remained. It was as if the coal dust was part of the fabric of the place.

'You'd think McCall's might be interested in the mining site out here?' Maddie said.

'No one knows what to do with it. It's all slagheaps with tunnels dug out. A nightmare for building on.'

'I suppose someone would have tried by now if it were viable,' Maddie mused.

They pulled into the front car park of Snowdown Recovery. The ground was made up of grey shingle and their movements kicked up clouds of dust. Most of the cars were covered in a decent layer of it. The sign pointing out *Reception* was a little misleading. On following its direction through a door, *Reception* turned out to be just a small hatch in a corridor. It had a glass frontage that was pulled opened as they approached. A man in a short-sleeved t-shirt, complete with oil stains and dust, opened it up and looked out expectantly.

'DI Blaker.' Harry held out his badge.

'The classic Land Rover, right?' the man said. His eyes dropped to hunt for something. He lifted a pair of keys into view and then disappeared. A bit further down the corridor a door opened and the man beckoned for them to follow. Maddie hung a few paces behind as they were led through into the main yard. It was fenced off and bigger than looked possible from the road. Cars were parked bumper-to-bumper — those that still had their bumpers attached at any rate. They all looked to be crash damaged in some way. Specimens ranged from minor dents or collapsed front wheels to a metal corpse with the roof cut cleanly free from the tops of the door frames. They crossed the yard and stopped outside a small warehouse. A box hung down with two buttons. The man jammed his thumb into one of them and a large metal door slid up on runners that squealed their contempt.

'The car's in here. This is our forensic storage now.' The man seemed proud.

'Forensic storage?' It wasn't a term Maddie had heard before outside of a police station.

'Yeah. We stick the cars under cover for your lot when they ask. We don't tow these either — they get a full lift. Seems you don't want our greasy backsides on the driver's seat!'

'Ah, I see,' Maddie said. She wasn't sure why the car of a victim of a hit and run would need his own car seized in such a manner but she was pretty certain that Harry wouldn't appreciate the question. Major Crime were well known for their belt and braces approach.

Harry spoke. 'It's been searched and swabbed. The car can be released. I'll let the wife know and she can come and pick it up. We're only here to collect his property. Apparently it's bagged up inside.'

'So I can open her up?' the man said.

'Yeah.'

Both men moved to the car. Maddie fixed on the one next to it, the only other one in there. It was a silver Ford of some sort, a family hatchback. The front had been staved in; the bonnet rippled up and peeled back like the untidy opening of a can of sardines. The windscreen was hanging out. She leaned in a little. Her eye was dragged to a child's seat that was pushed tight against the seat in front, too tight for even a tiny human to fit. Spent airbags hung limp from the steering wheel and the dash. The driver's dials and vents were spotted with what looked like blood. There was a larger stain in the foot well. She shivered and turned away. Harry was now clutching a clear bag with small items inside. It had a blue seal around the top, tied off in a gooseneck.

'That all you need for now?' the man asked.

'This is it. The wife will be back for the car. You can move it out of here if you need to.'

'Yeah, will do. We've got another fatal coming in, I think. Not sure where they're dragging that from but they usually ask for them to be put in here.'

Maddie glanced back over at the smashed up family car. She shivered again. Harry was already moving back out into the sunlight. She caught up with him.

'These places give me the creeps,' she said.

'They do have an atmosphere.' He didn't speak again until they got back in the car. He put the bag on her lap. 'Can you take the seal off? They can be tough. I want to drop it back in and speak to the wife.'

Maddie did as she was asked. There was no more conversation. She watched through the window as the setting became more rural again until they entered a town signposted as *DEAL*. Immediately the architecture changed: older, country-style cottages, thatched roofs, neat lawns and even castle ruins. They didn't go far into the town before pulling into a quieter road. The house they stopped outside was detached. It had flint walls with a wooden front door that looked smaller than was standard and had surely been made bespoke to fit.

'Do you want me to stay in the car?' Maddie asked.

'No.' The door closed, stilting any further conversation. Maddie climbed out. She stayed still, watching Harry walk towards the door. She considered staying where she was, making him come back for the property that she clutched in her hands as a sort of protest. But she was pretty certain it would change nothing. She moved around the car and walked up the path. Harry was already knocking. The door pulled open just a few seconds later.

'Are you the inspector?'

'Yes. Harry Blaker.'

'Someone called ahead. They said you would be coming.'

'That's good news. I asked for one of my team to let you know. Did they say why?'

'Yes.' Her eyes moved to the bag Maddie was carrying. 'Is that it? Are those his things?'

'Some of them. That's anything that was found as part of our initial searching. We haven't kept anything back.'

'Okay. Well, did you want to come in?'

'Yes please.' Harry stepped in. 'It's Mrs Beasle, is that right?'

'Yes, but Linda please.'

'Linda. Thank you. This is my colleague, DS Maddie Ives—'

'Maddie's just fine,' Maddie said, reaching forward to shake Linda's hand.

'Maddie. Nice to meet you.' She smiled but it fell away quickly. Her voice was low and on a set level, like an

162

undertaker arranging the final details, missing any emotion at all. No anger, no sadness, no nothing. Maddie had seen it before in the recently bereaved.

'Where should I set this down?' Maddie said.

'Oh!' Linda moved through to the kitchen. Maddie was tall, nearly six foot, and she had to stoop as she stepped through the doorway. The ceilings were low; the beams that ran along them even lower. 'Put them in here, could you?'

Maddie put the bag down on a rustic kitchen table. It was a natural wood, the edges rough and unfinished, the knots in the middle thick and rugged.

'That is an incredible table, Linda,' Maddie said. 'Beautiful.'

'Yes, isn't it? That was my treat to myself for my sixtieth. Ron — well, he had his Land Rover thing. That was his pride and joy that was. Shows you how different we are. I guess you could say this is *my* pride and joy. Sounds a bit sad really, doesn't it?'

'Not at all. I think if I had something like this in my home it would be mine, too. And is this the man himself?' Maddie gestured at a picture that was pinned to a downward beam. In it, Linda wore an evening dress and was slightly side-on to a tanned-looking man in a tuxedo whose smile beamed out from a face littered with laughter lines.

'That's him. That's my Ron. It was taken on a cruise we did — just last year. A wonderful trip. I take a little comfort in a strange way that it was our last. We couldn't have chosen better.'

'You should remember that. All the good times in fact.'

'We had a lot of those. Can I make you a tea?' Linda had been looking at the picture. She snatched her eyes from it and moved to a large cooker that was cut into a tiled alcove. A kettle sat on top of the stove.

'Yes, that would be lovely,' Harry said. He picked up the bag of property that Maddie had left undone and reached in to take out each item individually. Maddie noticed he was gentle as he placed them down. Nothing in the bag appeared to be of any real monetary value: a few dog biscuits, a small, tattered notepad, a black plastic watch, a silver-plated Saint Christopher necklace. There was also a hat and from inside it Harry tipped out a wallet, a phone with a cracked screen and a wedding ring.

'This is it then, is it?'

'No, Linda. There are more bits in the Land Rover. You can go and pick that up any time you want. Normally they charge sixty pounds a day for storage up there, but they're very good. They bill us for the initial recovery and then they tend not to worry for a day or two after that in these sorts of circumstances. So make sure you go up there today or tomorrow. Is that going to be okay?'

'Yes, that should be fine. I have a friend who has already offered to come along.'

'Is that John, by any chance?'

'It is, yes! How did you know that?'

'I spoke to a man named John up at the shooting club. He was obviously a good friend to your husband. He was shocked by the whole thing, of course, but I got the impression he would help you out all he could.'

'He's a good man. We see a lot of him and his wife. At least we did . . .'

'I'm sure that won't change, Linda.'

'It might. I mean, people are nice, but they're not going to want to spend time with me down in the doldrums, are they? Life's too short to surround yourself with miserable people. You know who told me that? My Ron.'

Harry said nothing for a moment, but his face carried a warmth that Maddie hadn't seen before. 'This is going to be hard on you, Linda, but you have the strength to get through it, that much I can tell. You'll need to use the people around you, friends and family, and I can *promise* you that no one will mind spending some time down in the doldrums with you, if it means they get to help lead you out.'

Linda beamed. She rushed in a breath like she was fighting her own emotions.

'So this stuff . . .' Harry continued, 'this is just what was on Ron's person generally. I think the wallet came from the car — we just didn't want to leave it in there. We've taken a forensic copy of the phone, but there's nothing relevant on there that we can see.'

'He couldn't even use the thing! Thank you.' She picked up the wedding ring. She turned it over in her hands a couple of times, then she made a fist around it and her knuckles whitened, her face suddenly wearing a grimace. She looked like she would never let it go, as if it was everything to her. Maddie didn't speak. Harry stepped forward, Linda kept her hand clenched but she reached out to him and stepped in for a tight hug. She expelled a loud sob that caught under the low ceiling to fill the kitchen.

Maddie's eyes fell to the table. She picked up the notebook for something to do, somewhere to look, and flicked idly through the pages. It was mainly rows of numbers that looked like scores, with some notes and names. Maddie guessed it was what he used to keep tallies for groups of shooters. It fell open at the front cover. Her eyes were drawn to a handwritten series of numbers and letters. The writing was awful but she could just make it out: *GN66 LGO*. Her pulse quickened suddenly and she looked up at Harry. He had his palms on Linda's shoulders, his head bent as he whispered more words of comfort.

'Harry, can I talk to you?' She knew she sounded abrupt, the urgency clear in her voice. Harry looked at her with sudden surprise. She could feel Linda looking at her too.

'Sure. Would you excuse us a moment, Linda?'

Linda wiped at her face. 'Of course. Let me make that tea I promised you!' She sniffed again and turned away. Maddie stepped out of the kitchen and took Ron's notebook with her.

'What's the matter?' Harry said. He sounded agitated.

Maddie held up the book, her finger under the handwritten numbers and letters. Harry glanced at it, then immediately back to her.

'Go on?' he said.

'This job. The running theory is that our man got hit by a truck and didn't see it coming, right?'

'It's all we have.'

'And your offender doesn't know the victim. Never has, never will?'

'What am I looking at, Maddie?'

'The registration number for one of the McCall's trucks. They were up on that board in the office. This is one of them.'

'The one that was burnt out?'

'I would guess so, but I don't know which one that is.'

'You're sure?' Harry bit down on his lip. He leaned in closer to study the book. Maddie could see the excitement in him too.

'You pick it up when you do what I've been doing. Reg numbers, phone numbers, that sort of thing. I'm one hundred percent sure that this was one of the reg numbers written on that board.'

'Can I see that?' He reached out for the book. 'Golf, November, six, six, Lima, golf, Oscar?' he read, looking straight at Maddie for a reaction.

'That was it.'

'We need to take this back with us. I need to make some calls, find out what the reg number was for that truck. I wasn't told it. The plates were either missing or melted. They identified it by a chassis number.' Harry rubbed at his head. 'So what are we saying here? There's some

dispute? Or one of the surveyors was a . . .' Harry moved back into the kitchen. He spoke directly to Linda, his tone immediately more urgent. 'Have you ever heard of a property developing company called McCall's?'

'McCall's? No. I . . . I don't think I have.'

'Do you own any property?'

'Well, yes, this one. But we don't own anything else. We're not into all that.'

Maddie spoke up. 'What about land, Linda? Do you own any land? Maybe where the shooting club is?'

'No! We don't own anything like that. The club is on a ninety-nine-year lease from some lord of something-or-other. I don't know much about it — just that they have permission and they pay a good levy for the use of it. There is . . .' She faded out.

'There is what, Linda? What were you going to say?' Maddie pressed her.

'Some land. Between here and Dover. It's not ours — it's Jimmy Leonard's place.'

'Who's Jimmy Leonard?'

'A good friend. Of both of us, really. He had a big farm, worked it all his life until he became unwell. Then he saw an opportunity to secure his family's future, you know. He was talking to some company about selling it for development. Apparently they renovate what's there or something. It's the only way you could get any sort of permission for housing on there. Jimmy didn't make it unfortunately. Cancer. He got bad and they were trying to rush something through, then he died and it was all up in the air. It still is. Jimmy asked my Ron to keep an eye on the land. They had a bit of bother up there with travellers.'

'What sort of bother?'

'It's out on its own. There are a few barns and bits. They had stuff suddenly appear in them. Some farm machinery, a couple of quad bikes, that sort of thing. It was all stolen. Ron reckoned they were left up there while the heat died off and then the travellers would come back for them. He's seen that happen before.'

'Travellers, you say?'

'Oh, well I don't know that he knew that. He didn't see who left it. I think he put two and two together.'

'So he didn't challenge anyone up there?'

'No. He was going to call the police but then the stolen gear was gone. He never actually saw anyone. Do you think it's got something to do with what happened to my Ron?'

Harry shook his head. 'I don't know, Linda. When was he there last? On the land?'

'I don't know for sure but probably Saturday. He would often check on it before he opened up the shoot. He certainly left early enough.'

'Okay, this notebook . . . I was going to give it back but do you mind if I keep hold of it for now? I need it for a little bit longer.'

'You can have that. I think that's his score book. Just a load of old tallies.'

Harry opened it up so the inside of the cover was showing. 'And this . . . is this his writing?'

She nodded. 'Yeah, that's all his. I don't know what he's written there, but, yes, it's his writing.'

'Great. Thanks for your help, Linda.' Harry pulled a card from his pocket. 'These are my contact details. If you need to speak to me, my number is on there. I will do my best to keep you informed, okay?'

'Thank you. Are you leaving? I didn't have chance to finish the tea yet?'

'Yes, Linda, sorry. We're going to have to get back to work.'

'Very good, then. I'll wait to hear from you.' Harry was already back to the front door. He pulled it open and the sunlight was like a burst of energy. He stepped out into it. Maddie stopped at the door to speak to Linda.

'You'll be hearing from us soon. Don't forget to pick up Ron's Land Rover as soon as you can.'

'Yes, I will.'

Maddie turned to the car. She could hear the engine revving. By the time she pulled the door shut Harry's phone was already ringing through the speakers.

'Boss.' It was a man's voice that Maddie didn't recognise.

'Mitch, I need a favour,' Harry snapped. The car pulled away with purpose. Maddie snatched at her seatbelt.

'Sure, what do you need?'

'Two things . . . Do you have the reg number to hand for that burnt-out vehicle? I only remember seeing a chassis number.'

'Hang on a sec.' It sounded to Maddie like Mitch was chewing something and she could hear clicking. 'I've got the PNC here somewhere. There was only a chassis but we did get a reg from running it through. Ah, here we are: golf, November, six, six, Lima, golf, Oscar. What else?'

Harry hesitated, like he was considering his next move. His eyes flicked to his watch. 'Find out what you can about Leonard's Farm in the Dover, Deal area. A Jimmy Leonard used to run it but he died recently. Find out if we attended the death — we should have details for next of kin. Also, can you do open source research on the farm itself.'

'Open source research on a farm, boss? It would help if I knew what angle we're coming from with this?'

'Angle? Assume you're a developer and you're interested in buying it. See what you can find out.'

'Okay, I'll let you know what I get.'

'Great — and one more thing, Mitch . . . We downloaded the victim's phone. I want it reassessed. I want every phone number on there reviewed for any links to property developers called McCall's — business numbers or the personal number of anyone linked to that company. As best you can.'

'Leave it with me.'

Harry ended the call. Maddie waited almost a minute before she prompted him.

'Do you want to tell me what you're thinking then, Harry?'

Harry looked pensive. His driving was noticeably quicker and Maddie had hold of the door. 'I'm thinking we should go to Leonard's Farm. I'm thinking that it might have been one of the last places our victim visited. I want to retrace his steps.'

'What do you expect to find up there?' Maddie asked.

'I don't know. Nothing, probably. I just want to see it for myself. Then we can get back to looking for your girl. I have some questions that need answers. Ron was looking after land that a property developer was interested in. That has to be McCall's. His wife thinks that Ron might have been on that land on Saturday morning and then later that day he was run down by a truck owned by McCall's. And when it ran him down, Ron had the registration number for the truck that killed him in his pocket. We'll go to Leonard's Farm so I know it at least. Then we'll go back to McCall's. Somewhere between those two places are some answers, Maddie. There have to be.'

Chapter 24

Maddie had to use her phone for guidance. Leonard's Farm was showing on her mapping app with three entrances. It covered a large area, crossing roads and other farm territories in a jumbled mass of land. The easiest entrance looked to be off a road that ran along the top of the cliffs towards Dover's famous castle. This was also somewhere she had visited as a schoolgirl. She could still remember its giant rooms, cobbled floors and far-reaching views. They were travelling from the Deal end and the castle wasn't even a speck in the distance before they needed to turn off. Maddie was almost disappointed not to see it up close again.

The farm track presented a real change in terrain. The car's higher suspension took turns in bouncing, then grounding out on the muddy ruts. The winter had been a sodden one, during which farm machinery had carved deep grooves into the mud. Since then the intense sunlight had scorched them into solid gullies with the tread of thick tractor tyres still visible. At least it forced Harry to slow down. They were soon surrounded by fields and Maddie could just make out a perimeter fence in the distance.

There were no signs of any crops, just solid mud with tufts of straw stripped close to the ground and wild grass growing around it. Maddie was no expert on farming but it looked to her as though the land hadn't been worked for some time.

They pressed on. The land had a natural curvature and resting on the horizon in front was a dark-coloured square. Maddie fixed on it. They edged closer and she could see it was a small barn. The track ran right past. Harry must have seen it too; the car sped up a little, the juddering through her seat becoming almost unbearable. They made it to the barn. Harry slowed and they were drifting past when he seemed to make a decision and stopped harshly. He backed up a little and turned off the engine. The silence was blissful. Maddie felt the straw stubble under her feet; it cracked and snapped as she walked around to the driver's side. Harry was already out and striding towards the barn.

'Be careful in there!' Maddie called out. The building looked rundown — more a ramshackle shell than a building. She lifted her head to inspect the roof. The half that remained looked precarious at best. She could see a steel container on the left side of the floor space. It looked like it had been pushed in close to the wall. She couldn't see the doors, they had to be on the other side, which suggested to her that it had been put there to get it out of the way rather than for any particular use or purpose. A few paces to the right of that was a metal bin. Its sides were scorched black, the lid came up to a funnel and it had holes punctured near the bottom. She recognised it as the sort of incinerator like she had seen used on allotments. Harry was standing over it, frowning.

'Can you smell that?'

'Yeah, smells like something's been burnt. I reckon I know where the source of the smell is!' She was joking. Harry ignored her. He moved towards the container.

'It's not smoke. I caught something on the breeze. Christ! It's stronger over here!'

Maddie turned to him. She had been looking down into the bin through the hole in the lid. It had been used — recently too, but there was nothing left that was identifiable. 'What is it?'

'Death!' Harry growled back. He stepped out of sight behind the container. She could hear the sound of metal scraping. She got to him just as he pulled a padlock clear. He tugged the door. It looked like a struggle; he had to use all his weight. The door swung open, spilling out a thick cloud of flies as it did so.

The smell washed over her like a wave. It was so pungent it was almost like taking a strike to the nose. She stepped back, lifting her hand to her face at the same time. 'What the hell . . .?' It was one of the most distinctive smells there is: rotting flesh. She took a step forward, suddenly feeling very unsure. Harry was in front of her but she could see past him. She braced herself.

The container looked empty.

Harry fiddled with his phone until it lit up as a torch. He directed the light into the space. Maddie was trying her best to breathe into her sleeve but it wasn't stopping the pungent stench getting through. She peered around to get a better view. Harry's light flashed around the inside. It settled on a marking high on the wall on the left side where the number *37* stood out in black letters on a white sticker. His light moved on until it stopped, settling on something small. Something that looked to Maddie like rolled up clothes — or a blanket, maybe — was heaped in a corner. Harry stepped in. Maddie stayed at the door. Harry had his hand over his mouth, too.

'A fox,' he called back. He sounded like he had been holding his breath. His words came with an expulsion of air.

'Dead, right?' Maddie managed.

'Not for long,' Harry said. She could see he was crouched down just a few inches from the animal. Big black flies swarmed around him and cast flickering shadows in his light. He lowered his face further and sniffed hard.

'What are you doing? Making sure?'

He didn't reply. He swept the light around for a second time, studying the sides and the ceiling again. He looked unsure about something. She could still hear him moving around when she moved away, longing to take in a lungful of air that wasn't contaminated by that stench.

Harry walked over to her. She was resting on the bonnet of the car.

'There is no worse smell on this planet, is there?' she said.

'No. It's particularly strong.'

'No shit.' Harry's eyes snatched up and she raised her palm. 'Sorry, okay? I forget the no cursing thing.'

'It doesn't seem right. A dead fox might smell like that eventually, but it looks too fresh in there. There are maggot casings all over the floor, too. Too many.'

'I'll take your word for it.'

'And how did it get in there? There are small rust holes in the corner that would explain the flies, but the fox . . .'

'Animals are like that, right? They can squeeze themselves into the tiniest of places and then he probably couldn't get out. It's boiling hot, it wouldn't have taken long for the creature to start chucking up.'

Harry didn't reply. He was still looking around. Maddie could tell that he wasn't sure. 'This doesn't feel right.'

'Was it locked?' Maddie said.

'What?'

'The padlock. You opened it easy enough. I assume it wasn't locked?'

'No, it was hanging open. But the door was shut. No way a fox was getting in there.'

'Did you see how old Mr Fox copped it? Maybe someone was up here training their dog illegally. We used

174

to get it up north in the rural bits — people training their dogs to catch foxes. They'd tear them apart. It was obvious what had gotten hold of them so they would hide the corpses — especially if they wanted to keep using the land. It must be prime up here for that sort of stuff . . . chasing foxes . . . hare-coursing. I bet it happens up here most nights. The gypsies are always looking for places out of the way to have a runabout. And Ron's wife mentioned trouble up here with gypsies.'

Harry bit his bottom lip. Maddie was quickly coming to recognise this meant he was contemplating something. 'You could be right.'

'Did that hurt? Saying that?' Maddie chuckled. Harry's face may have flickered a smile. She watched him move around to the driver's door and pull it open. She took the hint and took up her seat beside him. The car moved straight off and they drove further into the estate.

'Are we going to see the rest?'

'We might as well. We're here. I want to see what all the fuss is about with this land so I know what McCall's are talking about.'

Chapter 25

Lorraine was awake again. Immediately her body flinched and contorted, as the panic of the moments when she was last conscious came rushing back. She had been fighting for her life. Her mind tried to spark her arms into movement, to raise them up to defend herself — to lash out. She couldn't move them. The best she could manage was to flex her fingers. It didn't matter. There was no one there. Not anymore.

She tried to run back over what had happened in her mind. She remembered getting free. She had managed to sit up enough to run her hands over the metal walls. She had found a handle, something to get a grip on. She had managed to pull herself to her knees. She couldn't make it to her feet. It had been dark and she'd been trying to feel for a way out. The door had opened up from nowhere. She didn't know how long she had been kneeling there in the dark, pulling and pushing hopelessly against the cold metal. Then it just swung open.

Her mind was still fuzzy — the memories, too. He was so angry! She remembered that. She'd been knocked backwards. Something hit her so hard that she had really needed to focus to stay awake. She could feel the daylight around her; she knew this was her only chance. She had fought to stay conscious. She remembered being grabbed. She remembered a blade — *the knife! There'd been blood on it!* He said something, too — he was so close to her face. He said that they were trying to stop him, but they wouldn't. He said he would finish it. She'd closed her eyes, waiting for the final blow.

It never came.

She'd thought he had gone. She'd managed to roll onto her side so that she could see the door and she'd started to crawl towards it. She'd gotten halfway there by the time he reappeared. He had been grinning. He stepped in. She remembered seeing his foot swing. The last thing she remembered was accepting that this was it. That she would not be waking again.

But now she could see a strip of bright light. Her eyes hurt. She couldn't be dead. She felt the compulsion to blink but it was uncomfortable. Her eyes felt swollen; it was an effort to keep them open enough to see. She focussed on the light — different to the artificial light shining on her before. It ran in a straight line across the floor, like it was cutting the gloom in half. It was a few metres away. *Sunlight!* She yearned for it. She was naked. She couldn't move her head to confirm it but she could feel the coldness of the floor. She prayed she wouldn't shiver. It made her whole body tense up. It was painful, but the pain seemed lessened each time she awakened. It wasn't a stabbing pain anymore; it was more a dull ache. The coldness, too, was no longer as harsh. All her senses seemed a little dulled. Certainly her eyesight seemed fuzzy, despite it appearing a little lighter and she could no longer hear the buzzing of flies as intensely as she remembered. The overpowering smell was gone, too. One thing she did feel was a constant breeze.

She must have been moved. She concentrated. She thought she could remember moving, but only in flashes.

She remembered a floating sensation with warmth all around her. The light was much stronger; she had needed to close her eyes to it. Then she was being rocked; it was gentle and she must have fallen back to sleep. When she woke up she was back out in the sunshine. She recalled glimpses of a beautiful house with a boarded window that made her think of a black eye. Then the warmth was gone. She wasn't sure if that was her dreaming.

She was on her side now. She didn't think she was restricted anymore. She could see she'd been laid out on a stone floor, cold where it touched her skin. She felt the breeze again. It carried the scent of straw and animals and she had a sudden flush of happiness as she remembered childhood trips to her nan's farm.

She could feel the exhaustion coming on again. She was still trying to remember, still trying to sort her memories from her dreams. Something else had happened. A metallic sound — something had scraped over the floor. *She remembered!* A bowl had been pushed right up to her face. A metal bowl. It was like the one she had at home in her flat, left over from when she had a terrier — a muscly little bull terrier called Davo. Silly name. Silly dog. She smiled momentarily at the thought of him. She opened her eyes to hunt for the bowl. It was there! But it was further away. She didn't understand how it had moved so far. The strip of light was directly over it.

She remembered more. He had been here. He had dragged the bowl away. 'It's water, drink it,' he had said. The voice had been gentle, like it was mixed in with the breeze. Then it had changed — just like that. Suddenly it was threatening, mocking, telling her she could have a drink but she would have to work for it. That metal, scraping sound again as it moved away. He said something about how he would be watching. She didn't know why he was so angry — *why was he so angry?*

She didn't know anything. She was so confused and her mind felt so tired. She couldn't fight off the exhaustion any more. She had to sleep.

* * *

Harry's driving was much slower when they moved away from the barn and Maddie was thankful for it. The scenery became fields on both sides again. The track led downhill and they soon had an elevated view of a farmhouse that was surrounded on three sides by large barns. Harry stopped the car in the courtyard. They climbed out and stood still and silent.

The house itself was large. Built from red brick and topped with a slated roof, it looked almost symmetrical, with tall windows at all four corners and a front door in the middle. Two of the barns were further away from the house than they had looked from a distance. The third barn was almost touching the house and framed the same courtyard. Its front was open and it spilled decaying straw, while the stone floor was covered in brown stains where animals had been recently. There was nothing to this place now. The door was boarded over, along with one of the windows on the ground floor of the house. There was also a double garage block, detached from the house and only noticeable now they were closer. It looked old enough to have served some other purpose and Maddie was pretty certain it had been converted from a much smaller fourth barn. This one was probably part of the original estate. Two garage doors stretched across two thirds of the frontage and the final third was taken up by a wide wooden door that looked original and didn't quite meet with the bottom or the top of its frame. This door was locked by an oversized steel chain that looked new. She was drawn to it. The sound of her footsteps suddenly seemed intrusive against the gentle shushing of a huge tree that loomed over the garage, its drooping leaves brushing the pitched roof like they were offering it comfort.

She rattled the chain. It was heavy. The padlock securing it also looked brand new. She pushed up close to where the wood didn't quite meet the brick wall. The sunlight arrowed in through the gap and the sound of her feet scuffing on the ground echoed into the space. The beam of sunlight was the only light and she did her best not to block it as she peered inside. The beam illuminated some old tools that looked as if they had been simply thrown in a pile. She could make out part of a lawnmower against the far wall; some of its insides looked to be spilling out onto the floor next to it. Closer to her was a metal bowl, the sort you'd put down for a dog. It looked clean. She couldn't tell if there was water in it.

She stepped back. She could hear fidgeting, like a rodent of some sort, coming from inside. There were plenty of dark corners to be explored. It would be a rat's paradise.

Her attention was snatched to her left. A pigeon made a noise in the rafters of the big, open barn. It set off, its wings flapping, and it whistled as it flew away. Her eyes dropped to the decaying straw laid out on the floor of the barn. There was nothing left here — nothing of use, at least. She pressed back against the door. She fixed again on the dog bowl. Something about it seemed out of place — she couldn't say why. Perhaps it was simply that everything else was old and broken and the bowl looked brand new, glinting in the sunlight. There were some other items on either side of it that she couldn't quite make out. She pushed more firmly against the wood. There was at least a third of the barn that she couldn't see at all. The slit was too small. From what she could make out, the barn looked largely empty. She batted away a fly that suddenly made for her through the gap. When she stepped back she felt her clothes sticking to her and became aware of her discomfort overall. The sun was beating on her back; she needed some shade at least. She considered calling Harry over. He might have a theory about the water bowl.

'Come on!' Harry's tone carried frustration as he walked away from the boarded-up door. 'We're wasting our time here.' Maybe he was feeling the heat too. Certainly there was nothing here that could give them any answers.

'I could have told you that,' Maddie mumbled into the gap so Harry wouldn't pick up on it. 'I'm not even sure what we're looking for.' She moved back towards the car. 'It's so peaceful down here. I don't get why someone would move away. It looks like it's just been abandoned.'

'It doesn't seem right,' Harry agreed.

'I can see why there are developers interested in it. I guess they'll convert the barns and all sorts.'

'That's what they do.' Harry was in the driver's seat. Maddie got back into her side. They swung round to go back the way they had come. She took in the estate for a final time: the boarded-up farmhouse, the oppressive-looking chain on the outhouse, the barn that looked like it had once been full of life. She could see the potential of a site like this. Who wouldn't want to live here?

'Are we heading back to McCall's? You said you wanted to talk to them again.'

'It's getting late. I wanted to speak to someone a bit higher up. There probably won't be anyone there outside of office hours. I'll go first thing tomorrow morning. Then I'll check back in with the team around what they're doing with your missing girl. Don't think I've forgotten about her. I set a lot of actions. There should be a lot of work being done.'

'Actions?'

'We've got a standard response to high-risk missing persons. CCTV trawls, tracking bank accounts, speaking to friends and family and checking everywhere there's been a sighting that is recorded on police systems. I've also arranged for all the pubs and off-licences in a five-mile radius to be flashed her picture.'

'I had no idea so much was going on.'

'The boss will expect a lot. But we do need to find her soon. In my experience, the longer this sort of thing goes on . . .'

Maddie swallowed hard. This job had brought with it a bad feeling from the start.

'I thought you might have got them working on the hit-and-run job. I know it's important to you.'

'Ron Beasle is dead. He will stay dead. The first few days of an investigation are key, that is true, but compared to finding someone who might still be alive? I'd rather the team were looking for her. Once I've asked a few more questions of McCall's tomorrow, I'll be back looking for her too.'

'I'll come with you then. Just to make sure you do!'

'As long as you haven't got your own stuff to do?'

'I don't think anyone really cares *what* I'm doing. The guv'nor told me to work with you on the missing girl anyway.'

'Fine then. Be in for eight and we'll head straight up there. Depending on how helpful McCall's are, we should be back looking for your girl by late morning.'

'That sounds good.' Maddie hesitated. She was hunting for the right words. 'What are the chances, do you think? Of her just being on a binge and passed out somewhere?'

Harry's attention was fixed forward, back to negotiating ruts and bumps. They were near to the end of the track. He waited a few seconds until the tyres fell back on the smooth tarmac and he brought the Land Rover to a complete stop. He looked over at Maddie.

'After this long? I'm not expecting to find her alive.'

* * *

She heard an engine. She couldn't be dreaming, she could feel the breeze. It was still scented with farmyard animals. The noise must have woken her. Almost as soon as she had recognised it, the sound stopped. Then *clunks,* like car doors being pushed shut. She tried to scream. It was like one of those nightmares where you're willing your body to do something but nothing's happening. Her mind thrashed with frustration.

The light around her changed. She was so weak now her eyes were all she could move effectively and they flicked to the far wall. With her blurred vision she could see the door as a solid block with light leaking underneath and down one side. She could see two black outlines underneath. They were moving. *They were legs! Someone was here!*

She tried to shout out again. Her tongue lolled in her mouth, her lips opened and closed but nothing came out but her breath. She managed some movement: her foot writhed and scuffed behind her, her fingers scratched at the stone. The slit of sunlight was partially blocked. Her eyes flicked back to her own fingers desperately scrabbling to get a grip, reaching out towards the door.

Was that a voice?

She stopped her movement for just a second and focussed her hearing. She concentrated with everything she had left. *It was!* Two voices! One was close, *so close.*

'Come on! We're wasting our time here!' she heard. A loud voice but far away. An angry-sounding man. It sounded like he was shouting at her.

Then a woman's voice, softer, kinder: *'I could have told you that. I'm not even sure what we're looking for.'* The light changed again, it was brighter. The legs walked across the underside of the block of shadow.

She was moving away!

She could hear the footfalls; they scraped and kicked up the dust from the ground. She gave one last push, her hands and feet scuffing and scrabbling. She tried to move, to sit up, to shout out. Nothing happened. Her body wasn't responding. She had no control of anything. There was nothing left. She heard another two *clunks*. The engine

started again. It moved away. She held her eyes firmly shut
to try and stop the tears. It was no use.

* * *

Harry dropped Maddie back at the station. She was
already an hour late coming off-duty — something she was
making a habit of, it seemed — but she wanted to check
her email system before she went home. She was three
failed login attempts down when a message on her screen
warned her that she only had one more go at getting it
right — fail and she would be locked out. And the whole
system would probably·explode.

She cursed. She concentrated and made sure of every
letter as she typed the password she had written down on a
post-it stuck in her notebook. It worked. The screen
opened up with no explosions. Her inbox showed just one
email. It was from Detective Chief Inspector Lowe.

Maddie,

*I trust you are settling in okay. As part of your new role you
will be required to attend some meetings with returned missing persons
in order to conduct, or at least be present for their return interviews.
We have two such interviews scheduled for tomorrow and Friday.
These are two separate persons. Both are juveniles and their
interviews will take place at their respective schools. After the
interviews I would suggest it to be a good time to discuss with the
school how future instances can be avoided.*

*I know I asked for your assistance with our missing person
enquiry but this is absolutely key to your role and we have sufficient
Major Crime resources to cover.*

*I have asked PCSO Dawkins to make contact with you. She
will be accompanying you on both occasions. I have asked her to
conduct the interviews, giving you the opportunity to observe.*

JL

Maddie threw herself back in her chair. She didn't
enjoy being patronised and now she was being asked to

accompany a PCSO to watch how a missing person interview should be conducted for a school kid. Julian Lowe himself had assigned her to work with Harry on the missing girl. The fact that he had taken her off it told her all she needed to know.

His email signed off with a signature that included his phone number. She considered calling him there and then but thought better of it. She was angry and she knew she was no good at hiding her temper. They weren't used to her down here yet. Julian Lowe certainly wasn't. She clicked to reply to the email and stared at the blinking cursor. She couldn't think where to start.

She closed the system back down. She would head out with Harry first thing and then go and see the inspector face-to-face on her return. With any luck she would already have missed the school meeting and could play dumb. She would be sure to have her work phone switched off. For now, though, she was tired; she just wanted to go home — or rather back to her soulless hotel, which was the closest thing she had to home right now.

At least there was a bar there.

Chapter 26

By the time Maddie walked through the entrance to her hotel, she was very much ready for bed. She had planned on getting a drink, something strong enough to take the edge off the day, but decided she was too tired even for that. She pushed the button to call the lift instead. She caught the eye of the receptionist as she waited. The woman reacted like she had suddenly been stung.

'Oh, Miss Earnshaw!' she called out. Maddie was daydreaming, but switched on enough to remember the name with which she had been booked into the hotel, Greater Manchester Police being overcautious. The lift doors clunked apart in front of her. She put her foot in to hold it.

'Yes,' Maddie said.

'A male visitor came to the hotel asking for you.'

'A visitor?'

'Well, not really a visitor. He has a room. He asked for you to be made aware that he was here. I have his details here somewhere.' She fidgeted with some papers on her desk. She tutted like she couldn't lay her hands on what she wanted. 'It's here somewhere. Oh, it doesn't matter. I saw him come back down a few hours ago. I believe he is still in the bar if you want to go and see him. He's a tall man, wearing a blue suit jacket with patches.'

'How long is he staying for? I'm a little tired is all!' She did her best to sound casual. She felt her pocket, checking her phone was there if she needed it.

'Just one night. He did enquire if he could stay longer. We're not full at the moment.'

Maddie stepped away from the lift and the door slid shut. The entrance to the bar was to the right of the reception desk. She could just see in — not enough though to see who was in there. She walked to the entrance to the bar from where she could get a better view. It was busy with people. Most were talking in low tones. There was some sporadic laughter from a table where a group had overrun a corner with extra chairs. She couldn't see much of the restaurant area. She could see a man stood with his back to her at the bar. He lifted a glass to drink. He wore a blue jacket over darker blue jeans. The elbows had brown patches over them. His dark hair was neat, his back wide and strong. She didn't need to see any more of him: she recognised him immediately.

'Ah, here it is. Did you need his details, Miss Earnshaw?' The receptionist called out to Maddie. She looked back over.

'No need. Thank you.' She took a moment and sucked in a breath. She moved further into the bar.

The stool next to him was free. She sat on it. He was half-turned away from her. A barman walked over to her.

'A Jack Daniel's, please,' she said. 'Over ice.'

'Very good.' The barman started to turn. He stopped as the man in the blazer addressed him.

'You can put that onto Room 79,' he said. The barman nodded, his eyes flicked back to Maddie and then he turned again.

'I can buy my own drinks,' Maddie snapped. She peered around the bar. She didn't know what she might find, who she might see. Old habits. These people rarely travelled alone. She didn't like feeling that she'd been caught out. She had never liked surprises.

'And now you don't have to.'

'What are you doing here, Adam?'

'I could ask you the same question.'

'Working.'

'Well, I came to look for you! I was worried.'

'You never look for me and you're never worried.'

'I heard you got blown. From one of my blue contacts. No one on my side seems to know it. I was just making sure you're alright.'

'This blue contact . . . did he tell you where to find me, too?'

'He knew a county and a hire car. It was no small effort to find you from that. Did you really have to move 280 miles away? It wasn't that much of a mess, was it?'

'My bosses thought so.'

'Your bosses are idiots.'

'Actually, the fact you're here suggests they were absolutely bloody right.'

He laughed — loud enough to draw attention to them. It made Maddie flash angry. 'Shut up, Adam. You shouldn't be here. I need to get on with things. This is not a good time for me. I'm trying to pick up the pieces of what's left of my career.'

'You always were a bit of a drama queen.'

Her Jack D arrived. She waited for the barman to move away again. 'Adam, I never ask you for anything. I'm asking you now — go away. Please. Go back home and leave me alone.'

'Leave you alone? Could you not have told me that before you left? You could have spoken to me about it. You could have saved me a trip. Instead you just upped and left and didn't even think to talk to me.'

'I did tell you.'

'A text message. I got a text message saying what? *Working away. Will be gone a while.* What the hell does that mean?'

'What it says.'

'I thought we had something?' His expression was still light, good-humoured but Maddie knew him better. His face carried a constant half smile. It could lull unsuspecting onlookers into a false sense of security, but not Maddie. She knew who Adam Yarwood was — or, more importantly, who his brother was. Adam was the kid brother of Leon Yarwood, a man who had risen through the ranks of one of the most notorious criminal gangs in the North West of England. Adam had never admitted it openly, but there was no doubt he worked for his brother when it suited him. Maddie didn't want to know in what capacity. He was a big man and he had a temper. He could be useful to someone like Leon and not for his charm — although he could turn that on in spades when he wanted to. He had the looks to back it up too — a chiselled jaw with dark stubble and those dark eyes that you could find yourself lost in, the sort that seemed to always be half filled with mischief and the other half with lust. Like you were the most beautiful thing he had ever seen and he was working out how to get what he wanted. Even now.

She looked away, then spoke into her whiskey. 'We did. About once a week on average and then I wouldn't hear from you until the next time.'

'We were trying to keep you safe, remember? And they were your demands, not mine.'

'Keep me safe? And coming here is about that too, is it?'

'I was careful. We can't have my mates or yours following me down here, can we! I did like you always told me. I dumped my usual ride outside a hire-car place. It's probably a hundred miles from here. I got the train the rest of the way. And from the station to here took two taxi journeys with two different firms with a changeover somewhere remote. Over careful. Nobody's interested in me anyway. I barely see my brother. He's a liability at the moment. He seems to be enjoying the lifestyle a little too much — always off his head. Somebody will be along to take what he has if he's not careful.'

'You sound like you're considering it.'

'Me? It wouldn't suit me. Not any of it.'

'The money would.'

'Money suits everybody. Come on, Maddie, what the hell are you doing down here?'

'My job.'

'Are you down here undercover?' he lowered his voice and checked around. Maddie had trained him well. He knew what she did. In her previous life she'd been assigned to get close to Leon Yarwood. She hadn't reckoned on a cocky, good-looking man getting close to her while she was working. No one had even known he had a brother, let alone that Adam was him. The lack of information was the reason she'd been sent to work him in the first place. But Adam had been working too. Leon had sent him to get close enough to her to satisfy himself that she could be trusted. He was just about to endorse her when he had found out the truth. He had followed her to a meeting with her handler. She hadn't been careful enough. Had Adam reported back on what he had seen, she would have been killed — they both knew it. Fortunately for her, Adam couldn't let that happen.

'No. I think I might be out of that game now, Adam, don't you?'

'So what, you're down here acting the copper? Flashing your badge and introducing yourself as PC fucking plod?' Adam got angry quickly. He was an easy man to wind up. Maddie saw that a lot in people who were used to getting their own way.

'DS actually.'

'What?'

'I'm a sergeant.'

'You're a snitch. The people you've surrounded yourself with all this time hate the cops, you know that, you've heard it for yourself, but there's a specific type of cop they hate more than anything else. The undercover snake.'

'I didn't blow out completely. I didn't make too much noise. You found me because you were looking for me. Nobody else is.'

'You can't be sure. You can't guarantee you'll be safe down here.'

'So where should I go? Find an island somewhere and build myself something out of driftwood. I need a life. This will do for now.'

'Come with me. Be with me.'

Maddie was caught out for the second time that day. She hadn't expected him to say that. She took a few seconds. 'And I'll be safe with you, will I? What was that you just said about the undercover snake? How long do you think I would last in among your lot?'

'You'll be safe with me.'

'And what if I don't like it? Or when you go off with one of your hangers-on for a night or two? Am I supposed to put up with that shit?'

'It's a lifestyle, Maddie. A good one.'

'Oh I see! So I *am* one of the hangers-on!'

'No, never. You know I don't see you like that. That's not what I meant.'

'I know what you meant. The fact that you came down here at all, the fact that you only booked in for one night, I know exactly what you meant. You thought you would come down here, snap your fingers, dangle this made-up life in front of me at a time when you think I'm vulnerable and I would just hop on the back of your horse and we could ride off together. Life isn't like that, Adam. You certainly aren't.'

'Maybe you don't know me at all.'

'All the more reason not to give up everything I've ever known to come join you in one of your whims.'

'This isn't a whim, Maddie. I'm not some kid with a crush. There are plenty of girls out there that would jump at the chance to be with me. You know that, right?'

'And not one of them has the same chosen career as me. We can never *be* anything. We've known that from the start. This was a mistake, but we have an opportunity to move on from it now. We should take it.'

'A mistake?' He covered his reaction with his glass.

Maddie felt a brief pang of guilt. She knew that had sounded harsh but that didn't make it wrong. 'A mistake,' she repeated. 'Please, Adam, have a drink with me — I've had a shit day. We can talk like we used to, about anything other than what we do to earn our living. Then I'm gonna need an early night and in the morning, I am begging you, please go home.'

'I'm a plasterer, Maddie.'

'And I'm an escort.'

'Just proves we can be what we want to be. We're good at it.'

'Drink with me, Adam. That's all. We know we're good at that.'

Adam turned away and tapped on the bar with a large, gold ring. The barman made his way over. 'Two more please,' Adam said. When he turned back to Maddie, his eyes were one half mischief, one half lust.

Chapter 27

Maddie woke to the sound of her alarm. The blackout curtains were doing their job and there was barely enough light to find her phone to silence it. She sat up and rubbed at her head. The alcohol hung heavily and she felt fuzzy and dehydrated. She swung out her legs and looked back momentarily to where Adam was outlined in the bed next to her. She paced to the bathroom and turned on the light; it seemed like the brightest light in the world. She closed her eyes to it and rested the weight of her head on her palms as she leaned over the sink. Her eyes got a little more accustomed to the brightness. Squinting between her fingers at the large mirror in front of her, she sighed at her nakedness. How had she got to this point? She was right when she told Adam that this was their chance to move away from the mistakes they had made in the past but she hadn't listened to her own advice. She had made the same mistake again. It shouldn't have come as a surprise. This was how their relationship had started in the first place.

She ran the cold tap and took a swig of water. She caught some in her hands and washed it over her face, shivering as it ran down onto her neck and chest. She filled two glasses and walked back into the bedroom. Adam's bedside lamp was on and he was sitting up reading something on his phone.

'I've come to appreciate the rooms here, you know,' he said. 'This is not the sort of place I would normally choose to spend my nights but it's actually rather nice.'

'Nice? I've seen the sort of places you treat yourself to. I don't know why you thought you would be okay staying here.'

'I'm more than okay, Maddie. You're here.'

'How much do they know about me? Your people, I mean.'

'You mean my brother's people.'

'What do they know?'

'About you?'

'About me. About what happened.'

'Nothing much. Nobody's even talking about it anymore. They reckon some call girl was working as an informant for the blue side. The theory is that the cops had something over her and she had to stitch up Eddie Flint. Leon's got the hump a bit. Eddie was becoming a problem and the cops might have got in the way of him resolving that. But this escort . . . nobody thinks she's a cop. I even heard somebody say that he'd heard she was too hot to be a cop. I reckon I agree with that!'

'Were they Leon's men?'

'Who?'

'The two that came after him — after Eddie.'

'I've no idea what was going on with him. Leon's never shared his thoughts on a solution to that particular problem.'

Maddie smirked. She knew what *solution* meant. She picked up the previous night's clothes from a chair. She needed to get back to her own room for a shower and a clean set.

'You don't have to get dressed just yet, do you?' Adam said.

Maddie pulled on her underwear, then some trousers. She looked up at Adam. He patted the bed where she had just got out. 'Only I have to go back today. For at least a few days.'

'Where does this end, Adam?'

'Who says it has to end?'

'You know what they say . . . all good things . . .'

'This is a good thing then?' Adam said.

'This is a . . . thing.' Maddie was being a little more careful than the night before. She had been angry and tired then, but now . . . now she remembered that this was not a man who always reacted well to being told things straight — not things that he didn't agree with. And sleeping with him again had certainly not been the right way to build up to it either. Once again she was back to damage limitation.

'So let's just leave it as that for now then and see where this goes,' Adam said.

'This isn't good, though. Not for you and not for me or my career.'

'You talk like they're the same thing!'

'Well, aren't they? What else can I do?'

'I think I already answered that last night. You can walk away any day you want. I earn more than enough to keep you in the manner you're accustomed to. I've been considering a move out to Spain. I've got opportunities out there. It would be a clean break — and think of the life we could have!'

'Spain! You have some plastering out there do you?'

'You don't like how I earn my living and I don't like how you earn yours. At least I don't pretend like I'm righteous when I cash my cheques.' Adam threw back the duvet and strode naked to the bathroom. The door closed roughly behind him.

'Neither do I,' she said out loud but to herself. She heard the shower start up. She finished getting dressed and moved to the door. She pulled it open enough to be able to see out. The corridor was empty. Not that anyone knew or cared what she was doing or with whom. The fact that she skulked back to her room was a demonstration of how much of a mistake she considered last night to have been.

* * *

Maddie couldn't be sure if Harry was immediately disapproving when he looked at her or if that was just his normal frown and she was being hypersensitive. Her hangover was pretty much gone, drowned by three bottles of water and a handful of paracetamols. He was sitting at his desk. It was just after seven thirty in the morning and the office was quiet.

She had called out too early, a sign of nerves, Harry stopped what he was typing but he didn't reply.

'Morning. We still heading out to McCall's first thing?'

'We leave in half an hour.' He returned pointedly to his work. Maddie didn't have the energy to try and push for more of a conversation.

'Well, okay then. I tell you what, I'm going to walk to that coffee place to get a takeout. I'll leave you to it for half an hour. You want one?'

Harry stopped again and seemed to be considering it. 'Sure. Black.'

'Of course.' Maddie left hurriedly. Going out for a coffee suddenly seemed like a good idea to her. She didn't want to bump into the DCI and be reminded of the meeting he had planned for her — not yet anyway. She was going to go out with Harry first. And a coffee might be just the thing to move her on from last night. Physically at least.

* * *

The reaction when they walked back into the plush reception area of McCall's was instantly different from their visit the day before.

'Oh, I'm sorry!' The receptionist's smile was obviously forced. 'That door isn't supposed to be open yet. We're not open for visitors until nine!'

'It was open, though,' Harry growled. He stood directly in front of her and leaned on the desk with both hands.

'Yes, someone must have left it open.'

'Lucky they did. I didn't bring a jacket.'

Maddie stifled a chuckle. Outside, the heat wave was showing no signs of abating.

'Well, yes. Can I ask you to take a seat, please?'

'Don't you need to know who we are here to see?' Harry pressed.

'I will take those details from you at nine o'clock, sir. I have other matters to attend to before I can arrange visitors.'

'I need to speak to Mr McCall. He works here, right? I think if you call him and tell him that the police are here investigating a murder and they would like to speak to him, he might be able to fit me in outside of office hours, don't you?'

The woman's eyes burst wide. 'I . . . murder . . .' she muttered. 'Mr McCall arrives at 9 a.m. and even then he has a very full—'

'That shiny Jaguar outside . . . the registration ends *JMC*. Your company website lists him as James McCall. Now, you have to appreciate that an old detective like me already knows that he is in the building and you've just told me that you pack his diary from 9 a.m. onwards. So, we both know that right now he is here and he has a half-hour slot. That's right, isn't it?'

'I . . . well, I mean . . .' She was more flustered this time. Harry let her off the hook.

'I tell you what. You phone your boss and tell him the situation . . . that you have some pain in the ass down in reception asking to speak to him and we'll see if he'll fit me in. If not, let him know that I'll drop back later, during office hours, with a warrant to close the business while a search takes place for the evidence that I need. I'll wait over there, okay?' Harry moved to the seat before she had a chance to answer. Maddie watched her hurriedly pick up the phone.

Predictably someone was down within five minutes. It was a man in an expensive-looking suit and grey hair that was in a neat side-parting. Even his walk carried authority.

'You must be the detective inspector?' the man said, before the receptionist could find her tongue.

'Harry Blaker. And you are James McCall?'

'I am. I understand you wanted to speak to me. Did you want to come up to my office?'

Maddie stretched as she stood up. Mr McCall led them through a different corridor to their previous visit. This one seemed to run through the centre of the building. A lift took them two floors up. The plush surroundings continued on this floor. Maddie wasn't expecting a dusty, plastic chair this time and she wasn't disappointed. She ended up in a slim-backed, leather seat that flexed as she sat. McCall sat opposite. Harry didn't sit at all.

'So, how can we help?'

'Leonard's Farm. Do you know it?' Harry said.

'Leonard's Farm? I mean, no. Can you give me some sort of context?'

'I believe you are negotiating to buy it.'

'Ah! Okay, that makes sense. We are in the market for a few rural locations at the moment. We've always had good experiences with converting farm buildings. They have a certain charm to them, don't you think?'

'And how do you secure this *charm*?'

'How do you mean?'

'I had a brief chat with your man who runs your vehicle fleet. I got some information but I need a better understanding. So you have surveyors that you send out to available sites to scope out if they might be something you can build on? Is that about it?'

'What is this about? I thought you were assisting with the theft of one of our vehicles?'

'I am.'

'Okay. And yet you are asking questions about sites of interest. We don't normally discuss such things, you understand. I'm running a business where revealing too much of our future plans can ruin them completely.'

'I'm not a competitor, Mr McCall.'

'You're speaking like one.'

'I'm speaking like a man investigating a murder. Maybe those two things can be similar in the right circumstances?'

'I'm not sure what you're implying.'

'This is a competitive market. I've been involved with other cases where this level of competition has led to physical disputes. This wouldn't be the first.'

'And what makes you think that's what's happened here?'

'Nothing yet. That's why I'm here. I need to learn a bit more about your surveyors. So, like I said, you send surveyors out to potential places and they come back with a projected value to your company. Is that about right?'

McCall sat back in his seat. He brought his hands together in front of him and took a moment before he replied. 'Do I need a solicitor, Detective Inspector?'

'I can't advise you about solicitors, not about whether you need one or not. In my experience, the people who need solicitors are those who have something to hide. So, it's a little difficult for me to say.'

McCall gave a smile. It didn't look to Maddie like the good-humoured kind. 'With regard to our surveyors, that's about right — apart from the bit where we send them out. I mean we *can* do, but far more often now we get the surveyors coming back to us with proposals. They actively hunt properties that might be viable for maximising.'

'Maximising?'

'Yes. It's what we do. You get some property companies who specialise in securing land and then building from scratch. You will have seen all of the new-build sites and estates appearing across the country. We, however, specialise in purchasing an old rural estate, for example, or a disused factory in a city location. We then maximise what is already there. We renovate it and often convert it to a multi-occupancy site. It's higher-end development, our clients are typically in the high net worth bracket of the housing market. They have different needs to the clients who are buying off-plan in the new-build estates.'

'I'm sure they do. So I was right about it being a competitive business?'

'What business isn't these days, Inspector?'

'And your surveyors are paid for finding these sites, are they?'

'After a fashion.'

'After a fashion? What does that mean?'

'They are self-employed. We don't have full-time surveyors anymore. We only require their services when we are looking for new sites. We found we were regularly getting to the point where we were working a number of sites at the same time, at absolute capacity and no longer in the market for new opportunities. You could be left with surveyors sitting on their hands for twelve months. So now we just use them when we need them.'

'Which is now?'

'Which is *for* now.'

'So they're on commission?'

'They get paid set amounts for set tasks but, yes, if they come to us with an opportunity they will receive a percentage of any profit made on that site when the project is complete and the properties have been sold. It's a long process.'

'So these surveyors work for other companies?'

'They are free to. Now I've answered everything you've asked, perhaps you could give me some more information about just what is going on here? I'm told there has been a tragic incident involving one of our vehicles. I believe it was stolen at the time.'

'It wasn't reported stolen at the time. And neither has anyone been able to provide a scrap of evidence that that was actually the case.'

'I see. Well, I guess the evidence is very much your domain. I instructed our fleet manager to provide all the information that you requested. Is there something else you need from us?'

'He was going to provide me with names and details of your surveyors. I haven't had that yet. And of anyone who has access to those vehicles. I'm sure you can appreciate that's a significant line of enquiry.'

'I can indeed. That may be a significant number of individuals, however. I will be sure to chivvy him up.'

'Also, in relation to Leonard's Farm, can you confirm your interest in that site? Only you haven't as yet.'

Maddie was watching McCall closely. His lips flinched as if he was going to speak. He didn't, and he took another moment. 'I can tell you that we don't own that site. All the sites that we have acquired for past, present or future development are readily available on our website or other publicly available resources on the internet.'

'I'm not interested in past building. Are you in for that site?'

'We don't divulge locations that we have not yet secured. You said the word yourself: *competitive*. Knowledge is power, of course. This has never been truer than for this kind of business.'

'Like I said, I'm not a competitor. I need to see any documentation you have around that site. I also need details of any other sites that you're currently involved in negotiations for—'

'Why on earth would you need that? You're certainly acting more and more like a competitor.'

'Some of these sites may have security — manned — or CCTV at least. Say your man did a couple of visits on the same day, or ten minutes after that vehicle ran someone down. That's good evidence that he was driving it on that day. Unlikely perhaps, but you'd be surprised how often I've got a result from *unlikely*.'

'I can get you addresses. That's about it.'

'Addresses are fine for the list of sites. But for Leonard's Farm that won't do. I am particularly interested in who brought it to you as a proposal, as you call it. I also need to know who has visited the site and when and what they were doing there. Also any records you have of the current owners, their contact details and if you have had any interaction on that site with anyone who might be looking after it. Does that all make sense?'

'We are not obliged to provide that information, Inspector, and some of it will fall within data protection laws.'

'You're probably right. This is an informal request. I can have a formal request made via Legal Services, but that will mean bringing my own search team down, which will require the closure of this building and the seizure of your computers. All of them. I'm sure you can do without the disruption.' Harry leaned on the desk so that he was looking down over the seated man. 'And that's just the start.'

James sniffed. He stood up and straightened out his suit jacket. He proffered his hand.

'I can assure you, Inspector, I will do what I can to help — no less.'

'And no more,' Harry said as he took up the handshake. 'I'll put our search team off for now, then.'

Maddie followed Harry out. They didn't talk until they got back to the car.

'Those surveyors . . . they're the lifeblood of that place,' Harry said.

'They are. The incentives for bringing new projects must be pretty sizeable.'

'They must be, yeah. There's a link somewhere in all this. I just can't see it yet.'

'Was Ron causing some delay with the sale maybe?' Maddie said.

'I don't know. But I've got nothing better for a motive. I need to go and see someone from the Leonard estate. Someone who knows a bit more about what offers might be on the table and Ron Beasle's part in it all.'

'Leonard's wife? Let's go.' Maddie was aware that Harry had started the car but it wasn't moving off. She turned to see him looking at her.

'Sorry, kid. I'm under strict orders to bring you back in. The boss made me promise. He called me first thing. I don't have an address for the Leonards yet anyway.'

'Goddammit!' Maddie cussed.

'It might be for the best. Maybe you can get to focus on your missing girl? You should at least get to check in with my team and get an update.'

'I wish it were something like that. I have a good idea what it is.'

'What's that?'

'A complete waste of my time.'

Chapter 28

As she walked back into the police station, Maddie still clung to the faint hope that maybe there had been some breakthrough with her missing girl and she might be required to lead that investigation while Harry was tucked up with his hit and run. She sucked in a breath on the threshold of Julian Lowe's office. She let it out in an involuntary raspberry the second she saw a uniformed community support officer sat in the corner of Lowe's office. The woman looked stern.

'Ah, DS Ives,' Lowe greeted her as she walked in. 'This is Janet Warren. She's the PCSO for Canterbury Central and the college comes under her remit. You got my email, I assume?'

'I did, sir. I was hoping to talk to you about it. There's a lot going on at the moment as you know and I was hoping to continue to look—'

'You remember our conversation around your remit here, DS Ives? Your role is not to be out *looking* for our missing people. You are more the conductor of the orchestra. You work with those who are doing the looking. I know I asked you to assist, but right now you are needed elsewhere. Major Crime has good resources. The search is in very good hands.'

'I see. There is also the hit-and-run incident, sir. Harry is running that by himself as it stands, but I have been out with—'

'Harry Blaker is a man who likes to work alone. You will see that for yourself when you have been at this station for more than just a few days.'

Maddie bit down hard on her tongue. She didn't like being cut off and talked over, she didn't like being patronised and she didn't like the way Julian Lowe was now smiling at her. She wanted to wipe that smile off his face, to tell him that she wasn't some new girl with nothing to offer. Instead she took a second and then had one more try. 'He seems to have been quite willing for me to assist over the last couple of days. I think we are getting somewhere.'

'This hit-and-run incident is not something that needs any more resources. Right now, from the briefing I have received, we have a man hit by a speeding vehicle and the only reason we are *considering* any kind of murderous intention is because of a tied-up dog. DI Blaker is very sensitive around road traffic affairs and I am quite happy to lose him to that investigation while it is bottomed out. I cannot justify losing our misper liaison too. Not when a meeting is scheduled of the type that will become your bread and butter once your feet are under the table. You will learn a lot today, DS Ives, I can assure you of that. Janet here is very experienced in the world of schools liaison and missing persons. You will attend a meeting with the school and then meet one of our regular mispers. Unless you feel that this sort of task is not relevant to your new role? Or perhaps it is beneath you entirely?'

He paused for a reply. Maddie knew a loaded question when she heard one. She took a second to compose herself. A career in policing had taught her one thing for sure: pick your battles. This was not one she could win.

'Not at all. This sounds like it's very relevant. It's just a shame that all of these things have come at once. I didn't realise everything else was quite so covered off. What time do we need to leave?' The question was directed towards Janet but the chief inspector answered it for her.

'Well, there you are. Seems we are able to cover all bases just as well as your big city force. Who knew, eh? You'll need to leave straight away to be sure to get there on time.'

Maddie resisted telling him just what she thought of his ability to organise anything. 'I'll just get my things together.'

* * *

Maddie disguised a sigh as the tall, metal gates of Homewood School yawned open and sucked in their car from the residential streets surrounding the site. Janet was driving, and so far she hadn't done very well. She showed no signs of improving either and didn't seem to slow for the unnecessarily intrusive speed bumps as they moved into the school grounds before abandoning the car at a skewed angle across a clearly marked disabled space.

'Won't we get in trouble for parking here?' Maddie said.

'Nah. I park here all the time. They know me here.'

Janet walked quickly towards the door marked *Reception*. The car made a clunking sound as she locked it.

In the reception area, Janet spoke to someone behind the desk. They were chatting about one or the other's holiday. Maddie was handed a sticky label announcing her as a visitor. She stuck it to her chest.

'Usual room?' Janet said. The building looked relatively new to Maddie. It was a bland series of squared edges and long, plain corridors with box-shaped rooms coming off at regular intervals. All the doors leading into the rooms were identical and with just a slip of card labelling each one. They stopped at a door with the label

Room 1.9. Janet led the way in and the door fell closed behind them. It was too small to be a classroom. It was square-shaped, of course, but with soft chairs laid out for four people to sit on. They all faced one another. There were leaflets in a Perspex holder on the wall, each of them seemed to refer to *wellbeing* of some sort, connected with student counselling or support groups. This must be the room for talking about thoughts and feelings. Maddie's least favourite thing.

'So, you're not really into all this?' Janet said.

Maddie lifted her eyes and they carried her surprise. For a split second she considered that her colleague might be reading her thoughts. 'All this?'

'You know . . . working the schools an' that. Stopping the little shits going missing again. The boss said that it wasn't really your bag.'

Maddie realised why Janet had barely spoken to her the whole way and perhaps why her driving style could be described as 'angry.'

'He said that? That's a shame, really. I don't want to get off on the wrong foot, Janet. I know this is your job, too. I don't want you to think I'm not into it — of course I am. I came three hundred miles to do this job!'

'Not by choice though, right? And I heard you back in the office. There's more important stuff going on that you would rather be doing.'

Maddie licked her lips, considering her reply. 'I'm worried about one of my missing girls. I think she might be in danger. Our lad here today . . . he's not in any danger — not right now. I get that we need to stop him disappearing — he's vulnerable when he's off the radar — but right now I think I could be better used looking for that girl.'

'There are plenty of people out looking for her.'

'There are,' Maddie conceded. She didn't want to. She wanted to scream back that she had already been patronised once by the chief inspector and it wasn't open season for anyone else who wanted to have a go. She almost surprised herself. Restraint seemed to be a new quality she had been saving just for Lennockshire. She continued, doing her best to remain diplomatic: 'And right now we're the only ones here, so this is the most important thing I've got going on. I've read up on the case and I'm ready to do what I can to make sure that David doesn't go missing again and put himself in harm's way. I'm in!' Maddie tried a chuckle to see if she could soften Janet's harsh exterior.

'It's Dan,' Janet said. Her exterior remained very much intact.

The door pushed open. A young lad bundled in. He had a satchel over both shoulders and, despite the warm weather, he also wore a zipped top that was done right up under his chin. He sat down in one of the seats and slumped so far back he was almost facing the ceiling. His top rode up over his chin and, combined with his brown fringe that was long and swept across his brow, his face was almost completely covered. He had let the door close on a middle-aged woman who came in after him. She looked flustered. She had a hardback A4 book under her right arm, more paperwork in her left hand and a mug of tea that she was struggling to keep from spilling. Her cheeks were red and as she moved to take one of the seats she let out an exasperated sigh. She sat down and fanned herself with the paperwork.

'Sorry,' she said, 'did you want a drink?'

Janet declined for them both. Dan looked out from under his fringe. He looked at every part of Maddie except her eyes.

'Dan, how are you?' Janet said.

'I'm alright. Bit bored. Dunno why I'm here — this is my break time.'

'You do know why you're here, Dan,' the middle-aged woman cut in, looking even more flustered.

'Some shit about where I've been? I've already done that.'

'And you didn't tell me anything.'

'I don't have to tell you where I've been or where I'm going. I'm fifteen. I'm not a kid anymore.'

'Actually, Dan, in the eyes of the law that's exactly what you are,' Janet said.

'I don't give a shit about the law. I go where I want, when I want. My mum knows I weren't at school. I told her and she don't give a shit. I don't get why you do.'

'Did you tell her where you went? Or who with?'

'No. It's got nothing to do with her either.'

Janet looked over at Maddie. 'Dan, this is Detective Sergeant Ives. She needs to speak to you about going missing, about what it means to the police — resources wise. You need to sit and listen, okay?'

Dan's eyes flicked to Maddie very briefly. Then he pushed his legs out, his head lolled further back into the seat and his eyes lifted to the ceiling. He expelled a huge sigh, clearly for Maddie's benefit. She looked over at Janet. This wasn't exactly her definition of *observing*.

'Yeah, well, Dan . . .' Maddie cleared her throat. 'What you have to understand is that when you go missing we have a duty to try and find you. No matter how much of an adult or how streetwise you think you are. There are people out there that may be looking to cause you harm and we have the job of preventing that from happening. Does that make sense?'

Dan stayed looking at the ceiling. He gave no hint that he had even heard a single word she'd said.

'It ties up a lot of people . . .' she continued. 'Police officers, PCSOs, teachers and anyone else that we might use to try and find you. People that could be better used elsewhere, looking for people who are seriously at risk, or that might be looking to cause other people harm. Do you understand?'

'I never asked for nothing. I just wanna be left alone. The next time I'm missing, yeah, just type this into your little system or whatever . . . *leave him alone 'cause he's fine and he don't want to be found.* You get that?'

'Can't do that, Dan.'

Dan sat up suddenly. He leaned forward and his eyes panned over Maddie again from the feet up. He lingered on her chest. 'Unless you wanna come find me . . . you're alright, you.'

Maddie sniffed. She could feel her anger rising. 'You might be alright now, Dan. You might have been fine every time you've been missing so far. But one day you might not be. You're more at risk than you realise because, despite the fact that you probably only weigh eight stone when you're piss-wet through, you carry yourself like you're someone. But you're not, Dan. You're a nobody loser, and if some bloke was to scoop you up in his car and drive you somewhere where he can be alone with you for his own entertainment you wouldn't be missed for days. Not by anyone. I saw a kid in my last force after that had happened to him. When we found his body we could only identify him using his dental records and his arsehole was stretched so far open it was presumed to be the cause of death. So don't give me the Billy-big-bollocks routine and expect me to accept that you're 'ard enough to look after yourself. You're fuck-all Dan. You're someone's plaything if they want you to be, so you need to get smarter, unless you want your arsehole to be *your* cause of death?'

Dan sat back and squirmed. Then he swept his fringe out of his eyes and looked first to the middle-aged woman next to him, then to Janet before sinking back into the seat.

'You can't say things like that to me! I wanna speak to your boss!'

'Sit up straight when you talk to me, Dan. I'm not your teacher, your poor mother or one of your little mates. I'm a police officer. You ever speak to me like you just did again and I will drag you into the cells myself and rather than speaking to my boss you can speak to a custody sergeant. I'll think of something good enough to make sure you stay there for the full twenty-four hours. Now, the next time you go missing, I want you to think about me. I want you to remember that I don't give a shit if you're safe or not. But this is my job and I take my job very seriously, so I will be looking for you. And if it's me that finds you, you might just wish it *was* the bloke in his car. Any questions?'

Dan was holding eye contact with Maddie now, and he looked a lot less sure of himself. 'No. I got no questions.'

'I must have made myself clear then. Do you have a phone?'

'Yeah.'

'I'll take the number. You can make sure you take mine too and I want you to put it in your phone. Then, if you're reported missing again I'll call you and I'll know you'll see my name flash up on your screen. If you answer me, I'll know I can stop looking. If you don't, you *will* piss me off, Dan. You don't want to piss me off, do you?'

Dan huffed loudly. 'Nah, I don't mean to . . .' He sat up straighter, his head hung a little. He had his phone in his hand. He held it out for Maddie. The woman next to him was flushing a far deeper shade of red. She spoke next. Her voice took a second to get going, like her throat had tightened up.

'R-right th-then, Dan . . . if you're done with us then you should get to your next class. We'll catch up later, okay?'

'Yeah.'

Dan got to his feet and took his phone back. He gave Maddie one last look and then he was gone.

'Well!' The flustered woman clapped her hands together. She looked at Maddie and she seemed to be struggling to find something to say. 'That was certainly a different approach. I guess it might be the way to get through to him. We will have to see.'

'What would you normally do? Kids like that aren't going to listen to people telling them how many resources are being wasted looking for him. He doesn't care about the police and he certainly doesn't care about upsetting any of us. The only angle left is to tell him that he will get himself in trouble if he does it again.'

'Well, you certainly got that message across. Thanks for your time coming in today. Janet here knows the way out.' She scooped up her paperwork and her mug and left just as clumsily as she had entered. Maddie waited for the door to fall back shut.

'Did I upset her?' Maddie noticed that Janet was grinning for the first time.

'I think you did!'

'Oh, well . . .'

'I always thought she was too soft. They walk all over her here.'

'Who is she anyway? She never did introduce herself.'

'Sharon Hanson. She's the safeguarding lead here. It's her job to look after the welfare of all the kids. I don't envy her really, I wouldn't fancy that job.'

'I don't think I'd be much cop at it.'

'I think you'd be great!' Janet was still smiling. She seemed to have perked up quite a bit. 'Come on, let's get out of here. Maybe we can get a coffee on the way back in, seeing as how we're going to be working together a bit in the future. We've got a similar visit tomorrow for a start.'

'I thought we were going to talk to the school about how to prevent missing persons in the future or something like that?'

'We were. We usually have a chat after and bat around a few ideas for stopping the pupil going again, but Sharon obviously felt like you covered that in the meeting.'

'Oh. I really did upset her!'

'She'll be fine. Especially if your little chat has the desired effect on our mate in the future.'

'He'll go missing again,' Maddie said. 'Kids like that tend to do whatever they want.'

'I think you're right . . . he will go missing. But he'll definitely answer your call when he does!'

Chapter 29

Maddie tried Harry's number on the way back and got no answer. When Janet dropped her back at the station, she made for his desk rather than her own. Almost a whole day had passed and she wanted to see if he had any updates on her missing girl and also on his hit and run. She felt invested in both, even if the DCI wasn't letting her play much of a part in either. Harry wasn't there. She could see a couple of DCs and she walked over to the closest.

'Hey, I was looking for the inspector. Any idea where he might be?'

'He just went out. I think he's going to be a while.'

'Ah, okay. I don't suppose you're working the Lorraine Humphries missing person investigation, are you? I'm DS Ives, I'm the new, erm . . . misper liaison and I was just wondering if anything had happened around her case.'

'No, most of the team are tucked up on that though. I haven't heard any major updates. The team's numbers are all up on the board there if you want to call any of them.'

Maddie turned to where he was pointing. There was a whiteboard with handwritten names, phone numbers and shift patterns. 'No, it's okay. I'm sure Harry will keep me up to date with anything relevant.' She didn't really believe that. She would give him a call later.

When she made it back to her own desk, Julian Lowe was hanging out of his office talking to a DC. He finished the conversation hurriedly when he saw her.

'Ah, Maddie! How did it go? Come in.' He moved out of view. By the time Maddie got into his office he was already sitting down. He gestured for her to do the same. He leant back in his chair and steepled his fingers.

'It went fine. The lad was there. He's a bit of a shit, if you'll forgive the expression, and I'm not convinced he won't cause me an issue again, but I think we made some headway with him.'

'And an impression, I'm told.'

Maddie took a moment to process what he had said. 'You're told?'

'Yes. I know the Principal at that school. An old friend. I wanted to make sure you were getting on okay.'

'I see. A good impression, I hope?'

'The woman who deals with safeguarding there wasn't sure. I think they are of the same opinion as you . . . he will cause trouble again, he is likely to go missing again and there's nothing anyone can realistically do to stop that. She did pass on that your methods are quite different to what she is used to. She didn't elaborate.'

'Oh, really? We just had a conversation. The usual stuff. I explained the time and effort that we had to put into finding him when he is reported missing and asked him not to do it again. I assumed that was standard.'

'Yes, that is. I'm surprised then that they suggested your methods were a little *different*. I spoke to Janet too. In contrast she was singing your praises. She thinks you might have a bit of a knack when it comes to speaking to our young people. Let's hope that's the case. Maybe you're a natural in this role, Maddie.'

'Maybe.' Maddie was aware that the DCI was inspecting her closely.

'But you still think you could be better utilised elsewhere?'

'Those are not my decisions. What I think doesn't really matter, sir.'

'That's not true. I like to think I run things with an open-door policy. I will speak with Inspector Blaker and see where he is with the missing person investigation. If he could still use you then I will see if I can give you some time next week—'

'Next week? With respect, that might already be too late, sir.' She had been doing so well; she'd been calm up to now.

Lowe sighed. 'It might. But as we discussed earlier, there is a whole team of detectives working through the tasks that have been identified in the search for Lorraine Humphries. Putting more people in among that investigation could have a negative effect if anything. Someone such as yourself, brand new to the area, with techniques born of a city police force might find yourself to be more of a . . . hindrance, for want of a better word. And I know you have another school meeting tomorrow and there will be more multi-agency work next week for you to get your teeth into. If you wish for an attachment to Major Crime then maybe we can look at that as part of your development. But these things do not happen immediately, DS Ives. There are plenty of other sergeants out there who have requested the very same thing. I have to be fair. Do you understand?'

She did. She didn't agree, however. She wanted to scream at him, to tell him that until just a few days before she had been the go-to girl for Major Crime or the Serious and Organised Crime Unit if they needed intelligence gathering on the most dangerous criminals in the North West of England. Now she was *a hindrance* in a simple missing person enquiry. She kept her reply short so she wouldn't shed any emotion.

'Okay.'

'Right, then. That's good work so far. Back to it!'

Maddie was glad to leave his office. Back at her desk she had a new email. The details of her meeting the next day were on it. It was a two-hour slot in the middle of her day, with travelling either side. She wasn't going to be able to get anything more done tomorrow either. She stood back up and grabbed her bag. She needed to get out of here before she really did say something she would regret. She decided on the coffee shop. Her first week in and that place was already becoming something of a refuge.

* * *

She sat down with her coffee at a table by the window. It was relatively quiet in there for once, though the street outside was still busy. She always enjoyed people watching; she had damned near made a career of it. The people that passed seemed to be dressed for office work. Most seemed to have a phone pushed to their ear, their eyes glazed to the rest of the world as if they were doing something really important — important to them at least. Maddie longed to feel like that again. Her own phone disturbed her thoughts and she pulled it hurriedly from her pocket in a flash of pink — she needed to get rid of that case. Her screen was lit up with the name *Alan Jackson* — her old DCI from up north, the man responsible for moving her down here to a job no one cared about, least of all her.

'Sir! I was just thinking about you.'

'I'm sure you were, Maddie. All good I hope?'

'Not really, sir!' Maddie gave a chuckle but she didn't detect one at the other end.

'As I expected. You know I'm only trying to keep you safe down there, Maddie. I assume that's your problem? That you're all the way down there?'

'I don't have a problem with being somewhere else. You know how much I've travelled for work before. My problem is with being somewhere I have no real purpose.'

'These things take time. It won't take long for them to realise you're one of the good ones. Good enough to be trusted with the proper jobs. I'd be the same here if I was landed with someone new. I'd put them somewhere they couldn't do any damage for a while until I was sure they were capable.'

'Landed . . .?' Maddie exhaled.

'Poor choice of words. You know what I mean.'

'What were they told, sir? Regarding the reason for me coming down?'

'As much as they needed to know. That you might have been compromised as a UC asset and we were moving you out of the area to keep you safe.'

'Any suggestion that I was the reason for that compromise? That I might have messed up?'

'No. Whatever the circumstances of your move, that's not relevant to them down there.'

'Only that might explain how I'm being treated. You do think I messed up after all.'

'This isn't the conversation I called for, Maddie. We're not going over it again.'

'You're not calling to beg me to come back then, sir? A UC job that only I can help with?' Maddie lightened her tone and dared another chuckle.

'No, unfortunately. You know I would, though, if there was any other way.'

'So what do you need?'

'We have some intelligence that I need to share. I cannot put across enough how sensitive this intelligence is. You need to keep this to yourself or people could get killed. Am I coming across clearly?'

'Loud and clear. I assume we're talking source information?'

'Exactly that. We have some new sources that have come to light. It seems that a few of our organised crime groups have not had such a good time of it of late and the riches are not rolling downhill, if you know what I mean.

This latest source is good, too. Right in close to Adam Yarwood—'

'*Adam* Yarwood?' Maddie spluttered.

'I know!' Jackson's excitement was obvious, even down the phone. 'We've never gotten to anyone anywhere near the so-called innocent brother! But this could be good for us. That's how we know that business is down. There's a lot of competition by all accounts and we think Leon has involved his brother in expanding the reach.'

'Expanding?'

'Yes. Our intelligence puts Adam down the south of the country over the last few days. Apparently it was a *business trip*. A bit unusual for a plasterer, right? I'm in no doubt that this is of interest to us.'

Maddie felt her throat go a little tighter. She was sure it would show in her voice. 'Did you manage to firm it up? I'm always a bit suspicious of new sources.'

'The same source gave us a new car for him. We were able to track it using ANPR as far as the outskirts of London, close to a car rental place. We know that brother Leon has a past history of changing his car when he gets close to a meet location. We found CCTV from a petrol station that gave good images of the sole occupant — it was him! It was Adam Yarwood. Seems he's learnt a few counter-surveillance tricks. I think Leon is maybe having some trust issues and had to send his brother.'

'And you're sure he was doing a meet? Any ideas who with?'

'No specifics when it comes to his contacts, but the word is that he's got hold of a new supply in the London area and he's taking on a network who deal in the South — mostly coastal towns. They're largely untapped, the drug scenes run by locals. You get someone as well organised and as savage as Leon Yarwood in among that lot and he could do some real damage.'

'So why are you telling me this?' Maddie swallowed again, trying to get her throat to loosen enough to function properly.

'Like I said, I'm trying to keep you safe. You worked Yarwood, right?'

'Leon, sure. A long time ago. I never met the brother.'

'Okay, that's good. I'm just aware that we had the incident last weekend and then this Adam pops up a few hundred miles closer to where we sent you to be safe. I'll keep you informed. I know you never worked him specifically, but this might be the warm-up for Leon to come down. You know what these criminals are like around easy money — they're like sharks in the water. They can smell it from even 250 plus miles away. Stay on your toes, Maddie. I'll let you know of anything we get that's relevant.'

'Will do. Thanks for letting me know.'

The call ended and Maddie sat back. She peered round the café, suddenly aware that she might have been talking without a volume control. No one seemed to be taking any notice of her. As she stood up she could feel her pulse in her temple, strong and rapid. Her breathing was quick too, her breaths shallow. Her place of refuge suddenly felt like anything but. She needed to get out, to go somewhere else. She had no idea where.

Chapter 30

Harry pulled onto the neat block paving of his 1930s
bungalow. It was in a nice area, quiet and well presented.
His neighbours were largely retired. Harry and his wife had
bought it twelve years before and their own retirement
plans had been part of the decision-making progress. It
had never included the consideration that his wife might
not make it.

He tutted at his flowerbeds as he walked to his front
door. They needed doing again. They were just beginning
to lose their sharpness. You had to look hard to notice but
his wife had always been fussy about the garden. He was
determined to keep it up.

The daylight levels were low inside the house. He had
left the blinds shut in an effort to block the effects of the
blazing sun. Certainly it was the coolest he had been all
day. He continued through to the back of the house and
into the kitchen. He put his bag down on the bench and
ran a glass of water adding ice from the dispenser on the
front of the fridge. The warmth of the sun was
undiminished when he stepped into the conservatory and
he quickly pushed the double doors open and stepped out

onto the bright white patio. The ice clinked and tumbled when he took a sip.

He took a moment to inhale the scent of his oriental lilies, bunched together beside a straight path that bisected the neat lawn. He took the path up to a small pond and a bumble bee drifted in front of him. He watched it land clumsily in one of the flower heads. He sat on a bench beside his pond. Ivy was crawling up its legs and was now stretching across its back as if nature were slowly taking a firm grip of the thing. Harry put his glass down. He reached out for an ornate wooden robin on a wooden platform that also had a small wooden roof to keep the rain off. Its spindly legs were splayed for balance and its head dipped in a constant bow towards the bright green lily pads. He held it gently, like he had done every day since his wife had grown her own wings.

The carved bird had started as a romantic gesture back in the days when Harry was a cabinet maker and before murderers became his concern. Life seemed much simpler then. He'd made a robin for his then girlfriend. It was the obvious choice: her given name was Robin, after all. Harry had always loved that, but she had hated it. It was something she confessed for the first time as a reaction to Harry proudly revealing his painstakingly carved tribute. She made her admission and then instantly covered her mouth in horror. There was a pause that wasn't long enough to become awkward and then there was laughter. Harry laughed so hard it had started to hurt and the smile that was left had lasted every one of their thirty-odd years together. The wooden robin had always stayed with them, spending those years in the living rooms of four different houses, watching their love grow, then their family. Three summers before, it had finally moved outside, where it had taken up his wife's favourite spot when she no longer could.

'How was your day, Robin?' He smiled broadly. He had just popped in on his way back to the office. He had paperwork to do, a missing girl to find and a puzzle to solve. But that could all wait. The sun was warm on his face and the flowers drenched his senses with their colour and fragrance. On a day like this, his wife would have been in her element. She was always happiest when the sun was up and her garden was in full colour. Which meant that he was too.

Chapter 31

Maddie slept terribly. Her mind was restless. Harry hadn't come back to her and the conversations she'd had with her new chief inspector and her old superintendent were both on a permanent loop in her mind. And her room was stifling.

When she finally gave up and parted the curtains, the day's first light was weak. She got washed and dressed in time to be hanging by the door to the restaurant for breakfast.

'Early start?' An Asian woman greeted her as she opened up the double doors through to the restaurant and Maddie managed a weak smile. She ate on her own. A few others drifted in but she barely raised her eyes, concentrating instead on the strong coffee that was refilled twice.

She got to the police station for 7 a.m. She considered that this might mean she could knock off earlier, too, but then pondered what an early finish actually meant: a walk back to the hotel in time to catch some awful afternoon television and then waiting for it to be late enough to go to dinner or maybe run a bath. When she got involved in undercover policing she always knew that her social life would suffer — her life in general. She was warned that it would be lonely at times but it had never really bothered her. She couldn't recall wishing that she had taken a 'normal' nine-to-five job where people knew what she did and where it was safe to have friends and family around her. Now she was in that position she had never felt more alone.

She made it to her desk. The office was empty. A tired-looking DC nodded at her when she walked in, as he made his way out. Maddie guessed that he had been the night duty cover for CID — the creases in his shirt suggested it might have been slept in. She hesitated at her screen. There was nothing to wake it up for, save for some irrelevant dribble about missing schoolchildren. She stood back up. Maybe Harry was already in.

He was. He stood at a cupboard-sized photocopier as she walked out onto the floor.

'I thought you might be in,' she said.

He turned to her. 'I didn't think you would be.'

'When you do a job as important as mine you've got to get an early start you see.'

'You couldn't sleep then?' He scooped up some paper and walked back to his desk.

'No. I was lying in bed waiting for an excuse to get up.'

'And this place was the only excuse you could think of?'

'Sad, isn't it? And what about you? You couldn't stay away?'

'I got a call. I came in to follow up on a sighting.'

'What?'

'Of your missing girl. Someone sent me a report from overnight. Patrols attended a noise complaint at about 3 a.m. They broke up a party of drinkers in a flat. According to the list of people given, Lorraine Humphries was one of them.'

'You don't seem very happy about it. I assume she wasn't there?'

'No.'

'So she'd left. Did they talk to her? Where was it?'

Harry huffed, his frustration obvious so she fell silent.

'I was late. I got the call at 5 a.m. and got to the address for half past. It wasn't her. It was some other girl lying there in her own vomit.'

Harry was pushing buttons on the photocopier. He was losing his patience. He stepped back and kicked out at it. Maddie could see the screen flashing to indicate a 'jam.'

'So what now?'

'My team are still going through the standard checks. Wait and see what comes of them.'

'Wait and see? You seem in a bit too much of a rush for someone who is going back to *wait and see*.'

'Lorraine Humphries isn't the only case in the world!' Harry snapped. 'This morning has been a waste of time so far. I intend on making sure the rest of the day is a little more productive.'

'And that wasn't my fault,' Maddie bit back.

'I know.' Harry seemed to back down a little. 'That officer at 3 a.m., he should be waking her up and doing his job properly. You can't just start naming people as being there without checking. I'm upset with him, not with you.'

'No offence taken.'

Harry stopped to lean on the photocopier, his head bowed. 'I spoke to BTP late yesterday, too. They've got CCTV of Jonathan Lee heading to London on a Southeastern train. They've also got him changing to another train and continuing his journey up north.' Harry seemed exhausted, every part of him.

'So he was telling the truth.'

'We got CCTV from a couple of shops, too, and from the council that shows him in Northampton town centre at around the same time as Ron Beasle was being dragged under a truck. So, yeah, he was telling the truth.'

'Okay. So suddenly I see why you're upset.'

'I'm not upset! I'm behind. I need to start again. I want to go out and see April Leonard. I've only just got address details for her now. Maybe she'll know something that will take me somewhere.'

'April Leonard? Is she known to us?'

'No. McCall's are suddenly being very helpful. They provided the address for her. They also insist that they aren't officially in contact with her. They assure me there's a box of paperwork to pick up too. I've got someone out there for opening time.'

'Okay. What do you think the chances are of me accompanying you to see April?'

He turned to look at her. 'Very small. I'd take you out, but I know the guv'nor would get the hump. Trust me, it's not worth you making an enemy of him at this stage. You need to get to where I am.'

'And where's that?'

'Where he knows that it's not worth making an enemy of *me*.'

'I think I'm a long way from that. He would have to respect me for a start.'

Harry sighed. 'Look, he's just a little old-school.'

'What does that mean? Is it a sexism thing?'

'I don't think so. You need to prove yourself a little bit. He's like that with everyone. Especially when you're an unknown quantity. If I were you, I would play his game for a while. Make sure he knows that you're nobody's fool. He'll see that pretty quick and then you can have a conversation about working somewhere that suits you better.'

Maddie considered that Harry was being supportive in his own way. 'Thanks,' she said.

'Don't thank me. I'm not the one who has to do it. When I see him I'll tell him again that I could use you with what we've got going on. He agreed with me the last time but he's got a bee in his bonnet about something. I don't know why he took you straight back off it.'

'I don't know either. Can you remind him that he doesn't want you as an enemy when you tell him?'

'I'll think about it.'

'And you do need me. Both these jobs have become a lot more difficult.'

Harry took his time to reply. 'These investigations are never easy. Where would be the fun in that?' His face flickered a smile.

Maddie snorted a laugh. 'Harry Blaker having *fun*. I'm not sure I know what that looks like.'

'Not sure I do either.' He turned away immediately and Maddie thought she detected a little melancholy in his voice.

She watched him walk back to his desk.

Chapter 32

April Leonard's address was a smart-looking, whitewashed cottage, with a tightly thatched roof that seemed to droop over at the corners. The windows were criss-crossed with lead inserts. The front door was a solid piece of wood with a shiny brass handle in the middle. The hanging baskets on either side of it were bright with colour. They both dripped onto the block paving underneath. Despite it being early evening the heat was still oppressive. They must only just have been watered. Harry tapped on the door and it opened almost straight away.

He hadn't been able to tell April Leonard he was coming. He only had an address for her. She looked at him questioningly. She was a slim woman. She wore long, black shorts and a white vest top that was spotted with moisture. She had marigold gloves on both hands and pulled at the fingers as Harry spoke.

'Mrs Leonard?'

'Can I help?'

'I'm Detective Inspector Harry Blaker. I work for Major Crime and I'm investigating the murder of Ron Beasle. May I have a few minutes of your time?'

'Oh!' Her eyebrows lifted. She backed into her home. She seemed unsure which way to turn before moving off to the right. 'You'd better come in.'

Harry followed her into the kitchen. The gloves were discarded on a worktop. She bit down on her bottom lip and waited for Harry to talk.

'You know Ron Beasle, is that right?'

'Well. Yes. I know him very well. Or I knew him at least. Murder you said? I heard it was some awful accident.'

'That may yet be the case, Mrs Leonard, but I like to be sure about these things — as you can imagine. There are some parts of this that don't seem quite right to me.'

'Oh, I see. Well, no . . . you have to be sure. I'm not clear on how I can help though.'

'Just a few questions. Ron's wife seemed to think that he was looking out for a piece of land that belongs to you. Somewhere between Dover and Deal, is that right?'

'Oh, yes. We used to live there. Unfortunately we had some problems with the house. Major problems. We were there twenty years. The house has been there hundreds and we suddenly started getting cracks — small at first, then more substantial. We got someone out and we were told that the place was suffering from subsidence. One of the barns, too. They reckoned it was all part of the same thing. I don't really understand it. Can you imagine? Twenty years in a house — our home — and you're being forced out to let it crumble to the ground.'

'Subsidence?'

'Yes. The land is giving out underneath it. I don't understand it all too well — I mean I'd never heard of it at the time. I guess I know a little more about it now. It's the chalk cliffs apparently. There's always a small chance that you can get problems. The water can erode them and the land basically washes away from under you.'

'Ah, that certainly makes a little more sense.'

'Makes sense?'

'Sorry. We drove across the land — just to get a feel for it — and we saw that the house was boarded up and the barns looked as if they had been used until recently. My colleague and I both commented on how beautiful it is down there. We couldn't see why anyone would choose to move away.'

'No, quite. It is beautiful indeed. I can assure you we would never have considered it. That was our forever home. They did a survey of some sort and the results were not good. There are gullies and hollows threatening most of the buildings. It will get worse, too, we're told.'

'Sounds expensive.'

'Not financially viable, the insurance company said. There are simply no guarantees it can be fixed. I still don't fully understand it.'

'But you have some people interested in buying it to renovate it? They must know about the problem.'

'We're in talks at the moment and they know as much as we do. I think they plan on converting the barns up there. Two are quite old themselves — the smaller of them is just as old as the main house. One of the newer barns has been condemned too. It's the worst. We actually had a sink hole appear behind it. But there is still at least one that's been largely unaffected. It would seem it's on much firmer land. We considered doing it ourselves, but I just wanted to move away. I love that house. The last thing I wanted to do was stare out of my window every day and watch it fall down. And you never could be sure if and when that might happen . . . that's what we were told.'

'I guess not. Have your insurance people made an offer?'

'Yes. But it's based on the value of the house only. The building companies make offers based on the potential of all the buildings and a number of other factors. The difference is not even comparable.'

'They must see something your insurance company can't?'

'They're proposing to knock it down, I think. They'll convert the barns and there's an old cottage at one of the entrances, too, that can be renovated. The roof fell in on that a long time ago. We had visions for developing that, too, at one time, but you get old, don't you? There just wasn't the need. Maybe if Jim's health had been better. The big barns are good. There's another, smaller barn near to the southern entrance, but the roof has fallen in on that too. It's just a shelter for the rats, really. Once Jim's health failed and it meant that he couldn't use the land anymore, well, that's when we started looking at other options. We didn't have the money to be doing what's necessary. We bought this place outright and we figured we could happily retire on what came from the sale of the land.'

'And do you know who you are selling it to yet?'

'Still nothing certain. Jim tried to get something definite done. It was stressing him out. I sometimes wonder if it didn't speed up his . . . problems. Stress can do that, can't it?'

'It never helps. Are you aware of a company called McCall's?'

'Yes, of course. They're one of the firms that we've been talking to. I think they're the only one left in the frame, actually. The subsidence issues seem to have scared everyone else off.'

'But not McCall's?'

'It would seem not.'

'Have you had any contact with them?'

'Yes. They still seem keen. I hadn't had any contact initially, but when Jim died . . . Well, I had to pick it all up.'

'Did you approach them?'

'No. They were already talking to Jim. When he died they approached me. Pretty soon after as well. Jim wasn't even in the ground yet. I remember telling him that.'

'Him? Who was he?'

'Oh . . . I forget his name. There were two of them actually. Two different men.' Mrs Leonard tutted. She turned into the kitchen and pulled open a top drawer that was stuffed with paperwork. She pulled some out, put it on the side and continued her search.

'Two?'

'Yes. I had a phone call from one of them. He told me his name but I didn't write it down. It was the man that Jim had been dealing with and, bless him, he didn't know. When I told him, he was horrified that he had called so soon after Jim had gone. He couldn't have apologised more. It wasn't his fault — I told him that. I said I would call him back, a bit later, you know. He said to take my time, that it was nothing that couldn't wait. Then a different fella turned up at my door just a few days later. He said he knew all about Jim and that he was sorry, but it was obvious he was there to talk about the sale. I told him I wasn't ready. He was very insistent on giving me his card, on making sure it was him I called when I was ready. It's in here somewhere!' She continued to ferret until she called out in triumph. 'Ah!' She held a business card out. Harry took it and studied it: *Ryan Clarke — Acquisitions Surveyor*.

'Ryan Clarke?'

'That's it. He was the pushy one. I have a number for the other fella on my phone. That was the number I was going to call when I was ready, to be honest. I know how these things work. I know they all earn commission when they get sales. I've got no problem with them earning a bit, it's how the world works, but I'd rather the first fella got it. He'd done all the work with Jim and he was considerate with me.'

'Have you got his number to hand?'

'Eh, yes, of course.' Her phone was plugged in on the kitchen bench. She picked it up and turned the screen to face Harry. He wrote the details down.

'So you will be getting back in touch with them soon to get the deal done?'

'Yes. It was all systems go at first, but this sinkhole problem has scared them off one by one. I wouldn't buy a place up there now, would you?'

'No. I don't think I would.'

'I feel lucky anyone's interested at all. The insurance company's offer isn't really enough. It's time-limited, too, otherwise I'd need to go back through the rigmarole of filling out the claim details again. I can't work anymore and we were supposed to be sorted for our retirement years. You work all your life to make sure and then something like this happens. I really should get back on to McCall's to be honest — get this deal done while the going's good. I just haven't had the motivation. Me and Jim, we built our life on that land. I suppose a part of me thinks that when it goes, that's the last of what we had. Yes, I know. . . I'm a silly old bird!'

'Not at all. Makes sense to me. But I'm sure Jim would want you to be comfortable — financially, I mean. I reckon he would have wanted you to finish the deal.'

'Oh, yes — one hundred percent. It was a real bind on him towards the end. He wanted it all finished for that reason, but McCall's were dragging their heels. Ironic really. Now they're chasing me and fighting among themselves to get it done.'

Harry reached into his pocket and put his card down gently on the bench. 'This is my number, Mrs Leonard. I'm investigating what happened with Ron so I will be the man to phone if you think of anything significant. And don't hesitate — even if it seems silly. Give me a call.'

'Okay, thanks.'

'And if McCall's bother you, if this Ryan Clarke fella turns up again and you don't want him here, you let me know. I've met him actually. I feel like I could go and have a quiet little chat with him. Maybe his behaviour might change.'

'Thank you.'

They said their farewells. Mrs Leonard stayed leaning against the surround of her open front door as he moved off. Harry had missed a call from Maddie. He felt too tired for a conversation but he could sense that Maddie was starting to get sensitive about perceptions, that if he didn't return her call she might take it personally. He pressed to call her back and the phone rang through the speakers.

Maddie was quick to pick up. 'How did it go?'

'What?'

'You went to see Mrs Leonard.'

'Right. Just coming away.'

'So, what then? How did it go?'

'I didn't realise I was reporting back to you.'

'Really? I thought that would be obvious by now.'

Harry allowed himself a smile before he replied. 'You're tenacious, Maddie, I have to give you that. She's suffering. She's still grieving for her husband and trying to sort her life out at the same time.'

'I'm sure she is. Did she tell you anything useful?'

'She told me that McCall's have been bothering her about the land. That upsets me a little.'

'I get the impression people shouldn't upset you.'

'People shouldn't upset decent people who haven't long lost their husbands. Not when it's about money.'

'You tell her that?'

'I did. She got a call from our friend the fleet manager at McCall's. Seems he's a little more bothered about bringing in the projects than he led us to believe.'

'The money has to be good. If you get the right plot, I mean.'

'Well, yes. But this plot isn't as straightforward as it looks. There's subsidence up there. That's why it was abandoned. The house is basically condemned. It can happen on chalk apparently.'

'That makes more sense. I guess a building company is best placed to sort that out. They must still stand to make good money out of it.'

'You'd think so or they wouldn't be interested at all. She did say that everyone else had backed off. Maybe McCall's have more experience dealing with subsidence. I think I'll go and ask Ryan Clarke how it all works. He can explain to me how they can turn a profit. After he's explained his own actions towards Mrs Leonard.'

'Are you going now?'

'I figured I would. I have a box of employee details on my desk. His address should be in there. I was hoping he might be in on a Friday night so I could go ruin it for him.'

'You want some company?'

'No, Maddie. It's late.'

'You think I want to go back to my hotel? And I mean, ever again.'

'You don't like hotels?'

'Never have. I got to spend a lot of time in them in my previous job. You get to see what they're used for.'

'I bet you did. I'm heading back to the station now to pick up the details. I won't stop you coming out. I can't be bothered trying to talk you out of it anymore.'

'Very wise. I'll get the details. It's Ryan Clarke, right?'

'It is.'

'How far out are you?'

'I'm still sat outside the Leonards' place. I'm going to be twenty minutes.'

'Sat outside? Are you making sure she gets to sleep okay?'

'Don't forget yourself, Maddie. No, and I'm sure she won't be getting to sleep for a long time yet. You earn your retirement together. They should be planning the rest of their lives.'

'That genuinely bothers you, doesn't it? Harry Blaker — the caring detective. I didn't see that coming.'

'Because I'm a miserable old bastard?'

'Yes.'

Harry couldn't help but smile again. But as he pressed to end the call, his attention was drawn to Mrs Leonard's house. The sun had now dipped behind it and soon it would be dark. What might she be doing right now? It was a good few hours from when she might go to bed. Three years on from losing his wife, this was still the time of day he hated the most.

Chapter 33

Maddie narrowed her eyes to the lights of the Discovery as they dragged across the frontage of the police station, engulfing her for a brief moment. She walked over and climbed up into the passenger seat with a bundle of papers.

'Have you seen the amount of paperwork up there? There must be hundreds of people with access to that building and to those car keys!'

'It was never going to be a small number.' Harry was deadpan.

'McCall's employees are just the beginning. You've got suppliers, agency staff, temps, apprentices — even college kids. The list goes on.'

'We need to be smart. We'll factor in some criteria for narrowing the list down.'

'You mean like running them for criminal records?'

'It's a start.'

'Ryan Clarke . . . I ran him through PNC while I was waiting. He has three convictions for violence and a lot more arrests. The three convictions were for fighting on nights out. The arrests that came to nothing were all DV assaults.'

'She never supported?' Harry said.

'No. And there wasn't just one *she*. There are twenty or more reports so I only skimmed them, but I counted at least four different women. None of them ever went through with it.'

'We see a lot of murders between partners. Nine times out of ten the offender has been nicked before but released with no further action because the other half didn't support.'

'This guy must be scary. Scary enough that they don't think it's worth it.'

'Let's go find out, shall we?'

The address was after another twenty-minute drive towards the coast and in a village on the outskirts of Langthorne called Hawkinge. The first thing Maddie noticed when they drove through it was the sheer rate of expansion that must have gone on.

'It's like someone built a brand-new town!' she said, as street after street of similar looking, new-build houses passed her window. When they stopped, Maddie looked out at three big blocks of flats with the same white façades and stainless steel entrance doors. They were arranged in a sort of clumsy circle around a small green area.

Harry stepped out and headed towards the middle block. 'What number did you say?'

'Flat 7, Marsh House.' She took a second to assess: the streets were empty of people and cars. Harry was already at the communal door and he tugged it open.

'Trade button works,' he said. Maddie followed him in.

Flat 7 was up two flights of steps. The floor was carpeted but in a material that felt thin and cheap. Every step had a metal strip running along it — most of them were loose and they clanged with every footfall. There would be no sneaking up to the door. Harry didn't seem bothered by that. He strode right up close and hammered it with his fist. Maddie stayed back and waited. There was a light visible through the frosted panes either side of the door but it was weak, like it might be from a distant room. A minute passed, maybe more. Harry beat the door again. This time he didn't stop; he fell into a rhythm and stuck to it. Another minute passed before the door fell open.

'Alright, alright! Jesus! What the hell are you beating my door down for! I've got neighbours here.'

'Not nice is it, Ryan? Being harassed at home. We need to talk.' Harry stepped in far enough that the door couldn't be closed. The light was still weak but there was enough from the stairwell to positively ID Ryan Clarke. He was in just a navy blue robe. His hair was slick and damp and his skin flushed red. Maddie guessed they had disturbed him from a bath.

'I don't have the time to be talking to you. You'll have to come see me during work time. This is my time now and I've got plans.'

'I don't think you understand how the police work, Ryan. This isn't a work enquiry — this is about you.'

'Are you arresting me?'

'Are you letting me in?'

Clarke still held his ground. A front door opened elsewhere, possibly the level above. There were no footfalls or sounds of it closing again; they were attracting attention. He stepped back.

'Five minutes. But I ain't happy.'

'That makes two of us.' Harry moved into the flat and Maddie followed him in. They walked through the low light of the hallway to a much brighter living room.

Clarke fell into a sofa but Harry remained standing and positioned himself so that he was standing over him. Maddie leaned against the back of a table. The room looked like it ran the full width of the flat and there was a kitchen area down the other end. Clarke looked uncomfortable. He stood back up and moved backwards to lean against the window. He put his hands behind his back and his feet shoulder-width apart. He looked every bit a man who was bracing himself for an attack. Maddie got the impression that their visit was not entirely unexpected.

'The Leonards. Tell me about your business with them,' Harry growled.

'The Leonards?'

'Don't act dumb. You were the one talking about having plans tonight. I'm not here to waste anyone's time. I've spoken to the wife so I know you have too. So tell me about that.'

Ryan sniffed. His eyes moved off Harry to Maddie and then to the floor. 'What do you want to know?'

'Tell me what you know.'

'I know they have a place. They have some land. I know that the company are at the table to acquire it for development.'

'The company?'

'McCall's.'

'I know what company you work for, Ryan. I meant, are the company in talks or are *you*?'

'They're the same thing.'

'Anyone else at this table?' Harry spat his words.

'That's not my concern.'

'What did I say about wasting time? Talk straight or I will arrest you and you will spend at least the night in a custody cell. I will not play your game of ask-the-right-question.'

'I bet you're great at parties. You don't take a joke well, do you?'

'Not when I'm *fucking* APPALLED!' Maddie jumped just as much as Clarke at Harry's sudden outburst.

'Jesus, man. Calm yourself, yeah? I was just trying to lighten it all up a bit in here.' He chuckled but it was clearly his nerves talking. Harry didn't move his gaze away or say a word. Maddie didn't think she had ever met anyone who used silence even half as well. 'Look, I get why you're upset. I called her up not long after her old man . . . well, I knew what happened, yeah, and I thought that she wouldn't want the hassle. Not anymore. I knew she would just want that place gone. I thought I could help her out.'

'How much?'

'How much what?'

'How much did you stand to make from *helping her out*?'

'It wasn't about that!'

'How MUCH?'

Clarke flinched again. 'Look, it's a job. I was the only one taken on full time. They sold it to me like I was the lucky one. But I can't make anywhere near what the others do and I've been working with the firm longer than all of them put tog—'

'So you steal their leads?'

'No!'

'This wasn't your deal. One of your colleagues was negotiating that sale. I know that.'

Clarke moved towards the kitchen. Harry held his ground and Clarke had to walk around him. In the kitchen, he took a glass from a cupboard, filled it with water and turned around to lean by the sink. He near drained the glass as they waited.

'Look, I do what I'm told. I had no interest in Leonard's Farm, okay? When I was in the game full-time, I had a reputation for picking out the right places — the easy switch.'

'Easy switch?'

'Yeah, you know, it's all a game. A piece of land is just the start. There's planning permission, access, local residents, pressure groups — the whole thing is a bit of a minefield. But if you know what you're doing you can pick out the plots that will go easy. I used to do my homework, make sure the land was owned clean to start with — no disputes. Then I'd run it past a few contacts on the council and building regs side, slip them a sweetener for their trouble. I had contacts at the auction houses tipping me off and all sorts. Sometimes I could walk onto a plot for the first time with a deal already done. I wouldn't touch Leonard's Farm. That place has grief written all over it. You know there's subsidence there, right? It's not viable.'

'You're not making any sense now, Ryan. You need to start making more sense.'

'I get tasked. That's what this was. I get tasked to go and get a particular plot of land, or at least to do what I can. It's always a problem. The plots I get tasked with are never without grief. Most of the time I'll be the only one at the negotiating table.'

'Tasked?'

'The McCalls. They don't get on. I can only think that he's trying to damage the business out of spite.'

'He? Who's he?'

'Who's he? You've met the brothers, right?'

'The brothers?'

'The McCall brothers?'

'James McCall we've met. He never mentioned a brother.'

'Of course he didn't!' Clarke chuckled. He refilled his glass. He tightened his robe and took another deep breath. 'Jim McCall is a good businessman. He seems to make good choices at least. He started McCall's around twenty years ago. He was a sole trader and a good builder. He had good contacts doing the bits he wasn't able to, like you need when you're a small outfit. He got a good reputation and got busier — the usual story. Then he took a chance. He bought some land without any permissions or access. He saw the potential. He put in a few applications with the council and was rebutted. He kept working and almost forgot about it, but the housing crisis has changed the way councils work. A couple of changes happened at the top and he was able to get the permission he needed to build a small clump of houses just outside of Langthorne. Not too far from here. The only stipulation was that they had to be *high-end*. They were in a wealthy area and on the edge of an area of outstanding natural beauty, so they wanted to be sure they were getting the right people moving into them. Wealthy professionals, I suppose. Jim didn't have the money to build what they wanted. He considered selling the land along with the permission. He would still have made a nice profit for sure. But I suppose he was still a builder at heart. By that time he had a small building firm and he couldn't just give the project away. So he teamed up with Andy.'

'Andy?'

'Andy McCall. His brother. He's ex-army — although, at the time, I think he was still in. I think he got a few ranks above where he started — nothing amazing — but he was good with his money I heard. All the time he was in the army they were paying his board, his house, his food, everything. So he never really touched his earnings. He had tax reliefs as well — he was posted away a lot. He never married. Jim once told me that he's never even seen him with a woman. So all that money he was earning was just accumulating. Jim approached him with a proposition and they teamed up. The firm built the houses and Andy was put in place as a partner in the company, but very much a silent one. He had no idea about it all really. He used to come in a lot at first and I know he tried to get involved. He even went out on the tools as a sort of apprentice for a while, but it didn't last. He ended up sitting at the desk next to me out in that dusty Portakabin, giving out keys to the men doing the real work. He used to turn up a few times a week. Then it was once a week. Then I wouldn't see him. There always seemed to be some crisis going on, he was always moving house or going away for personal reasons, and when he did turn up he would often look beaten. Do you know what I mean?'

'Like beaten up?'

'No, not physically. I saw depression in my sister, God bless her soul. It had a real hold on her. It changes a person. They get, like, this black cloud round them. We used to talk about her and say, "She's got the black cloud back." I don't know, you can tell.'

'You think he was depressed?'

'No doubt. I spoke to Jim about it. He didn't disagree. I think Andy came back from the army a different bloke, but Jim didn't really talk about it much. Andy was into communication — that side of things at least.'

'So what are you saying? That this Andy tasks you?'

'Exactly that. I don't see him much at all anymore. I know him and his brother have had a couple of blowouts at work. It doesn't look good when it happens. Andy mostly stays away but then he'll suddenly come in with a site proposal. He'll generally pick my brains about it and he usually wants me to get involved. The conversations are odd. It's like he's trying to find the most difficult plots for us to do something with. He must be doing it to try and piss off his brother. There's no other reason.'

'But surely Jim just blocks his plans?'

'He did at first. Maybe that's what they argued about. Maybe now he figures that it's not worth the hassle. I don't know — I've never been there when they're speaking together. It's obvious they don't get on. Sometimes I get the story from them individually but it's never a complete story — just bits. They need to sort it out, really. It has to be hitting the company's bottom line.'

'So, Leonard's Farm . . . Andy came to you with that one?'

'Yeah. Two months ago, maybe. The usual thing . . . he comes in asking what I know. I told him. I said it was a site one of the lads had looked at but we had done some work around it and were going to pull out. The land has subsidence problems and we didn't think they were of the sort that could be resolved permanently. I told him it was total can of worms, that if we took it on we'd be looking at years of planning applications before we could even set foot on the site with purpose. That just seemed to make him want it more. I asked him if he had spoken to Jim about it and he got upset. He reminded me that he was a partner in the firm and suggested that I should value my job more. I don't think he would fire me — I'm not even sure he could — but I don't want to make an enemy out of him, you know? Not if I can help it. He's a very intense fella. I get the impression he might be the sort to hold a grudge.'

'When was the last time you went there?'

'Where?'

'Leonard's Farm.'

'I've never been there. I've been to the house where Mrs Leonard lives, but that's off-site. It's in Deal. I've never been to the site.'

'And was anyone opposing it? Giving you any trouble?'

'No — God, no! The owner's desperate to get rid of the place, there's no other houses around it to be upset. That's a rare thing. It was just this issue with the chalk voids that we would need to resolve. But I'm still not sure if that can be done at all. There's one good barn up there from the reports I've seen and there won't be enough profit in that to justify our interest — assuming anyone would actually spend money to live there when it's done.'

'And Andy . . . did he ever mention it to you again? Did he enquire about the status or ask if anything was holding it up?'

'He would check in. I'd get phone calls out of the blue asking me for updates. He was never chasing me to try and push something through. We're waiting on structural surveys and engineers, but Andy was quite happy about that. To be honest, I reckon if I told him that there was a bigger holdup he would be delighted. Like I said, he must be trying to get back at his brother and this is the only way he can.'

'Are there any other buildings or plots of land that he has an interest in?'

'Yeah, there are a few.'

'And they're all cans of worms?'

'They are. All of them.'

'I need you to get me a list of them. All of them. I want to know when they came onto your books and how long until something will be moving on each project.'

'Okay. You know I can't do anything from here?'

'I do. But you people work Saturdays, right?'

'I don't.'

'My next conversation is with Andy McCall then.' Harry glanced ostentatiously at his watch. 'And tonight. I'll be sure to tell him who sent me.'

'Alright! Shit! I swear this ain't right. I'll pop in tomorrow. Andy's asked for an update on it, too, oddly enough.'

'Do you have a number for him?'

'I don't. I did have an old one but he changes his number every few weeks. I swear it. He's an odd bloke.'

'When did you see him last?'

Clarke bit down on his lip. His answers had been quick up to this point. Harry shuffled his position but he made sure Clarke was the next person to talk.

'The same day I saw you, okay? I'd seen him just before. We talked about the truck that had gone missing. He got proper angry about it — like I've never seen him before. It was like it was my fault! He told me I needed to look after the trucks better. He reminded me that I was the fleet manager and said that I could start by cleaning them. I thought he was taking the piss — that's not part of my job. But he just stared at me. It was weird. So I took the keys that were up there and took one of them out to the wash bay. I just wanted to be out of there to be honest. When I got back he was sitting in the office until I walked down to get you. He was gone by the time I got back.'

'I remember talking to you about the car being clean,' Maddie interjected. 'You never mentioned Andy having access to those trucks.'

'I won't see him for weeks then he'll just turn up. It's not like it's a regular thing. I get the impression he's not a big fan of the police either. I didn't want to be the one that mentioned him driving them. I knew you'd want to speak to him. I guessed you would get his name from elsewhere and I wouldn't need to. I haven't seen him or heard from him since.'

Harry sniffed. 'Brave to the last. So he takes the trucks out . . . do you know what for?'

'He does what he likes. You need to understand that. I'm not his keeper. The trucks are up there on the board. I don't know why he would though. He can use any of the fleet and we've got some much nicer metal on the books.'

'I see . . .' Harry mused. Then he suddenly turned to Maddie. 'Anything you need to know?' Maddie was caught out by a question suddenly directed at her. She shook her head.

'We might need to know a bit more after you send the stuff through. Give me your number in case. Will you be here?'

'No plans for tomorrow. I expect I'll be here in the afternoon. But call me, yeah? You got no reason to come here.'

'We'll see about that,' Harry said. 'One thing I'm good at, Ryan, is inventing reasons. And I don't always knock.'

Harry exited the flat quickly and Maddie had to break into a jog to keep up. The car was already running when she clambered into her seat.

'What did you think?' Maddie said.

'I don't like him but I think most of what he was saying was true.' Harry had his phone out. The screen was lit. 'That box of employee information on my desk . . . I don't suppose you noticed if Andy McCall was in there, did you?'

'No, I only went through it until I found the details for Ryan Clarke. I didn't check it thoroughly. If I was to have a wager though, I don't reckon he will be.'

'I was thinking the same. I can't think who's on late turn back in the office. I could start them looking.'

'It'll probably take someone all night to go through that lot.'

'I was hoping for much quicker so I could go and see him.'

'Tonight?'

'No time like the present. I'll drop you back.'

'I wasn't complaining! From what our man said in there, though, I'm a lot less sure what motivation a McCall's employee could possibly have to run down Ron Beasle. Our theory was that Ron was getting in the way of the sale going through, now we're being told that McCall's wanted it delayed for as long as possible.'

'Well, one half of McCall's did.'

'And one half didn't. I still don't see the link to Ron being run down.'

'I don't either. It's just seems like the next logical step, to go and see this Andy. I wanted to take it before Clarke in there had the chance to speak to him. We've probably already lost that opportunity to be honest.'

'What's your thinking with getting the list of sites Andy has tasked Clarke with?'

'I'm not sure. It's just odd behaviour. It stands out. I want to understand why. I get the point about upsetting the brother but I can see easier ways of doing that. It's another reason to speak to Andy, too — to see if he tells us the same.'

'Okay. I'm happy to stay on. Let's go and see what we've got on him for a start. It sounds like he moves around a bit. We might not have an address.'

'We do have an address for Jim McCall. I want to speak to him again too, especially if his brother isn't in that box file — I'll want to know why not.' Harry gestured at his phone. 'And I've missed a call from the boss. I just need to call him back.'

'No problem. You want me to give you lovebirds a bit of privacy!?' Maddie smirked.

'Very funny. We need to get on our way.'

The speakers sounded with a dialling tone as the car moved off.

'Harry!' Julian Lowe's voice cut in on the second ring. 'I needed to talk to you an hour ago!'

'Sorry, boss, I've been out at—'

'Don't worry. Look, I can't really speak. I'm on the way to pick up the daughter. I'm on taxi duty tonight. I need a free week next week. I've got a load of meetings with some fella who has designs on becoming the next Police Commissioner. It's something of a favour. He's a bit of a twat but an old associate I gave my word to. I need you to attend some meetings for me. I have a diary full of the damned things, most of them are a waste of everyone's time.'

'And now mine,' Harry said.

'Yes, and now yours. Welcome to the club. I would swap if I could rather than spending time with a half-wit looking to make a fast impression. Speaking of which, I also need to look at what can be done with our newest addition.'

'New addition?' Harry said. Maddie looked over. She knew immediately who he meant, though Harry seemed oblivious.

'Yes, the problem that Manchester kindly sent us . . . DS Ives. I've had contact from someone at one of the schools — just about the only place she's actually been yet and already I've been given some feedback that concerns me. She needs to understand how we work down here and I think I might need to move her somewhere a little more suitable. I just don't know where that is yet. Somewhere dark and insignificant is my plan.'

The chief inspector was speaking quickly. Harry wouldn't have had a chance to chip in to stop him even if he had wanted to. Not that he seemed overly keen to try. Now he had to reply. He stayed looking forward.

'Okay . . . we spoke about Major Crime. Like I said, we're a skipper down. We have been for a while. I think she could do a job for us in—'

'Absolutely not! No way am I putting her anywhere near the high-profile stuff! If she's already attracting complaints from a welfare officer at a local school, imagine what could happen if I put her in front of someone who actually mattered! No, she's a long way off Major Crime. She did seem to think that she was coming down here to walk into whatever role she wanted but I'm starting to make things clear. I was thinking more of project-related work, something that keeps her in the damned building until she can understand the culture down here. We're not the biggest force. That means we have to use and respect our partners. She'll learn, Harry, one way or another. Look, I've got to go. I'll have Sandra send through some of the meetings. If there's anything you really can't make then let me know but I would really appreciate you sitting in for me. And forget about Maddie Ives, she's my problem to reallocate. I'm sorry I got you involved in that.'

The line was cut. Maddie was looking out the window. She could feel her cheeks burning. Harry waited a short time before he spoke.

'I'll talk to him.'

'Don't,' Maddie said. It was all she could manage.

'I'll drop you back. We'll call it a night. There's no need to do anything more today.'

Maddie kept staring out of the window.

Chapter 34

They made it back to the yard at Canterbury police station.

'What are you up to now?' Maddie said. Her voice had a rough edge to it, a combination of the tension in her body and not speaking for a while.

'I've got a few bits of paperwork before I can call it a day. Unless we have a definite address for this Andy I think that can wait. If a call was going in, it has already. You should get yourself home, get some rest and make the most of your weekend.'

'I should, yeah.' Maddie did nothing to hide the sarcasm in her voice. The engine fell silent.

'Monday is a new week, Maddie.'

'It is. A worse one, it would seem.'

'Things will get better.'

'I must have missed that bit.'

Harry still held the steering wheel. He was just an outline in the poor light. Maddie could tell he was searching for the right words. She appreciated that he was trying. She let him off the hook. 'Look, I'll make you a coffee. I know I'm not much good for anything else. I was going to stay for one. At least then I could kid myself that I had a drink with *someone* this Friday night.'

'A coffee at work . . . that counts, does it?'

'No, it probably doesn't. But maybe I can pick out a dark enough shadow for me to occupy come Monday. The alternative is going back to the hotel for a proper drink on my own. That worries me a little bit.'

'Well, if it becomes a problem, at least you know how the meetings work!'

Maddie smiled despite everything. 'True.'

Harry had turned towards her, his eyes stood out against the gloom. 'You really do hate that hotel, don't you?'

'It's hotel living I hate. It never used to matter when I loved the job. I need to get my chin up off the floor is all. I can start again.'

'Not tonight, though,' Harry said.

'Not tonight. Tonight I'm on the hard stuff. Black coffee for you, isn't it?'

'Fine then. But just the one.'

They walked through the station and Harry continued past his desk and into the incident room at the back of the Major Crime office. There was a kitchenette in the corner and a fridge for milk. The table in the middle had four large cardboard boxes all marked *Op Wooden*. On the wall were pictures of what Maddie reckoned was Harry's hit-and-run investigation. A couple of them were quite grim. She curled her lips at a close-up of the back of a man's head. It looked flatter and the front seemed to be mingled with the mud-covered bank.

'Ron Beasle?' she said.

'It was.'

'That's no way for him to end up is it?'

'It's not.'

Maddie took a sideways step. There were photos that took in more of the area surrounding where Ron was lying.

'I thought you said he didn't brake?'

'Who?'

'Your hit-and-run killer. I take it these skid marks are from the incident?'

'That's the theory.'

'So he did brake?'

'Only after. They're ten metres further on.'

'Ten metres? And you're sure they're from the same incident?'

'Well, we can't be sure. They were fresh enough at the time for traffic to include them in the report.'

'So what . . . our driver hits Ron and doesn't realise until he sees something kick out from under the car in his rear-view mirror, then he panics and pulls up?'

'The crash team said you couldn't not know. Even if the driver was looking away when the truck hit, he would've felt the impact.'

'So what's your theory?'

Harry shrugged. 'He hit Ron because he meant to. He dragged him as far as he would go and when he fell out the bottom he got a sudden need to check he had done the job right. He stood on the brakes and made sure Ron was dead.'

'That would explain the marks.'

'It would.'

'I can see why you're thinking murder.'

'I've never thought anything else.'

'We just can't explain the reason someone would want Ron Beasle dead, can we?' Maddie said.

'Not yet. And therein lies the key to finding who it was that stood over him and watched him die.'

'The life of a Major Crime guv'nor, hey? You get to deal with people at their worst.'

'It keeps us in a job.'

'*Us?* I got spotty kids who can't be arsed to go to school keeping me in a job. I'm hardly changing the world here, am I?' Maddie pulled herself away from the pictures.

She found some mugs on the draining board and busied herself with making the drinks.

'Are you always this hard on yourself?'

Maddie stopped what she was doing. Harry must have been using another silence on her. She'd missed it this time.

'What do you mean?'

'You've been down here, what? A week? They may have brought you down here to look after spotty kids or whatever but you're looking for a girl in trouble, sticking your nose into a murder investigation and generally upsetting senior management. All that in five working days! You'll be where you should be soon enough, trust me on that. People like you get to where they should be and people like DCI Lowe don't want the hassle. He'll relent and then you get to show him he was wrong all along. And you will. I've never seen someone so driven.'

Maddie sighed. 'Thanks. I've done all that though.' She dropped a drink onto the table in front of Harry. He picked it up and stood up at the same time. He flashed angry.

'So you keep saying! Maybe it's time to forget about who you were, what you did, what you think of yourself even. You've turned up with this attitude that you've got nothing to prove — well, maybe you have. No one knows who you are down here and quite frankly no one cares. You're very capable of showing people what you're worth so just get on with it.' Harry walked to the door. Maddie watched him until he turned at the door and walked out of sight. She was stunned into silence.

She slumped into a seat at the table. She nursed her coffee. Her eyes lifted to the boxes in front of her. She pulled the lid off the closest one. She checked Harry was out of sight. She stood back up to be able to see inside — her curiosity getting the better of her. Inside were folders stacked neatly beside one another. Their spines were facing up and they were variously labelled *Case Notes, Scenes, Third-*

Party Material, Unused, Witness Statements — it went on. She pulled out the folder marked *Scenes*. She sat back down with it and it fell open around the middle. There was a glossy photograph of a murder scene. The body was still in situ. It was a woman's body. She was turned on her side but face down, the photo was from the head down but too far away to make out many details. Her hip looked unnaturally prominent as it pointed up towards the sky. She was lying on a patch of crumbling concrete. Blocks of the stone looked to have come loose and were lying all around her — weeds, too. They pushed through the cracks at varying lengths. In the background was a smudge of a building. It was out of focus but it looked industrial — two different sized squares resting against each other — like a factory, perhaps.

Maddie concluded that she was looking at pictures from the Sussex murder of which she had briefly been made aware in the video conference. This would be the first girl. She remembered the second was found inside. She turned the page over. The back of the photograph had handwritten notes: *Unit 4, Dryden Estate, Dryden Road, Hastings, Sussex (CR/4).* From her knowledge of investigations she knew it to be the location where the photo had been taken and the initials of the officer exhibiting it.

There were more photos. Some captured the buildings in better focus. She had been right: it looked like a factory that had fallen into disrepair. She moved past the photos to the documentation. There were a number of legalistic items headed *Sussex County Council.* The crux of the matter seemed to be that the land was condemned as the result of some sort of pollution and there were numerous references to hazardous materials. There were figures too — they looked like costs attributed to the council clearing the site. The figures looked ridiculous — astronomical — as if someone had added extra zeros to them as a joke. She flicked through and her eyes rested on a letter to an agent.

It became clear that the land was up for sale. This document was dated 2014, almost four years earlier.

She closed the folder, went back to the box and pulled out *Third-Party Material* and flicked through it. She didn't really know what she was looking for and flicked past lists of vehicle registration numbers from fixed cameras, then a list of CCTV locations. She stopped at the printout of a webpage showing pictures streamed from a webcam. It had specifications and prices. It was being marketed as a security solution. It was designed to run from a phone app and a key feature was listed as being *ideal for remote locations*.

He liked to watch them rot!

Maddie stood up, scooped up both folders and walked out onto the floor with them behind her back. Harry was bent over his desk, his silver pen twitching under a desk lamp. The rest of the office was dark.

'Do you have that list of locations McCall's were going to send?'

'What?' Harry didn't look up. His pen didn't stop moving either.

'McCall's. They were going to send you a list of places they've registered an interest in.'

'They were.'

'Did they?'

'I saw something on my email from them. One of my jobs before I can go home was to have a look at it. That's if I ever get the chance.' His frustration was obvious as he sat back and let his pen drop with a *thwack* on the pad. Maddie ignored the dig.

'Was there a place in Hastings?'

'Hastings? No idea. Why?'

'Can you have a look?'

Harry sniffed.

'Look, Harry, just humour me, please. This could be important.'

Harry woke his screen with his mouse. It was big and bright and he squinted at it. She watched him open an email and a spreadsheet that was attached.

'You get anything more than Hastings?'

'Dryden Industrial Estate,' she said.

Harry typed. 'Dryden Industrial Estate, yeah.'

'Unit 4.'

'Unit 4,' Harry confirmed. 'So what?'

Maddie brought the folders around and laid them out on the table. She found the photo with the body in the foreground. She put it down on the desk.

'What the hell are you doing going through that, Maddie? It's all in order.'

'The killer of these women. He watched them rot, you said?' She scrabbled with the second folder. She found the page with the webcam.

'I said that, yeah.'

'Yes, you did . . .' she huffed her frustration. She stomped back to the incident room, back to photos of Ron Beasle's final resting place, pinned to the wall. She ripped down the one showing the skid marks and stomped back to Harry. She put that down on his desk too. 'Something else you said, Harry. About this hit and run. You said the killer stopped. You said he stood over him and watched him die. What if he wasn't making sure? What if he was watching because that's what he *does*?'

'Wait, you think he's the same man? Those killings are very different. In every way,' Harry said.

'Maybe not. The first victim in Sussex . . .' Maddie pushed the photo of the woman lying on her side towards him. 'McCall's are at the table to buy these grounds. There's documentation about some toxic sludge or similar on the site. It's going to cost squillions to make that site useable. I bet it will be years before it's resolved. I bet every other interested party has backed away from a deal. But not McCall's. Ron Beasle is looking after a site that's in an identical situation. What if Ron wasn't *delaying* McCall's?

What if he got in the way? Or he discovered something he shouldn't have.'

'Like someone dumping a body,' Harry said. He got to his feet and pored over the documents Maddie had laid out.

'Nothing else has made sense,' Maddie said. 'But someone linked to McCall's, who used their position to discover sites that they knew would sit empty for years on end? It's perfect if you wanted to dump a body there and watch it rot. That makes sense.'

'It does.' Harry scowled. 'Except the delay. If Ron had seen a body he would have called us straight away. He had a phone on him, we know that.'

Maddie's heart was beating so fast she felt like it might jump out of her chest. 'Maybe he was just in the way, then. Or getting too close. Maybe his death wasn't even necessary. But this fella likes it, doesn't he? He likes the killing part.'

'I think he does. And then he stops the McCall's truck he was driving to watch. Which means we think we know who, don't we?'

'Andy McCall,' Maddie said.

'Andy McCall.' Harry moved back to his computer screen. Still on his feet, he opened another document — another spreadsheet. He clicked through it. 'He's not listed on here.'

'What is that?'

'The list. It's supposed to be the complete list of employees. Anyone with access to those vehicles. It was on the same email and refers to the boxes of employee details.'

'Who sent it?'

'James McCall himself.'

'So why would he miss off his brother?'

'He needs to be asked that question. And I need to know where his brother is.' Harry stepped back from his machine and picked up his car keys.

259

'Great — let's go!' Maddie said.

Harry turned to her, hesitating.

'What?'

'The boss. You know he doesn't want you working this, Maddie. If we go out and get this fella in, it will be a lot of work for the arresting officers. You know what it's like. There'll be a forensic plan for custody, he'll probably be on constant for hours and that's before I start planning interviews, arranging searches and writing statements.'

'I'm not afraid of an all-nighter Harry, you should know that about me—'

'It's not that, Maddie!' Harry snapped. Maddie was shocked into silence. Harry continued in a softer tone. 'It would tuck you up for days if I took you out. The boss, he was clear where he wants you.'

'All the more reason to take me, though, right? If I'm tucked up in this he can't send me somewhere that doesn't matter.'

'No. He can't. And I know how he'll take that.'

'Shit Harry! You're *with* him, aren't you? You think I should just go and sit in my dark corner like a good little girl?'

'Don't be ridiculous. I'd have you working this in an instant, but we have to handle this right. I'll take uniform tonight.'

'This is my chance! This is it! When Lowe comes in on Monday and we've got a cold-blooded murder suspect who likes to watch women *decompose* he won't care that I'm in among the investigation — especially when you vouch for me, when you tell him how we got here.' Harry stared at her, using one of his silences. Maddie waited him out. He broke first with a measured reply.

'I will vouch for you, Maddie. This is how you get to where you want to be. He will know what you've done.'

'What I've *done*! I assume by that you mean I am *done*? I tell you what then, Harry . . . I'll run along now, shall I?

Back to my hotel? Let the real detectives sort this out from here?'

'That isn't wh—'

'Don't bother, Harry. Loud and clear.'

Maddie was already walking away. She cast one last look back into the incident room, her eyes flickered across the photos hanging on the wall. She snapped them away before making for the door. She didn't look back again.

Chapter 35

Lisa Simpkiss woke up confused. Something felt wrong as she sat up. Her bedroom curtains glowed weakly around the edges. She cast an eye at her alarm clock: 4:30 a.m., Saturday morning. A thump on the door! It was loud and sounded impatient, as if it was a second knock. The first must have been what had woken her.

She spun her legs to the floor and stood up. She was in a long t-shirt and knickers. Her mind filled with terrible possibilities straight away. Her mother's bedroom was next to hers and she stuck her head in. The bed sheets were pulled back — *but she wasn't in there!*

Lisa's pulse quickened. She sucked in a breath and made for the stairs. She took them two at a time and hit the hall where her socks slipped on the wooden flooring and she almost skidded into the door. She pushed the light on and tore open the long curtain that covered the frosted front door. She made out a tall figure on the other side, dressed in black and wearing a hat. The unmistakeable outline of a police officer.

She fumbled with the door locks. She had to stop and tell herself to calm down. When she tugged it open there were two police officers. They were stood on either side of her mother. Lisa finally breathed out.

'Mum!' she gasped. She leaned forward to hug her. Her mother shrugged her off. She pushed past her and walked into the lounge. Lisa watched her go. She felt angry, terrified and relieved all at the same time. She could feel tears building.

'I didn't even know she was gone!' Lisa blubbed. She turned back to the two officers. Both men looked uneasy.

'Happens all the time, ma'am. She's very confused. We were able to get the road where she lives out of her and then a milkman outside directed us to your door. I take it you've been here a while?'

'My mum . . . as long as I can remember.' Lisa held her hand over her mouth as she fought to regain her control.

'Is there anyone else here?' the officer asked. He leaned in a little, his head moving left and right.

'No. My dad . . . well, no. Look, do you want to come in for a minute? Maybe I can offer you a hot drink or something?'

'We do need to take some details if that's alright. It won't take long. Paperwork, you know. We need to make sure we're dropping your mum at the right place!'

Lisa stepped back. She knew what the officer meant: her mother had been dropped back before and on that occasion, the officer had explained that they needed to check that the environment was 'suitable.' Lisa had pressed him a little and he had admitted that they had to complete a *vulnerability assessment* or something. It was to make sure her mother wasn't at any risk. Lisa had taken it as a failing on her part, despite being assured that wasn't the point. She was feeling the same way now.

'I know how it works,' she said.

'Well, that's good. I'm PC Neals . . . this is PC Kent. I'll just take your details and we should be able to leave you to your day. Sorry for the wakeup call!'

'Not at all.' Lisa moved to the kitchen. She could hear the television coming from the living room now. Her mother must have made herself comfortable. 'Did you want tea?'

'No, thanks.' The officers spoke in unison. Lisa clicked the kettle on anyway; she knew her mother would take one.

'Is she okay?'

'She's fine. We had an ambulance crew check her over. They were just around the corner actually. She's not even cold. She's wearing pyjamas and that big old dressing gown. It's not cold out there at all.'

'Not this time,' Lisa said. 'The last time she went missing it was a freezing night. The police didn't think she could have lasted much longer.' Lisa's hands lifted to her face. The emotion was welling up again. She had slept right through it twice now. Maybe her stepdad was right: maybe she couldn't cope. Actually, he had said that she shouldn't have to, that she had enough on her plate. They'd got as far as looking at specialist places for her mum, but Lisa hadn't been able to go through with it. Maybe she should go and look again. She didn't know what she would do if her mum came to any harm when she was supposed to be the one looking after her.

'We should count our blessings, then. Do you mind if I take some details?' PC Neals took out a notebook and readied a pen. 'Can you just confirm your mum's name for me?'

'Yeah, it's Olive. Olive Simpkiss.'

'Excellent, that's what she gave.'

'And your name, please.'

'I'm Lisa Simpkiss.'

'Great. And your date of birth, Lisa?'

'Twenty-fifth of May, 1985.'

'Thank you. And this is your home address?'

'It is.'

'Okay, so Greenfield Street, Langthorne . . . What was the door number please?'

'Forty-seven.'

'And no one else lives here?'

'No. My stepdad, he used to. My real dad died. It's not been an easy ride.'

PC Neals looked up from his notebook. He had a kind face. 'It doesn't sound like it, Lisa. Does your stepdad help with her? Is he still on the scene?'

'No. When my mum . . . well, when she started getting worse, he couldn't cope. I don't blame him for that. She's a different woman. I guess this isn't what he signed up for! My mum wouldn't remarry either. She's never got over my dad really. You can't blame my stepdad for taking his opportunity!' She snorted a laugh. Her smile dropped away instantly. 'It makes him sound like a bad man, but he's the opposite. He tried for a while, but on a bad day she would call him all sorts. She lashes out and I think he took the brunt of it. It's the frustration. She's so angry a lot of the time and she doesn't even know why. She's worse at the moment. She stopped taking her medication a few days ago . . .' She petered out, suddenly aware that she was rambling.

'And what about now? Do you get the brunt?'

'Sometimes. I know what it is, though. She's angry with herself. She just takes it out on me. She doesn't lash out so much anymore, not with her fists. She's got a sharp tongue, though. I had a problem, a drink problem. I'm not proud of my past, but she never lets me forget how disappointed she is about that. The illness has taken a lot away from my mum but her tact and sympathy were the first things to go.'

'Cathy! CATHY!' Lisa bit down at her mum's shrill voice.

'Cathy's my sister. She couldn't cope either. She's moved away. She says it was for work but the timing was a little convenient. She left me to look after our mum. Most of the time she thinks I'm Cathy, and when she realises I'm not, she's gutted. Nice, eh?' Lisa smiled. Then she called out to answer, 'Yes, Mum?'

'Can I have my afternoon tea, love? I'm parched in here! I'd make it myself, but my legs feel tired.'

'Yes, Mum.'

'I'm not sure what time she thinks it is,' PC Neals shrugged. 'She was stopped about an hour ago. It was still dark, but she was talking like she was going to the shops. She even had a bag with her. I've come across it before with Alzheimer's — I assume that's what it is?'

'Alzheimer's . . . dementia — a touch of it all. Apparently it can happen. She gets a totally different idea of time to everyone else. But she's been so much better recently. We got her on these new drugs and they seemed to level her out. We even made it to the bingo the other day. She used to love it. I knew she wouldn't be able to cope but she insisted. Sure enough I was right and that seemed to really knock her. That's when she started to refuse the meds again. I just don't know what else to do from here.'

'It's not easy. There is help out there. There are places where she can go that are a little more secure. I know people hesitate sometimes before putting relatives in . . . well, places like that, but they are geared up to look after people like your mum. And she would be with other people all the time. It might take some of the strain off you?'

'I know. I've had a look. Even if I wanted to, there are costs involved. I mentioned it to my sister. I'm not working at the moment but there's enough in my mum's account and in this house to keep her going. My sister's dead against it. I know she doesn't want to be spending the inheritance on looking after our mum. I couldn't say that though. I suggested she move back closer so she could help out, but I wish I hadn't. It wasn't worth the argument.'

'It's never easy with families, is it? You just need to look after yourself as well as your mother. You said about the alcohol thing. You don't need any extra pressure, do you?'

'Well, no. She does have good days. She was having a good few weeks right up until this. There were times when it was like I had my mum back. She's been amazing for me. I would be dead now if it wasn't for her — or in a gutter somewhere. I owe her.'

'We all owe something to our parents. This might be the best thing for her, living here with you. But it might not.' PC Neals closed his notebook and pushed it into a zip pocket on the front of his vest. 'We should get back to it. Anything more you need from us?'

Lisa shook her head. 'No. Where did you find her by the way?'

'The bus station in the town. We had a call about an elderly female walking in just a dressing gown and slippers. She almost made it to Asda! She's done well.'

'Goodness, she has. That must be two miles from here?'

'Just about.' Both officers moved towards the front door. PC Neals leant round the door frame to talk to her mother.

'Bye now. Your daughter's making you a nice cup of tea, okay? You're very lucky, she's a lovely girl!'

'My Cathy? She's always been good to me, that one.'

'It's Lisa. Lisa's here making you a tea.'

'Lisa?' Lisa heard her mother's voice change immediately. She could see PC Neals' back. Her mother continued. 'That girl's a drinker, she is. Wasted her life. No good ever comes from the bottom of a bottle. I told her that. Did she listen?'

'She doesn't drink anymore. Seems like she did listen!'

'That's what she tells you!' her mother snapped.

PC Neals turned back to face her. He rolled his eyes and pulled the door open at the same time. 'Try and have a restful day,' he said. Lisa pushed the door shut behind them.

Lisa finished making the tea and walked it through to the living room. Some American drama was on the television. The volume was low. It looked at least twenty years old and with cheesy acting. Her mother was engrossed. Lisa put the tea down beside her. She moved around so that she was standing in front of her mother. Her mother leaned out so she could see around her, her face contorted into a grimace.

'I do love you, Mum. You know that, right?' Lisa said.

Her mother's eyes darted towards Lisa's. She seemed to think it over before her face broke into a warm smile.

'I know that! I love you too, Cathy.'

Lisa pursed her lips into a smile. She'd take that. Her mother was safe and well at least.

Chapter 36

Maddie eased her foot from the accelerator as her phone rang through the speakers. She had no intention of talking to anyone right now. She didn't know what she was going to do, but answering her phone was low on the list. That was until she read her screen: *Harry Blaker*. She was desperate for an update, not that she would admit it. She bit down on her bottom lip as she pressed to answer. She felt a flush of regret and didn't speak immediately.

'Maddie, you there?'

'Yeah . . . It's Saturday morning, Harry. You know that, right? My day off apparently.'

'Yes, I do. Thanks for telling me, though. Where are you?'

She was northbound on the M20. It couldn't hurt for Harry Blaker to know that; no reason not to tell him why either. If he asked.

'M20. Just passing Ashford, I think. Did you find Andy McCall?'

'No. We couldn't get hold of his brother. We've still got a few addresses left to try. I was arranging door-knocks this morning but I got waylaid. We've found a girl.'

Maddie's eyes flicked back to her display. When she lifted them she became aware of flashing headlamps in her rear-view mirror. She had slowed again but was still in the middle lane. She moved over to the slow lane. Someone was gesturing at her angrily from the car behind as they passed her. She ignored it.

'My girl?'

'Do you have plans for today?'

'Where?'

'Can you come?'

'Is she okay, Harry?'

'Can you come or not, Maddie?'

'Jesus, Harry. Why can't you tell me what's going on?'

'I don't know what's going on. That's why I need you.'

Maddie hesitated. She sighed heavily enough to be heard down the phone.

'You okay?' Harry said.

'What do you think? I'm going home, Harry.'

'To Manchester? Long way for a weekend?'

'To Manchester. Not just for the weekend.'

'What do you mean?'

'I'm going home. I gave it a week. I tried. No one down here wants to give me the time of day. I've spent all these years building something. A career. I've done good things. People respect me for it and then suddenly I'm out in the cold with no reference. I need to go back, at least to a force that knows what I'm capable of.'

'Because of last night?'

'Last night, last week, all of it.'

'I told you it would take time. Lowe will see. We all will.'

'I don't have the time to start again. There were other opportunities back up North. I think that's the better option. You were right . . . I've turned into this moaning ball of frustration, harking back to the good ol' days. I don't want to be that person. I had a career, I just need to go back to it.'

'I thought that could get you killed.'

'At least that would quick. It's a slow death down here. I'm miserable every day.'

'Come back. Finish it off. You've got business with Lorraine Humphries. Maybe I was wrong to cut you out last night.'

'You were wrong. Is she okay?'

'I'll send a postcode through. Put it in your satnav. If you've just passed Ashford you're only half an hour away.'

'Harry, I told you . . . Harry!' The speaker fell silent. The call had been cut. 'Again!' Maddie beat down on the steering wheel. The second sign notifying her of the Ashford turn-off passed her on the nearside. She ran over her options. She could still go back home; it didn't have to be today. She could take a half-hour drive, see what this was all about and then make a decision. Harry wasn't telling her enough for her to be able to do that otherwise. She was learning quickly that was his way. She took the exit. She was on the bridge crossing the road she had just travelled. She pulled over, bumping clumsily up a kerb to stay out of the way. She got another angry horn sound from behind her. She pressed her phone to call Harry back, she was careful to hide her user ID so he wouldn't know it was her.

'Harry Blaker.' His voice was as gruff as ever.

'There are rules,' she said immediately.

'There are what?'

'There are rules or I am gone.'

'Rules?'

'You want me back because you respect me. Or I don't come back. You want me back to work the case, or I don't come back. You talk to me and keep me up to date, maybe even give me something to do all by myself, or I don't come back. You agree to this because you respect me and you want me back. Or I don't come back.'

'Fine.' Harry didn't hesitate.

'So you do then? Respect me?'

'I like that it's important. Come back. I wouldn't have called you if I didn't. I'll make sure you're working cases, not touring schools. You happy?'

'One more thing.'

'Don't push your luck, kid.'

'And there it is. The *kid* thing. No more.'

'I'll give it my best.'

'Fine.' Maddie pushed to end the call this time. And on her terms.

* * *

The postcode took her out into the countryside, the arse end of nowhere. Her satnav showed a chequered flag and counted down to a hundred metres — still there was no building or reference point in sight. She was on a tiny sliver of a road with scorched, muddy banks either side and trees leaning over, their branches drooping as if they were melting in the heat. Suddenly a figure stepped out in front of her and she had to brake hard, the tyres squealing.

'Jesus, Harry!' she called out through her open window.

'You should look where you're going,' he said.

'The way I was going was clear.'

He walked round to the passenger side and she tried to read his expression. She should have known better. As ever, he gave nothing away. She was still looking at him when he climbed in and clipped in his belt.

'What?' he said.

'Where am I going?'

'In there.' Harry pointed to the right. Maddie edged forward where a concealed entrance finally revealed itself. Overgrown hedges jutted through a wide metal gate that had been pushed open. Long grass was flattened beneath it.

'If Lorraine's here, this isn't good.' Maddie was thinking out loud. Harry didn't reply. The track opened up a little. Maddie could see a building up ahead. It was long and slim and they were side-on. She drove another twenty metres or so. 'This place is massive! What the hell is it?'

'It *was* a chicken farm. It closed down a few years back. It's been nothing since then.'

'And we are here because?'

'Pull up here — over there.' Again, he pointed over to the right. There was an indent in the line of trees where she could now see Harry's oversized 4x4. Parked next to it was a police response vehicle and a white police van. It was marked *Forensics*.

'Shit! This isn't getting any better, is it?' Maddie said. Harry didn't complain about her language and he certainly didn't correct her. He stepped out of the car and Maddie followed. They walked across the front of the building rather than round the side. Maddie looked around. To her right she could see a road. This was far wider than the way they had driven in. Grass and weeds were pushing up through the tarmac. Further down she could see a flat sign on two steel posts. It was at an angle and turned away from her. Maddie guessed this had been the main entrance when the place was operating.

They made it to the end of the line of buildings and took an immediate left. The police tape was the first thing she saw, then a figure in a white overall and blue mask on their knees. A short distance away was a police officer with a cocker spaniel on a lead. It was sitting obediently. Man and beast both turned towards them as they approached. Harry stopped at the tape and bent down to reach a plastic tub. He pulled it open and threw Maddie a white forensic suit. She took it silently and pulled it on over her leggings and t-shirt. Next she took the blue face mask, matching gloves and shoe covers and fixed them in place. Harry lifted the tape and waited. Even before she stepped through she caught the strong and unmistakeable scent of death. There was no smell like it for lingering. Her hand rose instinctively to her mask to make sure it was on tight.

'This isn't a fox this time, is it, Harry?'

He didn't answer. She hadn't expected him to.

'You must be Maddie?' The white suit she had seen kneeling from a distance stood up to meet her. Her voice was muffled through the mask.

'Yeah.'

'I'm CSI Mace. Charley. Harry tells me you're investigating a missing person. Do you have a picture of her?'

'Not on me. I got a call to come here. I wasn't at work.'

As Charley turned away, Maddie caught a glimpse over her shoulder of a blue sheet weighted down at two of the corners. The end nearest to her flapped open a little in the breeze.

'Is that her?' Maddie said. 'Is that Lorraine?'

'Harry can't be sure. How long has Lorraine been missing?'

'Around a week all in.'

Charley shook her head at Harry. 'The weather's been hot. That would speed up some of the processes but our girl's been dead longer than a week.' She moved to the sheet and rolled back the blue plastic. Maddie could see an arm. It was a washed-out shade of white and it lay with the elbow joint facing up. It looked like it had a few nasty sores on it and the outer layer of skin was starting to slip away. She could see dark hair, too, spread out along the corpse's back. It fell either side of an ear that protruded out; its edges were black and depleted. Whoever she was, she was face down and Maddie wasn't going to be able to get confirmation from where she stood.

The CSI must have been thinking the same. 'You can get a little closer over there.' She pointed at a patch of grass a few metres away. Maddie moved to it. She was now at the head end and far closer. The hair was long, dark and matted beneath a layer of dried mud and dust. Maddie could see a little more of the face now; the head was up enough to be facing almost towards her. She could make out high cheekbones and shaped eyebrows. It wasn't a good angle. She couldn't see the face that well and it wasn't a natural expression. This woman had a lot of the same traits as Lorraine Humphries. The hair was right, the build too from what she could see and she was white.

'I don't think it's her but I still can't be sure.'

Charley tutted. 'No, I'm sorry, it's not great. Hang on.' She stood up and moved to a black bag. She lifted up a camera with a large lens and fiddled with it. She walked the camera over to Maddie. The screen on the back was on. It showed an image of the girl rolled onto her side. They must have taken it as part of the initial checks. It was a much better shot of the face. The woman's eyes were missing from their sockets. Her lips were gone, too, revealing the teeth behind and making her mouth look like it was twisted into a permanent grimace. She could see more sores on both cheeks.

'I don't think it looks like her.'

Charley left the screen in front of her for another couple of seconds. 'Okay. Can you be sure?' Charley said.

'Pretty sure, yeah. It's not easy to tell, there's bits of her missing . . . you know . . . bits that would really help.'

'The eyes are always the first to go. The bugs go for the soft bits.' Charley seemed so matter-of-fact.

'Jesus.' Maddie looked back down at the clump of hair in front of her. 'She's not been buried.' Maddie was talking more out loud than asking a question but Charley answered her anyway.

'No. Just dumped on the ground with a light covering of tree branches and leaves over her.'

'There are marks in the ground, though,' Harry said. 'Someone tried to start digging and probably realised that the soil has been baked solid. You'd need some heavy digging equipment to even stand a chance on this ground.'

'So they just dumped a load of branches over her?'

'Yeah, probably hoping it would go away,' Charley said. 'She hasn't been here long either. She's been put here recently. Those red marks on her are where the wildlife has made a start. I'd say twenty-four hours tops.'

'So she wasn't killed here?'

'Not in this spot, no. She wouldn't have lasted this long out in the open.'

'How was she found?'

'Like she is, pretty much,' Charley answered.

'I mean, how was she found to be here?' Maddie managed to lift her eyes. She took in the derelict building. She had almost forgotten it was there but now it seemed to loom over them. The breeze was intermittent but it came in now, rattling a sheet of corrugated plastic that was fastened crudely over a window. The building and its surroundings had the look of somewhere that had long since been abandoned. Certainly there wouldn't be any reason for anyone to be coming out here. 'This is a McCall's site, isn't it?'

Harry puckered his lips. 'I'm waiting for confirmation on that, but I'd stake my mortgage on it.'

'So how was she found?'

'The classic dog walker,' Harry said. 'At least that's the story we got first off. There's a bit more to it, but nothing sinister I don't think.'

'Nothing sinister about finding a dead body? What about in there?' Maddie gestured towards the building. 'We don't think there's anything of interest in there, do we?' Maddie shuddered involuntarily.

'No. Our friend over there is a cadaver dog.' Maddie turned to the spaniel. His tongue lolled out and his nose twitched with enthusiasm. 'He's done a sweep and found nothing. Dogs like Vamp don't miss bodies.'

'Vamp?' Maddie raised her voice a little for the benefit of the handler.

276

'Not his official title, ma'am,' the officer replied, instantly cheerful. 'Just that he has a talent for blood, see?'

'I think I do,' Maddie said. 'Great name.'

'I'll still have a search team go through the building,' Harry said. 'Vamp here's got the grounds to do, too, before his shift is done. We're just giving him a rest.'

'That's a good point actually, boss,' the dog handler said. 'I should move him away. You know . . . he'll get saturated here.'

'Understood. No rush. Go get him freshened up and let me know how you get on. I've got a POLSA on the way. If they ask why you left early you send them to me.'

'Will do. You know it will happen!'

Maddie had never worked with a POLSA before, her previous role had kept her away from most uniform procedures, but she knew a bit about what they did, that they basically ran searches, made sure no areas were missed and that everything was done in the right order by the right person. They were always police sergeants and usually from the tactical side of the business.

Maddie took in the area that would need to be searched. It was vast, including woodland, tracks, the abandoned factory — it was going to be quite a job. She lifted her eyes, suddenly aware of the previous MO around cameras. Harry must have picked up on that.

'I couldn't see anything obvious. Cameras, right? I'll brief the search team. They have kit that can search for electrical pulses. If there *is* one they'll find it.'

'This was done in a hurry. I don't think they'll find one. I know the other girl was dumped outside but he didn't try to hide her. This is different enough to be the handiwork of someone who was panicked, or in a rush at least.'

'I agree completely,' Harry said.

'Something's prompted it. Something we've done. Someone we've spoken to.'

Harry didn't reply.

Maddie was still looking around and was struck by the thought that this wasn't the most picturesque place for a dog walk either. 'So tell me about our man who pitched up here for a dog walk? You said there was more to it.' Harry must have seen Maddie's scowl.

'I know. All the beautiful woods and trails in the area and he comes here for a stroll. I think we've got to the bottom of it. He's a young lad from Thanet — not exactly local. I didn't buy his dog walking story so I told him he needed to do better. I was on the verge of having him in for murder and he suddenly tells me the truth.'

'The truth?'

'He was out scoping the place out as a venue.'

'For what?'

'He arranges illegal raves. Of course, when he explained it, he just said *raves* — I had to remind him of the illegal bit. We get a few of them out in the sticks. They put something out on their Snapchat, or whatever it is, and before you know it you've got a derelict chicken factory full of ravers. He obviously got wind of the site and he was using his dog as a cover story. He said he'd decided not to use it anyway — too dangerous in there, he reckons. He was leaving and his dog suddenly ran off. Must have caught the scent. When he found the dog he was tugging at something on the ground. That turned out to be the girl's left arm. The dog must have pulled her torso out with it.'

'And that's the truth? You believe him?' Maddie said.

'I never said that. His car was parked around the corner. He's got flyers in there for a recent event — that one looked legal at least. He had some sort of music equipment in the boot and when I ran the car through it came up with an intel report linking it to illegal raves. He's guilty of something, I'm sure, but nothing we'd be bothered about. I got two DCs to drive him home — a CSI is heading out there to take all his samples and swabs. We've seized his car too. They'll get his statement in full at his home address so we know for sure where he lives. They also have instructions to seize all the shoes they can find — belt and braces — and to teach him a lesson.'

'So what now?' Maddie said.

Charley answered. 'Well, I for one have a lot of work to do. The trees over our victim were cut down from the row over there. They were cut cleanly. I need to take photos in situ then I'll seize the trunks. I'll be able to show a mechanical fit if we can get hold of the tool.'

'I assume there were no cutting tools in our dog walker's car?' Maddie said.

'Not that I could see in plain sight. CSI will swab it and I'll have a team pull it apart to make sure we haven't missed anything stuffed in a void.' Charley was suddenly animated. 'We'll be able to rule the car out easy enough. If she was in there she'll have left a part of her behind. She'd be leaking fluids and DNA onto whatever she touched. She's got open wounds and bugs everywhere. I can't even go near the car though — any defence would cry cross-contamination if I so much as look through a window. I've put a call out for as many CSIs as we can get.'

'The scene will probably take a few days anyway, won't it?' Harry said.

'Easily. These are the worst sort. I'll be able to get DNA so we can identify her. But there will be a lot of waiting around. I can't do much until the entomologist has been out to collect up some of the bugs.'

'Collecting up bugs?' Maddie couldn't hide her disgust.

'Oh yes. With something like this they could tell us a lot. We'll take a good sample of the maggots and flies, some get boiled so they don't develop any further, some are left to continue their life cycle. If they've been feeding on her from the start, we can start tying up times. The soil samples will give us how long she's been here too, depending on how far the bodily fluids have spread. It's a fascinating science.'

'It's something alright.' Maddie could see that Charley was a lot more passionate about bodily fluids and bugs with their bellies full of dead flesh than she could ever be. 'Suddenly I can see why this all takes a while.'

'We'll get Vamp going soon,' Harry said. 'I want to be sure we don't have any more bodies hidden under conifer branches. This is a big site. This might have been the one we were supposed to find.'

'You think Lorraine might still be here somewhere?'

'I don't know. Depends who we're dealing with.'

Charley took back over. 'You're not dealing with someone nice, that's for sure. We rolled her very briefly, I can tell she's got a nasty stab wound in the stomach and her throat's been cut. Take your pick as to which one of those killed her. The throat is usually much quicker. We'll know more when I can start getting hands on.'

'Sounds familiar!' Maddie said.

'The DIs mentioned a similar case over in Sussex. I'm waiting for a phone call from the senior CSI on that case. I want to make sure we're consistent and doing all we can to prove any links. I'll get back to it.'

Maddie watched as Charley knelt next to the blue tarp that was still peeled back halfway. The woman's torso was exposed. Her hair moved in a breeze tainted by the stench of death. Maddie took the opportunity to move away and walked back across the front of the building. She kept going until the air was fresh, until that smell was gone. From here she could just see paths cracking with flowering weeds, swaying trees that lined the track down which she had driven and bluebells carpeting the forest floor either side of it.

'You okay, kid?' Harry's voice came from close behind.

'You forget already?' she said.

Harry looked a little blank. 'Oh, the *kid* thing. Yeah, I forgot.'

'Try not to!' She snapped.

'Noted.'

She took a breath. 'And, yeah. I'm fine. She's not my first dead body. I saw a lot when I was in uniform. A lot worse than this, too.'

'I'm sure you did. But we thought it was someone we were looking for.'

'It's not her.'

Harry held up his hands. 'I didn't think so either.'

'I thought it was, though. When I pulled up here. When I put the mask on and walked towards that blue mound. You didn't think to share your doubts over the phone? Or maybe even a little warning of what I was walking into?'

'No. I was going to, but there was something in your voice. I knew you were serious about leaving. I knew you didn't mean to come back.'

'So you had nothing to lose then, did you?'

'I did. If I had told you it was a body and not Lorraine, you might have kept on driving. And we would have lost you.'

'And that matters, does it?'

Harry smiled. 'Don't know yet.' He walked away to where the dog had reappeared with his handler. Maddie shook her head. This job seemed to attract people that were difficult to fathom. But Harry Blaker was on a whole new level.

Chapter 37

Lisa Simpkiss waved to her stepfather. She could still hear the car ticking over when she walked through the door of the some time Scout hut. As usual, she gave her name to the woman with the patronising smile and walked up the ramp into the stuffy room that smelt of dust and polish. She made for the coffee. Another week clean. Another week of fighting for structure, to make her plans and stick to them. It was getting harder, almost as hard as she could remember, and she knew what that could mean. She was yearning for a drink more and more. The pressure of caring for her mother was getting unbearable. She was desperate to forget, to not be worrying about her constantly, for just a few hours away from it all. Alcohol had been her escape once. It had taken her a long time to realise it was nothing of the sort.

That morning had been the worst possible start to her day. She'd considered not coming to the meeting but to have missed it would have been a break in her structure. She couldn't afford that. Maybe not ever again. Saturdays were the days where she showed herself that she was winning. She couldn't leave her mother alone, though. She had begged her best friend Naomi to come down and sit with her. She could trust Naomi.

She sat down on a plastic chair, wriggling to try and get comfortable. Her coffee was hot as hell and she put it down on the floor and rubbed at her face. More people were coming in. She didn't look up. The chair scraped next to her. She was still looking down at the floor but she recognised the Converse trainers of the man with the nice eyes who had shared her park bench the previous week. He was half-turned away with his arms crossed and biting down on his bottom lip. He wore an open shirt over a white vest. The shirt looked to be sticking to a moist patch on his back. He checked his phone with a jerk of his wrist before stuffing it into his shirt pocket.

'Watch my coffee this time, yeah?' she said. He turned to her. It seemed for a second like he hadn't heard her.

'Your coffee . . . yeah. No problem.' He smiled but it was hurried. He looked stressed. She looked away. She recognised someone who didn't want to talk. Normally that was her. She immediately regretted talking to him in the first place. She didn't know why she had done if she was honest. She wasn't there to make friends.

Ian, the man who led the sessions, appeared. He made his entrance as usual, dragging his chair from left to right in front of the loose circle until he was positioned directly opposite Lisa. He sat on the chair backwards, his arms resting on the back, like a teacher trying too hard. He gave the same story he did every week. Lisa looked round the room while he was doing it. There were a couple of new faces and at least one she hadn't seen for a while. There was an older man with long, greasy hair that he kept sweeping back out from his face. He wore cowboy boots and a short-sleeved shirt with popper buttons. He looked a lot worse than she remembered. She guessed that his latest fall off the wagon had been a hard one.

Ian finished his spiel and paused to look around the room. There were seven addicts in his audience, eight if you included him. He asked if anyone wanted to speak, to *kick them off.*

'I can't stop it.' The man with the Converse trainers was quick to speak first. She turned to him. He still hung his head and it was shaking from side to side. The desperation in his voice was thicker now; it coated his words, hung heavy on his broad shoulders. He didn't say any more. The room's attention was fixed on him. Ian took his opportunity.

'Bad week?' he remarked and fell back silent. It was just a prompt. The man looked like he was studying every detail on his pumps, but he suddenly raised his head.

'What if it was my best week ever?' he said. Lisa sensed genuine fear in his eyes. 'What if the only way I can be happy is . . .' he faded out. His head slumped forwards again. He was rubbing his hands together. The fidgeting that had been in his legs was now in his hips. He rocked from side to side.

'How about you tell us about it? About your best week ever. You might find that there are some opinions in here that can help. We might even have had the same sort of week as you, friend.' The question was left hanging. It was at least a full minute before it was taken up.

'I know I'm an addict. I didn't used to see it that way. I thought an addict was, like, hooked on heroin or drink or whatever, where you feel ill when you come off it, when you *feel* like you need something to survive. It's not like that for me — it's not something I physically *need*. I don't need this. But I can't live without it.' He lifted his head again. There were a few nods around the room. 'I was good at hiding it, for a long time, but that's all fallen apart and I don't even think I care anymore. This . . . *thing* . . . I need it to be happy. I need it to feel alive. Without it I'm just coasting through. I was just doing one day, then doing the next and trying to be like everyone else. And they all look so happy!' He was hunting around now, making eye contact wherever he could. 'Don't they?' He got a few more nods and they increased in vigour. 'But what it is that makes *me* feel alive, that makes *me* happy is something I can't have. It's something that hurts the people around me. I'm an addict. I know that now. So what do you do when you're an addict? You come to meetings like this. You get help to stop. But what if I stop? What then? I go back to coasting, to doing one day then doing the next. I *can't* stop. I don't want to fucking stop!' He paused long enough for the host to start a reply.

'Well, there's a lot—'

'I KNOW this is my last meeting!' He cut back in, renewed aggression in his voice. 'And that terrifies me. I don't know where I go from here.' His head fell back to the floor. Lisa looked up at Ian. He pushed off the back of the chair to sit straighter. His mouth opened a few times as if he was going to start again, but he didn't. Lisa spoke instead.

'Part of being addicted to something is not being able to see past it. Not being able to see what can replace it.'

What was she doing? She didn't want in on this debate! She could see the host was struggling; she could feel the quality of the silence that had settled on the room — it was a stunned silence. People were thinking, and Lisa was worried that they might be thinking that he had a point. He didn't. Lisa knew that she needed to be clear about that — for her own sake. And saying it out loud made it clearer.

'Nothing else makes me happy.' The man turned to her. His eyes were wide, Lisa wasn't sure it was still fear she was seeing written there. His forehead was slick with sweat; it was visible in the overhead lighting and a drop rolled over his temple.

'Happiness is a state of mind. It's the one thing that we're all addicted to. Everyone needs to be happy — we crave it. But it's just an end result. There's more than one way to get there,' Lisa said.

'Not for me.'

'She's right,' Ian said. 'Lisa's right. Our addictions are the walls that trap us. But not only do they trap us, they block our view. When I was addicted to painkillers I would walk down the street and no matter what was going on, all I would see was the dealers. I would see them sat on park benches, waiting on street corners or on their own front doorsteps. It wasn't that there was nothing else there. It was just that they were all I was looking for. I thought they were all that I needed. I was wrong. Don't stop coming here. Even if you just come for the free coffee! Just come and listen and try and leave at least a part of your mind open to the idea that you can find what you need from other things, from other sources.'

Lisa was watching him closely. Someone else spoke after Ian and another after that. They were trying to be supportive. But the man kept his eyes turned down throughout. She knew he wasn't listening at all. When he had said that he wasn't coming back to these meetings again, he'd meant it. She reckoned he had struggled to come to this one. His body language, his fear, his lack of attention all confirmed it. He had come here in desperation. It was his last chance to be saved. She had been there before. Just before she had started a drinking session that nearly killed her.

When the meeting came to an end, the man sprang to his feet as if he had been jabbed in the side and made for the door. Ian was calling after him but he didn't look back. She watched as Ian shook his head. He looked thoughtful for a second, as if he was about to go after the man. Lisa stepped in front of him.

'I'll go,' she said. She didn't know why. She never got involved with other people; she had enough on her plate. It was like the police officer had said at 5 a.m. in her kitchen: she needed to start looking after herself. But she was committed now.

He had crossed the road and was standing by the bench. She could see him from the back, hunched in, his elbows bent as if he was lighting a cigarette. Sure enough he straightened with a puff of white smoke and moved off. Lisa was halfway across the road when she called out.

'Hey!'

The man stopped and turned to face her. She could still see the emotion in his eyes.

'I was going to have a seat for a few minutes. Like last week. You need a chat?'

'No,' he said. But he didn't move off.

'Well, do you need to sit for a minute then?'

He looked around. The cigarette stayed between his lips. His eyes were narrowed to the smoke. He walked to the bench and sat on the edge. Lisa did the same.

'You normally sit out here with a coffee,' he said. 'That's what you told me.'

'I do. You ran off. I didn't have time to get a coffee today.'

'You should go back in and get one.'

'I've been there. Where you are. Where you lie to people. Where you manipulate them and get good at making them go away when you need them to. I could go and get a coffee, but you'd be gone by the time I got back.'

'I would.'

'I can wait.'

'You'd be better off going to get yourself a coffee. I'm telling you that now. People around me, they all get hurt. I've seen it enough. That's not what I want for them, but I can't help it.'

'So you keep saying. Like I said, I've been where you are. I've hurt people too—'

'Not like I have!' The venom was back.

'We all think we've got it the worst. Like no one else has ever been as addicted as we are. But I was there. I came out the other side. Never entirely — you don't ever want to think you're not at risk of being dragged back — but I've come a long way. You can too.'

'It's too late.'

Lisa felt her jeans pocket vibrate. She pulled her phone out. The screen read *Naomi*. She felt her heart flutter. Naomi had said she could cope. She said she wouldn't need to call and not to worry. Something had to be wrong. She stepped away to answer the call. 'Hey, you okay?' She braced herself for the reply.

'Sorry to call you, Lisa. It's your mum. She's getting aggie. She's usually fine with me but I can't talk to her today. She accused me of stealing something. I don't even know what. She's got it in her head that I'm a thief now.'

'Jesus. Where are you?'

'Stood outside your house! I'm on the front lawn. She was getting herself more and more wound up and I thought she might attack me at one point. I came out here so she could cool off a bit and I thought I'd give you a call. How long are you going to be?'

'I'm walking back. I'll be fifteen minutes. Hold on.'

'Fifteen minutes. Try a jog, will ya! I can hear banging in there, Lisa. I think she's okay but your stuff might not be!'

Lisa hung up the phone. The man was looking at her. He took the last drag on his cigarette. She ran over her options. Fifteen minutes was a fast walk. It would be less than five in a car.

'Did you drive here?' she said.

'Yes.'

'I need a lift. Can you run me, like, five minutes down the road? I'll owe you. Maybe you'll let me take you somewhere for a coffee? I just need to check on my mum. I think I can help you, but you need to help me first! Please. I wouldn't ask if I wasn't desperate.' She wouldn't have done either. It seemed like a bad idea the moment she said it but she couldn't think of any other solution.

He looked around again, then bit down on his bottom lip. That gesture again and that look in his eye, the one Lisa had interpreted as fear. She wasn't so sure that was what it was anymore.

'Okay. I'll run you back. I'm parked just over there.' He turned away from her, pressed a button on a key fob and the lights flashed twice on a white, new-looking truck. She could see *McCall's* in small writing down the side. She hesitated now. Maybe walking was a better idea. Fifteen minutes would give her mum enough time to calm down a little. Sometimes she could switch back just as quickly. Lisa could imagine coming home to find her cleaning up anything she might have broken. But Naomi was outside in their front garden. The risk that it all might escalate was too much. Lisa moved towards the passenger seat. As she did the door was pushed open. The man had leaned across and he straightened up as she got in.

'Where are we going?' His eyes were still pinned wide. He gripped the steering wheel so tightly that his knuckles showed white. 'And thanks for caring, I do appreciate it. I'm Andy, by the way.' The sweat still ran either side of those intense-looking eyes.

'Sure, no problem, Andy. Somebody has to, right? I'm Lisa.'

'Nice to meet you. Now, let's get you back to your mum.'

Lisa lifted her phone back to her ear. She was calling Naomi back. She would stay on the phone until she got there. She was suddenly aware she had put herself into a total stranger's car. That wasn't like her at all. Not recently. Her reckless days needed to be behind her now.

Chapter 38

Naomi's expression showed instant relief as Lisa walked up the front path.

'She's still in there. It was noisy for a while but it's gone quiet. I checked at the window but I couldn't see her. I didn't want to go in. I didn't want to upset her again.'

'Okay, thanks, Naomi. Take this . . .' Lisa handed her phone over. 'If she kicks off, just call the number on there under *doctors*. They came out last time she was like this. She listens to the doctor. They might even get her to take her medication.'

'Okay, no problem.'

Lisa readied her key. She pushed it into the lock and hesitated. She rested against the door. She couldn't hear anything from the other side. She turned the key and pushed it open.

The hallway was small. The stairs were straight ahead, the entrance to the living room almost immediately on the right and the kitchen was on the left. A pot plant lay on the floor, out of place. It was smashed to pieces and the soil looked like it was melting into the carpet.

'Mum!' Lisa called out.

'Yes, love? Is that you, Cathy?'

'Yes, Mum. You okay?' Lisa turned to make eye contact with Naomi, she was a pace or two behind her.

'I am now, love. That horrible girl was round here earlier. She broke my plant, she did! Your sister's friend — what's her name?' Lisa's mother finished her last word with a grunt, the sort that Lisa knew to mean that she was getting up. Her voice was coming from the living room.

'You need to go,' Lisa whispered quickly to Naomi. 'She seems to be calmer, but if she sees you she might go off on one again.'

'I never broke the pot plant!' Naomi hissed.

'I know! I'll give you a call later.'

'What if she kicks off with you? She was so angry earlier. I don't want to leave you with her, Lisa. She's getting worse.'

'I'll stick around.' Andy was a few steps further back still. Lisa hadn't even realised he had followed her down from where they had parked up the street. She'd almost forgotten about him.

'Who's this?' Naomi gestured to Andy with her thumb.

'Andy. We know each other from the meeting. He's . . . a friend.'

'I'll stick around for a few minutes,' Andy said. 'Just to make sure you're okay. My nan . . . she was similar. I know what they can get like. They're so brittle — you can't do anything to protect yourself. I'll just be here. I don't think she should see your friend. No offence.'

'Love?' Her mum's voice. She was close now. She appeared in the hall. 'Who are you talking to?'

'A . . . a friend, Mum. That's all. From work.'

'A friend? What friend?'

Lisa had pulled the front door almost completely closed. She opened it back up now. Naomi had stepped off to the side. Lisa could see her looking over. Andy stood in the doorway. He was smiling.

'Well, okay! He's a handsome one, isn't he?' Her mother chuckled. 'Aren't you going to invite him in?'

'Er, yes. He's only popping in for a few minutes, though, Mum.'

'Well, okay then. Did you want some dinner? I can put some on if you want some? What's this pot doing here? Did you break my plant?'

'No, Mum. I'm not sure what happened. Let me clean that up and then I'll put some dinner on. Don't you worry. Why don't you go and watch the telly? I think some of your programmes are on now, aren't they? You shouldn't be up worrying about dinner. That's what I'm here for!'

'You're such a good girl, Cathy.'

Lisa watched as her mother walked back into the living room. She exhaled in a sigh. She smiled weakly at Andy. 'Thanks. Look, this is above and beyond. She's going to be fine now. Maybe we should meet up for that drink some other time. I need to make sure she's okay.'

'I understand. But I can stay for that coffee now? That makes us even. And my leaving might confuse your mum more — she actually seemed to like me! Five minutes and I'll be happier that you're both going to be okay.'

Lisa glanced back to where Naomi had stepped back onto the path. She was smiling behind his back. It dropped away quickly when he turned to look at her.

'I'll make myself scarce, yeah?' Naomi said. 'I don't want to, er . . . upset your mum . . .' Naomi gave her biggest grin yet and then winked. It was all Lisa could do to stop herself laughing. For just a second the day seemed to be a lot less grim.

'I suppose a cup of coffee is the least I can do. I'll speak to you later, Naomi, okay?'

'Sure.' She was backing away down the path. Andy stepped in. He wouldn't be able to see Naomi making grabbing gestures towards his backside. She spun and walked away and Lisa led Andy into the kitchen.

'What do you want for dinner, Mum?' Lisa called out.

'Yes please, love!' came the reply. The television was playing loud. Lisa rolled her eyes at Andy and filled the kettle.

'I'll do her a tea first. She's had a long day. Good days and bad days, you know? This is as bad as it's been for a while.' She busied herself with prepping mugs and sugar. 'How do you take your coffee?'

'Coffee?' His tone was instantly different. All the tension and latent aggression was back. She looked over at him where he leant against the wall on the opposite side of the room. Both his hands were behind his back, one of his legs was lifted so the sole of his right foot was resting against the wall.

'Do you mind not putting your foot on the wall?' Lisa said.

'You don't want to be drinking coffee, Lisa. Why don't you drink what you want to drink?'

'Coffee does for me now.'

'No, it doesn't. Not if you're really honest with yourself. You're an addict, Lisa. Alcohol is your thing. That's who you are. Why are you fighting it?'

'This isn't really the time or the place. I thought you wanted a drink? Maybe you should just leave.'

'You're still a drunk, Lisa.'

'Maybe you're right. But you need to leave.'

'Now you want me to leave? You followed me out today. You stopped me from walking away so you could intervene. That's what this was, right? An intervention?'

'I don't know what it was. I saw you at the meeting. I remember being like that before. I had somebody to help me and I thought maybe you needed somebody, too — before you end up dead or worse.'

'Worse?'

'Worse. Alive and still a slave to the drink.'

'Who said I was ever a slave to *drink*?'

'Whatever your poison is. It doesn't matter anyway, not when you strip it down. They're all the same.'

'Mine isn't.'

'Really.'

'Really. My addiction is death.'

Lisa was reaching for the milk. She put it back down on the bench and stood so she was facing him directly. 'Death? What sort of addiction is that?'

'One I've been trying to shake. Harder than anyone has ever tried. I've been trying to find other ways of making myself feel alive, of making me feel like it's worth breathing, worth waking up for another day. Nothing else comes close — nothing at all. Today I was walking away, Lisa. You remember that.'

'Remember it when . . .?'

'When I'm watching you die.'

Lisa was ready for him when he lunged. He had been building towards it. All the signs were there. The final one was when his hands fell by his sides and he pushed off the wall. But he was only a few strides away and she could only manage a shout before she felt the punch to her stomach. It was firm — enough to knock all the air from her lungs and rob her of her voice in an instant. She felt her eyes bulge and her lips flexed helplessly, trying to suck in some oxygen. Andy's shoulder pushed against her cheek. He stepped into her. It felt to her like he was still pushing his bunched up fist into her stomach. He pulled it out and she stumbled a step forwards. She looked down at his fist. It was wrapped tightly around a stubby blade that dripped a thick red. She lifted her eyes to meet with his. They flashed wild with excitement. Her hands moved to her stomach and she felt the warmth of her own blood. Her voice was still incapable of more than a low moan.

'Are you making my tea, love?' Her mother stepped through the door, mostly hidden behind where Andy stood in the middle of the kitchen, arms by his side, his black shirt hung open to reveal the blood on his vest. His shirt had two bulging pockets and he pulled a dark cloth from one of them. He slid the blade of the knife through it and licked his lips. He kept facing her, away from her mother. She couldn't see what Lisa was seeing. She wouldn't be able to see Lisa's wound either.

'You've got to feed your addiction, Lisa. That's what I say. You've got to be who you are.' Andy's voice was low but carried the same menace.

There was a knock at the front door. Andy half-turned, the stubby blade still in his right fist. Her mother tutted and turned towards the door. Andy started towards her. Andy would be quicker — he'd get to her before she even made it out of the kitchen. Lisa tried to shout a warning but she still didn't have a voice; she could only take rasping breaths. She lunged forward, aiming for the arm that was holding the knife. She missed and her legs gave way but she grabbed his shirt on her way to the floor. Something gave and she heard a tearing sound — something heavy dropped to the floor. She managed to drag Andy down to his knees. His right hand flashed out, this time it was a solid fist, still gripped around the knife, which caught her with a stinging blow to the face. She felt a push to her chest and she rolled away. She still gripped a clump of torn material in her hand.

Lisa heard the door open and Andy ducked back into the kitchen. She heard her mother's voice: '*What do you want? You already broke my pot plant!*'

From her position on the floor, Lisa's eyes fixed on a black mobile phone. It must have been what had fallen from Andy's shirt pocket. It was within reach and her hand shot out for it while he was still looking away. She pulled it back just as his movement became a blur in front of her. He grabbed her by the scruff of her neck and pulled her further into the kitchen. She had to be bleeding freely — she could see that from the crimson smear left on the floor as she slid backwards until her shoulders found the kitchen units. She pushed the mobile phone out of sight under her buttocks.

'*I forgot to give your daughter something is all. Is she there? I've still got her phone.*' Naomi's voice – *Naomi had come back!* Lisa's relief turned to fear in an instant. Andy was looking down at her, his face a sneer. He held the stained knife to his lips — an instruction to be quiet. She was frozen in panic anyway and if she managed to call out he would surely finish her off. And what then for her mother and her best friend? She held her breath.

'*Yes of course she's here! She lives here, doesn't she?*'

'*Can I speak to her, Mrs Simpkiss? Just for a moment?*'

'*A moment, eh? What are you going to do about this pot plant?*' Her mother scolded.

'*I'll pay for it, sure. I'll bring the money right over or I'll go and pick you a new one. How about that?*'

'*No, no! You'll get one that's all wrong. I know what you young people are like . . . you've got no idea. Don't worry about it now. Is that all you wanted?*'

'*I just wanted to speak to your daughter. Is she there?*'

Lisa started to feel pain now. Maybe it was the way she was propped up against the units. Andy still had a handful of her top scrunched up in his fist. He lowered his face to within an inch of hers.

'You call through,' he said, through gritted teeth. 'You tell her to piss off. You do it nice and easy or I start stabbing anything that moves. Do you understand?' His breath smelt of stale cigarettes.

'Yeah,' she said. Her voice was low and gravelly but she had managed to get some air back in her lungs. He changed his grip. He stood up over her and yanked her up to her feet. Moving agitated her wound and it was all she could do to stop herself from crying out. He'd caught her by surprise, too; she hadn't had time to pick the phone back up. She couldn't stand completely straight. She was on her feet but bent double. She chanced a look to where the phone still lay, up against the kick board under the kitchen units. He dragged her a few steps closer to the door. She was still hidden from Naomi. Her t-shirt was sopping wet and stuck to her skin.

'Hey!' she called out, aware that her voice sounded weak. She needed to be stronger. She knew what it meant for all of them if Naomi stepped into the house. 'Hey, Naomi!' This time she sounded better.

'*Lisa, you okay?*' Naomi's tone carried concern.

'Yeah. Yeah, of course I'm okay.'

'*I've still got your phone. I never gave it back.*'

'Ah, yeah! Nice one. Keep hold of it, yeah? I'll get it later.'

Naomi was quiet for a brief moment. '*You don't want it? Where are you?*'

A pang of excruciating pain shot through Lisa. It seemed to course through her whole body from top to bottom. It was all she could do to stay on her feet. She sucked in a deep breath, making every effort to keep the distress from her voice.

'In the kitchen, mate. Just trying not to confuse anyone, if you know what I mean? I'll come and see you later.' Her last few words had been an effort; she knew they sounded forced.

'*Okay then.*' Naomi didn't sound sure. It wasn't unusual for Lisa to act different around her mother but she knew she was pushing it. She prayed Naomi would accept that. A few seconds passed and Naomi still hadn't answered. Lisa was still stooped forward and could still feel Andy's grip on her collar. She let her eyes fall closed and focussed on blocking out the pain. She muttered silently for Naomi to go. *Just leave!*

'*I'm sorry to bother you, Mrs Simpkiss,*' she heard Naomi say, and then the door clicked shut.

'*How are you getting on with that dinner in there, Cathy?*' her mother called out. '*You need anything?*'

'No . . . thanks, Mum,' Lisa managed. The television must have been paused because its sound now came roaring back. It was like a signal to Andy. He pulled her roughly across the kitchen floor to the back door. The key was in it and Andy unlocked it and tugged it open. He reached down for her. Once again she was wrenched to her feet. She felt her legs wobble, every part of her wanted to collapse, to curl up in a ball, to assess her wound. She knew she was seriously hurt, she could tell from the kitchen floor how much blood she was losing.

Rough hands pushed her out of the back door and she fell to her knees. The pain shot through her again as she tried to steady herself and she leaked more blood onto the concrete path that led along the side of the house to the little garden shed. He used his weight and one arm to pin her against the shed while he pulled the door open. Then he pushed her in amidst the clutter of garden implements and furniture and shut the door.

'Move or make the slightest noise and your mum comes with us. Do you understand?'

'Yes,' she managed. She heard him move away. She sucked in a breath, trying to quell her panic. She pushed herself against the wooden slats, trying to see out where the light leaked through. She couldn't. She gave up and lifted her top. She had been pressing the wound instinctively with her left hand. She moved it away. Blood was still seeping out. Her waistband and the tops of her jeans were soaked in it too. She looked around for something that might help — a weapon, something that could make a noise. There was nothing.

She heard the sound of an engine. It moved close enough for her to guess that it had been pulled up to the back gate just a metre away from where she was lying. They were going somewhere. Andy reappeared within a few seconds. She was angled so she could look up at him, she could see the look in his eyes. The excitement was unmistakeable now. She knew that feeling well. For her it had been the walk home from the shop with bottles in her bag. The anticipation. It was the look of an addict lost in the moment, getting his fix.

He wrenched his sleeves up and Lisa saw flashes of white scar tissue on his forearms as he reached and grabbed her again. She knew what was coming. She was already rocking to try and get up. She gritted her teeth to overcome the pain and could feel droplets of cold sweat running down her forehead. She stooped back out onto the path and through the open gate. The front passenger door was already open. She assumed it was for her but he pushed her roughly towards the lifted boot and she bumped into the protruding lip, causing her to bend and her abdomen shot with pain. She turned to remonstrate. She saw that excitement in his eyes again and had a moment of clarity. All her focus had been on getting him out of her house, away from her mother. Now her mind pounded out with a simple message: *if he gets you in there you're as good as dead.*

She opened her mouth to cry out, to shout for help. The words never came. She felt a blow to her face, a flashing pain in her nose and a blurring of her vision. She felt her back scraping, as if something sharp was raking down it. Her vision blurred further until there was only darkness.

* * *

Olive Simpkiss heard the car pull away. Cathy had to be going to the shops? She didn't know if they needed anything. She paused what she was watching on television. It was a show about doctors. She liked it most of the time but recently there had been a lot going on. Too much for her to keep up with. Why couldn't they just keep it simple? She stood up and her knee twinged with pain. It was getting worse. She couldn't remember if she had taken her medication that morning. She was supposed to rest it as much as she could, otherwise it would swell up and she could end up bed-bound. She hadn't been resting it. She had gone for a long walk. She couldn't remember why, but she had talked to a very nice policeman while she was out.

'They just keep getting younger!' Olive chuckled to herself. 'Cathy!' she called out. She stood still, waiting for the reply. It didn't come. Yes, she must have gone to the shops. She felt suddenly confused, a little unsure of why she had stood up. She looked around and tried to think back to what she had been doing. She remembered talking to Cathy — it was about dinner. Cathy was making her something to eat. No, that wasn't quite right. There was something else? It wasn't Cathy! Lisa was here! She remembered now. Lisa was making her dinner. Her friend had come round too. That had to be what the noises were.

'Lisa!' Again there was no reply. Olive tested her knee. She put one leg forward and shifted her weight. It held and she shuffled across the floor. Each step seemed a little easier as it loosened up and she walked through to the kitchen. The units were to her left, the table to her right. But no Lisa.

'Lisa!' She moved to look up the stairs from the hallway. 'LISA!'

Nothing. Strange.

Back in the kitchen, she couldn't hear the oven. No smells. No sign of activity at all save for the washing machine rolling lazily through its cycle. Her foot skidded. She tensed and steadied herself and the strain of it aggravated the pain in her leg. She reached out to steady herself on a kitchen worktop. The floor was wet. She looked down for the source but she didn't have her glasses on. There were two blurred, dark-coloured shapes on the floor. She reached down for one. It was a damp piece of cloth — cotton, she guessed. The second item stuck out from between the units. It felt wet too, but was more solid in her hand. She huffed as she straightened up for a better look. It was a mobile phone. A big one that she hadn't seen before. The screen lit up as she tilted it towards her face. She used to have one of these. Maybe this was it? She couldn't remember much about it. She tried to wipe the dampness off. Some of it came off in her hands. It was bright red and thick. Blood? It couldn't be. She wasn't bleeding. She checked her hands and arms. Nothing. Her knee ached all of a sudden. She slipped the mobile phone into her cardigan pocket so she wouldn't lose it again. She needed to sit back down, but in her comfortable chair where she could elevate her leg. She made her way slowly back into the living room.

When she got to her chair she almost fell into it. She was overdoing it; she knew that. Best to stay here until Cathy finished making her dinner. Her doctor programme was paused on the television. She liked this one. It had gotten a bit too complicated recently — she wasn't entirely sure who was who anymore. But she liked it all the same. Her glasses were on the arm of her chair. Sometimes they hurt her nose. She put them back on gently. The television was a little clearer. She pointed the remote and started it playing again.

Chapter 39

'Harry Blaker!' Harry barked into his phone with such ferocity it made Maddie jump. His phone had been going off almost non-stop since he had turned it back on. They had moved away from where Vamp was working, to sit back in Harry's car. He had moved his car across the entrance on the off-chance that a member of public tried to drive their own car in there. They were waiting for more resources to arrive. Harry had vented his spleen about how there was nothing more important than uniform officers manning the cordon, something he said should have been done hours ago. He'd since found out that the patrol sergeant — pleading a lack of resources — had decided that the murder scene was remote enough that he needn't send backup there straight away. The DI had taken just a few seconds to put an alternative opinion across. It had been such a loud opinion that Maddie had considered stepping out of the car. The volume was increasing again.

'When?' Harry lifted his eyes to Maddie. 'Okay, who's going? How far out?' He leaned forward to where the car keys hung from the ignition. 'Send the log through. Keep the response team running but we'll head over there now.

I'm with DS Ives. Mark us up as attending and show me making progress.' He finished the call and started the engine. 'We need to go!'

Maddie struggled with her seatbelt as Harry pulled away with a squeal in the tyres. 'My car's back there!'

'We'll get it later.'

'What's up?' Maddie said. The car accelerated hard. It was a short distance to Stone Street, the main road linking Langthorne with Canterbury. He pulled the car left towards Langthorne and handed his phone over to her.

'There should be an email coming through. We've had someone call in. My team have been monitoring the call logs for reports relating to AA meetings, groups of drinkers — anything like that really. A girl has called in and said that she dropped her mate back to her mum's house and she was with a guy she met at an AA meeting. She hadn't seen him before. She had to go back later to drop something off and she felt like there was something wrong. It bothered her and as she was walking back to the house, she saw the man leaving alone — she said he was in a white truck.'

'A white truck?'

'With a back on it, she said. She couldn't describe it any better, but I bet we could.'

'Like a McCall's truck.'

'Exactly that.'

'So where are we going?'

'That call was ten minutes ago. It's graded as a medium, which means uniform won't go out there for days. The informant's gone back home — she said she doesn't want to go in there on her own as the mum has dementia and she's taken a dislike to her. We're going round to check on the girl. Lisa someone.'

'Lisa Simpkiss,' Maddie said. The log had come through to her phone. It was written near the top. 'Born in eighty-five. She's a similar age to Lorraine.'

'She is.'

'I'm just reading through . . . there's no description for the male.' Maddie scanned down as quickly as she could. 'Harry!' she exclaimed. 'The girl who called in . . . she said this bloke's name was *Andy*!'

* * *

It took Harry nine minutes to reach the address. A few of the overtakes he did to get there were enough to make Maddie catch her breath — one in particular had her slamming her eyes shut completely — but they arrived in one piece.

Maddie hammered on the door. This time Harry was a few paces back, studying windows on the various floors and access points. The rear gate was pushed open, it banged against its own surround as the breeze moved down the side of the house. She didn't wait long until she hammered the door again. Suddenly she could see movement through the frosted glass. An outline of someone in dark clothing.

'Harry, someone's in!' she said.

The door pulled open. Just a bit. Enough for Maddie to see a pair of terrified eyes sunk into an elderly face. Maddie had her badge ready.

'Ma'am, so sorry to bother you. I'm a police officer and I need to speak with your daughter urgently. Is she in?'

'My daughter?' the woman said. She didn't budge and her expression didn't change. Her eyes settled on Harry.

'Yes, ma'am. Lisa. Lisa Simpkiss — she lives here, right?'

'She . . . no. It's just me and Cathy. I'll go and get her.' She pushed the door shut. Maddie shifted her foot just in time to stop it from closing. The elderly woman had already turned away. She was walking towards the kitchen and didn't seem to realise that the door had bounced back open.

Maddie looked back at Harry. 'She's got something on her hands. It looks like blood to me.' She moved into the house and called out. 'Sorry, ma'am?'

The old lady reappeared at the entrance to the kitchen. 'What are you doing in here? You can't come in here! I'll call the police. Get out!'

Maddie held her arms out to show she meant no harm. She let her badge fall back open in her right hand. 'I am the police, okay? We both are. We just need to speak to your daughter.'

'Well, you can't. I think she went out to the shops.'

'Okay. What is your name? So I know who I'm talking to.'

'Olive!'

'Olive . . . great. Are you okay, Olive? Did you cut your hand?'

'My hand? No!' She lifted her hands to inspect them. She seemed confused by the staining.

'Is that blood? Are you hurt?'

'No! I don't think so.' Her anger dropped away, it was confusion now. She raised watery eyes. 'I don't know!'

Maddie stepped towards her. She smiled, doing her best to be reassuring. 'Shall we sit you down? We just need to speak to you about Lisa, is all. I want to be sure you're both okay and then we will leave you alone.'

'Lisa? She's not here. What's that?' Her eyes were looking beyond where Maddie was standing. Maddie turned to see what she was indicating.

'Harry . . .' she said. Harry walked past her, looking down at the smears of red.

'Dammit!' He turned back to where Mrs Simpkiss was still staring wide-eyed. 'Do you know where Lisa is?' The woman was still looking down. 'Lisa! Do you know where she is?'

Her eyes snapped up to meet with his. The fear was back, it quickly turned to panic. 'Is she okay? Is Lisa okay?'

She became unsteady. Maddie reached out for her, pulled a seat out from under the dining table and helped her into it.

Harry paced gingerly across the kitchen. He stopped at the back door. He pulled his sleeve over his hand to pull the handle down. The door swung inwards and he stepped out.

'Sir?' Maddie said.

'She was dragged to here. There's more on the path.'

'My Lisa!' Mrs Simpkiss whined.

'What happened to her?' Maddie said. She watched Harry step out. He walked slowly across the window towards the far side of the house. His eyes were down. He stepped out of sight. Maddie was about to follow him out when he reappeared.

'The spots stop at the drive. There must have been a car.'

'I thought she went to the shops!'

'It's okay. Tell me what happened?' Maddie said. ' Was she here?'

'She was. She was here — I don't know when!'

'You have to think!' Harry cut in. 'You have to try and remember! There's a lot of blood. If this is one person's . . . if this is Lisa's and she's lost this much blood we need to find her. You need to think. You need to tell me what happened!' Olive's eyes flickered around the room and her mouth opened and closed. She was trying to speak, but she couldn't. Her breathing was suddenly quicker and she seemed to be struggling with it.

'I can't . . . I don't . . .' Her breathing got worse, quicker and shallower still. Harry was standing over her and Maddie pushed past him. She dropped to her knees in front of the woman. She took hold of her hand.

'Focus on me, Olive. Can you do that?'

Olive's eyes flicked around the room, her breathing faster still. She was losing control. Maddie recognised the start of a panic attack and tightened her grip on the old woman's hands. Olive looked down at them. When she lifted her eyes again they met with Maddie's.

'Good, that's good.' Maddie smiled, 'I know you can help us, I know you can — but you have to stay focussed on me. Can you hear me okay?'

The woman managed a jerked nod. 'I want you to do something for me, okay?' She got another nod. 'I want you to tell me five things that you can see. Can you do that?'

'Five . . .'

'Five things. I'll count them down.' She lifted her hand, she had her fingers splayed out. 'Tell me the first thing you can see,' she said.

'Y . . . you . . .' she managed.

Maddie dropped one of her fingers.

'Excellent. Give me four more.'

'My cooker . . .' she sniffed, 'the floor . . .' Her breathing was a little more controlled, a little less rushed. 'The chair . . . your hand.'

'That will do, Olive. Well done. Now, four things you can hear.'

She lifted her eyes. 'Your voice . . . the washing machine . . . I can hear me — my breathing.'

'You're doing so well.' Maddie reached out, took hold of her hand and pulled it towards her. 'Now tell me something you can feel.'

Her face creased, it was criss-crossed with wrinkles from a lifetime of smiles. They hadn't been revealed until now.

'You're holding my hand.' Her breathing was back to normal and the fear in her eyes had dissipated. She sniffed and her eyes flicked to Harry.

'Okay, Olive,' Maddie said. 'That's great . . . you did great. Do you remember why we came here?'

Her eyes suddenly lit again, like she had been caught out, she looked between the two detectives, suddenly worried.

'It's okay if you don't, Olive. That's our fault. We came here unannounced. Anybody would be a little confused. I'm sorry we disturbed you. We came to see Lisa.'

'Lisa's not here!'

'Okay, but maybe we should check she hasn't come back home again. Do you mind if I pop upstairs to check?'

'Well, I don't think she will be up there, but I suppose . . .'

'Great!' Maddie looked up at Harry. 'Stay with her. I'll see what I can find.' Harry nodded. She moved back into the hallway and across to the living room. The television was on and paused. Olive's seat was obvious, it was high-backed with extra cushions and a low table beside it that was cluttered with an asthma pump, an empty blister packet of pills, some discarded glasses and a listings magazine. From a quick check she could see no signs of disturbance, no obvious clues that Lisa had been in here and, crucially, no more blood.

Back in the hallway she cast her eye around quickly and looked up the stairs. The carpet was a dark blue. She turned the light on and bent forward a little to see if any patches of blood shimmered in the light. She couldn't see any. The banister and the walls were painted in a light vanilla shade. She checked them on the way up for any signs of splattering.

The stairs came up at one end of the landing. On the immediate right was the main bedroom. She stepped in. She guessed it was Olive's. The bed linen was floral and outdated, the bedside furniture the same. A cardigan hanging over the back of a chair looked to be similar to the one Olive was wearing.

She moved back out and across the landing into a box room. It had been the only door that was closed. It looked like it was used for storage — old clothes mainly — some piles of books and an old exercise machine with more clothes hanging off it.

The next room along was Lisa's for sure. It was sparse. It looked like the occupier hadn't quite unpacked yet — or was someone who wasn't unused to making anywhere home. The furniture, the single bed, it all seemed reminiscent of an adolescent Lisa. Maddie got the impression that she might have moved out a few times only to come back when she'd run out of options. This room was a little more untidy. There were clothes on the floor, the wardrobe was hanging open, with more clothes spewing out. She had numerous pairs of shoes lined up and an equal number of handbags thrown over the top of them. Maddie sifted through them quickly: lipsticks, makeup mirrors and the occasional packet of chewing gum — nothing that would be of any help to them.

The next room was the bathroom. She made sure to lift the soak-aways in the sink and the shower to check the undersides for blood. A good giveaway if someone had tried to clean up. She used the torch function on her phone to see right down the plughole for the same reason. The bath plug was fixed. She couldn't lift it out but she was able to ease it up just enough to be sure. The blood was isolated to the kitchen. And whoever it belonged to had been dragged outside from there. She ran down the stairs and back into the kitchen.

'She's not here.' Olive was still sitting at the kitchen table. Harry had taken a seat next to her, he was turned in and facing her. Olive had her hands on her lap and her head was bowed.

'Anything of note?' Harry asked.

'Nothing that stands out,' Maddie replied.

'I told you she wasn't here!' Olive said. Her handbag was on the table. She reached for it. She pulled a small packet of tissues out and blew her nose. She offered the packet around. Both detectives declined. She left the bag on her lap.

'We were just talking about Lisa,' Harry said. 'Olive, here, was saying that she saw her today. She was here with the police.'

'The police?'

'Yeah. They found you out on the streets this morning, didn't they, Olive? We're not sure what time.'

'And the police spoke with Lisa, did they?' Maddie said.

'We're not too sure, Maddie. Maybe we'll have a record?'

Maddie took the hint. She'd left her police radio in the car. She patted her pockets for her phone. She would call in to the force control room and find out what happened.

'Maybe she called me!' Olive exclaimed suddenly. 'I found my phone today! She always lets me know where she's going. I thought I had lost it. I found it just earlier! Now . . . where did I put it?' She sat up straighter, her eyes flicked around the room, scanning the surfaces. Harry stood up, keen to assist; Olive's phone would have her daughter's number at the very least. They might be able to use that to find her.

'I'll have a look if you like,' Harry said. 'You stay sat down. You told me about your bad knee there.'

Maddie swapped with him to sit next to the old woman. 'What happened to your knee?'

Olive flexed her leg gingerly and started describing her symptoms. Maddie wasn't really listening. Instead, her eyes followed Harry as he moved round the kitchen. He was searching the worktops and the drawers. He was being careful with his feet. Maddie took in the red smear across the floor. The blood surely had to be Lisa's and here was her mother talking casually about joint pain. She didn't seem to have a clue about the carnage that must have taken place in her own home — perhaps even while she sat watching her television.

'Do you have children?' The question punctured Maddie's thoughts and caught her out.

'I don't, Olive. Not yet. You have two, right?'

Olive suddenly broke into a wide smile. 'Two daughters. We tried for a boy, but it wasn't to be.' Olive's expression was suddenly melancholy. 'God didn't want us to be blessed with a boy. I reckoned it was his way of telling us that we needed to make the most of what we had. I tried. We both did. You can't live their lives for them, though, can you?'

'You can't. You can only bring them up the best you can.'

'They're good kids, though. We've had our problems. My Cathy, she's a real high-flyer, I always knew that about her. My husband, John, he used to say, "she's born ambitious that one." He was right, too. She puts me to shame. I've been a stay-at-home mum my whole life. I mean, it was different then. Now you can go out and do what you want. But back then, that's what you did.'

'Of course you had to.' Maddie could see Harry had stopped searching. He was the picture of frustration.

'But my Lisa . . . well, at least she might have got herself a man now. And he seemed nice. It's nice that she even brought him back here to meet me. I don't think she's ever done that before!'

'No, they don't, do they!' Maddie was still looking away but her attention suddenly switched back to Olive. 'A new man?'

Olive was beaming now, her eyes losing focus. 'Yes, he was here earlier. It must be early days. He seemed a bit nervous, you know, to meet me. The good ones always are. They want to make a good impression, see?'

'Do you remember his name, Olive — or anything about him?' Maddie tried to sound casual.

Olive grimaced. 'Oh, no, I don't. She would have told me, wouldn't she? She would have introduced him to me. I'll get into trouble! I should remember things like that . . . important things. But just recently, you know, I don't seem to—'

'It's okay, Olive. I'm sure she'll understand. I'm not very good with names either. Maybe they said where they were going?'

'I don't remember. I don't remember what she said.'

'Did you think they were going out somewhere nice? Was he treating her? Did she seem happy when they left?'

'I don't know! I think . . . I just don't know.'

'That's okay. Don't worry. Do you remember them leaving?'

'I . . . I think they went together? I'm a bit of a muddle. Oh I found my phone! When they left. It was just there. Maybe I should give her a call and see what time she wants me to put dinner on for.' Olive shifted her position so she could reach into her pocket. She pulled out a sleek smartphone. She grimaced again, her confusion obvious.

'Oh dear! I don't think I can work this one. Maybe this isn't mine after all?'

'Would you like me to have a try?' Maddie said, as she locked eyes with Harry. Olive handed it over without a second thought then went back to flexing her leg.

'I'm not supposed to walk on it,' Olive said.

'Sounds like good advice!' Maddie replied. She lifted the phone. She kept her voice low to speak with Harry. 'There's blood on it.' The glass front was spotted but there was a clearer smear down the side. Maddie was suddenly conscious that she shouldn't be handling it — too late for that. The screen demanded a passcode or a thumbprint. Maddie swore under her breath. She spun it round to show Harry.

'Have you got a second?' he said.

Maddie made her excuses to Olive and they moved as far as the hallway. She still faced back into the kitchen, where she could keep an eye on Olive. 'This must be Lisa's phone. We need to know what's on it.'

'We do. We can assume this Andy is known to her and she should have a number for him — maybe other

312

information that can help. I might know someone who can get into the phone.'

'On a Saturday morning?'

'I'll need to be persuasive. I'll get some more coppers here on the hurry up. We need to get a scene on and be away.'

'I agree,' Maddie said. 'We're not going to get anything more from here. We need to be doing something — and fast. We have to assume the daughter has been injured and dragged out. If we can't get into that phone though, we may need a plan B.' She paused for a moment. 'What did you do overnight? Around Andy McCall?'

'We don't have any addresses for him in the county. I spoke to Jim McCall, but only on the phone. He said he was out of the area on business. If he's to be believed he doesn't know where his brother is living. Apparently he moves around a lot. He did say that he thought he was living in Brighton and then Hastings at different times.'

'That ties in with the other girls.'

'It does.'

'Did you get a phone number from him?'

'Yes. I already ran a trace. It hasn't connected to a network for four months.'

'He's changed his phone.'

'Highly likely. His brother also said that the last time he saw Andy he was really angry — like, beside himself angry. He turned up at the office and was raging about Jonathan Lee getting arrested. He wanted to know what was going on — all the details. James McCall said he told him as much as he knew, which was that Jonathan had been arrested and someone had been knocked down by one of their trucks. James said he was furious about the arrest, about the police being at the office. It seemed strange to James at the time because he didn't think that Andy and the fella we arrested even knew each other.'

'You think he was angry because we were sniffing around?'

'I certainly do now.'

'So he moved the girl. He won't be using that site again, will he?'

'I wouldn't think so. I've tasked search teams with doing all the sites McCall's provided. There are seven in total — five in Lennockshire. The other two are in Sussex.'

'Makes sense.'

'It makes sense to search them to be sure, but it wouldn't make sense for him to use one of them. Not now.'

'So how do we find him?'

'You tell me! You wanted in on this, Maddie. Now's the time to pull something out of the hat!'

'That's hardly fair.'

'You're right.'

'We think he's in a McCall's truck. We can nominate the registration numbers on the ANPR system — just in case he runs a camera.'

'Okay.'

Maddie was still thinking. 'Did you speak to James McCall yourself?'

'I did. Over the phone.'

'And you think he was telling you everything he knows?'

'Hard to tell for sure. He sounded sure when he was speaking about his brother but he was a bit hesitant about his own whereabouts. I'm not convinced he's out of the area, put it that way.'

'Okay . . . I don't think his brother will change his MO.'

'So you think he'll use one of the sites?'

'Not one on that list he won't.'

'You think there are more?'

'At least one more. There has to be. Andy McCall would know that we've been in the office. Maybe there's a site that never even got to the negotiation stage.'

'And the only way for that to happen would be if James blocked it?'

'Exactly. Maybe he put his foot down.'

'Okay, so you want to go back to James McCall?'

'Or Ryan Clarke. But I think Ryan told us all he knew when we saw him. If you're not sure James did the same, then he might be the better bet. Especially if he is at home — we can catch him on the back foot if he lied about being away.'

'You're starting to think like a detective now, DS Ives, you should be careful with that.'

'It's plan B, though. That phone is still the best option.'

'I agree. I need to make some phone calls.'

Maddie nodded then turned back to Olive. She was still sat at her kitchen table — humming to herself in blissful ignorance.

Chapter 40

Robert Ford was Maddie's idea of a stereotypical techie. Harry had called him as they came away from Olive Simpkiss's house. Maddie's worries about leaving her were eased by the uniform officer who turned up, a middle-aged woman with a kindly disposition. It was the best she could have hoped for.

They were back at Canterbury police station. Robert lived within walking distance and was there waiting when they'd arrived. He wore khaki shorts and flip-flops and his hair was long and unkempt, as was his beard and the sizeable belly that threatened to push the creases right out of his Spiderman t-shirt.

'Let me see it then, but like I said on the phone, no promises. If it's Apple then you've got no chance.'

'It isn't. It says HTC.' Harry had the phone in an unsealed, clear bag. Rob took it off him and held it up.

'It's the Desire 10 — the pro version. We don't get many of these. We might have a chance. They tend to use older Android technology. I'll plug it in.' He turned to Harry. 'Just so you know, even if this is an instant fail, I'm still billing you for the full day's callout.'

'Just do what you can,' Harry said.

They were on the fourth floor. Rob and his fellow forensic media technicians, to give them their proper title, were tucked away at the end of a corridor where access could be controlled. The room was dark and the external windows had fixed shutters over them to prevent anyone from being able to see in — not that anybody was likely to see into the fourth floor, but the police had a responsibility to ensure they couldn't. This was one of the rooms used for viewing and downloading evidential material for all sorts of cases. That could be anything from drug dealer phones to devices containing child pornography. Maddie couldn't imagine the horrors that had been on display in this room. Rob seemed blasé about it all. He thumped a keyboard to wake a monitor. It had *Do not switch off!* handwritten on a peeling post-it note. The screen was cluttered with icons and Rob clicked on one. The screen changed and he reached for a lead. The other end ran behind the monitor.

'You're sure you want me to do this?'

'Do what exactly?' Harry asked.

'I'm going to plug it in. I'll be attempting to download whatever I can get from the phone but there are three possible reactions.'

'Three?'

'Yeah. It either bypasses the phone's operating system and sucks up all the data as it was designed to, or the security is effective enough that it does nothing at all, or — and this is entirely possible — it meets with an installed bot app that detects something is trying to bypass the security and wipes the contents of the phone completely. Anything on there is lost forever.'

'I see. What are the odds?'

'No idea. I assume you know more about the owner of this phone than I do. If the right app is installed then we're in trouble, but we won't be able to tell that in advance. Our best bet is to use the systems at

317

headquarters. They have something that can do a prelim scan. That gives you a pretty good indication of what applications are installed on the phone.'

'And if it did show that this app was installed, would we be able to do anything to stop it happening and still get the data?'

'Well, yeah, you get the phone's unlock code from the owner. There's no other way.'

'That's not an option. Plug in your gizmo.' Maddie was aware of Harry looking at her as he continued, 'let's hope your girl isn't security conscious, eh?'

'I can't see it,' Maddie said.

'Let's get it done then, shall we?' Rob took a seat at the desk. 'My time off is precious.' He connected the lead to the phone. It lit up and then fell back to black.

'What happened?' Harry said.

'Nothing yet. Patience!' Rob clicked the mouse and the screen changed again. A box came up asking if he was sure about something, but before Maddie could read the whole warning he had already clicked again and it disappeared. A box appeared with a pulsing horizontal line running through its middle. It started to fill from left to right . . . *very* slowly.

'Looks like we might be lucky,' Rob said. 'There must be a lot of data on there, though. This is going to take a while. I take one sugar.' He sat back and crossed his arms. Maddie could almost admire the front of the bloke. They *had* dragged him away from his precious time off, though, whatever the hell that meant. She watched the line build and relented.

'I can do coffee, that's all,' she said.

Harry turned to her. He still looked agitated but he snatched a nod. 'I'll call round for an update from the search teams.' For the first time, Maddie considered that the stress of their situation might be getting to Harry.

She made her way out. The coffee machine was on the next floor up. It was quiet. The only people that generally worked weekends were the response officers and they were too busy to stop for coffee. The machine burped and fizzed with the first of the drinks. She took a moment to check her phone. She had a text message. The sender was marked simply as '*A*.' That was how she'd labelled Adam Yarwood. She slid her thumb across her screen to open it up.

Hey. Coming back your way tomorrow I think. I'll book into the same place. I liked the rooms there.

Nothing more. It wasn't a question, he wasn't asking to meet and he wasn't asking if it was alright. He was just being Adam Yarwood and that meant doing whatever the hell he wanted while assuming everyone else would fall in line. That might be the very same attitude that had got her into him in the first place, but right now it was threatening her career more than ever. She needed to handle him better than this. In her previous life she had lived and worked out of sight, off the grid. She had made it work, but she couldn't do that anymore. She put her phone back in her pocket to start the next drink. It was a problem for later.

The digital line on the screen was just about full by the time she returned with the drinks. Harry was still pacing. He wasn't good at waiting for results. In her experience, detectives rarely were. The screen changed. A list of files quickly filled the screen from top to bottom.

'What's on there?'

'Shit, Harry! You gotta give me a second. There's a lot of data here.' Rob was shaking his head.

'Okay, focus on text messages. I need to know who she's been talking to and what she's been saying. And if we can get a phone number for the handset I can put in for a historic picture. We can see where she's been.'

'Messages? Well, there aren't many, so that should be easy enough. Ninety percent of the shit on this phone is video and images. Are you interested in them?'

'We'll have a look at a sample. I've not got time to be going through it in great detail now.'

Rob clicked and the monitor screen changed again. It seemed to mirror a smartphone home screen. It looked like a load of app tiles over a digital photo. Maddie gasped at it. She could make most of it out: a man in sunglasses, his arms crossed, his right foot up and resting on a white truck. 'That could be our Andy!' Maddie said.

'Can you get the tiles out of the way?' Harry growled.

'No. It's not like operating the actual phone. I might be able to find the photo, though.'

Maddie bit down on her lip. Rob clicked furiously. A folder opened with a grid of thumbnails. It looked like the top image was the photograph they wanted. Rob had seen it, too. He double-clicked to open it up.

'Look at the truck, Harry!' Maddie said. The *McCall's* livery could be seen clearly on the door. 'They must be an item?'

Harry stayed silent.

Rob clicked again. The image changed: the same man minus the sunglasses. It was a selfie, the glimpse of scenery behind looked to be woodland somewhere. After that came a screenshot from a website. It was a motion sensitive webcam similar to the one Maddie had seen in the material sent from Sussex.

'It's his phone!' Maddie breathed. 'It's Andy's!'

'It's his phone,' Harry repeated.

Rob clicked again. He had to scroll through more pages of webcams; they all seemed similar. He stopped when he got to a solid, dark square with a triangular *play* symbol in its centre. A video. Rob clicked to start it playing.

The blurring took a few seconds to resolve itself. Maddie leaned in to try and make something out. It wasn't obvious what she was looking at. The monitor was dark. She could make out vertical lines that were a slightly lighter shade. A timer counted up in the bottom right of the screen and it showed 22:04:17. Suddenly the screen flared white, every part of it. Another second passed and the camera adjusted. The screen was still white but other details came into focus. It was like a version of night vision. Maddie's eyes were drawn first to a number that stood out in the bright light as if it was glowing. The lines that she had seen as shades were now clearly recognisable as the sides of a metal box or a container. A number came into focus, its thick, black font standing out against the white background — *37*.

'Thirty-seven!' Harry exclaimed. 'We've seen that! Leonard's Farm — in that container!' He was now as animated as Maddie had seen ever him. He walked to the door, then stopped and turned as if he had changed his mind.

'This is what he was worried about. Ron Beasle *was* getting too close. I knew the fox wasn't right. We were stood right there! This was going to be one of his dump sites. He must have changed his mind after he killed Ron.'

Maddie shook her head. 'We couldn't have known. We weren't there looking for dump sites, Harry.' Her head was shaking; she knew she was consoling herself really.

Harry still didn't reply. He leant in closer to the screen. The video was still playing. The camera was fixed. At the bottom of the screen was something dark, it looked like a roll of carpet perhaps. There was movement. Maddie had to squint to make it out. She leant closer to the screen. Harry did too; they were almost touching. Definite movement. It was an arm. It seemed to reach out from the roll of carpet, the fingers on the hand were visible now and they scratched at the floor.

'Harry! She's alive!'

Harry didn't reply. Maddie held her breath. There was more movement on the screen. Now that Maddie had identified one body part the rest of the picture started to make sense. She could see the woman's head moving. The camera was at an angle, like it was in the corner and pointed down and across. The arm was reaching away, towards the door. The angle of the camera meant they were looking at the back of her head. There was another shape lying alongside her too. There was no movement from that. The picture quality wasn't good enough for Maddie to make out any details from it either; it was just a clump of darkness.

She felt Harry move away. He paced back to the door and then came back again as if he didn't know what to do with himself. 'I need to call the team who are out at Leonard's Farm,' he said. 'Damage limitation on the scene preservation. Rob, you need to keep this on your screen. I'll get a DC up here to go through it all to see what else we can get. I need you to do a full evidential download too. I can't have anything lost from that phone.'

'Okay. You don't want to see what else there is yourself? Quick? Looks like there's all sorts of—'

'Could we still activate one of those bot app things?'

'It is possible.'

'No then. Get your download done. That takes a while, right?'

'Two hours, based on the amount of material.'

'That video — is it dated?'

Rob clicked some more. 'It will be. Normally the date is in the title but these files haven't saved like that. They must be saved from a third-party app. I guess there's one on here that runs the camera. I can find out exactly when that video was saved to this phone but it'll take a while.'

'Okay, it doesn't matter right now. We need to be somewhere else. Can you just bring up the contacts list? I need to be sure of something.'

Rob clicked his mouse. The video screen was replaced by a list of names and numbers.

'There are hundreds of them.'

'Are they alphabetical?'

'No, but there's a search function.'

'Okay, search for James — or Jim.'

Rob typed then shook his head. Nothing.

'Jimmy?'

'No, that would have come up. Who's Jimmy?'

'If we're right about this, it's his brother. One last thing . . . can you bring up the call list?'

Rob typed something again. There was nothing inbound — maybe he'd deleted them — and just one of the outbound list showing on the screen as *Bruv*. There was a row of digits next to it and a date that was two days old. 'I guess that'll be your James then,' Rob said.

Harry took out his own phone for comparison. 'It's him. It's James McCall's number. We have to go!'

Maddie looked up to where the video was back up on the screen. It was paused where Rob had stopped it. The arm was reaching out towards the door. Maddie could feel the desperation. Harry was already out of the room. Maddie snatched her attention from the screen to go after him.

Chapter 41

Something shook Lisa Simpkiss awake. Something or somebody. She was aware of a flicker in front of her, as if someone had walked across the bright light that was forcing her to squint. The light was pouring in through a large bay window. She tried to follow the direction of the movement but the pain came rushing back, slamming her eyes shut so there was just darkness. She groaned and sucked air in hard, coating her throat with a layer of thick dust. The coughing that followed was agony, but she did her best to get still again. The pain didn't stop, but it dulled enough for her to bear it. She opened her eyes to the ground, away from the light. She could see exposed floorboards littered with dead insects that increased in number the closer they were to the window. She was in the room of a house. A front room: she could make out an old fireplace crudely papered over; the walls were scraped back to plasterboard and the dust was visible in layers.

She tried to recall the sequence of events leading to her being here. Her mind had been foggy but it came back with sudden clarity. She remembered the man in her kitchen, the smears of blood she had left behind, and the desperation to get him away from her mother. She felt her pulse quicken. Her breathing sped up with it and the movement agitated her abdomen. She had to stay calm.

She opened her eyes enough to squint at the window. It still flared painfully white. She was on her side. Under the window she could see a dark triangular shape. It was unmoving. For a terrifying moment she thought it was someone squatting down or hunched over but then she realised that it was a blue office chair with black legs on a chrome pedestal and castors. Her eyes were getting a little more accustomed to the light, too. Enough for her to see out of the window to a blue sky interrupted by the top of a tree. A small part of the window was open and she picked up birdsong and the shushing and creaking of tree branches in the wind.

She detected movement. Someone was pacing from left to right. The figure settled on the chair. It was Andy.

'You're going to die, Lisa. Here.' He stared at her for a few seconds. His stare broke off and he seemed to be looking around the room, looking for something perhaps. 'I don't know when. You've lost some blood but not enough. I will need to hasten things along. I don't know how yet.'

'What do you want?' Lisa's voice was quiet; it came out as a sigh almost. She was trying to limit her movement, trying to stay calm. Still she could feel the vibration of her own voice through her stomach. She moved her free hand to the wound and it felt warm to the touch. Her other hand was trapped beneath her body with no feeling.

'To watch,' he said. His voice was different from when they had spoken before and it wasn't just the acoustics of the empty room. He scuffed his feet and the sound filled the space. 'I know you understand,' he said.

'What?'

'We're addicts, Lisa. Me and you. You know what that means, you understand. We've spent our whole lives trying

325

to be understood but it's only ever other addicts that truly do.'

'I drink,' she managed.

'You do. You yearn for it. It's all you think about. It's the only time you really feel *alive*. Am I right? It is who you are, Lisa.'

'It isn't. I beat it.'

The noise was sudden and loud. The chair tumbled onto its side and scraped across the bare floor. She shut her eyes. When she opened them again, he had moved out of sight. The floor squeaked behind her. She could sense him. He was close. When he spoke this time she could feel his breath on her ear. 'You *beat* it? What does that even mean? You get to go to a meeting once a week and then pretend you're someone else the rest of the time? You can only be who you are. What's the point of being alive if you don't *feel* it?'

Lisa felt a surge of rage and she managed to move enough to rock onto her back and free up her left arm. It tingled with a million tiny pinpricks. She was facing up now, towards Andy and beyond to a stained, white ceiling with yellowed paper hanging down around a single bulb. Andy moved quickly out of sight. She couldn't twist enough to keep him in her field of vision.

'So this is how you get off, is it?' Lisa growled. 'I never stood a chance! A knife from nowhere like a fucking coward.' She spat her words towards the ceiling but she could sense him off to her left. Sure enough he appeared, looming over her. He had the same expression she had seen earlier, his excitement was peaking.

'Addicts like you and me don't care what people think, Lisa. I tried fighting it. I tried being what I thought everyone else wanted me to be, but I can't do it anymore. Soon everyone will know anyway. I messed up. I got sloppy and I was kicking myself about it at first but I always knew this time would come. The time when I

326

would have to take myself away from society completely. I don't fit.'

'You can still make it right. Call for help. Help me. We all want to give in sometimes, but you got to have the balls to fight it. It's easy just to say it's what you are, but I don't believe that. You can be anything you want.'

He moved away. She sucked in a big breath and gritted her teeth against the pain. She wriggled to try and get a view of where he had gone. She started a gentle rocking motion, building up to shifting onto her other side.

'It's too late for that.'

'It's never too late to start. You must remember that from the meetings, right?'

'You don't understand, Lisa. I can't make it right. Just ask her.'

Lisa made it all the way onto her other side in time to see Andy move again, but it was through a doorway and he was gone. Her eyes fell to a form next to her. She focussed on a woman's pale face, her blue lips were parted slightly, showing her teeth, and her dead eyes stared out at her. For a moment Lisa froze. It didn't look real. It was like a bad dream. She couldn't scream, nor could she stop her eyes from scanning down the entire figure. She wasn't clothed, she could see a rough and jagged wound slashed across the woman's neck. Then her eyes ran over the pale breasts, stalling on an ugly laceration on the abdomen. Her hand was half over it, her fingers bunched together over a mass of something that looked like grey bubble wrap. Lisa couldn't catch her breath. Her mind suddenly made sense of the picture in front of her. It put everything in place and it flashed up her own future. She flicked back up to where those dead eyes were still staring right at her. The dead eyes of a young woman with her throat slashed, holding in her own intestines.

Lisa's scream finally came. She spun away and rolled fully over. Her stomach flashed with a searing pain and she took in more dust as she gasped, her hands and feet clawing at the ground as she tried to scramble to her feet.

With a rush of adrenalin she managed to get to her feet — just in time for the door through which she'd had seen Andy leave slam shut. There was no handle. Her fingers scrabbled over its surface, searching desperately for a grip, some way to pull it open — there was nothing. She turned on the spot and scoured the room in desperation. The upended chair was the only item — there was nothing else. She spun to the window. If she could lift that chair she reckoned it would smash through the glass. She stumbled to her knees. Her hands rested on the chair leg; it was cool to the touch. Suddenly a shadow loomed from outside the window. She turned to it as a sheet of wood was lifted by two gloved hands and bumped against the glass, covering one of the panes completely. She stumbled to the window as she heard the shrill whine of an electric drill. She hammered on the glass. Her desperation increased as another sheet of wood was lifted to cover the next pane. The light in the room was depleted. She grabbed the chair. The pain from her stomach tore through her when she tried to lift it and she was brought back to her knees. She lifted her head as the final pane was covered and she heard the whine of the drill securing it in place. The light was all but gone now and the room was sealed like a tomb.

Chapter 42

James McCall's house was the sort of thing Maddie was expecting for the owner of a middle-sized development firm. It was large, but not overbearing and sat on its own plot behind double gates that hung open. They were at the edge of a pleasant-looking village called Bossingham, on the outskirts of Canterbury. There was a courtyard at the front that was closed in by the L-shaped property. The left side of the L looked like a recent extension and was joined to the main house by a gabled roof and the end pointing towards them was mostly glass. Maddie could see a mezzanine level on the top and a kitchen on the ground floor.

'Nice place,' she said.

Harry grunted his reply.

'So he's out of the area is he?'

'That's what he said on the phone. He has some business in the north of the country — apparently. I did send the night duty DC to knock on the door, just in case.'

'You thought he was lying?'

'Sure, why not? We get used to it, right?'

'I suppose we do.'

'They got his partner just before he went to bed, according to the update I've seen. He backed up his story but the detective who called round here wasn't convinced either.'

Maddie took in the site as a whole. On the opposite side of the courtyard was a separate garage. It looked to be a new addition. The door was huge. She made straight for it. There was a handle in its centre. She reached for it and the whole door lifted in a smooth movement. Maddie could see the backs of a couple of cars: one looked like a sports car, small and low to the ground; the other was a large saloon. She pulled the door back down and walked back over to where Harry had his arms crossed.

'We're not here to carry out illegal searches, Maddie.'

Maddie shrugged. 'I thought that might be the front door.' She walked to a light brown front door that was half way down the new extension. There was another front door in the original part of the house but this one seemed to show more signs of use. Her knock was firm. So was the expression of the man who answered the door.

'Can I help you?' he said. He was of large build and wore a short-sleeved shirt with red flecks running through it, hanging over board shorts and flip-flops. His face and arms looked to have been scalded red by the sun. He looked beyond Maddie to where Harry stood.

'Ah yes, I'm Detective Sergeant Ives. I'm here to speak with James. We have met before. If you could just tell him I'm here.'

'Do you have an appointment?' the man said. He fixed his attention on Maddie.

'No.'

'I see. Well, unfortunately Mr McCall is out of the area for a few days with his work. I can take a number if you need him to give you a call when he is back?'

'Where did he go?' Maddie said.

The man huffed. 'I gave all of this information to the police last night — in the middle of the night, I might add.

I'm still considering whether I should make a complaint about that. This visit doesn't exactly appease me.'

'Well I'm not here to appease you, sir. I'm here because we're trying to keep a very vulnerable young lady safe from harm. James knows something about that. Did he mention her to you?'

'A young lady? I can assure you he knows nothing about your young lady—'

'With respect, your assurances are not what I'm here for either.'

The man hesitated. His lips twitched then his tongue ran between them. Maddie recognised the tic of a man preparing himself to lie. 'Well, he isn't here.'

'So where is it he's gone?'

The man huffed again. 'I already told you people, Sussex somewhere.'

'Ah, okay. He mentioned he was looking at a site out in the countryside there. Some farm, I think. Is that about right?'

'Well, yes, that sounds about right.'

'No trains around there. I assume he drove?'

'Drove? Yes, he drove.'

'His Jag?'

'I . . .'

'He doesn't have any other cars registered to him is all. There's a little Alfa Romeo sports car registered at this address. I assume that's yours? Do you let him drive that?'

'Yes, he can drive that. But, no. I mean, he will have taken his car.'

'Can you get him please? It really is very important,' Maddie said.

'Get him?' The man became redder still. 'I don't appreciate you—'

'I don't appreciate being lied to.' Maddie was quick to cut in, her voice raised, 'not with something as important as this. His car's here, you're a terrible liar and we don't have the luxury of time. Get him to this door now or you will be arrested for obstruction.'

His huff this time was the biggest yet. He pushed the door and was out of sight. Maddie got her foot out in time to stop it closing completely. She could hear his flip-flops as they moved away. She glanced far enough into the house to see a smart, open-plan kitchen over wooden flooring.

'Desperate to make friends today, DS Ives?'

Maddie detected the flicker of a smile from her colleague. 'I don't like being fobbed off. And I've seen enough liars in my time. It's quite refreshing to be able to tell them for once.'

'Be careful with that tenacity, Maddie. And when did he say he was going to some farm in Sussex?'

'He didn't. Just like I didn't check what cars were registered here.'

The door was roughly pulled back open again — the same man appeared, redder than ever. 'You'd better come in.' He stepped back to allow them entry. Maddie didn't need a second invitation. She walked through to the expansive kitchen. Bi-fold doors were pushed open on the other side. They led through to a shaded patio. She could see a table and chairs. Beyond that was soft seating for two overlooking a neat lawn.

'Outside looks very pleasant,' Maddie said, pushing her luck. She was already walking towards the table. McCall appeared from the same direction. He must have heard her.

'Please, take a seat.' McCall gestured at the table and chairs. 'Can I offer you a drink?' Maddie turned to see the man who had answered the door scowl at James.

'No, we're a little short on time,' Maddie said.

'Well, if you'll excuse me . . .' The man who'd answered the door made his exit.

'Sorry. He's angry at me and he's right, too. I put him in a difficult situation,' McCall said. He was flushing a little himself.

'By asking him to lie for you?' Maddie pressed.

'Well, yes, I suppose so.'

'Why would you do that?'

'Please,' James gestured again for them to sit at the table. 'I was just going to make myself an iced tea. Are you sure you won't join me?'

'This will only take a minute.'

McCall hesitated, but he sat down. Harry did the same. Maddie leant on the back of her chair.

'So, you asked your partner to lie for you,' Maddie said. 'Once last night and then again today. Why would you do that?'

James looked from Maddie to the seated inspector. 'I don't believe we were introduced last time? Mr Blaker, here, was asking the questions as I recall.' Maddie recognised a man who was stalling.

'Maddie asks the questions when she's angry,' Harry said. 'I try not to get in her way.' He sat back further in his seat and crossed his arms. Maddie took it as a prompt to continue.

'I'm looking for a young woman who we believe to be in serious danger. That's all you need to know except that every second we are delayed is another second further away from finding her. She might already be dead, James, but if she isn't and you don't help . . .'

'Dead? What is this? I thought this was about this hit and run nonsense!'

'We have a theory. The hit and run was part of something bigger.'

'Bigger? And you think my company is involved?'

'Someone who works for it.'

'Who?'

'The list of employees you provided, the people with access to the vehicle keys — why wasn't Andrew on it?'

'Andrew?'

'Your brother, James. Andrew was not on that list. He's a partner at McCall's. So why wasn't he included?'

'My brother! A partner? I mean, yes, on paper he is exactly that, but in reality I can assure you he has nothing to do with my company.'

'He has access to those keys, though, doesn't he?'

'Well, yes. I mean, he can access the building so he can get to the keys in theory—'

'In theory? There's no theory about it, Mr McCall. He was a regular at your building at one point. He still turns up when he wants to. Does that annoy you?'

'Annoy me? I'm trying to run a business. But what is this about him being involved—'

'And he gets in the way.' Maddie cut back in. She would be the one asking the questions. She didn't have time for anything else.

'I don't know. I don't have much to do with him to be honest.'

'So you don't get on?'

James McCall's chair scraped the patio. He appeared to fix on something beyond Maddie. She turned to see the flushed man in the flip-flops leaning in the open doorway. He spoke.

'You're not considering defending him, are you? Tell them what he's like. Tell them *who* he is! You don't owe him any favours and they're not going to leave until you do.'

Maddie turned back to James. He paced a little, his head bent as if he was thinking it through.

'I don't really know what you want me to tell you. We don't get on. We never have, really. I tried, when we were younger and under each other's feet in the family home. I always thought it was the job of the older brother to look after the younger one. That's how it goes, right? It was never like that. He certainly didn't need anyone looking after him. My brother is not an easy man to get along with.'

'And now he owns half your business.'

'And it's rare a day goes by that I don't regret that. Simon and I . . . well, if I had only met Simon a few years earlier he would have been the obvious choice. We could have been partners in every sense!'

Maddie turned back to the man still leaning in the doorway. 'And you would be Simon.'

'I would.'

'Where is he, James?' Maddie's tone was a little warmer. She had gotten across the urgency now.

He snorted his response, 'What? You mean now? Where does he live? I have no idea! He's always been restless, shall we say. The army was the best place for him. I really thought he might find his place in this world. He couldn't even make that last.'

'Tell me about his army career. What happened?'

'He signed up. All he was interested in when he was a boy was the armed forces. He wanted to be a pilot to start with but he didn't get the grades. The RAF in general was out for him, I never really found out why. He tried again for the army and got in on the communications side of things.'

'Communications? Like the signals?'

'I'm not sure. He seemed to be good at it though. When he first came on board at McCall's we were having issues with people stealing from the sites. We were losing metal and tools hand over fist. He fitted motion cameras. They were linked up to all our phones but he would turn out if there was anything untoward. He was the best security you could ever have! For a couple of months there we had a good working relationship. I thought maybe we could build on that, get something closer to the kind of relationship two brothers should have. It didn't happen.'

'Why not?'

'He lost interest, like he always does. He moved onto something else no doubt.'

'Any idea what?'

'He doesn't talk to me. You should understand that. I don't know anything and I couldn't even suggest someone who might. I've never met another person who I would describe as a friend of Andy's—'

'Girlfriends?'

'Definitely not.'

'Has he ever been here?'

'No. He wouldn't come here. He doesn't agree with my . . . lifestyle.'

'Lifestyle?'

'Simon and I. He is not someone who seems to be able to understand that a man can be in a same-sex relationship, let alone his own brother. He seemed to take it personally, to be honest — like I was doing it just to upset him.'

'And what does he do to upset you?'

'What do you mean?'

'McCall's. You're at the table for a list of places that have grief written all over them. One of your employees has suggested this might be Andy's way of upsetting you.'

'Did he now? I've tried to play that all down . . . he's probably right. We're never going to exchange actual money for those sites. It's bad enough we're spending money on the surveys and permissions. I have no intention of buying them. They're not feasible.'

'You sent the information for all your potential sites. Are there any others?'

'No. That's everything.'

Maddie exchanged a glance with Harry. She wasn't getting what she needed. Maybe James wasn't the man to help. But who else?

'Do you have a picture here?'

'Of Andy? Sure. That one over there captured a very rare moment!'

Maddie looked towards a shelf where there were a number of photos in frames. One of them was of James McCall in a suit with his arm around the same man they'd seen in the woodland selfie. There was no doubt the phone from Lisa Simpkiss's kitchen was his. Harry had moved a little closer to the picture. He seemed satisfied.

'You said you don't talk,' he said. 'We know he called you two days ago.'

'Called me? Probably. He calls me a lot. I don't answer anymore. Conversations with Andy are never pleasant. Do you think my brother ran someone down in my truck? Is that what this is all about?'

Maddie fixed back on him. 'Do you think he's capable of doing something like that?'

James glanced at his partner.

'You need to tell them about him,' Simon said. 'They need to know.'

Maddie stayed focussed on James. He sighed heavily. 'I do.' His voice was quiet and his head drooped forwards. He moved back to the seat. 'He's always been a bit of an angry man. Not enough on its own, I know, but there's something else with him. He seems to have a . . . fascination.'

'A fascination?'

'Yes. With the macabre.'

'What makes you say that?'

'When we were teenagers, a long time ago admittedly, I found some material in his room. It was strange stuff — it turned my stomach. Nothing terrible, really. He'd obviously found a seagull, a dead seagull, and he'd taken pictures. But it was more than just a schoolboy snapping a picture to show their mates. He had photos of it from every angle, it was up close and it was . . . oh, Christ!'

'Tell them everything, James.' Simon's tone had now lost its edge; it was almost soothing.

'It was posed.'

'Posed?'

'He'd moved it around. Changed its position, but not like you might mock something up for comedy. You know, I saw a sick picture of some dead livestock at school once. Some jock had put a hat on it and a fag in its mouth. High jinks — lads messing about. This wasn't like that.'

'What was it like?'

'Like he was revelling in it. Like it did something to him. It was unhealthy.'

'What else?'

'He got into shooting. He started out beating for the gentry but then he got his own shotgun and he would just go off with it. Not on organised shoots, just whatever he could find . . . rabbits, foxes . . . all types of birds. And it was the same story. I found some more photos, some looked like people's pets! A dog, a few cats and a shocking white bunny. I remember the blood . . . a white bunny, you can imagine. I was worried about him. I mean, that's not normal is it?'

'It doesn't sound it,' Maddie said. 'Not to me.'

'Not to me either. I went to our mother. I didn't dare speak to my dad — he was a fearsome man. Our mother said she would talk to Andy about it. She took her time, but eventually she did and that was it. That was a real turning point in our relationship. I think he felt betrayed, I think he felt as if I was against him and that's where we've been ever since. Him on one side, me on the other. I think everything else, Simon included, is just an excuse to hate me.'

'Mr McCall,' Harry cut in with his growling tone and James McCall lifted heavy eyes. 'We think Andrew might have moved on from animals. We think he is getting his kicks from hurting young women and we need to find him before he hurts anyone else. We don't have anyone else we can talk to. We don't think anyone knows him better. Please, now you know the stakes here, if you can think of anything that might help.'

'Women! You said . . . has he . . . has he killed someone?'

'He might have,' Maddie said. 'We need to find him.'

'Oh God!' James's hand shot to his mouth. Maddie heard movement behind her. Simon walked round behind where James sat and pushed his hand over his shoulder where it rested on his chest. James patted it. 'I always feared that he was some sort of psycho, that he was dangerous. All the signs were there — I told mother that. She must have known it, too, but everyone was so scared of him. We were on eggshells with him, the whole time. The house was such a different place when he left for the army.'

'Your brother knows we have been at McCall's,' Harry said. 'He might assume that we know about the sites he has proposed and he has moved on. Is there anywhere else that he might use? He seems to favour derelict locations — sites that he knows are going to sit unused for a long time. Is there anywhere else he ever proposed or talked about?'

'The tunnel!' James suddenly snapped straighter in his chair. He pushed Simon's hand off. 'Ryan — the fleet manager — he mentioned a site to me, but it was a little while ago. He said he had been tipped off by one of his contacts that it might be sold off but there were big issues with access. If they could be overcome then it might be possible. I looked at it and I said no. The access issue there is never going to be resolved.'

'Where? What tunnel?'

'The channel tunnel!'

'In Langthorne?'

'Yes. The Eurotunnel site. It's a huge site, but it's also a mess of ownership. They built these huge reservoirs and put them on the outskirts of the site. It's like a bowl, you see . . . all the water runs off the steep hills of the North Downs and collects in these reservoirs. Apparently they needed these things as a contingency in case they ever got a fire in the tunnel. They can flush it through using the water from these reservoirs. I don't know how.'

'And they don't need them now?'

'No. Technology moves on, I guess.'

'So the land is up for sale.'

'No. Eurotunnel are haemorrhaging money. This reservoir site has an old school right in the middle of it. It was the village school for Peene originally. Then it was a family home, beautiful I would imagine, and then a horse-riding school, where it was extended quite extensively. It's a lovely building. If it was on a country plot it would be just our sort of thing, but it was a non-starter. I put my foot down on this one. I did a little bit of digging around. It's well within the inner perimeter of the site. It's gated and fenced and the only access is through the Eurotunnel site's own access roads. You couldn't create access to it either for national security reasons. Apparently the tunnel is deemed a primary target for terrorist attacks. Makes sense, I suppose.'

'And Andy knew about this?'

'If Ryan knew, Andy would know. Ryan was normally the man he would send to sound me out. Then, when I told him no, it would get back to my brother and the abuse would start . . . the intimidation . . . the general unpleasantness. Because I needed Andy for the money to grow the company he seems to think I owe him. He thinks he owns half of the company and starts demanding his share. It doesn't work like that. Construction companies are like a lot of companies . . . all our worth is tied up in buildings, equipment, plant and projects we haven't completed yet. Giving Andy half what the company is worth would mean selling it completely.'

'But you didn't relent on the Eurotunnel site?'

'No.'

'When was this?'

'Like I said, it was a while ago. Eighteen months, maybe. Long enough that I'd forgotten about it.'

'And he was upset about this one?'

'No, actually. He seemed to accept it for once. Maybe he saw how impossible it was too. All the other sites would be extremely difficult but there are possibilities at least. There's no such thing with this site — we couldn't even get to start negotiations.'

Maddie looked at Harry. He stood with his arms crossed. 'There is another theory . . .' she said. 'That he finally found a site where he knew *no one* was going to bother him. Not ever. He might even have regretted mentioning it.'

'His plan B,' Harry said. 'We need to go.'

Maddie was already on her feet.

'You'll keep me informed?' James said.

'I'll do my best.' Maddie gathered up her things. Harry was already walking across the kitchen towards the door.

'I hope you're wrong!' James called out. 'About my brother!'

Maddie pulled the door open. She peered back over. James was on his feet and Simon stood next to him. 'It's you that would have to be wrong about him, Mr McCall. Thank you for your help.' She pulled the door shut and jogged to the car.

Chapter 43

Sergeant Oliver 'Ollie' Craddock leaned back in his office chair and lifted his boots onto his desk in the Ports Control Room at the Channel Tunnel. He led a team of ten officers who manned five armed response vehicles. His team were tasked with covering the whole county and they were the first response to emergency shouts where an armed presence might be required. It was a busy job; the area was large and they were stretched thin. The exception was the shift at the tunnel. Most of the officers hated it, but Ollie didn't mind it at all. He would try and put himself on the rota for covering the site at least once in a set of shifts. It was always a brief respite for him. The Home Office demanded that there was a constant armed presence at the port and who was he to argue with the Home Secretary? The Operational Order stated that they should be 'visible,' which meant walking the platforms and ticket booths, interacting with members of the public as they got off their international trains. But Ollie Craddock had fifteen years' experience in the job and had realised some time ago that interacting with the public was his least favourite part of it. And it inevitably led to having to do some police work.

Today he was crewed up with PC Alan Edmonds, a man with an even longer service record and a very similar attitude. Ollie would always take Alan when he was covering the tunnel. They had brought a deck of cards and Sue Revell, one of the girls covering the desk, had just made them a brew.

The office was dimly lit compared to the bright furnace outside. The blinds were turned inwards and the bank of monitors was providing the main source of light. The control room desk phones were incessant. Ollie supped at his tea then called over.

'Sue! Can you turn them phones down? Can't hear myself think over here!' He splayed out his cards. He'd been dealt a good hand. He peered over at Alan to try and read any reaction. He knew he was wasting his time. Alan never gave anything away.

'It's for you, Ollie.' Sue stood up and held out the handset.

'Who is it?'

'Said it's a detective someone-or-other. He wants a favour down here I think.'

'Has he asked for me by name?'

Sue shook her head. 'Well . . . no. He said he wanted to speak to the firearms patrol at the tunnel. I figured he meant you.'

'Ah!' Ollie beamed. 'He meant Alan then! That, you see, is the virtue of rank. Alan, go and fob off the nice man, would you? The late turn will be on in two hours. This already sounds like something that can wait.'

'Too right it can.' Alan closed up his fan of cards and was careful to lay them face down. 'Don't you go peeking now, Sergeant.'

'What? And ruin the surprise?' Ollie said.

'PC Edmonds,' Alan huffed down the phone. Ollie saw him stiffen almost immediately. He reacted to the change in his colleague by pulling his feet off the table and sitting up straighter himself. 'Okay, sir. Understood.'

Sir. Shit! This already sounded like work and it was going to be tough to avoid an order from a senior officer. Ollie heard Alan make a few more listening noises and agree to a few more things. The phone call didn't last long. Ollie was expectant as Alan returned to his seat.

'Detective Inspector Blaker . . . do we know him?'

Ollie shook his head. 'The name rings a bell but I don't think I know him.'

'He's on his way.'

'Here? What's he coming here for?'

'They're looking for somebody. Apparently they've got search teams out at a few addresses across the county and they've just identified another location that's on site here. They want a perimeter around it until they can get a full team.'

'A perimeter? Shit, Alan, that's us late off. What makes them think he's here?'

'I don't know. He said it wasn't certain but it needed to be checked. I think they just want us to make sure no one leaves until the team get here and this guy's supposed to be dangerous.'

'Did he say where exactly?'

'Yeah, the old riding school.'

Ollie smirked. He knew that location well. It was on the bank of a large reservoir and in summers past they had spent time sat up there on its banks with disposable barbecues. That was before they put some senior management on the site. He couldn't imagine the fallout if they were seen up there now with sausages on a barbecue. Certainly it would be the end of cushy shifts at the tunnel for him.

'What, they think he's in there?'

'They think he might be.'

'I saw a briefing this morning that went out to the armed search teams. They had four or five places to do. It was looking like a long day. I can't imagine they'll have done them by now. If we get up there on a perimeter we could be stood there most of the night.'

'What about lates?'

'They'll keep us on for something like this. It sounded like quite a big deal this morning.'

'Nothing we can do, though, sarge, surely? He said he's half an hour out. He wants us to identify a rendezvous point and to let him know. He'll meet us there.'

'I bet he will. These shiny arse detectives . . . that's how they work. It's all slow time meetings and risk assessments. I bet you, we can head up there, have a recce round the place, work out there's no one about and hasn't been for months and then call him with the update. He certainly won't mind if we save him a trip down here, trust me on that.'

'I dunno, sarge . . . he seemed grumpy.'

'Grumpy? He hasn't seen me late off, has he? Especially when we end up getting kept here for no reason. We'll head out and do the check. We can be back here before the tea's gone cold.'

Alan shrugged. 'Alright then, if that's a lawful order.'

'It is!' Ollie chuckled. 'And if there really is a big, dangerous man up there, you can go first.'

The two men called out their goodbyes and stepped back out into the furnace.

Chapter 44

Maddie stepped out into the low roar of the Channel Tunnel site and took a moment to take in her surroundings. It was a cacophony of noises in truth, but the individual sounds of mechanical movement mingled into one constant tone.

Harry was already stomping across the hard standing towards the entrance door to the Ports Control Centre on the tunnel site. He was not happy. He hadn't received the call back with an RVP that he had requested and, according to him, they had now wasted another ten minutes going to the PCC, when they should be heading directly to meet the two officers. She wouldn't want to be in their shoes right now. Just a few seconds after walking into the building, she could tell that his mood wasn't about to improve.

'How long ago did they leave?' Harry was talking to a young woman wearing the standard civilian outfit of a white shirt with epaulettes tucked into blue trousers. She stood behind a busy-looking desk. Maddie counted four monitors and at least two desk phones. She looked over at a bank of clocks. Maddie could see she was wearing ID round her neck that said *Susan*.

'About twenty minutes ago.'

'So, straight after I called? Did they have their phones on them?' Harry growled.

'They usually do. We call them at all times.'

'Can you try now? I've been calling them for the last ten minutes and I've not got a thing.'

'Yes, of course. Hold on.' The woman fidgeted over a phone. She stared into space with the phone at her ear. After a short delay she made eye contact with Harry. 'They're not answering me either.'

'What CCTV have you got covering the site?' Harry demanded.

'It's really well covered. Where do you need to see?'

'There's a big reservoir, I'm told. There's a building next to it. Would that be covered?'

'The old school, you mean? Oh, no, that's not really part of the operational site. We used to have something from a distance, but I don't think we even have that anymore. It's not in use out there. None of it is.'

'Do you know where the school is from here?' Maddie's question was aimed at Harry but the woman answered.

'There's a map of the site on the wall there. I know it well, you can get to it by the service roads.'

Harry turned to her. 'Could you get to it if you were off-site?'

'Well, no. The old road to it was blocked off.'

'Blocked off how?' Harry said.

'I'm not entirely sure. You used to pick it up from the A20 roundabout, just off the main motorway. You could see a gate from the road when it was first blocked. You can't anymore. I think it's just further up. That road used to be Castle Hill. It was the village school before, so you would have needed access. Then it was a horse-riding school before the tunnel took it on.'

'I know where you mean. The A20 roundabout. We had some gypsies pitch up there before. They snapped the padlock on the gate. It wasn't difficult.'

'You think that's how he's got in?' Maddie said.

'If he's there, it's exactly how he's got in. We'll go that way. If the gate's still secure, it'll be an indicator that we might be wasting our time. And I would suggest that to be a good RVP. Who knows, maybe our mute firearms colleagues are there waiting.'

Harry was walking back towards the door. Maddie called out her thanks to the woman who lifted a radio in response.

'I'll try and raise them on air. They're not always good on their radios, though.'

Maddie gestured with a thumbs up and strode through the door. Harry was already in the car. She took the opportunity to open the rear door and pick out her kit belt. It felt cumbersome in her hands. She couldn't remember the last time she had worn one, let alone used anything off it. She wasn't going to wear it now either. She climbed into the front passenger seat and they moved off immediately.

'How far?' Maddie said. Her handcuffs banged against the interior as she dropped her kit belt into the foot well.

'Couple of minutes.'

It felt like less than that. They joined the motorway until the next exit. It was a small stretch. The roundabout offered three options: you could re-join the M20, take a right towards Langthorne or take a left up a slight gradient that seemed to be blocked by a metal farm-style gate. The gate was a little further up, just out of site from the roundabout. There was a chain wrapped tightly around its right side.

'I can't see a lock, though,' Maddie said. She pushed her door open and walked to the gate. Her suspicions were right. The chain unwrapped with no lock and little resistance. She pushed it open. It juddered and skipped over the tarmac. She had to use her body weight for it to scrape open the last few metres. Harry pulled the Land Rover up level and they continued on.

The road soon got much steeper and narrower. It was closed in by high mounds of mud and low hanging trees, their branches fidgeting to give the sunlight a freckle effect on the dusty surface.

'This wasn't what I was expecting. You think of the Eurotunnel site and you don't picture country lanes. It's a huge concrete slab.'

'These are the parts you don't see.'

A turning appeared on their left. There was another gate, but this one looked much sturdier. It was ten feet tall and topped with coiled razor wire that glinted in the bright sun. A prominent sign with angry red lettering on a white background warned against trespassing. There was the silhouette of a German shepherd dog to hammer home the point. But this gate wasn't secure either. Even from her vantage point in the car, Maddie could see the gap on the right side of it.

She stepped back out, pushed her fingers through the steel mesh and leaned on the gate. The midday sun was directly above her. The trees held their shadows close so there was nothing to shelter her from its glare. There was a breeze, but the air it moved was too warm for it to be pleasant. She couldn't see much on the other side, just a lot more green trees and a grassy track that wrapped around to the right and quickly out of sight. This gate was far easier to move.

'This doesn't feel right,' she said when she stepped back up into the car. Harry didn't reply. The car moved forward. The scenery opened up immediately and she could see small buildings to her left. The first was circular and made of breeze blocks. It had numerous signs warning of electrocution. The next reminded her of a pump house for a swimming pool. As they pressed on and got clear of the trees, the reservoir that James McCall had mentioned

349

came into view on her right side. She could actually see two of them. The closest was the biggest. Its water level looked low and was a lurid green where algae had formed in the standing water. There were metal steps like those you might see on the side of a swimming pool that dropped out of sight.

'I can't say it looks inviting,' she said. 'Even in this heat.' Harry still didn't reply. She was looking across him at the reservoir. He was looking straight ahead. There was an intensity in him as he brought the car to a rough stop.

'Maddie!' he growled.

She looked ahead of her to see what had caught his attention. The road continued past the reservoirs, which were surrounded on three sides by layers of thick trees that rose up in a sort of bowl. The service road led away to the left and the old riding school was directly ahead. The road didn't make it as far. Access to the old school was via a flat, stony surface that looked a lot rougher, with grass and weeds sprouting through it. Halfway between their Land Rover and the school, her eyes rested on a prone and still figure in a black police uniform.

'Is he alright?' Maddie gasped. 'Get over to him!'

Harry was still staring intently forward as the engine idled.

'Harry!' Maddie said.

'Get on the radio! Divert what you can here. We'll get him in the car and then we wait.'

Maddie's attention snapped to the floor where she had dumped her kit belt. She leaned forward to scoop it up but her radio had come loose and rolled into the furthest corner of the foot well. With the car accelerating forward and pressing her back into her seat, she struggled to reach it.

The first shot she was aware of took out the back window. It popped inwards followed by a *thwack* as another round smashed into the side of the car.

'Maddie! Shots fired!' Harry bellowed. 'My side! Stay down!' She felt the car lurch and then pick up speed. Suddenly the *thwacks* were all around her — it felt like they were filling the cabin. She was still crouched forward, she couldn't have sat up even if she'd wanted to.

'You need to get out your side and get to cover! NOW!' Harry shouted. She turned to him just as his window popped, the glass shattering like dropped ice. His head twitched and she was sprayed immediately with a warm fluid on her face and arms. Harry tilted slowly as if he was gently lying down. His shoulders met with the handbrake and his head lolled out of control. His eyes were wide and bright and they stared right at her. Beneath them was a mess of red and black: on one side, his cheek flapped; on the other was a jumble of exposed teeth and muscle. The muscle was trying to work, flexing and pulsing as he was tried to catch his breath. The whole mess dripped clumps of thick blood. Maddie gasped. She couldn't scream. She wanted to.

The steering wheel snapped left as the car hit something hard enough to throw her head forward into the glove box. She felt the car lift at her corner and could see treetops through Harry's broken window. Then it dropped back down hard. It was still moving forward but was slowing. '*Hey! Where you going?*' The shout drifted through the window. It sounded like the source was some distance away. '*You trying to get away from me?*' The voice was cheery, like a friendly neighbour. She could hear the crunch of footfalls; someone was running over. Harry was still staring at her. There were no words, just a low moan, but his eyes flashed wider and his left hand reached out to push her away. He was telling her to go. She hadn't seen the gunman; it was possible he hadn't seen her either. She took one last look at Harry. His right hand had moved to take hold of the steering wheel to steady it. He was still lying across the front of the car and was struggling to sit back up.

She stayed low and pushed her door open. She could hear the big tyres crunching over the loose surface. She hooked her kit belt over her arm, hung her legs out and pushed herself onto the ground. She landed heavily on her knees and hands, rolled quickly to her feet and stayed low, ignoring the pain shooting through her kneecaps and trying to stay alongside the car. She could see different sized punctures in the bodywork where rounds had ripped right through. She pushed the passenger door shut and looked around her. The Land Rover still moved forward at a brisk walking pace, still rolling towards the old school across open ground. She was desperate for some sort of reliable cover — a big tree . . . a building — but there was nothing close enough to make for without being seen or being hit. She knew there was somebody pacing her on the other side and she had to assume it was the gunman. He would surely stop the car and then there would be silence. She wouldn't be able to move away, not on loose stones, and the car was no cover against gunfire — she could see that for herself. Desperately, she looked around again. There was only one option she could see . . . *underneath*.

She half jogged, half crawled to get level with the front wheel. She didn't know if it was rolling slowly enough for her to get under the car before the back wheel caught up and crushed her. There was no time to think. She threw herself on her back. The back wheel was almost on her straight away; she had misjudged how fast it was going. She shuffled her hips desperately and reached up for the underside of the moving car. She bent her legs away from the wheel, pulled them in and reached upwards. Her left hand found something. It was flatter than she imagined and there wasn't much to hold onto. It felt like a mass of flat, dark plastic. Her right hand touched something hot and she had to pull it away immediately. Desperately she plunged her hands back up. She couldn't make out what she was grabbing. The car had nearly passed over her. In a second she would be left lying on the ground, completely exposed, her cover gone. Both her hands gripped something. It wasn't comfortable, sharp metal dug in to her fingers and palms, but it was good enough for now. She lifted her body off the ground as much as she could, her heels dragging along the concrete as the car pulled her along. She could feel one of her shoes being dragged off. She curled her toes to hold onto it but it was no good — she was going to lose it. She flicked her foot at the last minute and managed to send it out from under the car on the blind passenger side, where it bounced and rolled into the long grass. She could only hope it would be hidden. Suddenly she felt a flashing pain in her head. Instinctively she jerked away from the source: a rock that moved underneath her, picked and tore at her clothes and skin, sliced her leg and banged her heel.

Her kit belt dragged, too. It was over her shoulder and her baton handle was digging into the ground, pulling her down. She slammed her eyes shut and concentrated all her strength on her fingers. She couldn't let go.

The car seemed to roll forever. She heard a door pull open then there was another few seconds before the car jolted to a complete stop. She felt the jolt through her fingers, it shook her loose and she fell back onto the ground. Her fingers were stiff with pain and the back of her head throbbed. She froze. She could see boots on the ground to her left that had to belong to the gunman. He was just half a metre from where she was lying on her back. She held her breath.

'Nice try, old man!' That voice again. 'Well, look at you! You got hurt in all that, didn't you? I was only trying to scare you, too! Well now, what are you?'

One of the boots lifted out of sight. The car creaked and shuffled on its suspension. A few more seconds passed and both boots were back on the ground again. She could hear Harry moaning loudly — whether from pain, fear or anger, she couldn't know. She bit down on her lip to stop herself crying out.

'A detective inspector! This is your badge, right? Now, why would a detective inspector be out here all alone? I thought if your lot came it would be fucking SWAT! The whole shebang! Not some old man with a hole in his face. Granted, that bit's my fault . . . Your lot don't know I'm here, do they? Well, isn't that good news!'

Both boots lifted out of sight this time. The suspension creaked again. He was back in the car. Maddie's eyes flicked to the underside. He was inches from her. She could feel him. A few seconds later the boots came back down with a crunch.

'Unless you weren't on your own. Is that it, old man? Was there someone with you?'

Maddie was just taking rushed breaths as the boots moved. She heard them walk round the front of the Land Rover. They stopped when they were level with her again but on the other side. She turned her head. She heard a door pulled open, the one she had just closed. The suspension dipped again. One boot stayed on the floor. She saw it fidget. He had to be searching where she had been sitting. She tried to think, to remember if she had left anything telling in the cabin.

'Two phones, old man? And the pink case? Now, that don't seem like your style?'

Maddie cursed silently. That damned case! Now being polite was going to get her killed.

'Is this your radio? I think we'll keep hold of that. That will give us a bit of a heads-up now, won't it? Good thinking, Detective Inspector Blaker! So, was someone with you or not? They wouldn't have got far if they were.'

Maddie peered desperately out from under the car. She still couldn't see any cover. Nothing that was close enough. She had no chance if she ran. She turned her attention to the underside of the car again. She pushed her hands back up into the plastic. Her fingers still weren't working well but she did her best to search with them. They curled around a strut that seemed to run across the whole width of the vehicle. She got both hands on it. She risked a glance left. She could see his boots. They had shifted so they were side-on. A hand appeared, palm to the ground. *He was leaning down. He was going to look underneath!* She heaved herself back off the ground but she had to drop back down instantly. Her hair was hanging down in a ponytail and it reached the floor. It would give her away. She wrapped it round her head and gripped a clump of it in her teeth. It took a valuable second. She reached back up for the strut and got the best grip she could with both hands. She felt with her feet, trying to be gentle and silent. She found a gap with her right foot but couldn't find anything for her left. She heaved herself off the ground and held herself as close to the underside as she could. She had to suspend her left leg in the air, battling to keep it straight. The angle might just give her a chance. If he put his face right down to the ground she was dead. If he just knelt down, maybe he wouldn't see her. Her chest and arm muscles burned instantly. She wouldn't be able to do this for long.

She held her breath.

She couldn't see well past the hair that was bunched up in her mouth. Her cheek rested against the plastic. The floor crunched. She could make out part of a knee. She couldn't see a face but was certain he was looking under. Her arms developed a shake from holding up her own body weight. The ache in her fingers was excruciating. She could still see his knee. He was still searching. She clamped her eyes shut. She took a silent breath through her hair, glad that it was gagging her. Her right hand was coming loose; she couldn't hold it anymore. Her foot fell onto the ground and the sound was a million decibels to her. She held her eyes shut as she waited to be dragged out or for the sound of the shot. A second passed until she heard his voice.

'Well then, let's get you out. You can't be dying yet. I need to get you in front of the camera. I don't want to miss this!'

His voice was distant. She opened her eyes. His knee was gone. She turned to look the other way. She could see his boots back on the other side. She fell roughly onto her back. Her fingers were agony and her left leg was threatening to cramp up. The car shook and creaked above her and she heard grunts of exertion. Harry was dragged out and thrown to the ground. He rolled onto his front but his head was turned and he saw Maddie immediately. His eyes fixed on her. The whole of his jaw was a bloody mess and dust stuck to it. The car creaked and rocked; the gunman was clearly back inside. Harry's right hand reached under the car towards her. She didn't take hold of it straight away. Instead, she fumbled with her kit belt. She was trying to unhook her pepper spray but she couldn't get her fingers to work. She was starting to panic. She steadied herself and sucked in a quiet breath. The popper holding the spray finally gave and she snatched it out and moved it closer to Harry. As he took it, he rested his whole hand on hers and she felt its warmth. Amid the terror and the desperation she managed a smile. He gripped down tighter on her hand and his right eye winked. He couldn't speak but he was still conveying a message: *It'll be alright, kid.*

Hands appeared and formed a tight grip round Harry's shoulders. He snatched his hand away from Maddie's and made a fist around the spray to conceal it. Harry was turned so he was face up. Then his head was lifted out of sight and he was dragged away on his heels.

Maddie took a deep breath and wriggled around to get a view. Harry was being dragged slowly towards the building. The man dragging him was stepping backwards, his head was turned that way too. She now had a proper view of the downed police officer. It didn't look like he had moved. She turned her attention back to Harry. She didn't have much time. She had to do something now.

She scrambled over to the passenger side of the car and rolled out. The car had come to a stop resting against a wire fence. On the other side, she could see just long grass and weeds in what might once have been a paddock. She struggled to push the passenger door open wide enough to get back into the car, squeezed herself in and shuffled over into the driver's seat. The dash was still showing lights, the keys still hung from the ignition. She looked towards the building: Harry was just about to be dragged through the door.

She turned the key. The engine fired and she revved it hard, her eyes fixed on the two men. It had the desired effect: the dragging stopped and the gunman's head snapped up to face the noise. Harry was thrown to the floor and the man stepped over him and started pacing back towards her. He must have had his weapon hanging behind his back because now he spun a rifle into sight and levelled it. His pace quickened. Harry was scrambling to sit up behind him.

She pushed the gear lever to *drive*. The car shuddered as the engine engaged and she twisted the steering wheel to the right. The car was more ensnared in the fence than she realised. The steering wheel tried to whip back as the car jerked forward. She fought it. The car shuddered violently and some of the fence started to come away. It chewed up under the wheel and for a horrible second the car stopped and the engine sounded as if it might stall.

'Come on . . . *please*!' Maddie screamed. She pressed hard on the gas and the car gave its biggest shudder yet, but it came free. She straightened up, the car jerked forwards and she eased off. She looked up. The gunman had stopped still, he was twenty metres away, his weapon raised and set into his shoulder. Harry was now on his feet and stumbling towards him, making up ground. But he was too late. There were two loud cracks in quick succession. The windscreen took a hit off to her left; it didn't shatter but there was a neat hole and a terrific noise. A second round struck just as loudly and the rear-view mirror sprang loose. She ducked down and accelerated harder. There were more *cracks* of gunfire but nothing struck the car. She risked a glance out to check she remained on course. She saw that Harry was staggering away now. The gunman hadn't moved any closer and his weapon dropped to the ground. The firing had stopped and his head was bent. His free hand clawed at his face and eyes. Harry must have given him a shot of pepper spray. Maddie stamped on the accelerator, the nose of the Land Rover pointed right at him. The gunman stopped his clawing and lifted his head to the noise of the surging engine — his gun, too. The weapon fired a burst of rounds and the front of the vehicle took a spray of bullets. Maddie was crouched behind the dash with her foot still on the gas. She heard and felt a massive thump at the same time. Something thudded close to where she was ducked against the door. Her foot reached for the brake and she pushed it hard. Not hard enough. She sat back up just in time to see the wall of the school building approaching at speed. There was no time to scream.

Maddie took the hit through her right side. She felt the front lift and heard the engine surge. Then the car finally cut out and the roaring of the engine was replaced by the buzzing in her ears. An airbag hung in front of her and the car was thick with a floating powder that she sucked into her nose and mouth. She had to get out. She pushed the door. Her shoulder shot with pain. Her right arm hung forward at an odd angle. As she stepped out onto her right foot, her knee gave out immediately and she dropped clumsily onto her left side.

The car was silent. The front was pushed into the wall of the building she had last seen from a distance. She felt the warm breeze. Her eyes were a blur and darkness seemed to be encroaching from the sides, funnelling her vision. She heard a loud moan and it snapped her back to alertness.

'Harry?' she shouted. 'HARRY!' The moaning was the only response. She rolled enough to plant her left hand on the ground and struggled to her feet. She used the car, pushing herself against its side using just her left leg. Her knee was painful but she could stumble a few paces — enough to see Andy McCall lying out on the ground. She was close enough to recognise him as the man she had seen in the photos. He was on his front, his legs at obtuse angles behind him. He was dragging them through the dirt, his arms reaching out and clawing at the stony ground — inching towards his dropped rifle.

Maddie was quicker. She made up the ground to where Andy lay. She loomed over him but the darkness was getting thicker again and she could feel a pulse behind her eyes. For a terrifying second she thought she was going to pass out. She took a deep breath. Her vision cleared a little. She fought the urge to vomit. Andy twisted to look up at her. She could see the *Eurotunnel* logo on the overalls he was wearing.

'I got told off . . .' she rasped, her throat sore from the airbag powder. 'For standing on criminals . . . in a past life.' She moved her weight gently. Her right knee was sore but it took her weight. She rested her left foot on McCall's leg where it was clearly broken. She shifted all her weight onto it. He bellowed in pain. She pushed off him and walked to the rifle. It was heavier than she thought. The radio was nearby. She scooped that up next. She could just about hold it in her right hand. Harry was lying on his side another ten metres or so away. He was looking over. She picked up the weapon and walked to him. His eyes followed her. She collapsed clumsily next to him and laid the rifle across her lap.

'Customer facing, Harry,' she said. 'I love it.'

She pressed the red button on her radio. She felt it shake in her hands and then beep to confirm the emergency signal had been sent.

Help was coming.

Chapter 45

The light was bright enough to penetrate Maddie's eyelids and render her vision a yellow searing mass. Had she not felt the glare and the pain from just about everywhere, she might have thought that she was dreaming. She was groaning. The sound surprised her, like it was coming from someone else. Her eyes opened.

'It's okay! Calm down, you're okay!' She looked up at a man's face that blocked the worst of the sun. His smile was tinged with concern. He wore an army-style helmet, but it was navy blue and it had *Police* written across it in white lettering.

'You've taken a bit of a bump but you're going to be fine. Try not to move. Do you have any pain at all?'

Maddie couldn't remember where she was. Her mind thrashed with confusion. The man turned his head towards voices that were muffled to her, the sunlight arched past him, back into her eyes. She slammed them shut.

'Sorry! I'll try and block the sun.'

'My legs hurt,' she managed. Her shoulder did too. Her head was aching like she had never experienced before and she could feel a burning sensation on her cheeks.

'That's a good sign!' he said. 'Just keep still. We're going to get you up and moved just as soon as we can, okay?'

Maddie didn't reply. She licked her lips. They were dry and coarse. She had a metallic taste in her mouth. She could still hear muffled voices beside her. She tried turning towards them but her neck was being held straight. She could do nothing but face up. The man moved away again, the sun beat back down on her and she closed her eyes to it.

* * *

When she woke the next time, Chief Inspector Lowe's was the first face she saw. Someone was fussing around her legs and she felt restricted. Her limbs felt like they were all bound together and she still couldn't move her head. There was a ceiling above her now. She could see strip lighting and square, flecked tiles.

'Hey, Maddie. Nice to have you back with us!' Lowe said.

'What happened?'

'You were in a car accident. You're going to be fine. The doctor here, he just wants to ask you a question.'

Maddie felt a sudden scratch on the top of her foot. She jerked her leg and snarled her disdain.

'Sorry.' It was another new voice. A woman in a blouse leaned over her. 'I just wanted to be sure that hurt. Do you have any other pain?'

'I just feel sore.'

'You will. You've got a bit of concussion for sure. You've dislocated your collarbone and your knee's swollen, but it shouldn't be too serious. And a good few bumps and scrapes. I think we've been overcautious with the neck brace, though. There are no abnormalities on your spine. Hurting you was the last test!' Her smile broadened. 'And you passed.'

Maddie heard a clunk and then a whirring sound. She felt a gentle pressure on her back as she was pushed to a sitting position. She was still squinting her eyes. The blurriness cleared quickly. She was in a hospital bed. There was machinery around her but none of it seemed to be plugged into her or working. There was a curtain all the way around her bed, dull white with a cheery blue pattern. She could hear people walking past.

'Do you remember what happened, Maddie?' Lowe spoke to her. He had stepped back from the bed. She heard a gurgling sound, like someone pouring liquid into a glass. Her neck tickled. Something was pulled from around it and it felt cool now it was exposed. She ran her hand over the back of her neck and moved her head gently from side to side.

'No, I don't know why I'm here.' The doctor held out a glass of water. Maddie took it.

'You and Harry—'

'Harry!' Maddie's mind suddenly flashed with an image of Harry — he was critically injured, he was gripping her hand tightly, he looked terrified . . .

'He's going to be okay, Maddie.' The doctor's smile was back. She looked reassuring. 'He's got some recovery in front of him but he's going to get there. He'll need his mates around him.'

'He got shot! His face! It was all such a mess!'

'It looked worse than it was. We think it was a fragment of a bullet and mainly soft tissue. He was lucky.'

'Do you remember anyone else being there?' Lowe pressed.

'Yes. With a gun. He just kept shooting at the car.' She suddenly inhaled a sharp breath. 'I think I ran him down! Did he . . .?'

'You did. He's here, too. He broke some bones but he will be standing for his sentence, we're sure of that. We're still piecing it together down there, but you saved Harry's life — and your own. We also found an injured woman.

Seriously injured. She would have died. You should be very proud.'

Maddie took a few moments. She let the information sink in. She peered around the room. No one spoke to her; they let her take her time.

'Can I go home?' she said.

'To your hotel?' Lowe replied. 'I would rather you stayed in here overnight. I would rather you were with someone.'

'I can call someone. I won't be alone.' As much as she hated hotels, she was damned sure she hated hospitals more. No way was she staying here. She fixed her gaze on the doctor.

'I mean, I would rather you were with someone like your colleague here says. But if that can be arranged then we can't stop you discharging yourself. The concussion is our only lasting concern. I have made a bed available.'

'I'll go.'

'Okay then!'

'Who are you staying with Maddie?' Lowe asked. 'I'll arrange for a call to be made or we'll get someone round to pick them up.'

'No!' Maddie was aware that she had snapped her reply. 'It's fine, thank you. I'll make a call. It won't be a problem.'

'Are they close?'

'Yes. If you can get me to my hotel they won't be far behind.'

'I'll run you back myself. We'll need to take your account. It will be a full debrief. I know you're injured and you've had quite a day, but I would want to do that sooner rather than later.'

'I'll see how I feel. Not tonight, boss, with respect.'

'Goodness, no. Not tonight, Maddie. We'll see how you feel in the morning, maybe.'

'Can I see him? Harry, I mean?'

The doctor answered, 'He's in surgery. He'll be in and out of procedures for a few days, I would expect. He needs a bit of a rebuild. It might be later in the week.'

'But he's going to be okay?'

'He should be. Just focus on you for now.'

Lowe was nodding. 'I'll be seeing him the second we're allowed, Maddie. I'll make sure you're with me.'

'Thanks. Is there a phone I can use?'

The doctor's hand fell to her belt. She lifted up what looked like a landline. 'We'll give you a minute.'

Maddie waited while they stepped out. She could see silhouettes against the curtain. She waited until she couldn't anymore.

The call was answered on the second ring.

'Yeah.' The tone was hard and suspicious.

'Adam.'

'Mads! What you ringing me on?'

'It's the hospital's phone, I think.'

'Hospital? You okay?' Maybe it was his voice softening so quickly, maybe it was the sound of any friendly voice at all, or a combination — she broke down. She could barely speak. 'Can you come? I just need someone.'

'I'm just two hours away.'

Chapter 46

Maddie braced herself at the door. The nurse who had shown her through turned quickly on her heels to walk away. Maddie didn't move. When she glanced to her left the nurse was looking back over. She smiled and gestured with her hands.

'Go on, now. He'll be happy to see you!'

Maddie rested her good hand on the metal handle. Her left was supported in a sling. She took a breath and shook her head, trying to shake away the images of that day and the lingering feeling that she could have done something different.

She turned the handle and had to lean on the door a little; it was sticking on the thick carpet. Harry Blaker was in his own room on the private wing of the William Harvey Hospital, Ashford. It was a brand-new addition and it looked it. The bed was directly in front of her.

Harry was sitting up. He was bare-chested, with suckers covering much of his torso. Wires trailed from each one to bleeping machines. His head was wrapped in a tight white bandage that had oval chunks missing for his eyes — like some sort of bandage balaclava. His jaw was

365

covered with metal struts sticking out from under it and converging to a plastic pad that rested on his chest. There were more metal struts at the side, too, and she guessed around the back. His eyes fixed on her and he jutted out a thumb in greeting.

'Hey, Harry!' She moved into the room and peered around. She knew it was going to be a one-sided conversation but she still hadn't come prepared with the right thing to say — whatever that was. Harry had been communicating using written notes when he wanted to. The pad was to his left. He didn't even pick it up.

'I have to admit, I've not had too much practice at talking to people who can't answer back. The boss . . . he just said to give you an update. I think you might have had it already. He's been better with me, by the way — Mr Lowe. I'm not sure we're friends yet, but you getting shot seems to have improved our working relationship no end. So, thanks for that!' Maddie chuckled. She hesitated.

'I'm rambling, aren't I? So, an update . . .' She paused again to try and organise her thoughts. Just a few days had passed; it was all still very fresh but it was also very jumbled. She didn't know where to start. She knew Harry had asked for an update. She also knew that he had insisted that it came from her.

'We did good, Harry. Overall. Lisa Simpkiss was there. She was badly injured but she's going to be just fine. One of the coppers, too — he's just fine. And me and you . . . we're still here. I've been told often enough that we should call it a good result.' She took her time with the next bit. There was a tall-backed seat beside the bed. She stood behind it and rested her hand on its top. 'My girl didn't make it — Lorraine Humphries. They don't reckon she'd been dead long when we got there. The pathologist reckons she might have died when he moved her. She was a fighter, though, Harry — oh my goodness, did that girl fight. A week or more with her own intestines hanging out of her gut. He slashed her throat too, then left her for dead in that stinking box. He must have thought she was dead. But she wasn't going that easy. The post-mortem . . . They reckon he missed the main bits in her throat and when he wrapped her tight it compressed her stomach wound.' Maddie fought her emotions to be able to continue. She took a minute. She rubbed at the chair and focussed on the feel of the material through her fingertips. It was cool and smooth. A grounding technique she'd been taught for keeping calm. Different to the one she had used on Olive Simpkiss, but just as effective.

She raised her eyes again to meet with Harry's. His attention hadn't shifted from her. 'That house . . . where we found him . . . He was setting it up for who knows what. There were cameras in all the downstairs rooms. He had tinned food and water, enough to last them both a while. We're pretty sure the sick fuck was going to play with that girl and then who knows how many others. He was keeping her alive and in pain while he watched it all. She would have died though, in the end. Just like all the others. He seemed happy to talk in the first round of interviews. Your theory was almost spot-on. We thought he was going to those AA meetings to prey on the vulnerable. That wasn't quite right. Seems he went there because he was vulnerable himself. An addict. He just happened on a source of perfect victims. That woman we found at the chicken farm was a Polish girl last seen in Brighton seven weeks ago — Eva Makowitz. She'd come here for a better life but it didn't work out. She got into the drink. No one even reported her missing.'

Maddie peered around the room.

'Do you mind?' She pointed at a jug of water and a stack of plastic beakers on his bedside table. Not waiting for an answer, she took one and poured herself a drink. She took a long swig.

'The two coppers . . .' Maddie hesitated. She had voiced her concerns at telling Harry the whole story. Maybe he didn't need to know the ins and outs at this point. Lowe had insisted that he had been asking for it, that he wanted to know everything, so she continued.

'The firearms skipper, he didn't make it. There's a bit of a story around that but I'll let the lad he was with tell it to you. He tells it right. Ollie Craddock was the sergeant's name, and it sounds like he really stepped up when he needed to. His mate's alive because of what he did, no doubt about that. Seems our offender was dressed up to look like a Eurotunnel worker. They dropped their guard and he took one of them out with his own weapon. The same one he fired at us.' She took another swig. She swilled the water this time. Harry's eyes were still fixed on her. His breathing seemed to have deepened, his chest rising and falling with more prolonged movements. She could sense his emotion building. Maybe that was enough of an update.

'Oh! I got your instructions too. You have terrible handwriting!' Maddie lifted a carrier bag that she had been swinging absently under her arm. She carefully took out an intricately carved, wooden bird.

'A robin, right?' She cast her eyes around the room, looking for the best place to put it. Harry became more animated. He made a noise from his throat and when Maddie looked up at him he reached out his right hand, palm up. She stepped close enough for him to take hold of the wooden bird. He took it gently. His fingers curled round its little body. He moved it closer to his face and seemed to inhale its scent. His eyes closed completely and he breathed out in a long sigh. Maddie suddenly felt awkward. When his eyes opened again they looked to be heavy with emotion.

'As lovely as this water is, I'm gonna pop out and find a cup of tea, okay? I'll be back.' She walked to the door. She stopped on the threshold. Harry's big hand was still wrapped around the ornament. His eyes had fallen closed again.

'Oh, the doctor . . . she said you've got some recovery to be making, but she reckons you'll be back to full fitness. So there's no reason why we can't get this partnership back up and running again. That's what this is, see — in case you didn't know. That's why the instructions were for me, right? That's why you had me go to your house and pick up your stuff — you didn't trust anyone else, did you? You can't answer that, Harry, so it means it's true! The doctor also said that you'll need to build up the strength in your jaw and it will be painful for a while. She said I should expect you to be a man of few words and to be a bit grumpy too. I told her I think I can wait it out, you know, until you're back to talking incessantly and being so *damned* chipper!'

Maddie saw wrinkles appear around Harry's eyes, as if he was smiling under all that padding. She chuckled to herself then stepped back out of the door to give him a few moments. And to give herself the same.

THE END

Thank you for reading this book. If you enjoyed it please leave feedback on Amazon, and if there is anything we missed or you have a question about then please get in touch. The author and publishing team appreciate your feedback and time reading this book.

Our email is office@joffebooks.com

www.joffebooks.com

Made in the USA
San Bernardino, CA
12 April 2019